Bryce came home on a few days' furlough in the Highland Light Infantry's tartan trews and the bonnet with its jaunty red and white cockade. When he took her into his arms and kissed her, his uniform jacket felt stiff and scratchy, and she felt shy and ill at ease, as though she was with a stranger.

'I was thinkin',' he said awkwardly when he had released her, 'that it would be a rare comfort tae me tae know that you're here.'

'Where else would I be?'

'I don't mean here in Paisley, I mean here waitin' for me. Promised tae me.'

'Did we not agree just to be friends?'

'Aye, but that was before I went tae be a soldier. A man has tae have some hope.'

'You've got plenty of hope – and plenty of cheek as well. You always have had. So just keep on hoping.'

He heaved a gusty sigh. 'We can talk about it again when I get my next furlough,' he said.

THE DANCING STONE

Evelyn Hood

WARNER BOOKS

A *Warner* Book

First published in Great Britain in 1997
by Little, Brown and Company
This edition published by Warner Books in 1998

A CIP catalogue record for this book
is available from the British Library.

ISBN 0 7515 1700 3

Typeset in Times by
Palimpsest Book Production Limited,
Polmont, Stirlingshire
Printed and bound in Great Britain by
Clays Ltd, St Ives plc.

Warner Books
A Division of
Little, Brown and Company (UK)
Brettenham House
Lancaster Place
London WC2E 7EN

This book is dedicated with gratitude and affection to all the librarians and all the readers I met during Scottish Book Fortnight, 1996.

E.H.

1

Although moonlight washed the street, the pend leading to the back yard was an ink-black cave with no floor, walls or roof. Caitlin, who walked through it every day and had thought that she knew it well, hesitated, one foot poised on the line where moon-silver met menacing black, then stumbled as Bryce surged confidently past, drawing her after him into the darkness with a grip on her wrist.

'I can't see!'

'Ye don't need tae see,' he said gruffly. Then, as she tripped and slipped over the unseen cobbles, he released her wrist to put his two strong hands about her waist and swing her round. Her back came up against the house wall hard enough to make her gasp out a protest, but before the words were formed Bryce was kissing her, his open mouth covering hers and denying her breath. She struggled, suddenly panicking, and managed to push him away.

'What's amiss?'

Caitlin sucked in air. 'You are, Bryce Caldwell. D'you have to behave like an animal?'

'That's not what ye said when I pulled ye intae that close in Causeyside,' he said, hurt. 'Ye were all for kissin' me then.'

1

'I know, but . . .'

'But what?'

Although the September night was mild, Caitlin shivered. 'This is . . . different. It's too dark to see you.'

'We don't need tae see each other. Feelin's enough.' His hands slid round her back, drawing her away from the wall and close against his body while his mouth sought and found hers again.

He was right; after walking out with him for the best part of a year, she well knew how he fitted into her embrace, the touch of his hands and body, the smell of him. Now that her eyes were becoming accustomed to the darkness she could just make out the curve of the pend's roof over his head. Beyond those age-blackened bricks lay her small bedroom with its two windows, one looking to the street, the other to the lane leading to the yard and workshop, and behind her, across the width of the storeroom that had recently become a weaving shop, her mother and stepfather would be sitting companionably in the kitchen at that very moment, one on either side of the fire. She relaxed at the thought and gave herself up to the pleasure of Bryce's kisses.

When he finally drew back they were both breathless, and Bryce was trembling from head to foot, a sure sign that it was time for Caitlin to go into the house. Fond though she was of him, she had a good sense of right and wrong, and although she had firmly resisted all his attempts to get her to go further than cuddling and kissing, it didn't stop him from trying to introduce new intimacies whenever he got the chance.

'It's getting late,' she began, her fingers busy straightening and buttoning her jacket, and he groaned.

2

'You always say that just when we're gettin' cosy together.'

'It's true, though. We've both got work to go to tomorrow.'

'Has Todd said anythin' about the new workshop?'

The sudden change of conversation took her by surprise. 'What new workshop?'

'The one your Alex wants tae buy down by the river.'

'This is the first I've heard of it.'

'Aye, well, you're no' involved with the workshop, so nob'dy'd think tae say anythin' tae ye.'

His condescension stung, and her voice was sharp when she shot back at him, 'Nobody said because there's nothing to say. You're just havering.'

'I am not. Alex came from Glasgow this very mornin' tae talk tae Todd about it. He has it in mind tae buy some old mill over by the river an' set it up as a workshop with Todd in charge.'

'And sell this place?' Kirsty, Caitlin's mother, had inherited the house and the adjoining cabinet-maker's business from her father. Caitlin's half-brother, Alex, had since bought it from Kirsty; as the owner he had the right to sell, but Caitlin couldn't see him letting the family inheritance go.

'Alex says that the business is doin' so well that it needs tae expand. Todd'd run the new place, an' he an' the missus'd live in the wee house that goes with it. That means that I'd take over the runnin' of this place, and that means . . .' Bryce reached for her again, his breath warm on her cheek, 'that you an' me could get wed an' live here.'

Alarm twinged through Caitlin. 'You're taking an awful lot for granted!'

'Come on, lass, we've been walkin' out for years.'

'For ten months. And anyway, what makes you think I want to marry and run a house and look after you? I've got my own work to do.'

'Carin' for a man an' raisin' bairns is a woman's proper work,' Bryce assured her. 'We're the right age, Caitlin, an' we're well suited.' He pulled her close again, his voice muffled by her neck when he said, 'An' there's nob'dy else I'd want tae be wed tae but you.'

With surprising speed, he managed to unfasten the jacket she had just buttoned. One hand moved inside it, sliding over her blouse to find and cup a breast.

'Bryce . . .' she protested as he squeezed the soft flesh gently.

'Caitlin,' he groaned in answer against her mouth. 'Oh, my wee darlin'. Can we no' just . . .'

Without realising it, Caitlin had moved further along the pend during her attempts to say goodnight. Instead of leaning against the brick wall, she had reached the weaving shop's timbered door, and when it opened she swayed backwards, off balance, into the sudden void behind with a yelp of fright. Bryce almost tumbled after her; he pulled back with a startled oath as Caitlin was saved from toppling down the two steps into the shop by hands that caught at her shoulders from within the room.

'Are you all right?' Murdo Guthrie's soft, lilting voice said just above her head.

'D'ye have tae go creepin' round the place?' Bryce snapped.

'I didn't know that anyone was in the pend. I'm sorry if I frighted you.'

'So ye should be!' Bryce snatched Caitlin from the other man's grasp and tucked her possessively under one arm.

4

'I'm sure that Murdo was as startled as we were, Bryce,' Caitlin said swiftly, embarrassed at being caught spooning with her sweetheart. 'You're working late tonight, Murdo.'

'I was working on a piece of cloth that Mr MacDowall wants for the end of the week. I'll bid you a good night.' Murdo Guthrie brushed past them, his head and shoulders taking on a silvery outline as he stepped out of the pend and into the moonlight.

'Daft Highland devil!' Bryce snarled.

'Shh, he'll hear you!'

'What if he does? When I get tae be master here that one'll be out on his ear.'

'Alex won't allow that, and he's the one who employs Murdo.'

'I'll find a way.'

'What harm has Murdo Guthrie ever done to you?'

'None – yet. And he'll no' get the chance tae try, I can promise ye that. Not tae me or tae you.'

'Why should he harm any of us?'

Bryce hunched his shoulders. 'He's a sleekit Highlander, and ye cannae trust any of them. I don't like him skulking in the store at all hours, so close tae the house.'

'He told us that he was doing some work for Alex. All the man wants is to earn a living.'

'Takin' his side, are ye? Have ye a fancy for him, then?' Bryce sneered, and she felt her face begin to burn.

'Don't be so daft, I scarcely know him. I'm only saying that he's probably as decent as any of us.'

'But he's a Highlander . . . ,' Bryce began, and Caitlin gave up.

'I'm going in.'

This time, alerted by the sharp note in her voice,

he didn't try to detain her. 'I'll see ye tomorrow night?'

'I'll mebbe have to work on at the shop, for we've got a lot to do.'

'Suit yersel',' Bryce said huffily and turned away, stamping over the cobbles and throwing his hefty body round the corner into the street without offering, as he usually did, to walk the last few steps to the kitchen door with her. She didn't bother to call him back.

Caitlin had expected to find her mother and stepfather alone in the kitchen, but to her surprise the room was full when she went in through the back door. Her younger sister, Mary, was still up, sitting on the hearth rug with her head resting against her mother's knee and her eyes heavy with sleep, while Alex, Caitlin's half-brother, had turned a chair around from the table and straddled across it, his arms folded along the chair back.

'What's amiss?' Caitlin asked at once. It was rare to see twelve-year-old Mary still up and about and Alex in Paisley at that time of night.

'Nothin's amiss, lass.' Todd Paget's fireside chair stood with its high back to the door. A cloud of tobacco smoke drifted up into the air as he spoke.

'Nothing at all.' Alex smiled at her. 'I just came to see Mam and Todd about an idea I've had.' His normally solemn face was animated and his blue eyes sparkled. One look at the way his ruffled red hair glowed in the lamplight told Caitlin that Bryce hadn't been havering after all. Alex's hair always seemed to take on added colour when he was excited or elated.

'Is it about the new workshop?'

Kirsty Paget's needle had been dashing through a

6

length of blue cloth as though her life depended on finishing the seam she sewed. Now the needle stilled as she gaped at her daughter. 'How did you come to know about that?'

'From Bryce Caldwell.' Alex supplied the answer. 'I saw the man's ears wagging when I was talking to Todd earlier.'

'So it's true that you're thinking of buying an old mill here in Paisley?' Caitlin took off her hat and started to unfasten her recently buttoned jacket.

'Did he tell you the asking price and all?' Alex wanted to know dryly. 'Aye, it's true. Our customers have taken a liking to having furniture made specially for them, and I could do with expanding the workshop.'

'But you've already got your own wee place in Glasgow. Surely the two workshops can supply all the furniture you need?'

'I'm selling the Glasgow premises, for my father wants me to spend more time in the emporium,' Alex explained. 'The way he sees it, I'll be running the place one day, and he wants me to start getting used to the idea of being there.'

Alex's natural father, Angus MacDowall, owned a large furniture emporium in Glasgow. A cabinet-maker by trade and an artist by nature, Alex had introduced hand-decorated handmade furniture into the business, and it had done so well that MacDowall had publicly acknowledged the young man as his son and heir and set him up with his own cabinet-maker's business in Glasgow. In return, Alex had taken on his father's surname. Father and son had commissioned the small Paisley workshop Kirsty owned to make furniture exclusively for them.

'My father originally thought of asking you to run

the Glasgow factory, Todd, but I didn't see Mam wanting to move to the city.'

'You're right there,' Kirsty said firmly, and Alex grinned at her.

'You could have started up your own clothes shop in the city, Mam. Look at the success you've made of Jean's wee place.'

'That was a matter of helping an old friend, and in any case, it's Caitlin and Rose who've made the real success of Jean's shop. I'm content with what I've got – and where I am.'

'But you'd not be averse to moving just a few hundred yards or so, would you?' Alex coaxed. 'The mill's only at Hunterhill, so you'd still be near enough to the shop and Mary would still be near her school. There's a fine big gatehouse on the premises with plenty of room for the four of you. It's not been lived in for a good while, so it needs work done to it, but I'd see to all that for you. You could have the whole place done out just the way you want it, Mam,' Alex wheedled. 'And Todd would have more room to work, for the mill's several times larger than the wee workshop out the back. It's got three floors to it, as well as a good-sized yard.'

Todd shot a glance at his wife, then asked, 'What about this place?'

'We'll keep it, of course, since it's been in Mam's family for so long. Your journeyman could run it, and you'd be close enough to keep an eye on him.' Alex got to his feet. 'I must go or I'll miss the train back to Glasgow. I'll take the two of you to see the mill tomorrow or the next day.'

Mary, her eyes sheltered from the light by the material Kirsty was stitching, had fallen asleep against her mother's knee; while Todd went to the street door with Alex, Kirsty roused the girl and sent her upstairs, yawning and rubbing her eyes.

'Is that you doing my work, Mam?'

'I'd finished the darning, so I thought I'd just put a stitch or two into it for you.' Kirsty smoothed the material gently. 'It's bonny. I didn't get as much done to it as I'd wanted.'

Todd came back into the room, looking down at his wife with a bemused and slightly troubled expression on his normally placid face. 'What d'you think, Kirsty?'

She folded the cloth on her lap, tucking the needle securely through several layers of cloth. 'I'm too tired to think anything, so I'm going away to my bed, and so should you two. We can talk about it in the morning.'

Todd nodded, but Caitlin took the sewing from her mother and settled down in Todd's chair. 'I'll just get a bit more work done before I go to my bed.'

Alone with the ticking clock and an occasional crackle from the fire in the well-polished range, Caitlin considered the implications of Alex's news as her fingers bustled the needle in and out of the skirt she was making for one of her customers. The prospect of moving to another house didn't bother her, for she had only come to this one, and in fact to the town of Paisley, seven years earlier when her mother had inherited the house and workshop.

Caitlin's father, Matt Lennox, had been alive then; he had died almost four years ago. After three years of widowhood, Kirsty had married Todd, who had been journeyman to her father then to Matt. The marriage had met with approval from Kirsty's children, who liked Todd and appreciated his gentle, placid nature, so different from Matt's sudden bursts of temper.

9

On her return to Paisley, Kirsty had renewed her friendship with a former school friend, Jean Chisholm, who ran a second-hand clothes shop. After helping Jean with the shop, Kirsty had used her skills with a needle to introduce clothes alterations into the business. Some time after that, Rose Hamilton, the youngest daughter of a wealthy local family and an independent soul with no wish to emulate her sisters and her friends by following the usual path to marriage and a household of her own, had come in as a partner, buying the empty premises next door and expanding the original shop to include dressmaking for those who could afford it.

When Caitlin left school, her talent as a seamstress and her flair for design had helped to develop the dressmaking side of the business. She loved her work, and she and Rose shared plans, hopes and dreams of future expansion, which was why Bryce's plans for their future made her uneasy. He was a good worker, and no doubt, with Todd still in the area to keep an eye on him, he would run the workshop efficiently. He deserved the chance to better himself, but Caitlin had no desire to marry him, or anyone else, yet, although as Bryce had pointed out, they were both of marriageable age, he twenty-one and she nineteen.

Finding, after a short while, that the seam she was working on had begun to waver before her tired eyes, she put the work aside and turned off the gas lamps before going upstairs. As she passed the master bedroom, she heard her mother and Todd talking in low voices, no doubt discussing Alex's offer.

The moon, still high in a sky free of clouds, washed her small room with its silvery-blue light. Brushing her hair by the window, looking down into Espedair Street, empty at this hour of pedestrians and traffic, Caitlin remembered the way the light had haloed Murdo

Guthrie's head and shoulders as he'd stepped from the pend into the street, and she wondered if that same ethereal effect could be achieved with materials. A very dark blue cloth, perhaps, overlaid with silver lace, if she could find some among the collection of clothing in the back shop. The bulk of Jean's stock consisted of cast-offs from the women who lived in Paisley's big houses, and the best of materials was to be found among them.

She put the brush aside and slipped into bed. While her mother and stepfather talked on in the adjoining room, she fell asleep in the space of a minute.

2

Young Mrs Harper had set her heart on a costume with a long jacket in horizontally striped material, just like the drawing she had come across in her new fashion magazine. The model in the sketch was tall and slender, while Mrs Harper was small and of the type described in Caitlin's circles as 'a sonsy, well-set-up lassie'.

Caitlin, who in childhood had suffered nightmares after coming across a drawing of a hapless native trapped in the coils of a large snake, was keenly aware that that was just what Mrs Harper would look like in the stripes she craved. She had scoured the fashion magazines Rose brought to the shop, finally coming across the ideal outfit on the morning after Alex's visit.

Rose and Kirsty both approved of the choice, a smart high-waisted jacket with narrow, vertical embroidered panels running up the sleeves, bodice and collar.

'Much more slimming than the one she wants,' Rose said. 'What colour?'

'Something light – ivory,' Kirsty said, and Caitlin nodded.

'That's what I thought, too, with blues and reds in the embroidery. But it means having the embroidery done specially.'

'Isa Harper can afford it. I just wish,' Rose said for the hundredth time, 'that we could employ our own hand-embroiderers instead of having to farm the work out. That way everything could be done on our own premises instead of having to leave good materials in the embroideress's house. With all those children she has, I always worry in case the cloth gets torn or something's spilled on it.'

They were all in the small fitting room. Jean Chisholm, enjoying a cup of tea in peace before returning to her usual place behind the shop counter, sniffed loudly. 'If things had been left the way they were, nob'dy would have to traipse expensive material through the town,' she pointed out, and Rose smiled sweetly at her.

'If it had been left the way it was, Jean, you'd still be running your wee second-hand clothes shop and you'd not have me as your partner. Just think of the pleasure you'd have missed.'

Jean sniffed again, though the glimmer of a smile tugged at the corners of her mouth as she went through the curtained archway leading to the sewing room and the shop. Suspicious of Rose when she first suggested a partnership, she had grown to like the younger woman, but they still enjoyed the occasional tilt at each other.

'You know that we need more room, Kirsty, now that you and Caitlin have opened up the dressmaking side of things,' Rose persisted as the curtains fell back into place behind Jean's narrow back.

'It's you that's done most of the opening up, showing your new clothes off to your friends,' Kirsty said, and Rose preened herself.

'If you'd spent all your life feeling more like a giraffe than a person, you'd want to show off a bit too.'

Too tall, too thin and angular, Rose had until quite recently driven her socialite mother to despair with her inability to dress stylishly. When Caitlin had started working in the shop the situation had changed, for she had a natural affinity for colours, shapes and materials. The first person to recognise Rose's potential for elegance, she had designed and made several garments for her. They had aroused such interest and envy among Rose's friends, and so many of them had begun to make use of Caitlin's services, that Rose now referred to herself as Caitlin's sandwich-board woman.

Today Caitlin and Kirsty wore the shop uniform that Kirsty herself had introduced – a white blouse with a black bow at the throat and a black skirt. Rose's outfit was similar but topped by one of Caitlin's designs, a long, loose silk waistcoat made up of diamond shapes in all the colours of the rainbow. It was Rose's favourite garment and one she wore frequently.

Rose's insistence on going into commerce instead of making her parents happy by marrying well had made her something of a curiosity among the women of her own social class. Friends and acquaintances such as Mrs Harper tended to visit the shop, ostensibly to call on Rose while passing, but in actual fact to view the place she had chosen to become involved with and to spend most of her time in.

After looking round the shop with disdain and deeming it 'quaint', most of them swept back out to their waiting carriages, nose in the air, then enquired of Rose at some social function within the next two weeks if she could arrange for 'that little woman' who had made her gown, blouse or costume to make something for them. When that happened, Kirsty or, more and more frequently, Caitlin would call at their houses, armed with pattern books and samples of material.

A few hours after she, her mother and Rose had agreed on the perfect outfit for Mrs Harper, Caitlin, pink with triumph, hurried back to the shop from the large and elegant house opposite Brodie Park where the woman lived with her husband.

'Hello, Aggie,' she said affectionately to the dress-maker's dummy that always stood outside the shop, dressed in a different outfit every day, as she hurried past the shop door, choosing instead to use the door leading directly to the sewing room, Jean's original shop.

As usual, Teenie Stapleton was crouched over her sewing machine like a champion jockey riding a thoroughbred to victory on the race course. Her feet were rocking the treadle so hard that they were a mere blur of motion, and her turbaned head was bent so close to the material whizzing beneath the needle that she seemed in permanent danger of stitching her nose as well. Teenie was extremely short-sighted and, despite the wire-framed spectacles Rose had insisted on getting for her, she always worked with her face almost on the table so that from behind, her body seemed to be headless. Her sewing machine, Kirsty's machine on the table set against hers, and every surface in the room were hidden beneath heaped clothing and pieces of material. She paid Caitlin no heed at all.

After dropping her bag of samples and patterns on the floor, Caitlin stretched her back then took off her coat and hung it up neatly. Finally, she cleared a space on Teenie's table and rapped her knuckles sharply on the wood. 'Teenie!'

The machine roared to a standstill and Teenie lifted her head, her magnified grey eyes huge in her small face. 'It's yoursel', lassie.'

'Is Rose in the fitting room?'

'Aye, with your mother and a customer,' Teenie said, and went back to her work.

The customer was buttoning her blouse while Kirsty carefully folded a woollen coat and Rose made notes in a large exercise book. 'Next Thursday afternoon?' she said as Caitlin went in.

The woman's face fell. 'We're visitin' my man's old auntie on the Wednesday night, hen, an' she's that particular. He likes me tae look my best when we see her. Could ye no' . . . ?'

'I'll make certain that the coat's ready for you on Wednesday afternoon,' Kirsty promised, and the woman beamed.

'I'd be grateful, pet.' She reached out and stroked the coat gently. 'This'll fairly make her sit up and take notice,' she said, with a giggle of anticipation. 'I'll pay half now and the rest when I get it.'

'Miss Chisholm in the shop'll attend to that. I'll take you through.'

'Poor woman,' Rose said, when Kirsty had escorted the woman out. 'I hope the new coat stuns her auntie into silence for the entire visit. I've got an aunt just like that – she treats all her relatives like servants and her servants like slaves. She's the only person I've ever seen Mama grovelling before.' She made a final note in the book and slammed it shut with one of her usual quick movements. If Jean Chisholm, who was of a nervous disposition, had been in the room, she would have jumped at the noise, but Caitlin, used to Rose's ways, was unruffled.

'Mrs Harper's agreed to the costume we chose, with the embroidery and the velvet hat.' Caitlin, who had gone home to change into her visiting clothes before going to Brodie Park, took a long smock from a hook on the wall and began to put it on.

'Well done! I've heard that her husband's taking her off on a cruise next summer. If she likes the new costume well enough she might come to you for her holiday wardrobe.'

'How can we cope with an entire wardrobe when we've scarcely got room for the work we're already doing?' Caitlin gestured at the small room where they stood; like the sewing room, it was gradually being taken over by clothes that were half made, being altered or waiting their turn to go on display in the main shop.

'We'll just have to make room. If only the butcher next door would move out, we could rent his premises.'

'There are three generations working in that shop,' Kirsty said from the doorway. 'I don't see them closing down.'

'Then we must think of another way of expanding. We need a proper storeroom for materials instead of having to go out and buy what we need bit by—'

Kirsty cut her short. 'Rose, I've heard more than I want to about expansions in the past few hours. Caitlin, I need a hand with some sewing.'

'I'll come as soon as I've written Mrs Harper's details into the workbook. She's agreed . . .' Caitlin began eagerly, but her mother had already gone.

'I'll see to the workbook.' Rose took it from her. 'What's amiss with Kirsty today? She's jumping about the place like a hen on a hot griddle, and it's not like her to be so sharp.'

'She's fretting about Alex's plan to buy the old mill. Did she not tell you?' Caitlin asked when Rose looked puzzled.

'She did not.'

Caitlin's heart sank. 'She must have wanted to keep it to herself. Mebbe you'd best say nothing,' she said hurriedly, but it was too late. Rose had already forged past her and into the sewing room. 'Kirsty, what's that carrot-haired son of yours up to now?' she was saying when Caitlin scurried in behind her.

Rose pounced as soon as Alex arrived at the shop that afternoon, looking every inch the businessman in a grey pinstripe suit with a watch chain across his flat, waistcoated midriff. 'What's this I hear about you buying property in Paisley? I didn't know that there was a mill for sale.'

'It's only just come onto the market. It's been lying empty for a while, and I've had my eye on it, waiting for the owner's decision to sell.'

'Have you put in a definite offer?'

'Mebbe,' he said calmly, then turned to Kirsty. 'I've hired a cab. I thought I'd call for you first, then for Todd.'

'I'll come with you.' Rose reached for her coat. 'I'd like to have a look at the place.'

'You'll do nothing of the sort. I want Mam and Todd to see it without being influenced by your opinion,' Alex told her, and swept his mother from the sewing room, leaving Rose almost apoplectic with rage.

'The impertinence of the man! Who does he think he is?'

Teenie, used by now to Rose's outbursts, continued to thunder away on her machine, while Caitlin said apologetically from where she sat at her mother's sewing machine, 'You know Alex – he hates talking about his business ploys until they're settled.'

Rose sniffed loudly and stamped into the fitting room, her brown curly hair escaping from its restraining pins as it always did when she was upset or angry. Caitlin shook her head at the material flashing beneath her needle. Like Jean, Alex had been suspicious of Rose when they first met, and she had taken a dislike to him. They were both ambitious, stubborn and proud, both determined to fight for whatever they wanted against the odds. In Rose's case the enemy was her overpowering mother, who had done all she could to push the youngest of her three daughters into marriage as soon as she had completed her education, and in Alex's case it had been his stepfather, Matt Lennox, determined to dominate his family and see his own son prosper rather than Alex.

They had both won their personal battles, and in the process they had developed a cautious respect for each other. Over the years, respect had mellowed until, despite the fact that they still argued and disagreed frequently, both Teenie and Jean Chisholm had talked of them being almost like brother and sister.

Caitlin didn't agree. It seemed to her that if her half-brother and her friend would only desist from their arguing and fault finding, they might find themselves becoming even closer than siblings. In her view, it was bound to happen eventually.

Kirsty didn't return to the shop that afternoon, and when Caitlin arrived home midway through the evening she found Mary alone in the kitchen, busy with her school books.

'They're in by.' She jerked her head in the direction of the front parlour. 'Your dinner's being kept hot; I'll clear a space and put it out for you.'

'Have they said anything about the mill?' Caitlin asked as she ate at one side of the big kitchen table while Mary scribbled busily at the other.

'Not a word, but they still think of me as a wee lassie,' said Mary, who, as her mother often said, had made the move from child to elderly woman during her first year at school. The classroom had opened up a new world for her; she had learned to read almost at once, and lived now for books and school. The creative skills shared by Kirsty, Caitlin and Alex had passed Mary by; her interest lay in facts and figures. She was a fine housekeeper, well able to cook and clean, but in her case housework was approached with an almost mathematical precision as she first estimated the time necessary for each task, then set out to complete it faster.

During the family's first years in Paisley, Mary had been a timid child with a tendency to cling to her mother and sister. No little surprise, Caitlin thought as she looked at her sister's bent head, considering the troubles that had beset them. Fergus, the baby of the family, had died under the hooves of a carthorse in the pend; Alex had been driven from the family home and business by his stepfather's harshness; Ewan, Matt's son by an earlier marriage, had run off with Todd Paget's betrothed; and finally Matt had died.

It had seemed to Caitlin in those dark days that the move to Paisley had brought her family nothing but worry and misery, but time had improved their lives. The shop had prospered, and Alex had settled down well with his father in Glasgow. Todd's serenity, the very opposite of Matt Lennox's tensions and tempers, had enriched the entire household, and under his influence Mary's timidity had melted away.

The younger girl had gone off to bed when Kirsty and Todd finally came through to the kitchen, both looking as though they bore the cares of the world on their shoulders.

'You didn't like the mill,' Caitlin guessed.

'There's nothing wrong with it,' Todd said. 'It's just . . . a big step for both of us to take. That wee workshop at the end of the yard'd be lost in the mill.'

'You could do with some extra space.'

'Aye, but . . .' He looked apologetically at the two women, then burst out, 'I'm no' an ambitious man – nothin' like Alex. I'm no' sure that I could run a big place.'

'Of course you could,' Kirsty's voice was firm. 'Once you got into the way of things it'd be no bother to you at all. And you'd have more men under you and less to do yourself.'

'Aye.' Todd, who was allowed to smoke in the parlour but never did because he was afraid of spoiling his wife's good furniture and curtains, reached automatically for his pipe, tobacco pouch and matches. 'I'll just go out by for a wee smoke.'

'Stay in here; it's cold out tonight.'

He shook his head. 'I'll be out of the wind, for I've a mind tae go down tae the workshop.'

'Then put these on.' Kirsty lifted his scarf and jacket from the nail on the back door. 'I don't want you catching a chill.'

'I'm no' a babby,' Todd protested, but did as he was told, winking at his stepdaughter. Matt Lennox had suffered badly from rheumatism brought on by his move to the damp climate that had made Paisley's textile industry so successful, and as a result Kirsty tended to fuss over her family's wellbeing, especially in cold, damp weather.

'Would you be willing to make the move, Mam?' Caitlin asked when they were alone. Kirsty, making the tea that was a cure for all ills in Scotland, sighed.

'To tell the truth, I didn't want to come back to this house when I heard that my father had left it to me, for as a lassie I knew such unhappiness here after my mother died. But Matt was eager to come to Paisley, and it's a woman's place to do whatever her man wants.

Then for a while I blamed the house for the bad things that happened when we settled here, but now I'm not so sure that I want to leave.' She poured hot water from the kettle into the teapot then looked round the kitchen, her eyes misty with memories. 'The house is contented again, more like the way it was during my mother's time. It has a good feeling to it.'

'It's the people that make a house, not the other way round,' Caitlin said gently.

'Aye, I suppose it is. Your poor father was never really happy here, for all the hopes he'd had of the move. And if the head of the house isn't settled, nobody else is.'

'Todd isn't happy with the thought of a move.'

'All Todd's ever wanted was to earn a living and to know that those around him were contented. The thing is, Caitlin, if we decide to stay here, what are we going to say to Alex? He's set his heart on buying that mill and opening it as a wee factory.'

'It's early days yet. You and Todd should take time to think about it before you decide.'

'Aye, I suppose you're right. I just wish Alex hadn't found that mill, then we'd not have this worry.'

Todd returned a few minutes later. 'Murdo's still workin' away in the old store – I saw a chink of light through the shutters when I came back up the lane.'

'Poor man, he must be tired. Ask him would he not come in for a drink of hot tea.'

'It's no use, Kirsty, you know he'll never sit with us. I'll take a mug out tae him and mebbe keep him company for a wee while if he's in the mood for a bit of a crack.'

Todd was still out when Caitlin went up to her room, and there was no sound of the loom's steady clack beneath her feet. Undressing, she wondered whether the two men were talking or just sitting in as companionable a silence as anyone could enjoy in Murdo Guthrie's brooding company.

Alex had found Murdo sweeping floors in Angus MacDowall's store, and on discovering that the Highlander was a hand-loom weaver and therefore a rare find in 1913, he had brought him to Paisley. Kirsty's mother and grandfather had been weavers, and her grandfather's loom, found lying in pieces in a corner of the storeroom by the pend when the family first came to Paisley, had been carefully restored. It was Kirsty's dearest hope that one day it would work again, and it was as much for her sake as his own that Alex had turned the store into a weaving shop and commissioned Murdo to make material to upholster some of the furniture now made by MacDowall and Son.

Kirsty, overjoyed to hear the thump and clack of her grandfather's loom again, had immediately offered the freedom of her kitchen to the weaver, hoping that he would become part of the family. But Murdo, a silent and withdrawn man, chose to keep himself to himself, and not even Kirsty's kindness could reach him. He tolerated Todd's company on occasion, but nobody else's. Kirsty fretted about his wellbeing, while Bryce mistrusted him because of his secrecy and his soft, lilting accent, so unlike the harder, flat tones of the Lowlander. As for Caitlin, she wasn't quite sure whether she felt sorry for the man in his loneliness or feared his dark presence.

For the past few years Caitlin had been attending evening classes at Paisley's Technical College and Art School in George Street, studying drawing and design. Shortly after Murdo's arrival in Paisley he, too, began taking evening classes; she had seen him at the school but had never had the courage to approach him. Nor had she told anyone else that she had seen him there, feeling that she had no right to gossip about him.

Sometimes she heard snatches of music from the store below. Todd had told her that he had seen an old mouth organ lying on a shelf in the store, but Murdo had merely shrugged when asked about it. Whenever she heard the music, sometimes melancholy, sometimes surprisingly lively, Caitlin longed to go to the store where she could listen properly. But, knowing that if she as much as put a hand on the door latch the music would stop and the instrument would be slipped out of sight, she kept her distance and continued to puzzle over the enigma that was Murdo Guthrie.

3

A sudden pounding on the door knocker made Kirsty jump just as she was moving the heavy soup pot onto the range. Soup splashed over the rim and sizzled dry on the hot metal, leaving a stain.

'For any favour!' she muttered irritably, bustling into the hall to throw the door open. 'You didn't have to knock the door down,' she snapped. 'A wee tap would've brought me just as quick.'

The burly bearded man standing on the pavement was in no mood to apologise. 'I've other deliveries tae make, missus, and this wind's been cuttin' through me all day.'

Kirsty eyed the horse and cart at the gutter. From between the cart's wooden bars, a child stared sullenly back at her, and she saw that its small fingers, locked around two of the spars, were dark blue with cold.

'If you're making a delivery, you'll have to take it through the pend to the workshop yard.' She began to close the door, with some thought of hurrying upstairs in search of a pair of woollen gloves that she could give to the child before it was driven away, but the man put out a hand with a grubby handkerchief wrapped about the knuckles to stop her.

'There was nothin' said about any workshop.' He

brought his other hand close to his eyes and scowled at a piece of paper almost lost in its grip. 'Would Mr Lennox be at home?'

Kirsty stared. 'Mr Lennox has been dead these four years nearly.'

'Are you the widow then?'

'I'm . . . Yes, I'm his widow.'

'Then you'll do,' he said shortly, turning his back on her and stomping across the pavement. 'It's on the cart,' he said over his shoulder, 'and ye'll have tae fetch it down for yersel', for I'm havin' nothin' more tae dae wi' it.'

'What is it?' She followed him across the flag-stones.

'This.' He jerked his head, and Kirsty, studying the boxes and trunks and brown-paper parcels scattered over the wooden planks, took a moment to realise that he meant the child.

'What're you . . . ?'

'No sense in askin' me, missus. All I know is that I was paid tae bring it tae Mr Lennox at this address. And a time of it I've had an' all,' he added, glaring through the bars as though studying an animal in a zoo. The child glared back at him. 'Kickin' an' screamin' and carryin' on, an' every time I stopped it was off an' away an' had tae be fetched back. I'd've left it tae run, but there's still a shillin' tae pay.'

Looking closely, Kirsty saw to her horror that one of the child's wrists had been lashed to the bars. 'You've never tied the poor wee soul to the cart!'

'I had tae, it was the only way tae keep it from runnin' off.'

'Untie him . . . her,' Kirsty still had no idea whether the dirty little scrap of humanity was male or female, 'at once!'

'I'll have my shillin' first,' the carter demanded.

'You will not.'

'I will!'

'You'll untie that child or I'll fetch a policeman.'

He flourished the hand with the handkerchief under her nose. 'You dae that, missus. No doubt he'll cart it straight tae the jail for bitin' decent hard-workin' folk. An',' he added in the child's direction, 'he'll put it intae a black cell wi' nothin' tae eat but hard bread.'

'For goodness' sake!' Kirsty didn't know what to do for the best. If she went off to fetch Todd the man might drive away, and heaven knew what might happen to the poor child then. 'I'll fetch your shilling if you'll untie that rope,' she compromised.

'But—'

'Untie that rope or there'll be no shilling!' she almost shouted at him. He hesitated, eyes swinging back and forth between her and the little face pressed between the bars, then finally gave a reluctant nod. Kirsty hurried into the house, convinced that she was throwing her hard-earned money away but at a loss to know what else to do.

When she returned, the child had been freed and was standing on the pavement. One end of the rope was still tied about its wrist, and the carter grasped the other end at arm's length. The shabby skirt hanging to the child's ankles proclaimed that this was a girl.

When Kirsty held the money out the man snatched at it, at the same time pushing the rope's end into Kirsty's hand. 'Here ye are – an' ye're welcome tae it, missus.' He plucked a brown-paper parcel from the cart and handed it to Kirsty, together with the paper he had been holding, then he scrambled onto the cart and stirred the horse into action, leaving Kirsty and her delivery on the pavement.

'What's your name, pet?'

The child tucked her mouth into a thin firm line to indicate that she had no intention of answering. She was filthy, from the top of the shapeless felt hat jammed over her head to eyebrow level to the toes of her scuffed shoes. Two women passing by stared openly at her, then at Kirsty, who was still holding the rope. One seemed about to remonstrate, but the other caught her by the wrist and almost dragged her away. 'Don't get drawn into anything, Nancy,' her voice floated back. 'It's none of our business . . .'

Kirsty dropped the end of the rope as though it had caught fire, and took the child's hand instead. It was like touching a block of ice. 'Poor wee lamb, you're frozen. Come in and get warm.'

The small fingers in hers stiffened, and for a moment she thought that the child was going to resist. Filthy though she was, Kirsty nerved herself to pick her up and carry her indoors if need be. Then the child began to shuffle reluctantly, one foot at a time, across the pavement and into the house.

In the hallway, Kirsty knelt to unfasten the rope from the little girl's tiny wrist, exclaiming at the red marks on her soft skin. The poor little thing must have been trying to free herself by pulling at her bonds.

'Does it hurt?' Her lips were gripped between her teeth, but from where Kirsty knelt, on a level with the child's face, she saw the child's eyes for the first time, wide and clear blue and tilted up at the outer corners. She only got a glimpse before they were hidden beneath long-lashed lids.

In the kitchen the child immediately ducked out of sight beneath the table. Lifting one side of the chenille cloth that covered the table when it wasn't in use, Kirsty tried to coax her out but with no success.

'Just stay there, then, until you feel ready to come and speak to me,' she said helplessly and turned her attention to the paper she had been given. It was an envelope, addressed in a hurried scrawl to Mr Matthew Lennox, Cabinet-maker, Espedair Street, Paisley.

Opening it, Kirsty took one look at the signature then caught at the edge of the table for support. She read the few words on the single sheet of paper, read them again, then said in a voice only just above a whisper, 'I'll just . . . Stay where you are, pet, I'll be back in a minute,' and blundered towards the back door.

In the workshop, Todd's smile at the sight of her disappeared as he took in her expression. 'Kirsty? Has somethin' happened?'

'I need to talk to you – outside,' she added, acutely aware of the sudden interest being shown by Bryce and the apprentice. He came at once, joining her in the yard and closing the door against inquisitive ears.

'It's not Mary . . . or Caitlin?'

'No, no, it's nothing to do with them. Read this.' She thrust the letter at him.

'Not out here, it's too cold, and you're shiverin'. We'll go intae the house.'

'Not the house – not until you've read the letter,' she insisted, then, as he opened his mouth to argue, 'The wash house'll do.'

'For any favour, woman, what's wrong with the kitchen where it's warm?' he protested, but she would say no more, and he had no choice but to follow her along the lane and into the stone wash house that had been built on at the back of the house. Once the door had been closed against possible eavesdroppers, Kirsty, comforted by the familiar smells of soapy water, bleach and starch, sat down on the little chair mainly used to hold piles of clothes and handed the letter to her husband.

As she had done, he glanced at the signature first. His brown head, the hair just as thick as when she had first met him, though now it was well scattered with grey, came up swiftly. 'Ewan?' He stared at her. 'Ewan . . . after all these years?'

Kirsty's heart fluttered uncomfortably in her throat. 'Read the letter, Todd,' she ordered huskily, 'and read it aloud, for I'm not sure that I've made sense of it yet.'

'"Dear Father, . . ."' he began, and looked at her again, perplexed.

'He'll have no idea of Matt's death since we didn't know where he was to tell him. Read it, Todd!'

'"Dear Father, you'll be surprised to hear from me again, and maybe not much pleased, but I have nobody else to turn to. This is Rowena Lennox, born in wedlock on 28 July in the year 1909. Me and Beth wed each other, so at least your grandchild is not a bastard. As cir . . . circum . . ."' Todd, never a scholar, stumbled slightly over the word but finally managed it, '"cir – cum – stances have turned out, we are not together now, and I must go away for a while. I hope that you and Mam will care for the child in my absence and trust that you will not hold my sins against her, for none of them were of her making. I will write when I am more able. Your dutiful son, Ewan Lennox."'

Todd read the letter again, this time to himself while Kirsty watched his lips form each word, then he looked up.

'Ewan and Beth – they had a child.'

'They did, and she's in our kitchen right now, under the table. A carter brought her to the door. He'd tied her to his cart.'

'Why did you put her under the table?' Todd asked, thoroughly confused.

'I didn't, she went there of her own will!' Kirsty didn't know whether to laugh or cry. In the space of an hour, her ordinary, contented life had been turned upside down. 'She's . . . She'll not say a word. The carter says she bit him. What are we going to do, Todd?'

He shook his head slowly, still bemused, then went to peer out of the small window overlooking the yard and workshop. Realising that, like her, he needed a moment to collect his thoughts, Kirsty bit back the words that flooded forth and waited, hands tightly clasped in her lap, until her husband turned back to her.

'I suppose the first thing is tae try tae get the bairn out from beneath the table,' he said, 'then try tae find out what's been happenin', and where Ewan might be.'

Mary came home from school while they were both trying to coax Rowena from beneath the table. Todd had attempted to pull her out but had given up the idea when she lunged at his outstretched hand like a dog, sinking small but sharp teeth into his knuckles.

Not one to be easily ruffled, Mary listened to the tale of how Ewan's daughter had arrived at the door tied to a cart then lifted a corner of the tablecloth and peered underneath. 'She'll be hungry,' she said when she straightened up. 'She'll come out when the dinner's ready.'

Rowena did indeed crawl out when the aromatic broth was ladled into bowls, but only for long enough to take her bowl and the hunk of bread Mary offered her before disappearing beneath the table again. Normally the cloth was taken off and the plates put on the scrubbed boards, but today Kirsty decided to leave it where it was for once rather than deprive the child of her protection.

'Best to pretend she's not here,' Caitlin suggested when she arrived home. 'She'll be feeling strange in a place she's never seen with folk she's never met.'

It wasn't easy to behave normally while at the same time straining their ears to catch every movement from below. They ate in silence, darting glances at each other then looking away whenever their eyes met. 'It's a fancy sort of name, Rowena,' Mary finally ventured in a loud whisper.

'It's a name Beth always liked.' Todd, who normally had a large appetite, had been stirring his broth around his plate. 'She got me tae take her tae the theatre at Smithhills once tae see a play. I mind that one of the lassies in it was cried Rowena.'

Kirsty put down her spoon, her own appetite suddenly gone, and got up to dish out meat and potatoes. When everyone else had been served she put a plateful on the floor, and a small and very dirty hand darted out and pulled it beneath the cloth. After a moment the empty soup bowl was pushed out against her feet. That night Rowena had the heartiest appetite in the house.

She came out when the meal was finished and stood against the inner door, surveying them all with clear blue eyes that seemed able to pierce through skin and flesh and bone and look right into their minds and souls. They had agreed, in whispers and nods and winks, to behave as though she wasn't there until she got used to them, so the two girls busied themselves with washing and drying the dishes at the sink while

Kirsty swept the hearth and Todd settled in his chair with his pipe and newspaper.

When the dishes were done, Mary took it upon herself to pour milk into a mug and hand it to Rowena. The girl hesitated, then took it and drank deeply and noisily. When she eventually took her face from the mug Kirsty's heart melted at the sight of the milky moustache decorating the little face. She longed to lift the child and give her a hug, and longed even more to put her into a bath and clean her up, but she knew that she must bide her time.

'So,' Todd said comfortably when the mug had been emptied and the little girl had sidled over to put it by the sink, always keeping the table between herself and the others, 'you're Rowena, are you?'

She nodded, her chin wagging up and down.

'And ye've come tae stay with yer grandma?'

Mary giggled, her eyes flying to her mother's face. Kirsty, settling into her own chair opposite Todd, felt her jaw drop.

Rowena nodded again, then said in a surprisingly strong voice, 'Till my daddy comes for me.'

'And when'll that be, then?'

'When he can.'

'What about yer mammy, pet?'

Rowena stared at him, her eyes suddenly darkening. For a moment Kirsty thought that she was going to burst into tears, then her chin jutted out. 'She went away. It's just me and my daddy, and he's coming for me when he can.'

'While ye're waitin' for him ye might as well sit by the fire,' Todd suggested casually, then began to study his newspaper again, with great interest. Rowena fidgeted in a corner for a while, then, as Kirsty and Caitlin got on with their sewing and Mary spread her school books on the table, she sidled over to sit on the hearth rug. Soon the heat of the fire made her eyelids droop.

'You'll be ready for your bed?' Kirsty ventured. The little girl hesitated, her eyes darting round the room as though in search of escape, before nodding.

'A wee wash first, though.'

Rowena's face seemed to close down. Her mouth tightened, and she shook her head firmly.

'She'll have to have a bath,' Kirsty appealed to the rest of the family. 'She can't get in among clean sheets in that state.'

'It won't be easy,' Todd warned.

'Easy or not, she isn't getting into bed like that. She could be covered in fleas for all we know.'

'If she was, we'd all be scratching ourselves by now,' he pointed out, getting to his feet. 'I'll fetch the tub from the wash house, for she's too wee tae go intae the upstairs bath. Best wash in front of the fire. Put more water on tae heat, Caitlin,' he added over his shoulder as he opened the back door.

Rowena watched the preparations with mistrust. When the bath was ready, Todd and Mary went upstairs to pull the truckle bed from its storage place beneath Mary's bed and make it up, while Kirsty and Caitlin set about undressing and bathing Rowena.

As Todd had predicted, it wasn't an easy task. She fought tooth and nail, and by the time she was bathed, dried and dressed in a nightgown Mary had grown out of, Kirsty, Caitlin and the hearth rug were all soaked. Leaving Caitlin to empty the tub and start clearing up the mess, Kirsty carried the squirming child upstairs. It was like holding a barrowload of monkeys.

When they put her into the bed she jumped straight out again, and for a while it looked as though they were going to have to leave her to sleep on the floor. Then Mary scurried from the room and returned with a photograph, which she thrust below the child's nose. 'Look, Rowena, d'you see who that is?'

Rowena's blue eyes, sparkling with fury, swept over the picture. She stopped struggling and snatched the piece of board from Mary's fingers. 'That's my daddy. That's mine,' she said fiercely, clutching it to her chest, defying any of them to take it from her.

'Of course it's yours, that's why I gave it to you. Now,' Mary pulled the blankets back, 'take the picture to bed, and you and your daddy can have a good sleep.'

They left a lamp burning, and when Caitlin looked in five minutes later, Rowena was sound asleep and the corner of the photograph, which Ewan had had taken not long before leaving Paisley, could just be seen peeping from beneath the pillow. Caitlin stood by the bed for a moment, marvelling at how fierce the child had been when she was awake, and how innocent and vulnerable she looked in sleep, with her face washed and her hair dried and brushed. A rich chestnut colour, it was fine and silky. Beth Laidlaw, the beauty who had scandalised Paisley by running away with Ewan just days before her marriage to Todd Paget, had had hair of that texture, though hers had been black. The little girl's blue eyes had been inherited from Ewan, though the uptilted corners had come from Beth. She had her father's wide mouth, but beneath her baby chubbiness her mother's clearly defined cheekbones could be seen.

'She's asleep. There's little doubt as to whose bairn she is,' Caitlin said when she rejoined her family, and her mother and stepfather nodded.

'The only question is, what's happened to the two

of them?' Kirsty was unpacking the parcel Rowena had brought with her, shaking out the few clothes it held. 'There's not much here, and no letter to explain anything.'

'What are we going to do?' Mary asked from the table.

Todd puffed at his pipe. 'There's not much we can do but keep her until Ewan comes to claim her.'

'D'you think he will?' Knowing Ewan, and his dislike of responsibility, Caitlin was doubtful.

'She's determined that he will,' Todd answered, 'and that's enough tae be gettin' on with. The thing is, what are we goin' tae dae with her in the meantime?'

'The shop has more need of Caitlin than of me, so I'll stay at home tomorrow. I'll bring out my old sewing machine, and you can send some work round to me, Caitlin.' Kirsty hesitated, then went on, 'I think Beth's family should be told and given the chance to take her in.'

'What, old Mr Laidlaw and that sour-faced daughter of his? D'ye think they'd want her?' Todd asked in astonishment.

'They have the right to know what's happened. After all, she's Mr Laidlaw's grandchild as much as mine – even more, since Ewan isn't my flesh and blood – and I don't want any of them saying that we never asked them.' Kirsty looked round at her family, then added firmly, 'I'll take her over there tomorrow.'

4

Kirsty had been shaken by Todd's memory of the night he took Beth to the theatre. Still trying to come to terms with the realisation that she was a grandmother, albeit by marriage rather than by blood, she had forgotten until he'd spoken of Rowena's name that the child asleep in Mary's room had been borne by the woman he had once worshipped and planned to marry.

Getting ready for bed, she thought of Todd as she had first known him. He had seemed to her to be a mere lad then, though she later discovered that he was older than he looked. Almost all of his conversation in those days had been about Beth and his great fortune in being chosen by her as her future husband. When Beth had eloped with Kirsty's stepson, Ewan, just before her and Todd's wedding day the young journeyman had almost gone out of his mind with grief.

Kirsty had thought that those difficult days were long over and forgotten, but Rowena's arrival, she reflected unhappily as she climbed into bed, must have triggered off memories within him of the two people who had betrayed him and destroyed his dreams.

A few minutes later Todd turned the lamp off and slipped into bed beside her, leaning over to give her his usual goodnight kiss before settling down.

'What's amiss?' he asked, peering into her face. 'Is it the bairn coming? We'll manage, lass, don't fret about that. We can surely find food and board for a wee scliff of a thing like that.'

'I was just thinking . . . She might have been yours, Todd, if things had gone the way they should.'

'Mine?' The bed bounced as he settled by her side. 'Never mine,' he said, amused. 'Not with my looks. Anyone can see that that wee one had two bonnier parents than me.'

'Will it bother you to have her in the house?'

'Not a bit of it,' he said comfortably. 'Is that why ye're thinking of askin' the Laidlaws tae take her in? Tae spare my feelin's?'

'No,' she lied. 'I just think that they should have the chance.'

'They'll say no, Kirsty. I'm certain of that.'

Silence fell. Kirsty opened her mouth to speak several times, then closed it again. But the question nagged at her and finally she had to ask it. 'Todd, d'you ever think of Beth and what there might have been for you if she'd stayed in Paisley?'

'I have, on occasion. And each time I've thanked fate that things turned out the way they did.'

'D'you mean that?'

He fumbled beneath the sheet for her hand, which he took firmly into his. 'Beth and me were never right for each other, but I was too befuddled by her tae see that. If it hadnae been your Ewan, it'd have been someone else. It's as well it happened when it did, before her and me went up the aisle together.'

Kirsty squeezed his fingers, then said after another silence, 'She never cried . . . Rowena.'

'Is that not more of a blessin' than a curse?'

'It's not natural, Todd. She's only four years of age.

You'd think she'd be crying her poor wee eyes out at being deserted by her parents.'

'If and when she's ready, she'll cry and we'll comfort her,' he told her patiently. 'Now stop frettin' an' go tae sleep, for ye're goin' tae have yer hands full in the mornin' with that one.'

Five minutes later he was asleep, while Kirsty lay wide eyed by his side.

Rowena ate her breakfast at the table instead of beneath it, but even so she remained aloof, scarcely answering when spoken to, keeping her head down and darting swift glances at her new-found relatives when she thought they weren't looking at her. After the others had gone off to work and school, Kirsty washed the dishes then helped the little girl on with her coat, which had been brushed but was in need of a good wash. As she smoothed down the sleeves, she noticed with a pang that there were still faint marks on the delicate skin of Rowena's wrist where the carter's rope had chafed. Deciding that the felt hat was only fit for the dustbin, she brushed the child's hair before tying it with a ribbon. It was soft and thick and crackled beneath the brush.

'I'm going to take you to see your grandfather, Rowena, and your aunt and uncle. They've got a nice shop just across the road, and they'll mebbe want you to live there with them.'

Rowena's eyes were immediately hostile. 'If I go away from here, my daddy won't know where I am.' It was the longest sentence she had spoken so far; when she had barked it out she folded her lips tightly together in what had already become a familiar gesture.

'I'll tell him when he arrives, and he'll only have to cross the road to get to you.' Kirsty buttoned on the shabby shoes she had tried in vain to polish, then stood up. 'I want you to be a very good girl, Rowena.'

It had been a while since she had felt nervous going into the tobacconist's, but as she crossed the cobbled street with Rowena's hand small and unfamiliar in hers, Kirsty felt her stomach lurch slightly. During her childhood, old Mrs Laidlaw, who had owned the shop then, had been the scourge of the local children. In Kirsty's teens, when deep loneliness after her mother's death had driven her into the arms of her father's apprentice, Mrs Laidlaw had been the first to detect the signs of her pregnancy and had told her father, who had almost beaten the lad to death and banished Kirsty from Paisley.

On her return more than eighteen years later, she had been relieved to find that Mrs Laidlaw was in her grave and no longer able to torment her. But her childhood friends had insisted that old Mrs Laidlaw was a witch with the power to curse folk, and even in maturity, with a husband and a family of her own, Kirsty had had reason to think that the tales might be true and that Mrs Laidlaw had cursed her all those years ago. Although she herself had gone, her granddaughter, Beth, had taken her place behind the shop counter and had dazzled Ewan and spirited him off, breaking Todd's heart and leaving Matt, already crippled by rheumatism, to mourn the loss of his beloved son for the rest of his life.

After Beth's disappearance, her elder sister, Annie Mitchell, had returned to Paisley with her husband to run the shop and share the flat above with her father. Mr Laidlaw had been in indifferent health for some time and was rarely seen in the shop, but on that day he was sitting in a corner, a woollen shawl round his shoulders and a rug over his knees. From behind the counter, his daughter eyed Kirsty coldly. In spite of the fact that nobody had ever been able to dominate Beth Laidlaw, her family had long since determined that the elopement was entirely Ewan's doing.

'Yes?'

Kirsty pushed the little girl forward slightly, her hands on the small shoulders. 'This is Rowena – Beth and Ewan's wee girl. She arrived yesterday.'

The old man in the corner gave a muffled exclamation, while Annie Mitchell, who possessed none of her sister's beauty, flicked a glance at the two blue eyes that could just be seen above the top of the counter, then drew herself upright. Her face seemed to close in on itself. It was for all the world, Kirsty thought, fascinated, as though the woman possessed the ability to button up her features.

'What's that to us?'

The chill in her voice and in her eyes reminded Kirsty so strongly of old Mrs Laidlaw that she almost lost her resolve. It took all her determination to stand her ground. 'It seems from the letter Ewan sent with her that he and Beth are no longer together. He's asked us to look after Rowena until he comes for her. Since she's your sister's child I thought—'

'She has no sister!' the old man said in a creaky voice, thumping the floor with a walking stick clutched in one knotted hand.

'But—'

'My father's right, I have no sister. As far as we're concerned, Beth died the day she walked out of here.' Annie Mitchell spat the words out as though they were poison. Hostility twisted her features, ageing them and emphasising the resemblance to her grandmother. 'We want no more of her or her paramour – or her brat for that matter!'

'I only thought—'

Mr Laidlaw thumped the stick again. 'Get out of my shop!' It was the second time he had given Kirsty such an order. The first had been when she had tried to apologise to him for what Ewan had done.

Annie Mitchell swept round the counter and threw open the door. 'You heard what my father said – leave this shop at once and take that . . . that devil's child with you!'

Before Kirsty knew what was happening, Rowena wrenched her hand free and shot across to the shelves against the wall. Swinging one arm forward, she swept a hand along the shelf at shoulder height, sending a shower of pipes and packets of tobacco to the floor.

Annie Mitchell screeched, then screeched again as Rowena spun round and rushed straight at her to deliver a hefty kick on her shins.

'Old bitch!' the little girl shrieked, then as the shop door opened she spun again, full circle this time, and plunged out onto the pavement, crashing into the customer on his way in and almost knocking him over.

'Rowena!' Her heart in her mouth, Kirsty ran after her, careering into the startled customer in her turn but managing to catch the child by the shoulder just in time to prevent her from crossing the road under the hooves of a carthorse. The animal half-shied, the carter shouted angrily and Kirsty, with memories of the day her youngest child had died beneath a horse's iron-shod hooves in the pend, clutched at a lamppost with her free hand, a wave of nausea sweeping over her.

Rowena, scarlet faced and heedless of the near accident, twisted round beneath her grandmother's restraining hand and screeched 'Old bitch!' at the top of her voice. Annie Mitchell, peering through the window, reeled back in horror, as did an elderly woman passing by on the opposite pavement.

'Get into the house!' Kirsty, shocked into action, hurried the child across the road and fumbled at her door.

'Some children'd be the better for a good smacking,' she heard the passer-by say as the door opened. She rushed Rowena through it and closed it thankfully behind them.

'You promised you'd be a good girl!'

Rowena stood foursquare in the hall before her. 'You were going to give me to that old bitch!'

'I was not. I just wanted your auntie and your grandfather to know that you were here.'

'I hate you,' Rowena yelled, and stamped into the kitchen. When Kirsty followed her, she had again taken refuge beneath the table.

'Come out and I'll give you a biscuit.' When there was no reply, Kirsty added, 'You can't stay there for ever.'

'I'm staying here until my daddy comes. He told me to stay here, and I'm not going to live with that nasty smelly man and that old—'

'Nobody said you had to live with them. You'll stay with us,' Kirsty said wearily, accepting the inevitable. When Rowena remained silent, she went to make herself a very strong cup of tea.

'If Ewan's told her to wait here for him, at least we know that she'll not try to run away,' Caitlin said helpfully that night when Rowena had been put to bed. 'She seems to be more fond of him than of her mother.'

'What I want to know is, how long will it be before he comes for her?' Kirsty had had a bad day; Rowena had refused to speak to her, and she knew that it would be a while before she was forgiven for having taken the child to Mr Laidlaw's shop. She heartily wished that she had never thought of it.

'However long it takes, we're all the family the bairn's got.' Todd's face suddenly creased into a grin. 'I wish I'd seen Annie Mitchell's face when the wee one cleared the shelf then kicked her.'

'I wish you'd seen it too, instead of me.'

'What's going to happen to the shop if you have to look after her?' Caitlin wanted to know.

'If she's going to stay, Rowena must learn to fit in with the rest of us. I'll have to take her to the shop with me – just in the mornings at first, until she gets used to it.'

'What if she behaves in your shop the way she behaved in the Laidlaws'?' Mary put in.

After a quick look at his wife's face, Todd said hurriedly, 'She won't. She was upset today because Annie Mitchell called her names. She might be wee, but she's as sharp as a needle. Nothing gets by her. If she's treated right, she'll behave hersel'.'

'One thing's sure,' Kirsty said wearily, 'there'll be no move to the old mill for us now. How can we put our minds to settling into a new house and a new factory at a time like this? Besides, moving to another strange house would unsettle her.'

'Alex won't be pleased.'

'Alex'll just have to put Bryce in to run the new place or find another overseer, for I'm not moving.'

Todd said no more, but Kirsty thought that she saw relief in his face as he sucked thoughtfully at his pipe.

Alex was not at all pleased. He argued for an entire

evening, but Kirsty's mind was made up and she refused to change it.

'It's too much for Todd and me to deal with, Alex. There's the wee one to consider now. I'll find it difficult enough caring for her and doing my work at the shop without making the move to a new house as well.'

'But there's more room in the mill house, and we could make a wee garden at the back for her to play in.'

'Matt and me brought five bairns here, and there was room for us all. In any case, the other house is too close to the river. I'd be fretting every minute of the day in case she fell in and drowned.'

'She seems a sensible lassie from what I've seen of her.'

'You've not seen her at her worst. I'd not put it past her to drown herself out of spite, and then what would I say to Ewan when he came to fetch her?'

'You think he will? If you ask me he's gone back to his old life now he's shot of her and Beth. You surely mind how much Ewan liked his freedom.'

'If you're right it means that Rowena's going to be with us until she's grown, and to my mind that gives all the more reason for us to stay here. Put Bryce into the new place and find another journeyman for Todd.'

'Bryce is too young.'

'He's not much younger than you are.'

'Four years, and not that long past his apprenticeship. I know he's a good worker, but there's still a restlessness about him,' Alex fretted, and Todd nodded agreement.

'Alex is right. The lad's a touch impulsive. He'd mebbe try tae be too clever too soon, just tae impress Alex.'

'Then take on a new manager.'

'Trustworthy men aren't that easy to find,' Alex told his mother sharply. 'That's why I wanted Todd. I'd not have had a minute's worry with him running the new place and he would still be close enough to keep an eye on what Bryce was up to here.'

Caitlin, keeping well out of the discussion but listening to every word, felt relief wash over her. She knew what Todd meant about Bryce being too eager to impress. He would be disappointed to hear that Todd was staying on in Espedair Street, but since he wasn't going to get the house after all, he would have to relinquish all hopes of marriage.

'You realise that this means giving up the idea of buying the mill?' Alex was saying.

'That's your decision, son.' Kirsty put her hand briefly on his. 'I'd have liked fine to please you, but I must think of my responsibilities towards that wee lassie upstairs.'

'Don't act hastily, Alex. Give yourself time to consider things,' Todd advised. Like Caitlin, he was relieved by the way things had turned out.

When he was leaving to catch the Glasgow train, Alex paused at the door. 'Ewan often caused trouble when he was living under this roof,' he said bitterly. 'Who'd have thought that he'd still be doing it? And him not even here!'

It was Mary, calling at the shop next day to hand in some work that Kirsty had completed at home, who told Rose Hamilton that there was to be no move to the mill house.

'My mam says that she's got enough to worry about just now, and it wouldn't be fair on wee Rowena to move her to another strange house.'

'You'll be sorry about that.'

Mary shrugged. 'I'm not bothered.'

'So Alex'll be putting someone in to manage the new place?'

'He says it'd be too much trouble.'

Sudden interest sharpened Rose's blue eyes. 'You mean that he's not going to buy the mill after all?'

'He tried to make out that it was Mam's fault, but she'd have none of it,' Mary said in her old-woman way, and departed.

Caitlin, busy with Mrs Harper's new costume, was vague when Rose questioned her. 'Alex'll get over the disappointment, and so will Bryce. I think Todd's pleased, though. He didn't care for the thought of overseeing a bigger place and more men. D'you think this material would do for the lapels, or should I see what else I can find? I wonder,' she said thoughtfully, 'if Alex would let us use the ends of the cloth Murdo weaves. It's good, strong material, and it's thrown away once it's cut off the loom.'

That evening Rose went to a supper party with John Brodie, the young lawyer who had drawn up the partnership between herself and Kirsty and Jean Chisholm. Family friends since childhood, they often accompanied each other to social events, much to the delight of both mothers. Rose looked on John as nothing more than a friend and, especially that evening, as a shrewd business partner.

By the end of the evening she had persuaded him to view the mill with her the following morning.

Twenty-four hours later, Rose had bought it.

5

Alex MacDowall strode up the long driveway, across the sweep of gravel fronting the Hamilton house, then surged up the steps to rap on the door.

The uniformed maid who answered his knock smiled politely at the well-dressed visitor, then stiffened visibly as he barked at her, 'I want to speak to Rose.'

'I'll enquire as to Miss Rose's whereabouts, sir, if you give me your n—' she began, then fell back with an outraged gasp as Alex put the flat of his hand on the door, pushed it wide and stepped past her into the large entry hall.

'The name's Alex MacDowall, and you needn't bother enquiring. Either she's in or she isn't, and if she isn't I want to know where I can find her.'

'Alex?' Rose said from the landing, then came swiftly, lightly down the stairs.

He went to meet her. 'You bought the mill!'

Arriving in the hall, she glanced up into his face. 'We can talk in the dining room. It's all right, Morag.'

The maid bobbed a curtsey then fled to the safety of the door behind the stairs as Rose led her visitor into a large panelled room dominated by a polished table running almost its full length.

'Sit down, Alex.'

He stayed on his feet, tossing his hat onto the table and ignoring the portraits ranged along the walls, the huge windows opening onto the terrace, the bowls of flowers and leaves placed at careful intervals along the table, their colours reflected in its rich depths.

'You bought the mill,' he said again, 'the mill that I had earmarked for myself.'

Rose pulled out one of the many high-backed chairs at the table and sat down. 'You changed your mind about buying it.'

'I did nothing of the sort!'

She frowned. 'But surely Todd and Kirsty have decided to stay in Espedair Street.'

'That has nothing to do with it. I was still considering the mill.'

'The factor told us that no definite offer had been made.'

'Damn it, Rose, you knew I had my eye on it!'

'Mary told me—'

'Oh, I see.' Alex took a few steps towards one of the windows, then swung back to face her, his voice cutting. 'You took Mary's word for it – and since when has my schoolgirl sister been my business partner?'

Rose's long face flushed. 'I assumed—'

'You've a habit of assuming things, Rose,' Alex told her icily. 'It comes of having more money than sense.'

Her face crimsoned, and she jumped to her feet, but he swept on.

'Years ago when you cost my mother her job here, you assumed that she would come crawling back when you wanted her to. Then you assumed that you had the right to poke your nose into the way Jean Chisholm ran her wee shop—'

'The three of us have done well with that shop!'

'Thanks to the hard work Jean and Mam and Caitlin have put into it.'

'That's most unfair, Alex! If it hadn't been for my money, we could never have expanded.'

'And if it hadn't been for your money and your God-given assumption that you should get everything you want, I wouldn't have lost that mill!'

Rose slammed her palms on the table. 'Don't blame me, Alex MacDowall – you lost that mill because you hesitated and I didn't!'

'I lost it because you took Mary's word for Gospel instead of speaking to me. I lost it because you and your friend Brodie went to the factor behind my back . . . and no doubt,' he sneered, 'you both used your family names as an additional lever.'

'We did nothing underhand. John's a lawyer.'

'John,' Alex spat the name out contemptuously, 'is your lapdog and so besotted with you that he'd do anything to please you, as you very well know.'

'You . . . How dare you.' She came round the table towards him like a whirlwind. He took a step forward to meet her just as the door opened and Mrs Hamilton's small, dumpy figure bustled into the room. She stopped short, one hand flying to the triple row of pearls at her throat.

'Rose? Who is this . . . person?'

'This is Alex MacDowall, Mother.' Rose's voice was clipped, her eyes still locked with his. 'And we have business to discuss.'

'We have nothing to discuss,' Alex corrected her, snatching up his hat and giving her mother a brief nod of the head. 'Mrs Hamilton . . .'

As he went towards the door the woman scuttled hastily to one side, out of his way.

'Alex . . .' The door closed behind him, and Mrs Hamilton blocked Rose's move to follow him.

'Who was that rude man?'

'I told you, Mama. It was Alex MacDowall.' Rose went to the window and watched Alex stride away along the drive.

'MacDowall.' Mrs Hamilton pursed her lips. 'Do we know his family?'

'I work with his mother, Kirsty Lennox.'

Mrs Hamilton winced, as she always did when she heard the word 'work' on her daughter's lips. 'I'm not even going to ask why they have different surnames. He strikes me as a very disagreeable person, Rose, and I trust that you will not encourage him to call at my house again.'

Alex was out of sight, hidden by the bushes lining the driveway. Rose turned from the window. 'I don't believe he will, Mama,' she said bleakly. 'In fact, I'm quite sure of it.'

'You'll never make this place a fashion house.' Caitlin stood in the middle of the mill's first floor, turning round slowly to take in the space, the pillars, the large but grimy windows.

'Of course we will.'

'We?'

'You're surely not going to leave me to run the place on my own. I'm hoping that you'll come in as designer.'

Caitlin gaped, then said weakly, 'Designer? But I've not got the experience.'

'You're taking design at night school, aren't you?'

'Yes, but . . .'

'And you're good at designing already. Look at Mrs Harper and the others – they've been pleased with the clothes you've made for them. That's one of the reasons why I bought this place. You need to get the chance to do more designing, and the best way to learn is to do it. You will come in with me, won't you?'

Caitlin nodded, scarcely able to believe her good fortune.

'Once it's cleaned and painted and some decent flooring has been installed, it'll be perfect.' As Rose paced, the ends of her long woollen scarf drifted out behind her. 'This floor can be the sewing room – just think how many machines it will hold! Our offices and the fitting rooms will be on the ground floor, as well as two pleasant salons where clients can wait to be seen.'

'Why two?'

'One for the comfortably off, and one for the ladies who fancy themselves to be too important to mix with the others. Instead of you having to go to their homes, they will come here to you. And the top floor will be the store. Just think of it, Caitlin. You'll be able to buy all the cloth and ribbons and everything you need beforehand instead of by the yard as you require it. Our ladies will be able to choose colours and materials, and we can have our own embroideress, or two, or more.'

It was unusually cold for October and the mill, unheated for some time, was chilly. Caitlin wrapped her arms about herself for warmth and exhaled a cloud of steam when she said, 'It'll have to be warmer than it is now.'

'Mmm.' Rose studied the antiquated stove in the middle of the floor. 'I doubt if this ever gave out much heat. We'll have to put in a good system that'll heat the whole place.'

'That,' said Caitlin, 'will take a lot of money.'

'Don't you worry about that. I'll manage, and John's agreed to put some of his money in as well.'

Rose had changed in the past week, Caitlin thought, watching her pace the floor. She had become . . . She searched for the right word and decided that brittle best described her friend. She shivered and thought longingly of the comparative warmth of the back shop as Rose went on.

'The yard below will be ideal for the clients' motor cars . . .'

For the first few weeks after her arrival, Rowena had asked on several occasions when her daddy was coming for her, but after that the questions stopped. She was still very much an outsider, speaking only when she had to and refusing to have anything to do with the children who sometimes played in the street.

Each day she went with Kirsty to the shop, where she sat in a corner twisting bits of cloth round empty bobbins or stood for hours watching the sewing machines at work, her vivid blue eyes peering over the edge of the table.

'She's like a wee old woman, listenin' tae every word that's said and watchin' every move,' Jean Chisholm marvelled. 'It's not natural for lassies of her age tae be so quiet.'

'I'm just grateful that she's behaving herself and hasn't bitten anyone,' Kirsty said with relief. Occasionally Rowena ventured into the front shop, where a number of customers had tried to make friends with her. Kirsty had held her breath, anxious in case the child should take it into her head to unleash one of her rages, but Rowena had studied each face gravely before turning away to slip, shadow-like, into the back shop.

Although she had kept well away from him at first, Todd turned out to be the only person able to make any headway with her. In the evenings she tended to sit on the floor at his feet, and on occasion he took her to the workshop, where she played with odd pieces of wood and the sweet-smelling drifts of curled shavings by the workbench.

Bryce found her presence unnerving. 'She slips in and out like a ghostie,' he complained to Caitlin. 'Ye don't know she's there until ye feel those eyes of hers on the back of yer skull. There's somethin' sleekit about her – mebbe old Satan's put his mark on her.'

'Don't be daft, she's just a wee girl.'

'She doesnae behave like one,' said Bryce, who came from a large and noisy family. Then he added, with a sideways glance, 'Our bairns'll no' be like that, I can tell ye.'

'Are you not a wee bit ahead of yourself with such talk, Bryce?' she said sharply, and he shrugged, undeterred. 'No sense in leavin' things too late.'

A slight chill touched Caitlin every time he said such things. Now that the mill was well on the way to becoming a fashion house, she was looking forward to working there and more determined than ever to retain her independence.

Rowena was doing what her father had told her to do – keeping quiet and minding her manners. If she did as she was bid, he had said before lifting her onto the cart and walking away from her, her grandparents would let her stay with them until he came to fetch her back.

It had been difficult at first. The carter had shouted at her and slapped her when she wept for her father, and in her opinion he had fully deserved to be bitten. Her daddy had warned that her grandfather was a cross old man who would smack her arse if she misbehaved and might even put her out on the streets, but she herself had found him to be gentle and quiet voiced. Confused, she at first suspected that he was setting some sort of trap for her, but as time passed without him raising his voice, let alone his hand, she gradually came to trust him as much as she would allow herself to trust anybody.

Days turned into weeks, and weeks into months. The end of November found Rowena still waiting for her father to come for her as he had promised. With December looming, Kirsty took time away from the shop when she could, bent on ensuring that her house would be spotless when the new year arrived, and sending Rowena out of the way to play in the back yard. Tiring of her own company on one such day, the little girl wandered to the work yard, where she slipped in through the open door. There was no sign of her grandfather, and Bryce and the apprentice were busy with a difficult piece of furniture.

Rowena made for the corner where the wood shavings were piled, burrowing into them and relishing their fresh, clean smell. She scooped up handfuls, scattering them over herself until she was almost completely covered and peering out at the workshop through a thin veil.

Neither of the men had noticed her arrival or heard the rustling in the corner. It wasn't until Rowena sneezed, just as Bryce was reaching for a hammer from the shelf above the shavings, that he realised she was there.

The sudden explosion of sound from just in front of his feet startled him. Letting out an instinctive yelp, he sprang back as Rowena rose from the corner, scattering shavings everywhere. Then he yelled again as the hammer slipped from his fingers and landed painfully on one of his feet.

A burst of laughter from the apprentice, a lad with a strong sense of humour, added to the journeyman's shock, pain and humiliation.

'You!' Bryce forgot about his sore toes. 'Ye wee bugger, ye!' He reached for Rowena, who in her four years had become wily in the ways of self-preservation. She eeled out from beneath the clutching hands and fled towards the door. Going after her, Bryce managed to catch a good handful of her long chestnut hair. He hauled back on it, and Rowena, within inches of freedom, screeched with pain and rage as she was almost lifted from her feet.

'Hold on there,' the apprentice protested. 'She's just a wee lassie!'

'She's a wee devil – and the spawn of devils, from what I've heard. It's time someone taught her a lesson.'

Bryce caught the child by the shoulders and spun her around, then lifted her off her feet, shaking her until her head juddered on the slender stem of her neck. Both arms were pinned to her sides by his grip, and she wasn't close enough to bite, but her feet were free, so she lashed out with them as though running in midair. Bryce's 'Right, milady,' gave way to a startled 'Oof!' as the tip of a sturdy boot, with all the muscle Rowena could muster behind it, caught him in the pit of the stomach. He doubled up, dropping her. She landed hard on the floor, winded, but managed to roll over, get onto her hands and knees and scramble rapidly towards the door. Once there, she got to her feet and fled without a backward glance.

'Get a hold o' her!'

'She's only a wee lassie,' the apprentice said again, then grabbed at Bryce's sleeve as the older man lunged for the door. 'For pity's sake, man, what d'ye think ye're at?'

'I'll teach her tae make a fool of me!'

It was the apprentice's view that Bryce had made a fool of himself, but he had the sense to keep that to himself. Aloud he said, 'The master's fond of her – ye'll only get intae trouble if ye go after her. Ye dropped her with a right bang as it was. It's tae be hoped that ye didnae hurt her.' As Bryce glared at the door then at him, the apprentice added, 'Leave it be. Mr Paget'll be back soon. We'd best get this place put tae rights an' say nothin' about it.'

He seized a broom and began to sweep the scattered shavings up, watching anxiously out of the corner of one eye. To his relief, Bryce finally shrugged and limped back to the workbench, rubbing his stomach gingerly.

'With any luck she'll run through the pend and under the wheels of some motor,' he said. 'Then we'll be rid of her.'

With any luck, the apprentice thought, putting the broom away and returning to his work, she wouldn't tell anyone about what had happened.

Rowena had indeed bolted through the pend and onto the pavement, only to stop short as she saw Annie Mitchell at the door of the tobacconist's shop, turning to help her father down the single step to the pavement.

The child immediately ducked back out of sight, then peered round the corner. Old Mr Laidlaw was making heavy weather of negotiating the step. When he was safely on the pavement and supported on one side by his daughter's arm and on the other by his walking stick, he began moving slowly along the pavement on a course that would take him past the pend, though on the opposite side of the road.

Slowly Rowena retreated through the pend, keeping close to the brick wall and trying to make herself as small as possible in case the couple parading along the pavement glanced over and saw her. On the day she'd been taken to the tobacconist's her gran had referred to this old man, who had shouted at her and banged his stick on the floor, as her grandfather. This meant that she had two grandfathers – and old Mr Laidlaw might be the one her father had warned her about.

The last thing she wanted was to be sent to live with him and his sour-faced daughter, which meant that she had no option but to return to her gran and face whatever punishment she might get for making Bryce angry.

Her hand, brushing along the brick wall, suddenly swung into space. Startled, Rowena turned and saw that a door was set in the wall. From behind it she could make out a strange thumping beat. She pushed tentatively with both hands, and the door opened just enough to allow entry. Rowena stepped through, and suddenly there was no floor and she was falling for the second time. For a moment she lay where she landed, cold, hard damp-smelling earth beneath her cheek. The thumping stopped, and hands lifted her and set her back on her feet.

'Are ye all right, lass?'

Although light came through the windows, the place was shadowy compared to outside. Rowena blinked, adjusting her eyes to the difference.

'Are ye hurt?' asked the man hunkered down in front of her.

She moved back, twitching herself out of his grasp.
'No.'

'You fell down the step with a right wallop,' he
said. Then: 'Where are you from?'

His voice was soft, with a lilt in it that she had
never heard before.

'The house,' she said, ready to run if he tried to
touch her again.

'You're biding with the Pagets?' he asked. Then,
when she gave a quick nod of the head: 'So you've
come to see what I'm up to in my wee room here, have
you?' He got up and gave her a slight bow. 'Welcome
to my weaving shop,' he said, then reached for a plain
wooden chair against one wall and brought it forward.
'Sit yourself down,' he invited, and went to sit on a
bench behind a large wooden contraption that filled
most of the room.

6

As Rowena scrambled onto the chair with some difficulty – her entire body was beginning to ache after her two falls – the strangely spoken man began to work his machine and the rhythmic beat began again. She watched, fascinated, noting how he operated wooden treadles with his feet and how his body swayed from side to side on the bench as he reached out, first with one hand and then with the other, to pull at strings on either side of the framework before him.

Each time he pulled, a collection of wooden rods holding threads lifted and a small something shot through the threads, passing just in front of him, to hit the opposite post with a sharp clack. Then the rods closed down behind it, lifting again when he pulled at the other string.

Curious, Rowena wriggled down from the chair and ventured closer to man and machine. The rods and the swift little thing, she gradually realised, created the thump-and-clack rhythm she had heard from outside. It was as though he was part of the wooden machine. He didn't stop work or look at her when she came closer, but said easily, 'I'm making cloth. See how the yarn's lifted? These threads are the warp, and the weft's carried across them by the shuttle. There's a box of shuttles behind me, if you care to look at them.'

She peered into the box at the little wooden things, her stomach contracting with homesickness as she saw that they were quite like the little wooden boats her father had sometimes carved for her. Occasionally, when he had been in a good mood, he had taken her to sail the boats in the small burn near where they lived. After her mother had gone away, though, there had been no more playing with boats.

She blinked against the tears that had come to her eyes at the memory and slid a quick glance at the man, wondering if he had witnessed her weakness. He was still swaying, still working and seemingly oblivious to her, but even so she kept her head down over the box, staring hard at the little boats. Soon the battle against the tears was won. Each boat, she saw when her vision cleared, was hollow in the middle, and each hollow carried a reel of coloured thread. There were all sorts of colours in the box – reds and greens and blues and yellows and purples.

The man stopped work, and the machine fell silent as he got to his feet, stretching his arms until his fists almost brushed the ceiling. 'Will folk be wondering where you are?' His voice was soft and unhurried, like clear water running over stones.

She shook her head, and he sat down on the bench, this time with his back to the machine, reaching for a shabby cloth bag on a nearby shelf. 'You'll have a wee bite to eat, then,' he said, bringing some bread and a thick slab of cheese from the bag. He broke off a piece of bread and handed it to her, followed by a chunk of cheese cut from the slab by a knife he produced from a pocket.

She looked at the food, then at her host, uncertain

of what to do. He bit off a piece of cheese, then a piece of bread, and Rowena did the same, not realising that she was hungry until she tasted the food. They ate in companionable silence, then he drew a bottle from the bag.

'It's only cold tea, and I have no mug, for I didn't know I'd have company.' He unstoppered the bottle, wiped the neck carefully with a handkerchief, and offered it to her. While she drank, one of his big hands helped to support the bottle, and when some of the liquid slopped round the sides of her mouth and ran down her chin, he used the cloth to wipe it away. Then he drank from the bottle himself before setting it aside and taking something else from the bag.

'We'll have a wee bit of music to finish with, then you'll go back to your gran.' He put the instrument to his mouth, cupping both hands round it, and blew into it.

Rowena stood before him, her eyes on his, her ears drinking in the music he made. The notes, like his voice, were slow and soft; they spoke to her of home and her mother, long gone, and her father, who still hadn't come for her. Loneliness, and the longing that had almost overcome her when she looked at the little boats, began to creep back again.

As always when he played his mouth organ, Murdo Guthrie was lost in memories of his own, but they suddenly fell away when he happened to glance at the child standing before him and saw that her small round face, slightly grubby but as open and innocent as a flower, was beginning to melt into tragedy. Swiftly, he broke into a new rhythm, a dance so quick and light and mischievous that the mist gathering in the little girl's clear blue eyes vanished and her mouth curved upwards at the corners into a smile.

Her feet shifted and her body began to twitch as though it wanted to break free and dance across the hard-packed earth floor. Just as it seemed that it would, the door opened and Murdo immediately stopped playing, the notes cut off as sharply as if he had taken a honed knife to them.

Kirsty, busy turning out the room she and Todd slept in, wasn't aware of the passing time until Caitlin arrived from the shop with a message from Jean.

'What time is it?'

'Half past eleven.'

'Mercy!' Kirsty swept past her daughter and down the stairs to the kitchen. 'You'll all be in for your dinners in half an hour and me with not a thing started yet. Set the table, Caitlin, while I peel some potatoes.'

'I must go back to the shop before I have my dinner.' Caitlin scooped cutlery out of the drawer. 'Where's Rowena?'

'Out at the back,' Kirsty was at the sink, running water into a basin.

'She wasn't there when I came through the pend.'

'She'll be with Todd then,' Kirsty said, then added as an afterthought, 'Let the table be, and run to the workshop, just to make sure.'

Caitlin opened her mouth to say that the child would be fine, then closed it and went out, leaving the cutlery in a pile on the table. Her mother was overanxious where Rowena was concerned, but Caitlin could understand why; she had lost one of her own children during a moment's inattention, and she would have no wish to lose Ewan's child as well. Better for her to be reassured.

But Rowena wasn't in the workshop. 'I've not seen

her,' Todd said, adding, 'Mind you, I've been out for a good part of the mornin'. Did the bairn come lookin' for me?' he asked Bryce.

'We've not seen her.' He glanced at the apprentice. 'Have we?' The lad gave a quick shake of the head without looking up from his work.

'Was she playing in the back yard when you came back?'

'No. I thought she was in the house with Kirsty.' Todd began to look concerned. 'D'ye think she's run off?'

'If she was going to do that she'd have done it by now,' Caitlin assured him, though she herself was getting anxious. 'I'll look in the wash house.'

Finding the wash house empty, she hesitated at the back door, then, unwilling to face her mother, hurried to the pend. Rowena wasn't in it, nor was she to be seen on the pavement, when Caitlin went out onto the street and looked both ways. Starting back to the yard to enlist Todd's help, Caitlin paused, hearing strains of music waft from beyond the weaving shop's partially open door. Hoping that Murdo Guthrie might have seen or heard something of the missing child, she pushed the door open further, and the music stopped at once.

'Murdo?' Caitlin stepped down into the shop, nervous about intruding into the Highlander's domain. 'I wondered . . .' She stopped as the man began to rise from the bench and the little girl standing before him whirled round. Both looked guilty, but Caitlin, weak with relief, paid no heed. 'Rowena! Oh, Rowena, we thought . . .'

As Caitlin went into the room, Rowena moved back, her face closing in on itself, until she was against Murdo's legs. He put a reassuring hand on her shoulder 'She heard the sound of the loom and came to call on me. There was no harm in it.'

'Of course there wasn't,' Caitlin said swiftly, struck to the heart by the way Rowena had cringed as though expecting to be punished. She stayed where she was, extending a hand as though trying to reassure a nervous dog. 'We just wondered where she'd got to, that's all. Your dinner's nearly ready.'

Rowena started to shake her head, then Caitlin saw the hand on her shoulder push her gently forwards. The little girl twisted to look up at the man, and when he nodded she stepped obediently towards Caitlin, who exclaimed as she stepped into a ray of light from the window and it touched the beginnings of a bruise on the side of the small face. 'What happened to you?'

'She fell down the stairs coming in the door,' Murdo said, and Rowena nodded firmly, and said, 'I hit my face on the floor.'

'We'll put something on it to make it better before you have your dinner.'

Murdo cleared his throat. 'I've mebbe spoiled her appetite, for I gave her some of my bread and cheese.'

'I'm sure she'll manage to eat something else.' Caitlin hesitated, then said, 'And you'd be welcome to join us.'

The firm shake of his dark head was very like Rowena's. 'Thank you, but I'm fine with what I have,' he said courteously.

Rowena hung back for a moment as she was led to the door. 'Can I come another day to see the cloth being made?'

'Mr Guthrie'll not want to be bothered—' Caitlin began, but his soft lilting voice said from behind her, 'She'd be no bother, if your parents will allow her to come in now and again.'

'We'll see.'

Rowena paused on the step, twisting her head over her shoulder. 'I'll be back,' she announced to the weaver, then went with Caitlin into the house, where she ate every scrap of her midday meal.

'If you did without the panelling . . . ,' John Brodie suggested.

'How can I? We're talking about the salon where clients will wait to be seen. You know these women as well as I do, John. Can you see them sitting comfortably in a room with whitewashed stone walls?'

'Panelling will swallow up more money than you can afford.'

Rose stopped pacing her father's library and glared at him. 'You sound just like a pompous lawyer.'

He was hurt. 'Not pompous, surely. But I am a lawyer – your lawyer.'

'And my friend,' Rose said sweetly.

'I most certainly hope so, but as your lawyer,' John pressed on, fully aware that she was trying to divert him from the business in hand, 'it's my duty to try to make you see reason. You only have a certain amount of money to spend on the mill.'

'I must have that panelling!'

'Then you'll have to give up something else.'

She swooped down on the table, planting both hands on its surface and leaning towards him. 'Such as?'

'The heating costs a great deal. I know,' he said as she began to speak, 'you have to keep the place warm for your clients.'

'And for the staff.'

'What about staff . . . and furniture?'

'The clients must have somewhere to sit, and our employees must have sewing machines and chairs, not

to mention cloth to stitch and thread to stitch with!'
She spun away and started pacing again, with the long
mannish steps that Caitlin had tried so hard to tame.
When she concentrated, Rose could move like a lady,
but her long legs tended to carry her along swiftly when
she was angry, excited or worried. Today she was
moving over her parents' thick, expensive carpeting
so quickly that she had to change direction every few
steps to avoid bumping into furniture.

'I wish I'd never bought the place!'

'I did point out at the time that it might not be a
good purchase.'

'Nonsense,' Rose said at once. 'It's ideal. It will be
perfect.' She swept back and forth for a moment, then
said, 'I could leave the old gatehouse as it is for the
moment.' She had had plans to renovate the building
by the mill gate and turn it into a home for herself.

'Since you've not allocated any money to the gatehouse yet,' John pointed out, 'leaving it as it is won't
make much difference.'

'John, are you determined to vex me? You're talking
like a lawyer again!'

'I'd certainly advise against trying to raise any
further loans, unless they come from friends or family.'
Then, as the grandfather clock in the hall chimed, he
said, 'Good Lord, is that the time already?' and began
stuffing his papers into a briefcase. 'I'm sorry, Rose,
but I really must go. We'll talk again tomorrow.'

Mrs Hamilton came downstairs just as they crossed
the hall. 'John, my dear, surely you're having lunch
with us?'

'Nothing would please me more, Mrs Hamilton,
but unfortunately I have another appointment,' he
apologised.

'Next time, then.' When John had left, she followed

Rose into the library and began to fuss over the writing table, rearranging the blotter and pen set. 'John's such a charming boy, so well brought up,' she said, giving her daughter a sidelong glance. Rose, staring out of the window and twiddling her fingers, wasn't listening.

'Mama, I was wondering . . .'

Mrs Hamilton was more shrewd than she looked. 'If it's about money for this new venture of yours, Rose, you can save your breath. Not a penny of mine will be thrown away on it.'

Rose turned towards her, hurt. 'I'm talking about a loan, not a gift. I'd pay it all back, with interest.'

'Not a penny.'

'Then I shall ask Father.'

'You may certainly ask, but he and I are firmly agreed on the matter,' her mother said with obvious glee, 'and he won't change his mind any more than I will.'

'So you've discussed it.'

'Of course we discussed it – after John's mother told me what you were up to. It was very hurtful, Rose, to have to hear of my own daughter's actions from someone else.'

'I was going to tell you.'

'If you need money, why don't you take your grandmother's inheritance back from that shop?'

'I can't. Jean and Kirsty couldn't afford to lose it all.'

'You see? I knew at the time that it was a foolish move, but you assured me that the money was still yours.'

'It is still mine, but it's tied up in sewing machines and materials and wages.'

'Your poor grandmother would turn in her grave if she knew how you had thrown away her inheritance.'

Rose summoned up all her patience. 'I did not throw it away, Mama, I invested it, and it pays me a good dividend.' She ignored her mother's exaggerated wince at her use of masculine terms like investment and dividend. 'It has already earned me enough to buy the mill, but at the moment I need a little more for renovation and furnishing.'

'Then you must look elsewhere for it, my dear.' Mrs Hamilton said, and swept out of the room, pausing at the door to add, 'It seems to me, Rose, that the only way you'll ever learn the value of money is by losing it!'

Alone, Rose chewed on a fingernail, wishing that she could talk her problems over with Alex MacDowall. Although they disagreed on almost everything else, they were alike when it came to business, often trying out new ideas on each other, confident of receiving practical advice free of sentiment or extreme caution. On several occasions Alex had thrown cold water on Rose's grandiose ideas, and she had had to admit, in hindsight, that he had been quite right to do so.

But her impetuous action in buying the mill without making certain that he no longer held any interest in it had destroyed their friendship. Just when she needed him most, he would have nothing to do with her.

She struck the heel of one hand hard against her forehead. 'You're a fool, Rose Hamilton,' she muttered, 'such a fool!'

7

Kirsty's hope that Ewan would contact his family at New Year, even through a brief note, came to nothing, and 1914 arrived without a word from him. If Rowena, too, had expected her father to make contact, she didn't mention it; since she'd begun visiting Murdo Guthrie in the weaving shop every day she had settled down, and now she rarely asked when Ewan was coming to fetch her.

At first Kirsty was uneasy about the child's sudden interest in Murdo Guthrie. 'We know nothing about the man,' she fretted to her husband. 'He could be a thief – or a murderer, even.'

'I doubt a villain'd be content tae live in a lodgin' house and spend most of his working hours at a loom. Alex is pleased enough with the man's work, and Rowena's no fool for all that she's so young. She'd not spend time with Guthrie if she didnae trust him. If anyone should be frettin' about her preference for the man it's me, for she never comes intae the workshop now, and I have tae say that I miss seein' the wee soul playin' about the floor.'

'She should be with children her own age.'

'Ye've tried that, and it didnae work. Things are hard enough for the bairn, Kirsty, havin' tae fit in with folk she knew nothin' of until that carter brought her here. Now that she's found someone she can be easy with, let her be.'

'I don't know what Ewan'll think when he comes for her and mebbe finds her sitting in that dark room with a stranger.'

'If he comes for her,' Todd corrected, a slight edge creeping into his voice. 'Face facts, lass, there's not been one scrape of a pen from him since she arrived. He's not tried tae find out how she is, let alone told us if or when he'll come tae fetch her. It seems tae me that Ewan's the one who'll need tae dae some explainin' if he ever turns up, not you.'

By mid-January a new heating system had been installed in the old mill and an army of women had cleaned the place out. The painters arrived to whitewash the walls inside and out before builders began partitioning off rooms on the ground floor. Broken paving stones in the yard were replaced, the fencing repaired and painted.

Most of Rose's time was spent at the mill. At first she bubbled over with enthusiasm during her spasmodic visits to the shop, but as time went by the others began to notice that she had become unusually silent, often staring into space and having to be spoken to twice before she heard anything.

'If ye ask me,' Jean said to Kirsty, 'that mill's causin' trouble for her. Buyin' it's been a poor day's work; I'm sure that this time the lassie's bitten off more than even she can chew.'

'But she can surely start small and work up, the way everyone else does.'

'Rose Hamilton?' Jean said, astonished. 'Have ye ever known Rose Hamilton tae behave the way everyone else does?'

Caitlin said nothing to the others, but she, too, was concerned about Rose's silence, and she had become unsure of her own future. After being told by Rose that she was to become an important part of the new fashion house, she had pinned all her hopes and ambitions on the prospect, working extra hard at night school and studying books on design borrowed from the public library. She had even started working on a design portfolio in secret so that when the day came she would have something to offer to her clients.

Rose appeared at the shop one afternoon just after it had closed. Teenie had already gone home, and the others were preparing to leave when she arrived, sombre faced, and asked them to give her a few moments in the back room. She looked round the circle of faces, biting her lips to summon up the courage to speak.

'We've always worked together, the four of us, and it's only fair that you should all know what's happening at the mill. The truth is that although I've put every penny I can scrape together into the place and borrowed all that I could as well, it needed more doing to it than I first thought.' She looked down at her hands. 'I had a long talk with John this afternoon, and the fact is that there's still not enough money to furnish the place and take on the seamstresses we'll need, not to mention buying in the materials.'

'Are ye lookin' tae take back the money ye put intae the shop?' Jean's face was pinched with apprehension.

'Oh no,' Rose hurried to reassure her. 'I'd not dream of doing something like that to you. In any case, there would be no sense in losing everything we've built up here just so that I can start elsewhere,' she added, and Jean gave a gusty sigh of relief.

Kirsty offered her suggestion about starting in a small way and building the new business up, but Rose, jumping to her feet to stride as best she could about the small sewing room, rejected it out of hand. 'If the place starts small, it'll stay that way.'

'I don't see why that should be.'

'Kirsty, this is Paisley, not Glasgow or London. If we're going to give this town a fashion house it must be a proper fashion house from the start. Folk'll come if they think it's going to be worth their while, but starting small would be just like opening another shop. If I try that, they'll all decide to stay away until such time as it expands, and without their custom that will never happen.'

'Mebbe you should just sell it and settle for this place,' Jean said.

'John already suggested that, but it's too late. The ground floor's already been divided into separate rooms, and the panelling's being installed at this moment. The place could never be used as a mill again, and as it is now it's of no use to anyone but me – and please don't tell me that I should never have bought it, Jean,' Rose added, trying to smile but not succeeding, 'for I couldn't bear it just at the moment.'

'The thought never entered my head!'

'Of course it did, and you're quite right. I should have waited until I found a large shop that didn't need as much doing to it as the mill. But there's no sense in going over what should have happened now. Instead of waiting I went ahead with my idea, and now I've got to open the fashion house or have folk pointing the finger and crowing over me for being such a fool.'

Kirsty bridled. 'If you mean Alex, he'd not do such a thing.'

Normally Rose would have flared back at her, but today she just turned a wan face towards her friend. 'I didn't mean just him, though I'd not blame him if he did. I'm sure I would, if the boot was on the other foot.' She straightened her shoulders. 'But as I said, I'm determined that nobody's going to get the chance to point a finger, even if I've to sell my body to raise the money I need.'

To Caitlin's surprise the shocked gasp came from her mother and not from Jean, who merely asked, 'How much d'ye think ye'd get for it?'

Rose glanced down at her bony frame. 'Not nearly enough,' she admitted, and laughed for the first time in weeks. Then, sobering, she said, 'There's only one way I can raise more money.' For the first time she looked directly at Caitlin. 'I've always planned the fashion house as a partnership between you and me, Caitlin, with me providing the money, welcoming the clients and dealing with the running of the place while you designed the clothes and supervised the making of them, but as John pointed out . . .'

She faltered slightly, putting a hand to her mouth. Caitlin, who already knew what her friend was going to say, couldn't bear to let the misery go on for another moment. She swallowed hard, then said levelly, 'As things stand, Rose, you must find a designer who can put money into the business by buying a partnership.'

Rose's mouth fell open. 'How did you know?' she said into the shocked silence.

'It was easy enough. We've all known for weeks that you were worried, and I'd an idea that it must be to do with money. John's quite right. It makes sense to look for a designer who wants a partnership and is able to buy into the business. That's just what you need at the moment.'

'What I need,' Rose said fiercely, 'is you and your lovely designs. But you're right.' She gave a small, hopeless shrug. 'I can't afford you, Caitlin, though you have my firm word that as soon as the business starts to prosper you'll be brought in as the second designer.'

Caitlin, painfully aware without looking at her mother and Jean of the sympathy in their eyes, smiled brightly at a spot somewhere beyond Rose's right ear. 'I'll look forward to it,' she said, then bounced to her feet and made for the door. 'I think I'll just finish off the work I was doing on Mrs Forsyth's skirt before I go home, Mam.'

The three of them had the sense to leave her be. Long after they left, she worked on in the small lamplit room, finishing Mrs Forsyth's skirt then moving restlessly on to the work left in her mother's sewing machine. As the hours passed she pumped the treadle and rushed the cloth along beneath the pounding needle as fast as Teenie ever had, her face set and her eyes dry, although deep inside she was weeping and raging with grief for her lost hopes and dreams. Finally, exhausted and cold, she locked up the shop and walked slowly home through the dark night to face her mother's pity, and Todd's and Mary's.

But when she got to Espedair Street it was to discover that her family was involved in a drama of its own. Rowena, who should have been in bed long since, stamped around the kitchen in her nightdress, her face buttoned into a fearsome scowl, with Kirsty trying in vain to coax her to eat her supper. Todd studied his newspaper in his fireside chair, keeping his head well down, and Mary pored over her books at the table, her hands clamped over her ears. Even during her holidays Mary kept up to date with lessons.

'Just a wee mouthful,' Kirsty was saying when Caitlin went in. Rowena tightened her mouth until it almost disappeared and shook her head.

'What's amiss?'

'She wants to go to a ceilidh,' Mary said calmly.

'A what?'

'A cay – lay,' Mary pronounced the word distinctly. 'You know, one of these parties that the Highlanders like to hold in their church hall.'

'Is that what they call them?' There were a number of Highlanders in Paisley, and most of them attended the Gaelic chapel in Oakshawhill. Caitlin knew that they held social events in the small hall adjacent to the church; sometimes if she and Bryce happened to be walking through the area of an evening, they heard lilting music, the sound of voices and even the stamping of feet coming from the small hall. On these occasions, Bryce always wrinkled up his nose and muttered something about heathens.

Mary turned a page of her book. 'Murdo Guthrie told Rowena that he was playing his mouth organ at the next ceilidh, and now she wants to go.'

'She came in with her head full of it,' Kirsty said despairingly, 'and flew into a right temper when I said no.'

'These parties are just for the Highlanders, Rowena,' Caitlin tried to reason with the little girl. 'Mebbe one day when you're older they'll let you go to one, but you're too wee just now.'

Rowena crossed her arms over her chest and scowled. 'Am not!' she said, and Kirsty tried to take advantage of the moment and pop the spoon into her open mouth. But Rowena was too quick for her. She buttoned her lips up again and the spoon almost went flying.

'Think of it, Rowena – Murdo'll be too busy playing

his mouth organ to look after you. You need to be with someone.'

'We'll all go, then.'

'Not me,' Todd said hastily. 'I cannae understand the Highlanders at all, and I'm surely not puttin' mysel' in among them. The rest of ye can go if ye've a mind.'

'Not me,' Mary snapped shut her book. 'I'm going to bed.'

'Mam?'

Kirsty looked at her daughter as though Caitlin had just invited her to jump into the River Cart fully clothed. 'I don't understand the Highlanders either. I'd not dream of going to one of their hoolies.'

'Ceilidhs.' Mary threw the word back over her shoulder as she went out of the room.

'What sort of daft-like word is that, for a start?'

'It's Gaelic, Mam, the language Murdo and his friends speak when they're at home. Gaelic can't hurt you.'

'It's not going to get the chance.'

Rowena remained mute, her eyes fixed on Caitlin, who sighed. 'I'm not promising anything, but I'll ask Murdo about the ceilidh,' she said reluctantly. 'But only if you eat your supper and go to bed like a good girl.'

The scowl was wiped off Rowena's face as if by magic, to be replaced by a smile so sweet that it almost took Caitlin's breath away.

'She's got her father's charm,' she said wryly when Rowena had eaten and been taken off to bed by Kirsty. Todd grunted and turned a page of his newspaper noisily, and she had the sense to hold her tongue and say no more. Ewan's warm smile could indeed have charmed the birds from the trees, while Beth's did little more than display her neat white front teeth.

The only people who ever saw a real smile from Beth were the men she was intent on winning over.

Caitlin wondered, briefly, who was at the receiving end of one of Beth's smiles now. The woman always needed to be on a man's arm, and she had surely deserted Ewan for someone able to offer her more than he could.

'You shouldn't encourage the lassie, Caitlin,' Kirsty scolded when she came back into the kitchen. 'It's just giving in to her.'

'It was the only way to get her to go to her bed. I was in no mood for one of her scenes tonight.' Caitlin caught the swift look that passed between her mother and stepfather and knew that Todd had been told of what had happened in the shop.

'I think I'll go to my bed,' she said as Todd cleared his throat as if to speak. She couldn't face a discussion about her future.

'You've not eaten anything.'

'I'm not hungry,' Caitlin said, and escaped before Kirsty could argue.

'Leave her be,' Todd advised as his wife made to follow Caitlin out into the hall. 'The lassie's hurtin', and she needs time on her own.'

Kirsty returned to her chair reluctantly. 'I wish there was something we could do. She's a good girl, Caitlin, and she works so hard in the shop. She deserves the chance to use more of her designs, and I know that Rose wanted to work with her.'

'Aye, well . . . Money rules us all, if we let it. And right now Rose Hamilton's allowin' it tae lead her by the neb like a bull bein' taken tae auction.'

'It's her way, I suppose. Rose grew up with money; she's used to buying what she wants.'

They sat for a while in silence, then Kirsty said, 'You don't think that Alex . . . ?'

'I'd keep Alex out of it, if I was you. He's hurtin' tae, because of Rose buyin' the mill.'

'But surely he'd want to help his own sister!'

Todd turned a page of his paper. 'It's up tae yersel', Kirsty, though for my part I'd just as well keep right out of it and let things lie where they fall. Between you and me,' he added, peering at her over the top of the paper, 'I'm just glad tae know that I'm stayin' put and not havin' tae move intae the mill and start all over again. I owe that much tae wee Rowena, at least.'

Upstairs, Caitlin wept into her pillow, her tears hot and fierce and angry. She would have given anything to have been able to bawl and rage and stamp around as Rowena did during one of her temper storms, kicking furniture and slapping at the wall. But she had to satisfy herself with a silent rage, stuffing the sheet into her mouth and every now and again punching at her pillow until a tiny but ominous ripping sound warned her that she would have to give up even that luxury. The last thing she wanted was for her mother to see the room covered with feathers from a torn pillow in the morning.

She cried until she was emptied of tears, then got up and washed her face in the china bowl by the street window. The night sky was cloudy, and the moon shone only fitfully on the silent cobbled street below. As she got back into bed she heard Kirsty and Todd coming upstairs, moving about their bedroom, talking quietly. Then silence fell again, and Caitlin found that she hadn't rid herself of all her tears after all.

She was determinedly cheerful in the morning, and

nobody, at home or in the shop, where she made a point of working in the sewing room all day, was tactless enough to comment on her swollen eyes. Teenie had obviously been told what had happened, for she, like the others, treated Caitlin with tender consideration. Rose was about the shop quite often that day. There was a haunted look about her, and she kept her distance from Caitlin, who could finally stand it no longer.

'Is it your mother?' she asked abruptly when Rose, coming into the back shop and finding her alone, shied back and tried to retreat without being seen.

'What?'

'You've given in at last and hit her over the head with something?'

Rose, trapped in the doorway, ventured a step forward. 'I don't know what you're talking about.'

'I'm talking about you creeping round this place as if you've hidden a body and you're waiting for the police to come and arrest you.'

'I wish I had,' the other girl said mournfully. 'At least I'd feel better than I do now.'

'For goodness' sake . . .' Caitlin put down the garment she was about to cut into and faced her friend. 'Rose, you've got no choice but to find a designer who can put money into the fashion house. I understand that. It makes sense.'

'But it's not fair! It was always going to be me and you running the place together. That's what I wanted!'

'It's what I wanted too, and there's no point in denying it, for I know that I've been walking round all day looking like a dumpling.' Caitlin briefly put a hand to her puffy eyes.

'You couldn't look like a dumpling if you tried.'

'Don't try to flatter me, Rose Hamilton, I'm not a bairn. I'm old enough to deal with disappointment now and again. And you've said that you'll take me into your fashion house as soon as you can.'

'I will – the very minute I can afford your wages.'

'Until then, can you stop looking so haunted?'

Rose gave her a dazzling smile and a swift hug. 'You're such an angel, Caitlin.'

It was a relief when she went out, for the backs of Caitlin's eyes had begun to prickle ominously. Alone, she gave an almighty sniff and blinked hard, telling herself sharply, *Behave, for goodness' sake!* There was always work for her in the shop, certainly enough to keep her busy until Rose could afford to take her into the fashion house. For one thing, she still had her portfolio to work on.

She sniffed again and blew her nose, then picked up the scissors and got on with her work.

8

Caitlin and Murdo Guthrie both attended classes at Paisley College later that week. As she spotted him going out of the main door just ahead of her, Caitlin said a swift goodnight to the girl she was with and pushed her way through the other students. Reaching the steps, she saw him cross George Street and begin to stride towards Causeyside Street, moving fast. She had to run to catch up with him; he didn't hear when she called his name, and she had to put on a spurt of extra speed and shout again before he swung round, a surprised glower on his broad face.

He halted, looking puzzled when he saw who it was. 'You're looking for me?'

'Yes.' Breathless from her run, and from embarrassment, she would have given anything to have been free to walk away in the other direction, but she had made a promise to Rowena. 'It's . . . it's about Rowena.'

He stiffened slightly, his face expressionless. 'She's no bother, but if your mother would prefer her not to come into the weaving shop . . .'

'It's got nothing to do with that. In fact, it's good of you not to mind her visits.'

'She's a decent, quiet wee lass,' he said, and Caitlin wondered what Kirsty would say if she heard that.

'She doesn't get in the way, and she likes hearing the music.'

'That's what I wanted to ask you about. Rowena mentioned that you were playing at a ceilidh.'

'Aye, next week at the chapel hall. I do, on occasion, though I'm not one for the dancing.'

'Rowena's got it into her head that she wants to go to it.'

His brows lifted slightly. 'She never said a word of it to me. Not that I'd have the right to say yes or no.'

'She's determined to go, and I said I'd speak to you about it. Mebbe it's only for adults,' Caitlin said hopefully.

'A ceilidh's for anyone that wants to go,' he informed her. 'Those that have bairns are always welcome to take them along, for it's just dancing and a bit of singing, and a bit of a talk. I'm sure you'd be welcome to bring her if you'd a mind.'

'I don't know . . .' she faltered, and again he stiffened.

'Of course not everybody in this town cares to mix with Highlanders.' Although his voice was usually soft, she discovered that it could also sound as hard and sharp as a honed steel blade. 'They think all Highlanders are tarred with the same brush, and that we're all tinkers and mebbe thieves or worse, and they'll not mix with the likes of us.'

He turned and began to walk away from her, and again she had to run to catch up with him. 'I didn't—'

'It can happen when you have to leave your home and all that, you know, and go to new places where the customs are not your own,' he said tightly, without looking at her. 'That's why the folk meet for their ceilidhs, so's they can be with those who know what their lives used to be like.'

83

'Murdo!' She clapped a hand on his arm and he swung round to face her. 'D'you have to be so . . . so stubborn?' she asked, finding a flash of anger of her own. 'I meant no criticism of you or your friends. I know that you've suffered from some folks' behaviour, and I'm truly sorry about that. It's because of it that I wondered if me and Rowena would be welcome – or do Highlanders think that all Lowlanders are tarred with the same brush too?'

He blinked, then had the grace to look embarrassed. 'Forgive me, I've been behaving badly towards you,' he said. 'You and Rowena will be made welcome among us, have no fear of that. I'll meet you outside the church at seven o'clock on Friday and take you in with me. Goodnight, Miss Lennox.'

He turned and walked away, not looking back. Watching him, Caitlin realised that the whole thing had been arranged without her having the chance to agree or disagree.

Rowena was overjoyed when she heard the news the next morning.

'Mind, you'll only go if you're a good girl until then,' Kirsty warned, making the most of the opportunity, and the child tucked her hands firmly behind her back and nodded agreement.

Caitlin had hoped that the others might attend the ceilidh as well, but they all refused. Given Bryce's antagonism towards Murdo and all Highlanders, she decided against inviting him.

Against Todd's advice, Kirsty told Alex about Caitlin's disappointment when he next visited Paisley. He listened, his long lean face expressionless, until she had finished speaking, then said, 'And you're expecting me to pay Caitlin's way into Rose's business?'

'I'm expecting nothing.'

'But you're hoping that I'll agree to hand over the money.'

'She's your sister, after all.' Kirsty felt her hackles rising. She knew that Alex could be as stubborn as the next man when he put his mind to it, but at the moment all her sympathies lay with Caitlin.

'Sister or not, what you're really asking me to do is to put money into Rose Hamilton's new venture.' His green-blue eyes, very like Caitlin's, became dark and stormy.

'The money's not for Rose, it's for Caitlin.'

'It'll be to Rose's benefit – and she's the one who snatched that mill from beneath my very nose.'

Kirsty's temper snapped. 'For goodness' sake, Alex, why should a daft quarrel between you and Rose spoil your sister's life? Have you no thought for Caitlin? Even though you're with your own father now, she's still a part of your family.'

'Family's one thing, Mam, and business is another. If Caitlin needed the money for something else – anything else – I'd do all that I could to help her. But this matter concerns—'

'It concerns your hurt pride, and you care more about that than you do about your own flesh and blood.' Kirsty snatched up an armful of clothes and pushed past him towards the back door. Ignoring his call, she slammed the door behind her and stormed into the wash house, where she pushed the clothing down into the steaming water in the tub then snatched up the long-handled wooden tongs and used them to ram the clothes below the surface. She didn't turn her head when the door opened.

'Mam, can you not see—'

She rounded on him, her face flushed with the

water's heat, the tongs steaming and dripping in her hand. 'Don't fash yourself, Alex, I'll find another way to help my daughter,' she said. Then, as he tried again to say something: 'I'd not want to be more beholden to you than I already am.'

For a moment he stood by the door. Then, he said, 'Please yourself,' and went out.

Kirsty pushed the tongs viciously at a sleeve that had dared to scramble back to the surface, then jerked away as a few drops of near boiling water spattered over her arm.

Rowena had been exceptionally good all week; now, as Caitlin walked along Causeyside Street to the town centre, known as the Cross, she skipped ahead, disappearing into the darkness, continually having to stop and wait for her aunt or run back to her.

'You'll be tired out by the time we get there,' Caitlin scolded gently, but the little girl just shook her head, ignoring the proferred hand, and danced off again. Rowena was not one for holding hands.

They had reached the Cross and were heading for Moss Street when they met Bryce and a group of his friends. Caitlin's heart sank as he halted in front of her. Rowena, about to scamper ahead, sidled against her aunt's legs instead, and to her surprise Caitlin felt a small mittened hand slip into hers.

'On ye go, I'll catch up with ye,' Bryce ordered his friends. Then he said to Caitlin, 'I thought you'd work tae dae this evenin'.'

'Rowena was too restless to go to bed, so I said I'd take her for a walk to tire her,' she improvised hurriedly.

'Is that right?' He glanced at her dark blue skirt and wrapover jacket, and Caitlin was thankful that she had decided against dressing up for the ceilidh. Even so, he said, 'You look very smart.'

'You know that I like to dress well. Sometimes it encourages folk to buy their clothes from Jean's shop.'

'I'll walk with you,' he offered.

'There's no need. We'll be turning back soon, and your friends are waiting.' The other young men had halted and formed a tight group beneath a gas lamp, eyeing Bryce and Caitlin from under the skips of their caps and murmuring to each other.

'Ach, let them wait. We can put the bairn intae the house and have a wee while on our own.' His voice dropped to an intimate murmur and heat began to kindle in his eyes.

'I promised her that it'd just be the two of us tonight,' she protested, and Rowena chimed in, 'Come on, Aunt Caitlin, we'll be late.'

'Late for what?'

'Late getting back,' Caitlin said swiftly. 'It'll soon be past her bedtime.'

'I could get rid of them,' Bryce jerked his head in the general direction of his friends, 'and meet you outside your house later.'

'Not tonight. I've still got that work to do after we get back.'

He began to argue, but Rowena, edging round to stand in front of Caitlin, glared up at him and said loudly, 'Go away!'

'Rowena!'

Rowena ignored her. 'We don't want you!'

Bryce's face darkened, and he bent down towards her. 'Wee lassies should mind their ain—' He yelped as Rowena's foot connected squarely with his ankle. A burst of noisy laughter came from his cronies as he skipped away from her.

'She's a bonnier fighter than what you are, Bryce!' one of them shouted.

'Rowena!' Caitlin said, scandalised, then 'Bryce!' as he snarled, 'Wee bitch!'

He glared at her, his face crimson with pain and mortification. 'What are ye yellin' at me for when she's damned near maimed me?'

'She's too wee to hurt you that badly, and anyway she's sorry, aren't you, Rowena?'

'Go away!'

'We're the ones who're going. Come away at once.' Caitlin dragged her away.

'I'll see you later, then.'

'Not tonight, Bryce.' She threw the words over her shoulder. 'You'd better go home and get a poultice on that sore leg of yours.'

She almost ran into Moss Street, dragging Rowena after her, convinced that Bryce was following. But when she glanced back there was no sign of him.

'You don't deserve to go to the ceilidh,' she scolded as the two of them started up School Wynd. 'You were a very bad girl.'

Rowena's head was well down, so that her muttered, 'He's a bad man,' only just reached Caitlin's ears. She recalled the way the small, childish body had trembled against her legs even while Rowena was ordering Bryce to go away. 'What d'you mean? Has Bryce been bad to you?'

Rowena, concentrating on climbing the steep hill, said nothing, and Caitlin, remembering the venom in Bryce's face and voice when he swore at the child, decided to let the subject drop for the time being.

Murdo was waiting for them outside the Gaelic chapel hall. 'You came, then?'

'Why wouldn't we?' Caitlin asked sharply, still jumpy from her meeting with Bryce. He said nothing, but turned towards the hall door. Rowena, deserting her aunt, hurried to his side and grasped one of his fingers firmly. The two of them walked into the hall together, with Caitlin trailing behind.

The place was already busy, but people obligingly made room for the newcomers on one of the benches lining the walls.

'This is Mhairi.' Murdo indicated the woman sitting beside Caitlin. 'She'll look after you, won't you, Mhairi?'

'I will indeed. Off you go now, man, for my toes are itching to dance.' Mhairi leaned forward and smiled past Caitlin at Rowena. 'You've got a bonny wee lass there.'

'She's my brother's child.'

'Indeed? I've not seen you here before.'

'We've never been to a ceilidh before.'

Mhairi patted Caitlin's knee. 'Then you've got a treat before you, my dear.' She was small and plump, with a round rosy face and bright blue eyes, and snow-white hair escaping in soft little curls from the knot at the back of her head. Caitlin took to her at once and didn't mind answering her probing questions. After all, she was a stranger in the midst of people who clearly knew each other well. When Mhairi had satisfied herself as to who the newcomers were, she turned to convey the information in Gaelic to the others, who had been eyeing Caitlin and Rowena with open curiosity. 'You'll not mind me telling them, my dear. We always like to welcome folk.'

They did. There were smiles and nods and some hand-shaking before the musicians on a small dais at one end of the hall began to play, setting off an immediate scurry to find partners. Almost at once the floor was filled with dancers of all ages, from quite small children bouncing about in pairs or by themselves to elderly men and women whirling, and in some cases hobbling, round the floor. The clothing, too, was varied, with some well dressed and others wearing patched and darned garments; it made no difference to their enjoyment. Even those still on the benches were moving to the lively music, while Mhairi thumped her feet on the wooden floor in time to the beat and slapped her open palms so hard on her thighs that Caitlin was sure the woman's legs would be covered in bruises in the morning.

By her side, Rowena twitched then bounced on the wooden bench, finally slipping down to the floor to jig on the spot, her eyes on the dancers, her small face entranced as she tried to follow their steps. Now and then, as the dancers swung apart, Caitlin caught glimpses of the musicians. There were two fiddlers, an accordionist and a stick-thin lad with a flat drum not much larger than a good-sized dinner plate strapped to one hand. In the other he held a short baton, laced through his fingers so that he could flick either end rapidly against the drum. He and the other musicians were grinning from ear to ear, but Murdo, standing to one side of the group, was as sombre as ever. Not that it was possible to smile while playing the mouth organ, Caitlin thought.

Within a few moments a middle-aged man had whisked Mhairi from the bench and into the thick of the dancers. Every now and again Caitlin caught sight of her stamping and spinning with the best of them. The dances ranged from fast, with a great deal of hooching from the dancers, to slow, with elegant, almost ritualistic steps. Now and again, to give the dancers a chance to catch their breath, a singer stepped onto the dais. During an interval for food and drink, Murdo appeared by Caitlin's side. 'Are you enjoying yourselves?' He had taken his jacket and cravat off and loosened his shirt at the throat; his face was flushed, and damp strands of slightly overlong brown hair clung to his forehead and cheeks.

'I am, but mebbe it's time Rowena was in her bed.'

Rowena, thirstily drinking lemonade and eyeing some children shyly over the rim of her mug, whirled round at once. 'I've not done any dancing yet. Show me how to dance, Murdo!' She ran at him and tugged on his trouser leg while Caitlin marvelled at the child's easy informality with this silent, somewhat frightening man.

'How can I dance when I'm playing the music as well?'

'I'll show you how,' a young lad offered, and Rowena beamed at him. Once she was on the floor there was no question of taking her home early, and soon Caitlin, too, was drawn to her feet to stumble through unfamiliar steps. Rowena picked up the rhythms faster than she did, but nobody seemed to mind when, on occasion, her ignorance spoiled the rhythm of the dances.

'You'll come again,' Mhairi said when they were leaving the hall at the end of the evening. 'You'll be more than welcome – the two of you.'

The small hall, filled to capacity, had been warm, and the cold wind cut through them when they stepped outside. A few snowflakes danced at them from the darkness. 'I'll see you safe home,' Murdo said, and scooped Rowena up, ignoring Caitlin's polite protests.

The little girl put her arms round his neck and almost at once began to snore softly against his shoulder while, in silence, he and Caitlin walked to Espedair Street together.

9

'Whatever you want, lass, is fine by me,' Todd Paget told his wife placidly.

'It's your money as well as mine. You have to be in agreement, Todd.'

'I am. The only thing I'm wonderin' is what your Alex'll have tae say when he hears about it.'

Kirsty's mouth tightened slightly. 'I don't see that it's any of his concern. He'd his chance to help his sister and he refused. I can't understand him, Todd. In the old days Alex would've given any one of us the shirt off his own back if need be. I don't like the way he's changed.'

Todd puffed gently on his pipe. 'It's hard work, runnin' a big Glasgow shop and thon workshop as well. He's had tae grow up, that's all.'

Kirsty couldn't let the matter go at that. 'D'you think that working alongside his father's hardened him? When I first knew Sandy he was such a gentle lad, but it's a different man who's come back into our lives.'

'Can ye blame him?' By now Todd knew the story of Alex's parentage well. 'After bein' near murdered by yer father then thrown out of the town with nothin' but the rags on his back, the man had tae fight for everythin' he has. Folk that've had it hard cannae survive without changin'.'

'But Alex hasn't had to suffer nearly as much as his father.'

'Even so, he's a grown man, Kirsty, and ye have tae let him make his own decisions, even when ye cannae agree with them. Ye have tae let him go his own way as he sees fit.'

'I suppose you're right,' she said sadly, thinking of the caring lad her Alex had once been. Then, her chin coming up, she added, 'And I must go my way as I see fit, so if you're willing, I'm going to help Caitlin, for she deserves it.'

'Fine.' Glad that the discussion was over, Todd reached for his newspaper. For a while the kitchen was silent, then Kirsty looked at the clock.

'Should they not be back yet? It's long past Rowena's bedtime.'

'They'll be enjoyin' themselves.'

She opened the back door then shut it at once, shivering. 'It's starting to snow. Mebbe you should take a walk along the road, Todd. You might meet them.'

He sighed inwardly but put the paper aside, knowing that his wife wouldn't be content until he did as she wished. As he got to his feet, the back door opened and Caitlin came in, Murdo Guthrie looming behind her with Rowena in his arms. For a moment both Kirsty and Todd were taken aback at sight of the weaver on their doorstep, but Kirsty recovered swiftly. 'You'll have a cup of tea with us, Mr Guthrie.'

'I'd not want to keep you from your beds.' Murdo began to ease Rowena carefully from his shoulder.

'Ye're no' keepin' us back at all, man,' Todd told him heartily. 'Come in, come in.' Then, hopefully: 'Ye'd mebbe sooner have a dram than tea?'

But Murdo refused to go over the doorstep. 'I've an early start in the morning, so I'll bid you goodnight,' he said, and handed over the child's small body before melting into the darkness.

Todd closed the door with his free hand, shaking his head as he turned to the women. 'I swear I don't know what tae make of that man.'

'Give her to me, poor lamb.' Kirsty claimed the little girl. 'You're just vexed because you missed the chance of a wee whisky.'

'What're ye talkin' about, woman? I can have a dram in my own kitchen whenever I want tae!' Todd reached for the bottle on its shelf.

'This bairn's exhausted! You should have brought her home sooner, Caitlin.'

'I couldn't get her to come away.'

'Well, she can sleep in her wee semmit and drawers for once, for I don't want to disturb her more than I must. The tea's fresh made,' Kirsty said over her shoulder as she carried Rowena out of the room.

'Mebbe I'll just have a cup with ye.' His point made, Todd replaced the whisky bottle and fetched mugs from the draining board by the sink for himself and his stepdaughter. 'Did the bairn enjoy hersel'?'

'She did that.'

'And did you have a good time an' all?'

Caitlin sank into a chair. 'I did. I really did.'

'Then that's all that matters,' Todd said comfortably, pouring tea.

When Kirsty came downstairs to report that she had managed to stow Rowena safely in her bed without rousing her, Caitlin got to her feet, too tired to face her mother's searching questions about the ceilidh. But Kirsty put out a hand to stop her.

'Sit down a minute. There's something me and

Todd want to say.' Kirsty took a seat at the table, smoothing her skirt nervously, darting glances at her husband as though hoping that he might deliver the news. But Todd just smiled serenely back at her and sipped at his tea.

'It's your idea, Kirsty. You tell the lassie.'

'It's like this.' Kirsty took a deep breath and plunged into her speech. 'We both know how disappointed you were when Rose decided to bring in a designer who could put money into her fashion house.'

'I was, but it's all right now. I'm going to join her as soon as she can afford my wages, you know that.'

'Wheesht when I'm speaking to you. You'll get my words in a muddle,' Kirsty rapped nervously, then took another breath as her daughter subsided. 'The thing is, you're a good hard-working lass, and me and Todd think you should have your chance. So we're going to pay Rose the money she needs so that you can work with her as her partner.'

It was the last thing Caitlin had expected to hear. She sat upright in her chair, her tiredness gone, staring at her mother then at her stepfather. 'But how . . . where'll you get the money?'

'Don't look at me, it was all your mother's idea – though I'm all for it,' Todd added swiftly.

'Mam?'

Now that her idea was out in the open, Kirsty's nerves had vanished, and she was beaming. 'It's the money Alex and his father paid to me for the workshop.'

'I can't take it!'

'Of course you can. Money's for using, not for lying idle in a bank.'

'But that was meant to keep you and Todd in comfort when you stop working.'

'Tuts, lassie, that'll not happen for a good long time yet. Todd'll stay in the workshop and I'll stay with Jean until we're both too old to be of use to anyone, and by then you and Rose'll have paid the money back.'

Caitlin looked from one to the other. 'It doesn't seem right,' she said weakly, but already a faint glow had begun to tingle and grow deep inside her.

'Of course it's right. It's what you want, and what we want for you. Is that not right, Todd?'

'Right enough,' he agreed amiably.

Caitlin's knees were weak when she stood up. She hugged her mother, then Todd, who gave an embarrassed chuckle. 'I don't know what to say.'

Kirsty gave her a slight push towards the door. 'There's nothing to say. Just get off to your bed – and mind that that mill's part yours now, so you'll have to make a go of it.'

'I will!' At the hall door, Caitlin turned. 'What'll Alex say about you giving his money to me?'

'It's not his money,' her mother told her firmly. 'It's ours, in payment for the workshop. What we do with it is no business of Alex's.'

Despite her exhaustion, Caitlin was still awake long after the house had settled into silence for the night. Apart from her excitement, the music she had heard during the evening echoed through her mind, sometimes fast and light-hearted, sometimes slow and sad. She finally got up and lit the paraffin lamp on the small table, then brought out her sketchbook and leafed through it. The designs already on its pages had been part of her collection for the distant future, but now, it seemed, they might become reality within the next twelvemonth.

Inside her skull the fiddles rippled up and down

the scale and the accordion wove its ribbon of sound, underlaid by the swift, exciting beat of the drum, and all of them were linked by the sound of Murdo Guthrie's mouth organ. Looking through the window into the dark night, she saw the dancers' flushed smiling faces, hair and skirts and coat tails twisting and flying, remembering the moments when these same laughing faces had stilled as they listened to the other music, slow and lonely, recalling memories of places far from Paisley's streets.

She turned to a blank page, reached for her crayons and began to draw.

Jean was shocked when Rose, on hearing Caitlin's news, rushed out and brought back a bottle of champagne.

'Ye'd think it was Ne'erday all over again!'

'It's even better than Ne'erday,' Rose told her, beaming as she filled the motley assortment of mugs normally used for their tea. 'Ne'erday's only the beginning of a new year – this is the beginning of a new life. A toast!'

'But it's not ten o'clock yet. It's far too early tae be drinkin'. We'll all be fleein' by noon, and us with a shop tae run.'

'It's only the once, Jean, an' it makes a nice wee change from tea.' Teenie eyed her mugful thirstily.

'You'd not grudge us a celebration on a day like this, surely.' Rose clinked her mug against Jean's, her smile almost splitting her long face in half. 'To all of us and what we've achieved so far, and to me and Caitlin in our new venture!'

'Ach, why not?' said Jean, and downed her mugful. 'Right enough, it sets up a nice wee glow,' she admitted, and joined in a second toast when John Brodie, summoned from his office, arrived with another bottle and insisted on filling the mugs again.

'To . . .' he paused, then asked, 'Have you thought of a name for the new place yet?'

'The House of Rose,' Teenie suggested, but Rose shook her head.

'No, it has to be both names or something else entirely. We'll think of something.' Then she raised her mug. 'To us again!'

'I was wondering,' Rose said later to Caitlin, 'if MacDowall and Son might be willing to make the chairs and small tables we'll need for the salons.'

'You're going to ask Alex?'

Rose flushed. 'It's only fair to give the business to folk we know, and it means that we can describe just what we want. I'd like to see some of his hand-painted chairs in our salon, and you never know, the clients might like them too and give him some orders.'

'I don't know, Rose . . .'

'Ask him and see. Nobody can deny that Alex is a businessman through and through,' Rose said with a slight edge to her voice, 'and I doubt if he'll turn down the chance of selling some of his work, even to me.'

Caitlin had reached the corner of Espedair Street on her way home that night when Bryce, who had been leaning against a wall, straightened up and moved into her path.

'I thought you'd be finished work long since.'

'I have, but I wanted tae speak tae ye.'

'I've got something to tell you, too.' She had been walking on air all day, longing to run into the street and shout her news to the entire town. 'Bryce, you'll never guess what's happened!'

'I know fine and well what happened.' His face was dark, his voice tense. 'Ye didnae know that ye were seen, did ye?'

'Seen where?'

'Walkin' along Causeyside Street last night with that . . . that Highlander!' He spat the word out as though it had a foul taste. 'And it was long past the time ye told me ye were tae be in by. Where were ye?'

As she stared up into his angry eyes, Caitlin came back to earth with a bump, elation ebbing and anger taking its place. 'What business is it of yours where I was last night and who I was with?'

'It's my business if ye're seein' him behind my back!'

'If you must know, Rowena wanted to go to the ceilidh at the Gaelic chapel, so I took her.'

'Ye were dancin' with that weaver? An' me standin' here like a fool waitin' for ye tae come out walkin' with me?'

'You were here last night?'

'I said I'd be waitin' for ye.'

'And I told you not to bother.'

'Aye, because ye'd work tae dae, you said. Some work!' He turned away and spat into the gutter. 'Dancin' with the likes o' him!'

'I was not dancing with Murdo Guthrie – he was playing his mouth organ all evening.'

'Then he walked ye home.'

'Rowena was tired and he carried her back home for me. Did your loose-mouthed friend not tell you that it was her in his arms and not me?' Caitlin made to walk past him into the pend, but he caught at her arm.

'I'll not have ye goin' out wi' him, Caitlin!'

'I've not been out with him at all. I told you, it was for Rowena.'

'I'll not have my lassie seen out wi' the likes o' him.'

'I'm not yours, Bryce.'

'Ye are,' he said almost pleadingly. 'Ach, Caitlin, everyone knows we walk out together.'

'Then you'll just have to tell everyone that they're wrong, since we're not walking out together any longer. And you can tell them that it was your stupid jealousy that put an end to it!' Furious now, she pulled away from his grip. 'I've got more to do than argue with you,' she said curtly, and pushed past him into the pend without looking back.

When Alex next came to Paisley, Caitlin seized her chance and offered to walk to the station with him when he left. It was hard for her to introduce the subject of the proposed fashion house; she made several attempts at it, but they all trickled away into silence, and they had almost reached the station entrance when he said, 'I know fine that you've got something on your mind, and if you don't hurry up with it I'll be halfway to Glasgow and none the wiser.'

'It's not me, it's . . .'

'Well?' His brow crinkled in a frown. 'You're never scared of me, Caitlin. I might have taken on my father's name and moved to Glasgow, but I'm surely still your brother.'

She took a deep breath. 'We'd like . . . Rose and me would like you to make some furniture for our new fashion house.'

His eyebrows shot up. 'You're still going into that business with her?'

She beamed at him. 'I'm going to be the designer.'

'But I thought she was looking for a designer who could be a paying partner—' he began, then stopped abruptly.

'How did you know about that?'

'It was just something Mam mentioned,' Alex said vaguely. 'So Rose decided she didn't need the extra money after all?'

'She's still getting it. Mam and Todd are buying the partnership for me.'

'What?' Alex, about to start down the steps to the station, halted abruptly. Caitlin, already part of the way down, turned with one hand on the rail.

'It was their idea, not mine, but they were determined to do it.' She stopped, then said in a small voice, 'You didn't know that they were giving me the money you gave to them.'

The lamplight in the street behind him meant that his face was in deep shadow, so she had no way of seeing his expression. 'The money for the workshop belongs to Mam and Todd, and they can spend it as they wish,' he said, and began to descend the stairs again.

Caitlin scurried down ahead of him. 'You're not pleased, though.'

'It's none of my business, though I think you're taking a risk, going into a new venture from the start.'

'I don't think so. Rose and I know what we're doing, and I'm sure it'll work. We're both determined to make it work.'

The train had been signalled, and the few people already waiting on the platform were moving towards the edge. 'You really care about this idea of hers, don't you?'

'More than anything in the world. Imagine me getting the chance to design clothes for folk instead of just altering them!'

'And is it you who thought of asking me if MacDowall

and Son would make some furniture for the place? If so, you'd be advised to see what Rose thinks before I give you an answer, for I doubt if she'd approve.'

His refusal to believe anything good of Rose began to annoy her. 'You're quite wrong, Alex. It was Rose's idea, and she asked me to speak to you about it.'

'Do you want me to do it?'

'Of course I do. We couldn't do any better than have some of your hand-painted furniture in the place.'

A whistle blew, and looking back beneath the bridge she saw the engine coming, steam puffing from its funnel.

'What sort of furniture?' Alex had to raise his voice above the noise as the train thundered into the station then slowed with a screech of brakes.

'About six decorated chairs for the main salon and one or two small tables to match. That's all we can afford to begin with.'

'I'd want to visit the mill and see the setting before I started working on the furniture.'

'Of course, though you'll need to wait until the workmen have finished with it. Does that mean you'll do it?'

'I'll do it – for you,' he said, and made for the nearest carriage.

When the train had gone, Caitlin ran up the steps and almost danced home, smiling at everyone she passed on the way, light-headed with the relief of knowing that the ordeal was over and he had agreed. He would visit the mill, he would meet Rose there, and perhaps the two of them would settle their differences. If that happened, Caitlin's life would become as close to perfect as it ever had.

Alex made a point of returning to Paisley within a

few days, choosing a time when he thought his mother would be at home and knocking at the street door instead of taking his usual route through the pend to the back yard. He wanted to see Kirsty rather than Todd. When she opened the door, her apprehension changed to surprise, then alarm at the sight of her son on the step.

'What's amiss?'

'Nothing at all. I just came to see you.'

'Then why not come round the back?'

'Because I wanted a word with you on your own.' He stepped inside and closed the door.

'Something is wrong!'

'No it's not, Mam. Can we go into the kitchen, or are we going to have to talk out here in the hall?'

'You know fine and well that the street door's for visitors and bad news,' Kirsty scolded, and bustled ahead of him into the kitchen, which smelled pleasantly of home baking. 'Everyone else comes round the back.'

The big table was covered with flour, and Rowena, swathed in an apron, was kneeling on a chair and working away at a lump of dough.

'We're making buns for Grandad's dinner,' Kirsty explained. 'You go on with it, pet, while your uncle Alex and me have a wee talk.'

But at the sight of the visitor the little girl had already dropped the dough, grey and greasy from her manipulation, and was scrambling down from the chair, trying to pull the apron off at the same time.

Kirsty helped her, wiping her hands carefully while Alex held his tongue and waited with what patience he could find.

'Go and play upstairs,' Kirsty coaxed, but Rowena shook her head and made for the door leading to the yard. She was called back and pushed into a warm coat before finally being released outside.

'She's still that timid with folk she doesn't see every day,' Kirsty fretted, reaching as usual for the teapot. 'That'll be her away to the weaving shop, to that Murdo Guthrie.'

'There's no harm in her spending time with him as long as she doesn't get in the way of his work. Mam, Caitlin tells me that you and Todd are buying her a partnership in Rose Hamilton's new venture.'

Kirsty, who had just finished pouring boiling water onto tea leaves, paused with her back to him, the kettle still poised in one hand. 'Aye, that's right,' she said at last.

'There's no need for you to put your hand in your pocket. Since Caitlin seems to have set her heart on it, I'll give her the money.'

'It's already been paid over.' Kirsty put the empty kettle down and brushed a drift of flour into the middle of the table with the back of one hand to clear a space before taking clean cups from the cupboard.

'Then I'll give you your money back.'

'You'll not bother,' she said flatly.

'But . . . Look, Mam, she's my sister and I should never have refused you the way I did. I was angered with Rose Hamilton and I stupidly took it out on you and Caitlin. Now I want to put things right.'

Kirsty said nothing, concentrating on pouring milk into one cup then the other. She filled each cup with tea then stirred sugar in as though getting everything right was of the utmost importance.

'So how much was it?'

Kirsty pushed his cup towards him and sat down. 'That's our business, Alex. You'd already refused to help, so we did what we thought best.'

'But that money was meant to make you feel more secure about your future.'

'We do feel secure. Rose and Caitlin'll pay the money back to us, and mebbe some extra besides.' Kirsty sipped at her tea, then put the cup down and looked levelly at her son. 'John Brodie explained everything to us and drew up the papers. Isn't that how a lot of business folk make their wealth?'

'Yes, but they don't invest every penny that they own. Let me pay the money back to you, then it'll be me that takes the risk. I can afford it better than you can.'

'You refused to help Caitlin when I asked you to. Why should you help her now?'

'I've already admitted that I took my anger with Rose out on Caitlin. It was a daft thing to do and I'm sorry about it.'

'I'm glad to hear you say that, son,' Kirsty said with almost formal dignity.

'And now I'm going to make amends.'

'Alex, Todd and me decided to use our money to help Caitlin, and that's the way things are going to stay. You don't need to do anything. We'll get the money back in good time.'

'Are you certain of that?'

'As certain as anybody can be about anything. You don't understand, do you?' Kirsty said almost kindly. 'There's business, and there's family. You refused to pay the money over because, as you saw it, it would help Rose to set up in the mill that you'd wanted for yourself. That's business. Todd and me just wanted to help Caitlin, and that's family.'

'But I'm family too, and I want to put things right!'

'There's no need,' she said, as though trying to

explain something to a child. 'It's all been seen to, and we're going to let things stand as they are.'

He argued, reasoned, argued again, but nothing he said would change her mind. Finally, realising that time was passing and he was due to return to Glasgow, he left the house.

As his train rattled towards the city he stared out of the window without seeing the tenements that presented their shabby backs to the railway line. When his natural father had suddenly come into his life, offering work, his name, and a secure future, Alex had seized the chance to escape from an increasingly difficult life with his dominating stepfather. In his own eyes he had remained part of the Paisley family, but now a gulf seemed to be opening between his present life and his past.

He would have liked to go straight to the small factory where he spent a good part of his day. There he would find solace in the familiar surroundings of timber and tools and sawdust, the calmness of craftsmen going about their business, the pleasure of creating furniture from wood that had grown over centuries in huge forests. But he and his father had agreed to meet an important new client, so instead he had to walk from the station to the large and imposing emporium with 'MacDowall and Son' in bold letters over the door and above the windows on both outer walls.

As he made his way to the offices on the top floor, the counter assistants, supervisors and even some of the regular customers who knew him nodded and smiled. Their recognition was usually soothing, but not today.

Angus MacDowall was waiting in his office. 'I've just sent a lad down to the factory. I thought you might have forgotten our meeting.' Despite the hard life he had known in his earlier years, and despite the extra flesh that age and comfortable living had laid over his bones, he was as straight backed and quick in his movements as a much younger man.

'I had to go to Paisley.' Alex hung up his coat and hat and glanced into the mirror by the hatstand.

'Nothing wrong, I hope?'

'No.'

Angus eyed his son closely. 'Is your mother in good health?'

'She's very well.'

'Good.' Apart from a few brief meetings when he had first gone to Paisley to find Alex, Angus had had no other contact in recent years with his son's mother. Once they had meant everything to each other, but only for a short time; after that, their lives had gone along widely divergent lines, and they had become strangers, with only Alex's existence to remind them of what had been.

Angus consulted the gold watch chained across his slightly rounded stomach. 'They're late.'

'Father, have you ever made a mistake?'

'Me?' Angus grunted an abrupt laugh. 'I've made more of them than you've eaten hot dinners.'

'I'm talking about mistakes you regretted.'

'So am I.'

'And when you felt regret, how did you go about making amends?'

Angus leaned forward, hands on his large handsome desk. 'Are you going to tell me what this is about?'

'I don't believe I am.'

'Quite right.' Although they respected each other highly and, in their own ways, cared for each other, the relationship between father and son had always been more businesslike than familiar. They both preferred it that way; when it came to open warmth, Alex had his Paisley family, and Angus his daughter, Fiona, Alex's half-sister, now married and living in Fort William.

'If you want my opinion, lad, you can never make amends,' Angus said bluntly. 'Best to let the matter be, whatever it is, and make up your mind to be more careful with your decisions in future.'

Then the door opened; the awaited clients were ushered in, and the matter was dropped.

10

Todd waited that night until he and his wife were alone in their bedroom before saying, 'Ye've been awful quiet all evenin', lass. Has somethin' happened tae upset ye?'

'Alex was here.'

'Alex? But he never came tae the workshop.'

'He didn't stay for long. I sent him away with a flea in his ear,' Kirsty admitted, 'and now I'm wondering if I did the right thing.'

'I'll not be able tae advise ye as tae that till ye tell me more about it.' Todd, already in bed, patted the pillow beside his. 'Come over here.'

'I've not brushed my hair yet.'

'It can wait.'

When she joined him, he put an arm about her and drew her close to his warm body, listening to what she had to say without comment until she finished.

'I've been vexed with the way he refused to help Caitlin, I'll admit that. But even so, mebbe I dealt with him too severely today. D'you think I was acting out of spite, Todd – doing to Alex what he did to me and Caitlin when he refused the money in the first place?' Then, when her husband said nothing: 'I just felt that someone had to make him see the difference between

110

an act of business and helping out one of your own family.'

Todd had rested his chin comfortably on the top of her head. 'If an itch bothers ye, scratch it,' he told her. 'It seems tae me that Alex set up a right itch in ye when he refused tae lend the money in the first place. And today ye had a good scratch.'

'But what if I've driven him away from me?'

'I doubt if the matter's gone that far. It's a poor sort of son who'd deny his own mother just because he didnae get everythin' his way,' Todd gave a huge yawn, '—an' your Alex is a better man than that any day of the week.'

In less than a minute he was breathing slowly and regularly, the matter discussed and his mind at rest. Unwilling to disturb him, Kirsty stayed where she was, her mind reaching back over the past to long before she had met Todd or her first husband, Matt. She had been only sixteen when she had given birth to Alex; her father had packed her off to live with his sister, who had agreed with him that the child would be put up for adoption immediately after its birth. Instead Kirsty had run away with her newborn baby and had had a hard struggle to support the two of them before meeting and marrying Matt Lennox.

She hadn't even known that Sandy's full name was Angus MacDowall until the day he had turned up at Espedair Street, wealthy and successful and eager for a son to run his large furniture store with him, and eventually take it over. It had almost broken her heart when Alex had chosen to throw in his lot with his father, though she had known, and still knew, that Angus could offer him a far better future than he could expect with her. But he had been her son, her precious first-born. Now, despite Todd's reassurance, she felt that things had changed for the worse.

Todd snored slightly, then settled again, his arm tightening about her. The hollow between his neck and shoulder was warm and safe and, despite her worries, Kirsty, too, drifted into sleep, her hair unbrushed and the lamp still burning on the table.

By the beginning of February the former mill had been painted inside and out, and the ground floor had been divided into several rooms. New, larger windows had been installed throughout, the yard where weeds had struggled up through broken cobbles had been relaid with flagstones and the railings round the property had been cleared of rust and painted. On the evening of the day the workmen finished, Caitlin, John and Rose toured the mill, breathing in the smell of fresh wood and paint.

'This salon,' Rose spread her arms out, revolving slowly, 'will be for the very wealthy, and the other one will be for the rest, though we won't let the rest know that there's any difference.'

'We'll just furnish this one until you start bringing in clients,' John put in warningly. He had brought a sheaf of papers with him and was making lists of all that still had to be done. They had agreed to retain the space on the first floor, which had once held machinery, as a sewing room, with two large cutting tables in the centre – 'One to start with,' John said – flanked by sewing machines. At one end stood the new stove, which would pipe its heat through the entire building, and at the other, doors opened into two small rooms that had once been occupied by overseers. One, it had been decided, would be occupied by a forewoman, when they could afford such a luxury, while the other would be used for specialists, such as embroiderers.

A flight of stairs took them to the top floor; here the small windows had been retained, shelving had been installed round the walls to hold bolts of cloth and cupboards stood along the centre of the room, waiting to be filled with small items such as threads, needles and ribbons.

In its original state the mill had appeared poky to Caitlin, but now that it had been cleaned and the walls whitewashed and larger windows installed, she was appalled by the size of the place. 'We'll never fill it!' she said as they went back downstairs.

'We will, given time,' Rose said confidently. 'We can build up gradually.' She settled herself on a broad stone windowsill in the main salon. 'Now, I'd like to open in April, with a small fashion display on the first day to show some of Caitlin's designs.'

'April?' Caitlin, leaning against the wall, straightened up. 'That's too soon!'

'It's a good time of year to start a new business.'

'But you're not giving me enough time to provide all the new designs we'd need for a display!'

'I was thinking of using some of the designs you've already done as well as a few new ones. If we ask some of the people we've already made clothes for to wear them in the display, it would show what we've – you've – already achieved. They would love it – think of the fun they could have! And who knows, it might tempt them to order more clothes.'

'It sounds quite interesting – not that I know anything about clothes,' John added hurriedly.

'As to new clothes, if you could manage to make one or two items, Caitlin, I'm sure that John and I could persuade some of those empty-headed girls we meet at parties to model them for us,' Rose rushed on, 'especially if we allowed them to buy the garments they model at a reduced price. And we'll frame some of the other designs and hang them on the walls for the guests to look at. I'm sure we'd bring in a few orders on that first day.'

'First of all,' John interrupted, 'we have to find out if Caitlin will be able to do everything in the time you're allowing her.'

Caitlin's mind was racing. She had been doing some further work on the sketches inspired by the ceilidh, and it excited her to think that she might be able to develop them quite soon. 'I might get it done on time, if I start right away. You'd need to find the models quickly.'

'I will,' Rose promised. 'You and I will need to go to Glasgow next week to shop for materials.'

'We'd never manage to make all the clothes at Causeyside Street in the time, not with the orders that are lying there already.'

'Then we'd best get some sewing women for this place as soon as possible and buy in machines for them.' John made a note. 'I'll put advertisements in the *Express* and the *Gazette* for experienced seamstresses. How many?'

'Six,' Rose said, just as Caitlin said, 'Three.'

John looked from one to the other. 'Three to begin with. Furniture . . . As I said, we could start by furnishing just one salon and one fitting room, and perhaps you two could share the larger office until we're established. I believe that your brother's going to make the furniture for this room, Caitlin.'

'Yes. He hopes to visit Paisley next Friday morning to see the place and talk about what we want.'

'That's decided, then.' Rose stood up, dusting her

hands and beaming at her partners. 'I can't wait to see Mama's face when we tell her that we open in April!'

Rowena's interest in dancing, awakened by her night at the ceilidh in the Gaelic chapel, took up most of her attention and kept her out of mischief. With her quick mind she had memorised some of the basic steps, and she practised them tirelessly in the kitchen, in the weaving shop whenever Murdo had time to play his mouth organ and, as winter lost its grip and the weather began to improve, on a large flagstone set into the small patch of grass in the back yard.

The flagstone quickly became her special dancing stone, where she happily hopped and skipped and twirled to music that only she could hear. Occasionally she managed to coax Murdo from the weaving shop during his midday break to play the mouth organ while she danced.

Although most of Caitlin's evenings were spent with books and her sketch pad, working and reworking new designs for the fashion house, Rowena persuaded her to go to another ceilidh. This time Mary went too, and admitted, as they walked home at the end of the evening, enjoying herself.

'I'd wondered how it would be, with Highlanders so different from us Lowlanders, but they're nice enough folk.'

'Especially that lad you kept dancing with.'

'Mmmm.' Mary refused to be drawn. 'Murdo Guthrie's a strange man,' she said, staring at his back. He and Rowena, deep in conversation, were walking a few yards ahead. 'I wonder what's happened to him in his life.'

'I've wondered that myself, but I doubt if he'll ever tell us.'

'Mebbe that's why he gets on well with Rowena. Mebbe she's the only one to take him as he is, without question. They're alike – both trying to fit into a place that isn't theirs. That can't be easy.'

'I feel a bit like that myself with the new fashion house,' Caitlin admitted. 'Now that I'm having to go to Rose's house some evenings to meet the lassies she's bringing in as models for the opening, it's as if I'm in a different country, among folk I don't understand.'

'Away you go,' Mary told her roundly. 'There's nothing strange or different about rich folk.'

'But they don't speak like us, and they lead such different lives.'

'That's the sort of folk you'll be dealing with all the time once the fashion house opens.'

'I know. There's times I wonder if I've done the right thing, going in with Rose.'

'Of course you've done the right thing! I wish I could see inside a big house like hers.'

'It's lovely, and you'd like her big bedroom with its thick carpet and its velvet curtains right down to the floor – you could put our whole house into that one room, Mary. And the maid that brings us tea and wee sandwiches is nice enough. It's the times I meet Mrs Hamilton in the entrance hall or on the stairs that I hate.' It was a relief to tell someone. 'She looks at me as if I was after the silver or as if I smelled bad.'

'She does, does she? Cheeky old witch,' Mary snorted. 'Just you put your own neb in the air next time she tries that.'

'I can't. When folk look at you as if you're dirt, it makes you feel like dirt.'

'You're far too soft, Caitlin Lennox. You'll have to

learn to be just as snooty as they are. No, not snooty,'
Mary corrected herself. 'Calm and ladylike, with just a
hint of subservience, because they need to think they're
superior. It keeps them happy. But at the same time
you have to remind them that you know more about
clothes than they do, and they're dependent on you to
make them look stylish.'

'How do you know about that?'

'You can learn a lot from books.' Mary linked her
arm through Caitlin's as they swung round a corner.
'I'll teach you,' she said confidently.

Rose and Caitlin had arranged to go to the mill together
on Friday morning to meet Alex, but when Rose arrived
at the shop she found Caitlin in a panic.

'It's Mrs Gilbert – she tried to alter her new jacket
herself but she only succeeded in spoiling it, and she's
due to wear it at a special luncheon party in Glasgow.'

'So someone must go to the house to try to put things
right.' Mrs Gilbert had a tendency to try to make her
own alterations, despite the fact that she usually got
everything wrong. 'Can't Kirsty go, or Teenie?'

'I'm the one who made the jacket, and you know that
she's promised to let us make her winter clothes.'

'Yes, I know. We'll need her custom.' Rose sighed,
then said, 'I'll just have to meet Alex on my own.'

'You don't mind?'

'We can't leave him to cool his heels outside, can
we? Someone has to do it, and I certainly can't do
anything about Mrs Gilbert's jacket.'

'I'll be at the mill as soon as I can.'

'Or sooner, if possible,' Rose said, feeling like a
condemned woman about to take her final walk to the
scaffold.

*   *   *

Alex MacDowall paused at the mill gate, taking in the newly painted exterior of the building he had once intended to buy. There were even tubs of flowers flanking the entrance. Then his heart sank at the sight of a familiar bicycle propped against the wall by the door. He had hoped against hope that Rose wouldn't be present.

He took a deep breath, pulled down the front of his jacket and walked across the courtyard to the door. The two steps up to it, which he recalled as having been hollowed in the centre from use, had been replaced.

He had to wait for so long for an answer to his knock that he began to wonder if there was anyone in the building at all. But finally Rose opened the door, saying abruptly as soon as she saw him standing on the step, 'Caitlin's been delayed. She had to go and see an important customer, but she'll be here as soon as she can get away.'

He nodded, then as she stood in the doorway, looking at him warily, he said, 'Would you prefer me to wait on the step for her?'

He had meant it to be a light remark, but he regretted it when her face went beetroot red. She took a swift, clumsy step back, opening the door wide. 'Of course not. Come in.'

'I'm sorry, that was boorish of me,' he said as he stepped into the big square entrance hall. Since they had been thrown into each other's company, there was no sense in starting off on the wrong footing.

'Yes, it was, but I should have been prepared for it.' They eyed each other with hostility for a moment, then Rose's shoulders slumped. 'And now, I suppose, it's my turn to apologise. You and I always seem to bring out the worst in each other, Alex. I knew as soon as Caitlin was called away that you and I would end up quarrelling. Can we start again?' She stuck out her right hand.

He shook her hand formally, his lips twitching. 'I'd certainly agree on a truce, if only for Caitlin's sake.'

'John had hoped to be here as well, but he's been detained at his office. You should probably see what we've done to the place first.' Rose opened the nearest door to reveal a spacious room, well lit by three windows overlooking the mill race. At that moment the room held a kitchen table and three upright chairs, making an elaborately carved triangular cupboard in one corner look out of place. 'This will be Caitlin's design office, though she and I will share it until the smaller room can be furnished for me. We've allowed space in here for another two designers, when we can afford them.'

As they went through the ground-floor rooms, then upstairs to the other two levels, they began to relax a little. Rose's nervousness was replaced by her pride in the restoration and her plans for the future, while Alex was impressed, despite himself, by the skilful way in which the mill had been adapted to suit its new purpose.

Back in the design room, Rose opened the corner cupboard to reveal a decanter, a bottle and some glasses. 'Can I offer you something to drink? We have sherry, or there's whisky if you prefer it.'

He chose whisky.

'The cupboard and its contents are from my parents' home,' Rose explained as she poured. 'My father says that our clients may enjoy a small glass of sherry when they visit, and their husbands, should they be brought in to approve their wives' purchases, will need the whisky. With a wife and three daughters, he knows about such things.' She handed him his drink in a handsome cut-glass tumbler. 'I suspect that he has a certain admiration for what we've achieved – not that he'd admit it, of course. In any case, my mother would be furious if he dared.'

Alex took a deep swallow of the whisky then raised his eyebrows. 'He must admire you to present you with such a fine malt.'

'I thought that Caitlin would have been here by now.' She crossed the floor to stare out of the window at the mill race, then turned swiftly with what he always thought of as a Rose-like movement, so that her dark blue skirt belled out and the bright colours of the loose multi-coloured silk waistcoat she wore shimmered in the light from the window. 'Before she comes, Alex, I want you to know how much I regret having gone behind your back to buy this place as I did.'

'There's no—'

'Yes there is,' Rose interrupted. 'I've wanted so much to apologise, but I've not had the chance until now. I'd have written, but I find it difficult to put my true feelings down on paper.' Her face was scarlet; he felt sorry for her, knowing how much Rose Hamilton had always hated having to admit that she had been in the wrong.

'I could have behaved better myself at the time. In any case, it's all in the past now.'

Again, she held out her hand to him. 'Then can we consider ourselves to be friends again?' Her face was bright with relief. 'I've missed our arguments.'

'The Glasgow folk are a bit on the mild side for me,' Alex admitted. 'Not one of them possesses a temper like yours.'

The main door opened and Caitlin called out.

'We're in here,' Rose answered, releasing Alex's

hand and moving back towards the window as Caitlin came in, breathless from running and full of apologies for her absence, looking anxiously from one to the other. 'You should use a bicycle, like me,' Rose told her. 'It's much easier than running everywhere.'

'I'd have to learn to ride one first, and you've got me working so hard that I haven't the time for that.' Caitlin beamed at her brother. 'So, Alex, what do you think of our fashion house?'

'I have to say that now I've seen it I believe that this place suits your purpose better than it would have suited mine. When do you hope to open?'

'In April.' Rose took his empty glass back to the cupboard. 'Though we still have to think of a suitable name.' As she closed the cupboard doors and turned back to face them, Alex's attention was caught again by the way the light shimmered on the colourful diamond shapes that made up her waistcoat.

'Harlequin,' he said without stopping to think. The other two looked at each other.

'Harlequin? Isn't that some sort of fool?' Rose asked doubtfully, and he wished he had kept his mouth shut.

'If so I didn't know it. I thought Harlequin was a performer who wore bright colours. It was your waistcoat that brought the word to my mind.'

Rose looked down at the silky material. 'Of course – you based it on Harlequin's costume, didn't you, Caitlin? It's a perfect name!'

'It certainly denotes colour and design,' Caitlin agreed.

'And the theatrical side of it is apt too.' Rose laughed aloud. 'My mother certainly thinks I'm some kind of fool to want to risk every penny I have.'

Alex felt his face warming. 'I didn't mean—'

he began, but Rose stopped him with a wave of the hand.

'Don't spoil it by trying to explain. The House of Harlequin . . . Harlequin House of Fashion. How clever you are!'

'If you're certain of it, I'll paint a sign to put above the door. Something bright and eye-catching.'

'How soon could you show us the design for it?'

'Next week?' he suggested. It was like old times, Caitlin thought. Clearly Alex and Rose had settled their differences during their enforced time together.

'And we could use the same design on our paper-work.' Rose smiled on them both. 'Now there's no reason why we shouldn't open in April.'

'Perhaps there's just one reason,' Alex said. 'If you want furniture made and painted for an opening in April, isn't it time we discussed it?'

11

There had been a flood of applicants in response to John Brodie's advertisement for sewing women. Every one of them had to be interviewed, and Caitlin found it very hard to narrow the decision down to just three.

'They all need the money.'

'That's not our concern,' Rose told her firmly. 'If we give work to every single person who needs it we'll end up with an army of people who aren't up to our standards.'

'Couldn't you make the final decision? After all, you're running the business.'

'And you'll be working with the seamstresses, so you must decide whether or not they're suitable.'

Caitlin looked down the list, trying to fit faces to the names, and finally settled on three women, two in their early twenties and the third, Grace Watson, ten years older and with experience in a Glasgow dress shop.

John had acquired three sewing machines and a big cutting table, all second-hand but in good condition. They were installed immediately in the old mill, and Kirsty agreed to work on the new clothes there with the two most experienced women, while the third moved into Jean's shop to do some alteration work under Teenie's watchful eye. Caitlin divided her time between shop and mill, while John and Rose under-took the task of furnishing the other rooms, visiting auction rooms and house sales in an attempt to keep down costs.

There were times when Caitlin regretted telling Mary about her worries over dealing with clients. Her sister pored over fashion magazines in the shop, borrowed books on etiquette from the library, and at every opportunity made Caitlin parade up and down the parlour with a pile of books balanced on her head. She also introduced exercises involving smiling, speaking, sitting and standing, turning, picking things up and putting things down. Mary was an excellent tutor, though hard to please; nothing short of perfection would do, and at times Caitlin rebelled.

'How can anyone be expected to walk about with a pile of books on her head?' she wailed one evening when they crashed to the floor yet again.

'In some countries the women carry big jugs of water on their heads.'

'Try to make me do that,' Caitlin threatened, making for the door, 'and I'll empty the jug over you. I'm going for a walk.'

'We'll go together. The fresh air might cheer you up.' Mary scooped up a bundle of books and held them out. 'You can balance these on your head while we stroll along.'

Caitlin glared and took the books, steadying them atop her brown head before pacing from window to fireplace for the umpteenth time.

Although Caitlin was busy working at her designs and trying to learn how to deal with the gentry, and Rose spent a considerable amount of time in search of furniture at economical prices, the two women managed to spend several hectic days in Glasgow, choosing materials for Caitlin's new designs and selecting cloth, thread and the dozens of other items required for the new fashion house.

Afterwards, delighted with the success of their day, they visited the MacDowalls' small factory to look at the chairs and tables Alex and his staff were making for the salon.

Before they returned to Paisley, Alex insisted on taking the two of them for high tea. 'And cream cakes. You deserve something special after the day you've had,' he insisted when they tried to argue. He picked up a sketchbook as he shepherded them out of the building. 'In any case, I want your opinions on the sign I'm planning to make for you.'

The restaurant he took them to was extremely smart, and Caitlin found herself glad of Mary's ruthless training as she followed Alex and Rose to their table. The two of them suited the stylish decor, Alex in a grey lounge suit with matching waistcoat and bowler hat, and Rose in a green checked woollen costume that fitted her tall, slender figure admirably.

Alex had planned a black background, which would stand out against the building's whitewashed walls, with 'Harlequin' painted across it in multicoloured letters. The harlequin diamond pattern filled in the top of the *A* and the centre of the *Q*.

'It's wonderful,' Rose enthused. 'You must give me a copy of it so that I can have it copied on cards and letterheads.'

Alex took an envelope from his pocket. 'I took the liberty of getting the printer we use to give me some samples.'

Caitlin was glad to see how comfortable her brother

and her friend seemed to be in each other's company; not, perhaps, as relaxed as before their furious quarrel, but certainly at ease. She cared deeply about them both and hated to see them at odds.

As March gave way to April, it seemed to Caitlin that hours became minutes, days became hours and time began to rush downhill like an out-of-control steam engine, with her trapped inside. Sewing machines thundered through her sleep, and in her dreams she chased designs that leaped from the pages of her scrapbook and danced away, out of reach and out of sight.

In her waking hours, though, she could see that everything was beginning to come together. Under Kirsty, Teenie and Caitlin's supervision, the new seamstresses had given a good account of themselves, and her designs for the opening day fashion display were taking shape. Rose had persuaded several clients to model clothes designed for them by Caitlin and a considerable number of invitations had been sent out. John had ordered enough stationery to last their first year. In secret, Caitlin marvelled over the cards with her own name neatly printed beneath the Harlequin logo and the words 'Fashion Designer' below.

Lights blazed in every mill window on the night before the opening. Todd and John Brodie had brought the sewing machines from the shop earlier so that the costumes could be completed, and John had volunteered to transport glasses, cutlery and china from his home and Rose's. Alex had arrived that afternoon from Glasgow, bringing the salon furniture and the sign with him. After the tables and chairs had been installed and the sign put in position, he sent the van driver away, planning to stay the night in Espedair Street and attend the opening the following day.

While her elders worked, Rowena scampered happily through all the rooms, supposedly helping but in fact getting in the way. Kirsty and Todd took her home when she began to droop.

'You get back to help the lassies,' Todd told his wife when Rowena had been put to bed. 'I'll keep an eye on the bairn.'

'Are you sure? It doesn't seem right to leave you here on your lone.'

'Ach, away ye go, woman – I'm happier with my pipe and my paper, and ye know ye're fair dyin' tae get back and see what's been goin' on behind yer back. Anyway, they've need of ye.'

They had indeed. While Alex and John got the ground floor rooms ready and hung Caitlin's designs, carefully framed, on the walls under Mary's watchful eye, all five sewing machines were kept busy in the sewing room above. In the small rooms to one side, Rose and Jean helped six giggling young women into the garments they were to model, and Caitlin was kept busy darting between seamstresses and models, checking, advising, making last-minute alterations and worrying.

It was close to midnight by the time everything was finished.

'You've brought in an awful lot,' Kirsty said doubtfully, surveying the glasses and teacups laid out on trestle tables covered by great stretches of white linen. 'D'you think you'll get enough folk to use it all?'

'Their noses'll bring them, if nothing else does,' Rose told her. They were all more than ready to go home. The models crowded into the Hamiltons' car, which had been waiting outside for Rose, and John managed to squeeze Mary, Jean, Teenie, Kirsty and Caitlin into his car, promising to come back for Rose, who had been persuaded to leave her bicycle at home for once. Alex opted to walk but returned almost at once, startling Rose, who was making a last-minute check of all the rooms before leaving.

'I just noticed when I was looking back at the place that the sign's crooked. D'you have a ladder? I sent mine back in the van.'

'Only the one you and John used to hang the designs on the walls. It's not big enough for outside.'

'It'll do.' He made for the smaller, unused office.

'Leave it, Alex,' she said. 'We'll get a proper ladder in the morning.' But he was already struggling out of the room with the ladder.

'I'll not be able to sleep until I get it right. Give me a hand,' he ordered, and Rose rolled her eyes before doing as she was told. Between them they got the ladder out into the April twilight. Alex put it in position then hurried back into the building for the hammer and nails. Rose stepped back and eyed the ladder uneasily.

'It's too small – and it's rickety into the bargain,' she protested when Alex came out.

'I'll manage.' He stuffed the nails into one pocket and the hammer into another. 'It's just a wee adjustment.'

'At least wait until John comes back.'

'Stop fussing and hold the ladder steady,' he ordered, and started to climb. Rose clung to the struts, feeling the whole contraption shake as he made his way to the top. Glancing up, she saw to her horror that he was balancing himself precariously on the very top step and working on the sign with both hands.

'Alex!'

'Wheesht, you're distracting me,' he said breathlessly, positioning a nail and hammering it home with blows that made the entire ladder creak and shake. 'Walk back a bit and see how it looks now.'

'I'm not going to let go of this ladder!'

'For goodness' sake, I'm balancing myself against the wall. I'm quite safe. Will you do as you're told for once?'

Reluctantly Rose released the ladder and backed off across the yard.

'Well?'

In the semidarkness she could barely make out the sign. 'It's grand.'

'Are you sure?'

'I'm positive!' she shouted at him.

As he twisted round to say something to her over his shoulder, the ladder began to sway beneath him. Rose screamed his name and rushed over to throw her weight against the supports.

'I'm all right.' He began to scramble down, then stopped and asked irritably, 'Rose, how can I get to the ground with you lying across the treads?'

As soon as she knew that he was almost on the ground again, and therefore safe, she stormed into the building. When Alex had put the ladder away he went looking for her and found her huddled on one of his hand-painted chairs in the salon, shaking.

'What's the matter?'

'You're the matter, Alex MacDowall, great daft lummox that you are! You could have got yourself killed!'

'Don't be daft. I'd not have had far to fall even from the top of that ladder.'

'You could have landed on top of me and killed the two of us, or you could have fallen onto the flagstones and broken your neck or your skull. What sort of opening would I have had with folk having to step over your blood to get in the door?'

'Rose . . .' Bewildered, he put a hand on her shoulder, but she twitched away, furious with him for having given her such a fright and with herself for giving in to weakness – and with him again for being there to witness her weakness. 'Just g-go on back to Espedair St-street!' Her childhood habit of stuttering at times of stress returned.

He moved away, and hearing the clink of glass against glass, she looked up to see that he had opened one of the bottles and was pouring something into two glasses.

'That's supposed to be for the g-guests tomorrow.'

'Your need's greater than theirs. Anyway, there's plenty for tomorrow.' He put a glass into her hand. 'Drink it down properly and never mind sipping at it.'

She did as she was told. He had given her brandy; it made her cough, but at the same time it burned down into her stomach and restored her backbone.

'Feeling better?' Alex asked, and she summoned up a faint smile.

'I'm sorry.'

'That's all right. It's nerves, with the place opening tomorrow.'

She took another drink. 'It has nothing to do with nerves. I don't have many good friends, and I can't afford to let one of them kill himself.'

He gave a brief, embarrassed laugh. 'It'd take a lot more than a shaky ladder to put an end to me,' he said, and began to wander round the room, giving her time to steady herself. 'This is very elegant, now that I see it all put together.'

Caitlin had opted for cream curtain material in all the ground-floor windows, trimmed with deep red and held back with red sashes. The chairs and small tables were also cream, and Alex had painted sprays of deep red roses over the back and arms of each chair. Delicate and yet sturdy, the furniture fitted in well with the airy, panelled room and the pastel-patterned rugs scattered over the polished wooden floor.

Alex tossed a wry smile at Rose. 'It's hard to remember now that it was once a mill and that I was planning to turn it into a wee factory.'

'Alex, what if my parents are right and I'm making a terrible mistake? What if Harlequin fails?'

'It won't fail. Just keep telling yourself that.'

She shook her head. 'But if it did – it's not just me; Caitlin and Kirsty stand to lose more than money if things go wrong.'

'You're just doubting yourself because you're tired. D'you want another drink?'

'Best not. John will be here in a minute.' She put her empty glass on the table, then said, 'You've got a streak of dust across your cheek from that sign. Here.' She took a handkerchief from her bag and held it out. 'Spit,' she ordered, and when he had moistened the cloth she scrubbed at his face.

He screwed his eyes up. 'That stings!'

'You can't go through the streets with a dirty face.'

'Why not? Enough,' he protested, then reached up to stay her hand as she rubbed harder. 'It's like being wee again, with Mam trying to skin me with the face flannel.'

'And I suppose you made a fuss then, too, bairn that you are. There, that's you clean and tidy again.' She put the handkerchief aside.

'Have you taken the skin off?'

'No, but there's a red mark.' She touched his cheek, smoothing the skin beneath her fingertips. 'It'll fade . . .' she began. Her voice died away and her smile faded as Alex put his hand up to cover hers and hold it against his cheek.

His cheek tensed beneath her fingers, and she was close enough to hear him swallow and to see his throat muscles move smoothly beneath their covering of skin.

'Rose . . . ,' he said. Her hand was still trapped by his, but her thumb was free; of its own volition it moved to caress the line of his jaw.

The air between them seemed to crystallise; it seemed to Rose that they were standing at some unseen crossroads, where her next movement, or his, could change the entire course of their lives. She caught her breath. Then John's car turned in at the gate, car horn parping, and the moment was gone.

Alex declined the offer of a lift to Espedair Street. He closed the yard gates behind the car, and when Rose twisted round in her seat to wave, she saw that he was standing, hands in his pockets, watching them drive away. He didn't return the wave.

Strains of 'Alexander's Ragtime Band', one of Rose's favourite pieces of music, wafted through the crowded ground floor from a gramophone in one of the fitting rooms. The brief fashion display was over, and now the models were mingling with the guests to allow them a closer look at the gowns. Rose, striking in a dark-blue layered skirt beneath a long, loose tunic in broad vertical stripes of deep red and paler blue, moved from group to group, notebook and pencil in hand.

'Nasty American noise,' Caitlin heard an elderly woman say as she went by.

'Not at all, Mama. It's the latest fashion, and such fun to dance to,' chirruped the girl with her. 'Let's go over there. I want you to have a closer look at that little afternoon gown.'

They moved away, and John Brodie appeared by Caitlin's side. 'Perhaps "Clair de Lune" would have charmed Mrs Bruce,' he murmured. 'But on the other hand, I think her daughter, Adele, may well become a client. She adores dancing, the wilder the better. Is that one of your designs Rose is wearing?'

'Yes.' Once, Rose had said airily that she looked on clothing merely as a way of avoiding the embarrassment to others of appearing naked in the street. Now almost all of her clothes were specially designed for her by Caitlin.

'She looks wonderful. When I think of the clumsy, gawky person she used to be . . .'

'She's still the same Rose.'

'I know, but now she looks so . . .' John cleared his throat, then asked, 'Does Rose ever mention me, Caitlin?'

'Frequently.'

'I don't mean as a lawyer or as a friend. I mean, does she ever talk about me in another way? Dammit, Caitlin,' he said as she looked blankly at him. 'Does she ever show any interest in me as a man?'

'Oh.' She had known full well what he meant, but it embarrassed her to talk about Rose behind her back. 'You know Rose – her mind's usually on things to do with the shop or Harlequin.'

'So she hasn't said anything about me?'

'Not really.'

'Or about any other man?'

'She's said nothing, John.'

He coloured. 'The fact is, Caitlin, I used to think very little of Rose other than her being more of a good sport than other women – and having a damned good business brain, too. But now . . . well, I rarely seem to be thinking of anyone else. D'you think that if I was to take her out somewhere quiet for dinner or a drive, I could venture to—'

'What on earth are you doing in a fashion house, John Brodie?' A plump, heavily scented young woman squeezed herself between them, her back to Caitlin.

'I have an interest in Harlequin, Isa, as you well know.'

'I did hear something of it. Did you see me in the fashion display?' Mrs Harper swept on.

'I did indeed, and you were quite amazing.'

'Oh, you flatterer!' Mrs Harper said coyly, and Caitlin bit her lip hard, wondering how John could keep such a straight face. Rose's friends had done quite well as models, but her idea of using real clients of various ages and sizes to augment the display had caused some anxious moments, particularly with Mrs Harper, who had graciously agreed to model the costume made for her by Caitlin seven months earlier. Unfortunately the woman had put on weight since then, and fitting her into it had been, as Jean remarked afterwards, like trying to fit a small shoe onto a large foot. They had succeeded, but Caitlin's heart had been in her mouth when the woman's turn had come and she had paraded round the salon, her high-waisted jacket and straight skirt straining at every seam. Mrs Harper, she noticed, had changed her outfit immediately after the display.

'You know Caitlin Lennox.' John reached out and drew her to his side. Mrs Harper inclined her head graciously.

'Ah yes, you're the seamstress who made my costume.'

John frowned and opened his mouth, but Caitlin spoke first, Mary's instructions ringing in her ears – *Neck straight, a very slight inclination of the head, lips curved in a faint smile that doesn't reach the eyes.* 'I designed your costume, Mrs Harper. I also made part of it, but now that I am Harlequin's designer and an equal partner, I'll rarely have time to do any sewing.' As fortune had it, she was standing by a small table with a scattering of cards on its surface; Caitlin took one and presented it to the woman. 'When you feel the need to replenish your wardrobe, I would be happy to assist, if you care to make an appointment.'

She smiled sweetly into the woman's astonished gape and moved away, telling herself that she must find the time soon to make a really nice blouse for Mary.

12

Alex was nowhere to be seen, and Caitlin, eager to get away from the crush and the noise and the mingled perfumes that thickened the air, went in search of him. He was sitting on a deep windowsill in the sewing room, looking down on the river below. He looked up with a faint smile.

'Had enough?' he asked.

'Yes, but it's going well.'

'With Rose Hamilton at the helm, could it fail?'

'Are you looking for somewhere else in Paisley?'

'No. We've been talking of expanding the Glasgow workshop and bringing in a manager so that I can spend more time in the shop, but I'm not sure if we will. Things are . . . happening.'

'At MacDowall and Son's?'

'In Europe. There may be a war.'

It was the first Caitlin had heard of it. 'Surely not,' she protested. 'Why would anyone want to go to war?'

'We must hope that nobody will,' he said, and turned his attention to the river again.

'Alex, is there something wrong between you and Mam?'

'No,' he said, after a hesitation so slight that it was scarcely to be noticed. But Caitlin had noticed it.

'This morning, at home, the two of you seemed . . . ,' she searched for the right word, 'formal with each other.'

'It's a good long while since we lived beneath the same roof. I know that it was hard for her when I moved to Glasgow.'

She didn't believe him. All her life she had known of her mother's secret preference for Alex. It hadn't bothered her or Mary, although Ewan had resented it, but then Ewan had tended to resent a lot of things. Watching Alex and their mother that morning, Caitlin had been reminded of a broken china plate so skilfully repaired that the crack could scarcely be seen with the naked eye, although it was still there. The break she sensed between her mother and her half-brother had been caused by something more serious and more recent than Alex's move to Glasgow years before. She was trying to find some way of delving deeper without angering him when he got to his feet and held out a hand to her.

'Time to go back downstairs and face your guests. They'll be wondering where you are.'

'Six definite appointments, and almost all the cards we left out have been taken away,' Rose said gleefully two hours later. The last of the guests had departed, and Alex had returned to Glasgow. The others were gathered in the design office – Caitlin, Rose and John with glasses in their hands; Kirsty, Jean, Teenie and the three seamstresses with cups of tea.

'It's a good start.' John drained his glass. 'Now I must get back to the office.'

'And we've got this place tae put tae rights for the mornin'.' Teenie got to her feet.

'You're not going to start cleaning now, are you?' Rose protested, and Teenie gave her a scathing look.

'The fairies arenae goin' tae creep in at night and wave their wands. I brought my apron – or have ye got a cleaner all arranged?'

Rose and John looked at each other. 'I forgot about a cleaner,' she admitted, while he asked, 'How much will it cost?'

Teenie shook her head pityingly. 'I'll away and get my apron.'

In June, Mary left school and started work in the boiling shop of Robertson's Marmalade Factory, close by Espedair Street. Each day she came home with the rich aroma of boiling fruit clinging to her clothes, and Todd claimed that just being in the same room as her when she was fresh from her work made him feel hungry.

It was her ambition to work in the office, where she could use her talent for figures. Until then she was content to stay where she was, despite the constant battle the jam workers fought with wasps drawn to the place by the smell of the fruit. Mary was proud to bring home a weekly pay packet, but she soon lost her taste for preserves.

'It must be the sight and smell of fruit all day long that does it,' she told Caitlin mournfully. 'After a few weeks you don't notice it any more, but the notion to eat the stuff seems to have left me.'

There was one consolation; Lachie, the Highland boy she had met at her first visit to a ceilidh worked at Robertson's as a van boy, and within a month he and Mary had started walking out together.

The ceilidhs had ended for the summer months, but to Rowena's delight one of the women had offered to give the child dancing lessons for a few pence a week.

Caitlin, with more work than she could handle at the fashion house, was alarmed when her mother, who still held a deep mistrust of Highlanders, showed signs of turning down the offer. For her own part, she was eager to agree to anything that would keep Rowena contented and avoid further problems at home.

'You must admit that Rowena's been more settled since she discovered dancing,' she pointed out, 'and that's what matters. Mary and I both know Flora McCall, and Rowena'll not come to any harm with her. I'll pay for the lessons as her birthday present,' she added. To her relief, Kirsty gave in.

'I don't know what it is with folk,' Caitlin said later to Mary. 'Bryce doesn't like Murdo because he doesn't understand him, but you'd have thought Mam would have been more understanding.'

Her sister shrugged. 'During the '45 rebellion there were Lowlanders who thought that Highlanders ate babies. Mebbe Mam heard about that once and it's stuck in her mind. Anyway, she still thinks Ewan'll turn up one day, and she frets in case he finds fault with the way she's raised his daughter.'

'Mebbe he'll come for the bairn's birthday. That would be the best present she could have.'

'After nearly a year without a word from him, the moon's more likely to fall from the sky. But if he does come to Paisley he should go down on his knees to thank Mam for what she's done for Rowena – and I'll be looking for him to do a bit of kneeling before me, and all,' Mary added tartly.

Ewan didn't arrive for his daughter's fifth birthday at the end of July, nor did he make any contact.

Nothing was said about his absence or his continued silence, but the rest of the family worked to make the occasion as festive as possible for Rowena. As family tradition demanded, Kirsty made a clootie dumpling, large and round and rich with fruit. A threepenny piece wrapped in greaseproof paper had been included in the mixture, and Kirsty made certain that it appeared in Rowena's slice.

Even Alex came to Paisley for the occasion, bringing with him a small hand-painted chair. Caitlin made the little girl a winter coat from the ends of cloth woven by Murdo Guthrie, while Kirsty made a cambric pinafore dress with a braid-trimmed sailor collar. Mary bought coloured hair ribbons and a pair of buttoned shoes, which Rowena promptly designated as her dancing shoes. Todd won a sparkling smile when he presented a pretty gilt frame for Ewan's photograph, which she kept beneath her pillow at all times.

Murdo had declined an invitation to attend the party. 'It'd not be right with Mr MacDowall there, and him my employer,' he told Caitlin when she tried to persuade him to change his mind.

'He'd like you to be there. You've done so well with Rowena, she'll be disappointed if you don't come.'

He was treating the yarn stretched tightly over the rollers with paste to strengthen it, using a wide, soft brush.

'Ach, I'm not one for gatherings,' he said, without looking up from his work, and she left him in peace, realising that he had made up his mind and would not be swayed.

When the meal was over, Rowena insisted on going to the weaving shop to show him her presents. 'She's going to be a beauty when she grows up,' Alex said as he and Caitlin followed her, carrying a plate of still-warm dumpling for Murdo and a mug of tea to wash it down with. 'She's got the best of Ewan and Beth's looks.' Then, as they turned into the pend, he added grimly, 'I just hope she hasn't inherited the worst of their natures.'

Murdo, who had stopped work and turned on the wooden bench, known to weavers as the saytree, to watch Rowena pirouetting around the hard earth floor, the skirt of her new dress held out to either side to show its width, jumped to his feet as soon as his employer walked in.

'Sit down, man, and eat this while it's still warm.' Alex thrust the plate into his hands. Caitlin, putting the mug on the windowsill, was certain that the Highlander would have preferred to eat and drink on his own, but Rowena ran to lean on his knee, demanding to see if there was a threepenny bit in his slice of dumpling. He had no option but to eat. Alex examined the cloth on the loom, a soft blue with a small dark green pattern running across it.

'It looks fine. You'll have it ready by next Friday?' Alex asked and, as Murdo nodded, his mouth too full of dumpling for speech, Alex sniffed at the air. 'What's that smell?'

'It's the pinks,' Rowena told him importantly, pointing at the pot of flowers on the windowsill. 'Murdo grows them 'cos all the weavers used to have them in their shops.' She began to poke her fingers into what was left of the dumpling.

'Rowena . . .' Caitlin swooped down on her. 'Will you let the man eat his food in peace?'

'I only wanted to see if Murdo's got money in his bit of dumpling too.'

The weaver scooped up the mauled remains and pushed them into his mouth, washing them down with tea.

'Not a penny,' he told the little girl, who dipped a hand into the pocket of her new dress and brought out her threepenny piece, still wrapped in its paper.

'Here – you take that one.'

'I cannae take your money!'

'It's all right. I've got other things.'

'But this is your birthday, the day folk give things to you.' He gently folded her small fingers over the coin, then reached behind the pot of pinks and brought out a tiny glass vase filled with fresh wild flowers. 'This is for you.'

Rowena put the threepenny piece back into her pocket and took the vase carefully in both hands. 'Look, Aunt Caitlin!'

It was made of cheap glass, but it had been delicately cut, and the light from the window sparkled off its facets.

'It's beautiful,' Caitlin agreed, smiling over Rowena's head at the weaver, touched by his thoughtfulness. His dark brown eyes were fixed on the little girl, his mouth curved in a faint smile.

'Where did you get the flowers?' Rowena wanted to know.

'They grow by the river and up in the braes.'

'Will you take me to see them?'

'Aye, if your grandmother allows it.'

Rowena handed the vase carefully to Caitlin then turned and stretched up on tiptoe to catch a handful of the weaver's long dark hair, tugging on it so that his face was pulled down towards hers. She brushed his cheek with her lips, and Alex laughed at his embarrassment.

'D'you not think it's strange that, of all of us, Rowena's the one who's made friends with Murdo?' Caitlin asked as she walked with Alex to the station later.

'Mebbe it's because she doesn't want anything from him.'

'D'you know anything of his past?'

'Why d'you ask that?'

'I was just wondering what happened to make him the way he is.'

'He's just a man that likes to keep himself to himself. I'm a bit like that myself – or have you never noticed?'

'I've noticed you're more contented living your own life in Glasgow than you ever were here.'

'It's not a case of being contented,' Alex said. 'Our house was always too busy for me, with Mam worrying about us all and Mary such a wee frightened skelf of a thing in those days, and Ewan full of himself, and the old man . . .'

She felt the need to defend her long-dead father. 'He wasn't so bad before the rheumatics got hold of him.'

'Mebbe not, but it was always made clear to me that Ewan was the favourite – though I suppose that was just natural, with Ewan being his own flesh and blood. Not that that made him special.' A bitter note crept into Alex's voice. 'He caused nothing but trouble and heartbreak, running away with Beth as he did and then sending his bairn back here without a word of explanation.'

'Evenin' tae ye, Caitlin, Mr Lennox,' Bryce Caldwell said just then. 'It's a fine night.'

'It's yourself, Bryce. Aye, it's a fine night, right enough. Are you on your way home?' Alex asked affably.

'Aye.' Bryce whipped his cap off, twisting it between his hands and shifting from one foot to the other, his eyes on Caitlin.

'Then you'll mebbe see my sister back home for me.'

Alex put a hand on Caitlin's elbow and began to turn her round to face the way she had come. 'My train'll be along in just a minute anyway.'

Bryce needed no urging. He said a cheerful goodbye to his employer and reached out to take Caitlin's arm.

'Just a minute,' she told him, and hurried after Alex, who was disappearing down the station steps.

'You know fine that me and Bryce aren't speaking!' she hissed at him, and he grinned up at her. 'I'm just lending a helping hand, the way you did when you left me and Rose Hamilton waiting for you in the old mill that day.'

'I was with a client!'

'So you said. Here's my train.' He continued down the steps, and Caitlin had no option but to fall into step beside Bryce, who had the sense to keep quiet until they were in Espedair Street before asking tentatively, 'How have ye been?'

'Fine.' They had reached the pend. 'Goodnight, Bryce,' she said. 'Thank you for walking back with me.' She would have ducked in below the stone arch if he hadn't put a hand on her arm. 'Caitlin . . .'

'What?' She glared at his fingers, and they fell away.

'I'm . . . I'm right vexed about what I said tae ye before.'

'I can't remember what you said.'

He swallowed audibly. 'About you an' thon Highlander.'

'What Highlander?' Caitlin asked, finding a certain pleasure in making him squirm.

'Thon Murdo Guthrie. I was wrong tae accuse ye of walkin' out with him.'

'Yes, you were.'

'It was . . . it's . . . Ach, Caitlin,' he burst out, 'I'm

that fond of ye, an' at times it makes me say daft things.'

'You're right there, Bryce Caldwell.'

'If I promise not to do it again will ye go back tae walkin' out with me?'

'I don't know about that.'

'Caitlin,' he said wretchedly, 'I miss bein' in yer company. There's just somethin' about ye that the other lassies don't have.'

'You've tried some, have you?'

He must have heard the amusement in her voice, for suddenly he was on the defensive. 'If ye must know, aye, I have! And some were well enough, but they're not you. Surely a man's got a right tae ask—'

'I will.'

'What?' asked Bryce, taken by surprise.

'I said I'll start walking out with you again – but just as friends, mind. And there's to be no more of your silly jealousy.'

'I promise!' Before she realised his intentions, he had caught her up in his arms and kissed her soundly. 'Tomorrow, eight o'clock?' he asked, beaming, and when she nodded he went racing off along the pavement, leaping to slap one hand against a lamp standard as he went.

Caitlin laughed and shook her head. He still behaved like a child at times, she thought, as she made for the back door. But there was no real malice in him.

It wasn't until much later that she realised that Alex hadn't answered her questions about Murdo.

13

As most of Caitlin's time was spent in the sewing room, she got to know the three seamstresses well. A natural hierarchy was swiftly established, with Lizzie Galloway and Iris Menzies more than content to let Grace Watson, the oldest of the three, take on the position of supervisor. It suited Caitlin, too, for it meant that she dealt mainly with Grace, a hard worker with a quick mind. The younger women were unmarried, and Grace was a widow, her husband having drunk himself into an early grave, leaving Grace with an elderly mother-in-law and three children to feed, house and clothe.

'The seven other bairns were taken from me,' she told Caitlin as a matter of fact, 'four just after they came into the world, an' three from the diphtheria.'

Caitlin thought of her own little brother, Fergus, killed in his second year. 'How could you bear to lose seven children?'

'It's the way of things. You just have to keep lookin' after them that're spared to you. I mind hearin' a minister sayin' once that God moves in mysterious ways, and I suppose He does, for when you think of it I could never have managed to care for ten. We'd have ended up in the workhouse.'

Local interest in Harlequin was still high, and Caitlin was kept so busy that on several occasions, to her disappointment, she had to forego the pleasure of buying materials from the Glasgow warehouse and let Rose go in her stead. Mr and Mrs Hamilton had left Paisley at the end of June to spend their usual long summer holiday in England; to her mother's annoyance, Rose had refused to leave Caitlin on her own so soon after Harlequin's launch.

In Causeyside Street, Kirsty, Jean and Teenie had their hands full getting the shop back to normal now that the others had their own premises. It had been agreed that the shop and fashion house would be run separately, though with Rose keeping the books for both premises.

Life moved on serenely, with Rowena absorbed in her dancing, Mary enjoying her new working life and her friendship with Lachie, and Todd kept busy in the workshop. When he'd read aloud from his newspaper about the assassination of an Austrian archduke and his wife in the faraway Balkans a few days before Rowena's birthday, Kirsty had tutted over the way some folk seemed unable to live with their fellow men in peace. Caitlin had paid little heed, for all her energies had been concentrated on Harlequin.

So it came as a considerable shock to them as well as to most ordinary folk when, on 4 August, Britain went to war with Germany.

Bryce Caldwell was among the first to volunteer to join the army.

'What did you do that for?' Caitlin wanted to know when he told her.

He looked hurt. 'What's wrong with wantin' tae fight for yer country?'

'But you're not a soldier, you're a cabinet-maker. What's Todd going to do while you're away?'

'He'll manage. They're sayin' that it'll no' last long. It's one way of seein' a bit of the world. I thought ye'd be proud of me.'

'I just wish you'd given the matter some thought first. There are regular soldiers in the army who know a lot more than you do about fighting.'

He preened himself. 'Are ye scared in case I get killed?'

'It's nothing to do with being scared,' she snapped at him. The declaration of war had caught her unawares; she still didn't know what it was all about, and Bryce's decision to enlist seemed to bring the whole business too close to home for her liking. 'I'm just saying that you should mebbe leave the fighting to the men that have been trained for it.'

'Well I didn't, and now I've taken the King's shillin' there's no sense in goin' on at me.'

'I suppose not. When do you go away?'

'They'll let me know, but it's bound tae be quite soon. They say it'll be sorted out by Ne'erday,' he said reassuringly. A week later, he was gone.

The declaration of war had ended the Hamiltons' holiday abruptly, to their daughter's annoyance. Rose had enjoyed her freedom and began to talk of having the old mill gatehouse renovated.

'You and I could both live there,' she told Caitlin enthusiastically. 'There's enough room, and just think how convenient it would be.'

'But we can't afford to spend a single penny on the place.'

'Not this year, that's true. But next, surely.'

'What if the war continues?'

'It won't,' Rose assured her blithely.

Recruiting posters blossomed on walls, recruitment drives were held, marching bands played in the streets and housewives hurried to stock up their larders, fearful of food shortages. Caitlin was grateful when Murdo, under pressure from Rowena, agreed to take the two of them to the Gleniffer Braes, west of Paisley, for an afternoon's walk.

Once they reached the Bonnie Wee Well they left the narrow, climbing road and took to the grass, Rowena running ahead and sometimes plunging into stretches of fern so tall that she was hidden from sight, with only an agitation among the fern tips to show where she was. The other two followed at their own pace, walking several feet apart. Caitlin had learned long since not to expect any conversation from Murdo; indeed, the silence soothed her after the thrum of sewing machines, the seamstresses' chatter and the fussing of clients in the fitting room. Up here, looking down on Paisley and picking out the abbey, the church spires and the John Neilston School's green dome like an upended porridge bowl, she felt as though she was on the roof of the world. In the distance, hazy in the sunlight, she could see Ben Lomond's peak and broad shoulders beyond the Kilpatrick Hills.

Sitting on a fallen tree, watching Murdo and Rowena's heads close together as they crouched by a stream a few feet away, dabbling in the water, she was suddenly struck by the fact that although everything about her was green – mosses, grasses, ferns and shrubs – there was a wealth of different shades. Next time, she decided, she would bring her notebook and some crayons.

Caitlin watched as Murdo produced a handkerchief and used it to carefully dry his and Rowena's hands, then he got to his feet and came to where Caitlin sat, the little girl skipping along behind him. 'Time we started back,' he said.

'Can we come back another day?' Rowena clamoured.

'If Murdo agrees,' Caitlin told her, and was pleased when he nodded.

Bryce came home on a few days' furlough in the Highland Light Infantry's tartan trews and the bonnet with its jaunty red and white cockade. When he took her into his arms and kissed her, his uniform jacket felt stiff and scratchy, and she felt shy and ill at ease, as though she was with a stranger.

'I was thinkin',' he said awkwardly when he had released her, 'that it would be a rare comfort tae me tae know that you're here.'

'Where else would I be?'

'I don't mean here in Paisley, I mean here waitin' for me. Promised tae me.'

'Promised?' Caitlin asked cautiously.

'With some sort of understandin', like. Some of the lads've got sweethearts waitin' for them an' the promise of marriage when this business is all over, an' I thought that—'

She caught his drift. 'You did, did you? Well, you can just think again, Bryce Caldwell.'

'Ach, Caitlin!'

'Did we not agree just to be friends?'

'Aye, but that was before I went tae be a soldier. A man has tae have some hope,' he said, then scooped her into his arms again, kissing her until she was almost suffocated.

'You've got plenty of hope – and plenty of cheek as well,' she said when she could speak again. 'You always have had. So just keep on hoping.'

'Will ye no' even wish me well?'

'I do wish you well, Bryce, and a safe return too. But that's as far as it goes for now.'

He heaved a gusty sigh. 'We can talk about it again when I get my next furlough,' he said.

Todd took a retired cabinet-maker on in Bryce's place, and in MacDowalls' shop and factory Alex, too, had to find other workers to replace younger men who had enlisted.

It wasn't until the first reports of British casualties, at a Belgian town called Mons, appeared in the newspapers late in August that Caitlin took in the fact that there really was a war going on. By then the household was involved in a battle of its own, for Rowena's first day as a pupil at the South School had arrived.

'I'm not going,' she announced that morning.

'You are so,' Mary told her firmly. Since the marmalade factory was near the school, she had been chosen to deliver the little girl there before going to work. 'There's folk that I know still at that school, so don't you give me a showing up!'

Rowena scowled at her and backed into the corner between the sink and the tall cupboard where the dishes were kept. Kirsty, too, glared at her daughter.

'Don't fright her, Mary,' she admonished, and Mary rolled her eyes to the ceiling. 'Rowena, hen, all the wee girls and laddies have to go to the school,' Kirsty wheedled. 'You'll learn to read and to write and to count, and you'll meet new friends.' When the child said nothing but squeezed herself further into the corner with an all-too-familiar buttoning of the features, she added placatingly, 'Just think how pleased your daddy'll be when he comes for you and finds that you can read and write.'

Caitlin and her stepfather exchanged glances across the breakfast table, while Rowena, seizing on the name, said from her niche, 'I want my daddy to take me to the school.'

'He can't take you today because he's . . . still away somewhere.'

'Then I'm not going!'

It took a lot of coaxing to get her to agree to go, and even then she dragged behind Mary, who held her firmly by the hand.

They were both subdued that evening. Rowena refused to answer any questions about her first day at school and Mary, tight lipped, ignored the little girl. Before and after her evening meal, Rowena sat outside on her dancing stone, hugging her father's photograph and staring moodily at the grass.

'I'm not taking her tomorrow,' Mary burst out as soon as the little girl had gone to bed. 'She gave me a right showing up!'

Kirsty, tired after a busy day at the shop, sighed and put aside the magazine she had brought home with her. 'I knew something had gone wrong, but she'd not say a word to me when I fetched her home. She wouldn't even look at me. What happened?'

'First of all I had to drag her all the way there, then when we reached the place she refused to go in. It took me and Miss Livingstone to carry her into the classroom, and when I left she was sitting at her desk without a word for anyone. Then,' said Mary, crimson with mortification, 'I was called out of work during the wee ones' playtime because she'd tried to run away. Everybody stared at me, and my supervisor said it wasn't to happen again. I didn't know where to put my face!'

'Did you catch her?' Todd asked from behind his newspaper.

'It seems that she ran full tilt into a policeman going down the road, then she tried to bite him when he got a hold of her. It's just fortunate for us that he's used to catching criminals, for he avoided the bite and he was carrying her back in when I arrived.' Mary squirmed, reliving the memory. 'She was nothing but trouble!'

'You should have told us sooner, Mary.'

'And let her be the centre of attention? If you ask me, that's what she wants. But I'm not taking her tomorrow, or any other day!'

'She's got to go,' Kirsty fretted. 'We'll have the law after us if she doesn't, and what'll her father think when he—'

'Don't fret yourself, hen. I'll take her tomorrow.' Todd came out from behind his newspaper. 'She'll be fine with me.'

Mary sniffed and gave him a sidelong glance. 'You think so?'

'I was much the same when I first went tae the school. I mind my father had tae give me a good leatherin' before I'd settle.'

Mary said darkly, 'Mebbe that would be a good thing for Rowena too.'

Todd's attempt to coax Rowena to settle into school life had no more success than Mary's. She tried to run away several times on the short journey to the school buildings, and in the end he was forced to carry her, mute and rigid, into the classroom.

'Puttin' her intae her wee seat was worse than tryin' tae thread a needle,' he told his family that night.

'You've never threaded a needle in your life, man!' Kirsty snapped, sick with worry.

'I've seen you often enough tryin' tae get that bit of thread through the wee hole in the needle. That's what it felt like, with the bairn stiff as a board and her knees bangin' against her desk till I was feared we'd hurt her.'

At least Rowena hadn't tried to run away during the school day, but when Todd went to fetch her, he was told by the thin-lipped teacher that she had flown at a little boy who'd jeered at her in the playground, and scratched his face. On the way home she had eluded her grandfather, racing ahead and out of his sight.

'Luckily when I got back she was where I expected tae find her – in the weavin' shop with Murdo.'

'She could have fallen under the wheels of a van or a cart,' Kirsty fretted. Mary said nothing, but her face showed clearly that she wouldn't have minded if Rowena had been mown down.

Caitlin sighed and offered to take the child to school the following day.

'You'll regret it,' Mary told her when their mother was out of the kitchen.

'I know I will, but I have to try. Mam looks worn out with the worry.'

'She'll settle eventually. Everyone has tae,' Todd predicted.

'Rowena,' said Mary, 'isn't like everyone.'

'I'm not going!' Rowena stormed as Caitlin buttoned her into her jacket.

'You'll like the school well enough once you get used to it.'

'I won't.' She refused to take her aunt's hand, marching instead along the inside of the pavement and letting the shoulder of her good jacket brush against the damp stone walls as she went. Knowing that she was watching out of the slanted corners of her eyes for a reaction, Caitlin held her tongue and concentrated all her attention on getting the child into the school building, then into her classroom.

They had just reached the playground, which was swarming with children bellowing at the tops of their voices, when she realised that Rowena had disappeared like a wisp of smoke. Caitlin looked up and down the street, and even peered through the railings in the vain hope that the child had somehow slipped in through the gate unnoticed, but she wasn't to be seen among the throng in the yard. Panic-stricken, recalling Kirsty's worry about Rowena being run over, Caitlin began to retrace her steps at a run.

As she turned the corner into Espedair Street, she caught sight of a small figure scudding along the pavement ahead of her.

'Rowena, come back here!'

The child ignored her, hunching her head down and rushing across the road. Caitlin's hands flew to her mouth in horror as the small figure slipped in a puddle and almost fell in front of a small motorised van, but miraculously Rowena recovered her balance just in time and leapt onto the opposite pavement, landing in front of Murdo Guthrie on his way to the weaving shop. Pedestrians turned to see what was going on as the van screeched to a halt, its horn blaring an off-key protest.

Caitlin ran across the road to find Murdo staring down at Rowena, who had locked her arms tightly about one of his legs.

'Oh, Rowena!' She tried to gather the child into her arms and was rewarded with a backward kick that grazed her shin.

'I'm not going!' Rowena screeched into Murdo's trouser leg as the van driver jumped down from his cab.

'Ye wee monkey, ye . . . ye could have got yersel' killed! What d'ye think ye were playin' at?' He pushed Caitlin aside and tried to wrench the child round to face him. Murdo's hand clamped over his wrist.

'Leave her alone.'

'Leave her, is it?' the man spluttered, turning to appeal to the small crowd that was gathering. 'And her nearly murderin' herself under my wheels? Whose fault would it have been then, eh?' He thrust his face aggressively into the Highlander's. 'What would ye have done tae me if that had happened, eh? An' what would the polis have done?'

'Leave her be.' Murdo put his free hand protectively over the head pressed against his thigh. 'Just let her alone,' he repeated, his voice quiet but at the same time hard. 'We'll see to her.'

'I'm sorry about what she did, and I'll make sure she doesn't do it again. But nobody was hurt.' Caitlin tried to calm the situation.

'No thanks tae her, missus,' the man said. He wrenched his wrist free. 'Ach, I've got work tae dae.' He stamped back to his van, the watchers scattering to let him through. Looking after him, Caitlin saw Annie Mitchell, Beth's sister, standing with her husband and a knot of onlookers at the door of the tobacconist's shop.

'If ye've got any sense ye'll give her a right thrashin',' the van driver yelled from the open window as he drove away. 'It's the only way tae teach them right from wrong!'

The onlookers murmured their agreement, and a woman's voice said clearly, 'If folk cannae look after their bairns, they've got no right tae birth them!'

Murdo swung Rowena up into his arms and carried her into the pend. Casting an apologetic glance round at the bystanders, Caitlin saw that Annie Mitchell, arms folded tightly across her bosom, was holding forth to the people with her. No doubt, she thought as she followed Murdo, the woman was portraying Rowena as the wayward product of wayward parents – without admitting to her listeners that one of the parents was her own sister.

In the weaving shop, Murdo was seated on the saytree with Rowena standing before him. At the sight of Caitlin, she tried to move nearer to him, but he held her back gently at arm's length.

'Now, what's amiss with you?' he asked Rowena.

'I'll not go!'

Anger flashed across his face as he looked up at Caitlin accusingly. 'You're sending her away?'

'Only to the school.'

His face cleared. 'Is that what it's all about? You don't want to go to the school?'

'I won't go!' Rowena whirled round and shouted at her aunt. 'I'll not go and you can't make me!'

'That's enough, now.' There was a steely note in Murdo's voice that neither of them had heard before. As Rowena's mouth fell open, he added to Caitlin, 'You've got mud on your skirt.'

She looked down and gave a vexed exclamation at the sight of the black wet smear on the pale-grey material.

'Why don't you go into the kitchen and clean it off while me and Rowena have a wee talk?' Murdo suggested, so completely in control of the situation that she did as she was told without question.

Caitlin had sponged the skirt and was holding it out to let the heat of the fire dry it when Murdo arrived at the open door, Rowena small and subdued by his side.

'We're walking to the school now. I'd be grateful if you'd come along, for she'll be late, and no doubt her teacher would prefer an explanation from one of her family and not a stranger.'

Rowena, declining the offer of a hand, stamped ahead of them while Caitlin, keenly aware of the wet patch still marring her skirt, and Murdo followed. At the school door Murdo detained Rowena with a big hand on her shoulder and squatted, turning her to face him. 'Mind what I said now. I'll weave that much cloth . . . ,' he held his big hands out at a distance apart from each other, 'then I'll have a bite to eat and I'll practise the music you like best for when you're finished here. After that I'll weave this much cloth . . . ,' again he spread his hands out, 'then I'll walk along from Espedair Street and be waiting for you when you come out. While we walk back home you can tell me all about what you've been doing in the school. D'you understand what I'm saying to you?'

She stuck her bottom lip out but nodded reluctantly.

'That's a good lass. Now your aunt'll take you in and explain to the teacher that it's not your fault you're late.' For a moment he let his hand rest on her head, then he straightened to his full height and told Caitlin solemnly, 'You can take her in now.'

When she emerged, he was waiting by the gate.

'Your skirt looks fine now,' he said, falling into step with her. 'Has she settled all right?'

'I think so. What did you say to her?' He shrugged. 'Oh, we just had a wee bit of a crack, her and me. If your parents are willing, I'll walk with her to the school in the mornings and walk home with her as well until she's more comfortable there.'

'I don't see that happening.'

'She'll be grand,' said Murdo Guthrie easily. 'It's just that the bairn's still trying to find a place for herself.'

'We've done all we could to make her feel welcome,' Caitlin said, stung by what she saw as criticism.

'I've no doubt you have, but making the step from one life to another's a hard business for an adult, let alone a wee bairn. It's only someone who's been through it that can understand.'

'Someone like you?'

They had reached the turning into Espedair Street.

'It's all right, then, if I fetch her home?' he asked, and when she nodded he went off briskly in the direction of his weaving shop without a backward glance.

14

Although he lived in a city spilling over with opportunities for the social pleasures of every class, Alex MacDowall was a solitary man and content to be so. By day he was either in his father's large furniture emporium or in the factory where, until recently, he had spent much of his working day.

His free time was taken up with visiting his family in Paisley or working on furniture designs in his spacious tenement flat on the first floor of a building his father owned just off Paisley Road West.

A capable cook-housekeeper came in every day to clean the flat and prepare his meals, and every Friday evening he travelled by tramcar to Pollokshields to dine at his father's large house, set in the middle of a well-cared-for garden and sheltered from the road by a small shrubbery.

The house, bought originally for Angus MacDowall and his daughter, Fiona, was large for just one person, but although Angus had talked of moving to a smaller place when Fiona married and settled in Fort William, he liked his house and had gradually given up all idea of a move. Neither father nor son had mentioned the likelihood of Alex moving in when he first settled in the city; they were both fond of their privacy, and after living cheek by jowl with the rest of his family in cramped housing all his life, it suited Alex to have a place of his own. He revelled in his right to spend his free time exactly as he chose without having to consider other people's wishes.

Alex travelled to his father's house as usual on a pleasant evening in mid-September, getting off the tram a few stops earlier than usual in order to extend his walk. The trees on either side of the road had not yet begun to relinquish their leaves to autumn and through the branches sunshine dappled the broad pavements pleasantly as Alex swung in at the double gate and up the driveway, humming 'Alexander's Ragtime Band' to himself.

Angus kept a good staff around him to cater for his needs. There was a full-time gardener with an assistant, an excellent cook, a scullery maid and two upstairs maids, the older also acting as a housekeeper, and a laundry woman who came in twice a week. He had never had a valet, believing that there was something wrong with a man who was unable to dress himself unaided.

The younger of the upstairs maids opened the door.

'Good evening, Ellen. Isn't it a pleasant evening?' Alex handed over his hat and stick. 'Is Mr MacDowall in the drawing room?'

'He's not come downstairs yet, sir, but—'

'No hurry, I'll wait for him.' In the drawing room Alex, who felt quite at home in this house, went towards the small table where his father kept decanters and glasses. Angus enjoyed a glass of whisky before his evening meal.

'Good evening, Alex.'

Startled, he swung round, and at the sight of the

woman by the fireplace his heart gave a double thump before seeming to stop in his chest.

'Fiona!'

She smiled, giving him a glimpse of small white teeth. 'You're surprised to see me.'

'I . . . I'd no idea. I thought you were in Fort William.'

'I came from there today. Perhaps you will pour some sherry for me.'

He was glad of the excuse to collect his thoughts and to give his heart time to return to a regular beat, though faster than usual. To his annoyance his hands were shaking, so that the neck of the decanter rattled against the glass in his other hand.

'Let me.' Fiona appeared by his side and took the decanter and glass from him. 'I'm used to pouring drinks for George.'

Her sleeve brushed against his, and her perfume brought back memories. Alex turned away from her, towards the windows, thrusting his hands into his pockets. Ever since that terrible time when he had discovered that the girl he had fallen in love with was his half-sister, he had kept well away from this house on the few occasions when Fiona had visited their father.

'Seeing me here must be quite a shock to you,' she said, as though reading his thoughts. 'Papa couldn't warn you, for he didn't know that I was coming. I decided to make the journey at short notice.'

Her hand swam into his vision, bearing a glass. He took it, grateful to see that it held a generous measure of whisky. He took a quick, deep swallow of the liquid before turning back into the room. Fiona had seated herself on a large sofa by the fire, a long-stemmed glass in her hand; she patted the cushions by her side in invitation, but Alex chose an upright chair opposite.

'To your good health,' she said demurely, raising her glass.

'And to yours.' He took another good swallow of his drink, wishing himself anywhere but in his father's drawing room with Fiona.

A silence fell between them. Aware that she was using his inarticulate embarrassment to study him, Alex cleared his throat then asked, 'Are you staying in Glasgow for long?' To his relief, his voice was fairly normal.

'Until the end of the year at least. George – my husband – is in the Naval Reserve and has been called to service. I had no great wish to stay on in Fort William without him, so I decided to come to Glasgow instead.' She stretched out a slender, silk-clad arm to take her glass from the small table by her side, took a tiny sip from it and added, 'The social life in Glasgow is much more interesting.'

Angus MacDowall hurried in just then. 'I didn't realise you'd arrived until the girl told me, Alex.' He glanced anxiously from one to the other, and Alex jumped up to fetch his father's drink.

It was a relief when the maid announced that dinner was awaiting them in the dining room, where Angus had no option but to take his usual place at the head of the long table, which meant that his son and daughter sat to his left and right, facing each other.

There was never much conversation at Angus MacDowall's dinner table, for he enjoyed his food and liked to concentrate on it in silence. Afterwards, he and Alex usually talked about the week's work and their plans for the following week over brandy and cigars. As he toyed with his food, his appetite completely gone, Alex sneaked swift glances across the table. Fiona was still the beautiful woman he had fallen helplessly in love with when he had first set eyes on her at a furniture exhibition. Beneath an overdress of dark-red chiffon, the neat-fitting embroidered bodice of her shell-pink dinner gown was cut low enough to reveal the upper slopes of her breasts. Her hair, the colour of honey in sunlight, was swept back from her face and secured behind her head with a jewelled pin, and diamond drop earrings fell almost to her shoulders.

Time seemed to have passed her by, though once when she flicked a swift glance across at Alex, catching him unawares, he saw that her gold-flecked brown eyes, though still wide and thick lashed, had lost their youthful sparkle. And on another occasion, when she was staring down at her plate, he detected a faint downward turn to the corners of her mouth.

She waited until dessert was served before saying, 'So . . . you haven't volunteered to go to war, Alex.'

Even the sound of his name on her lips reawakened memories. He glanced at his father, then as Angus remained silent, said, 'If conscription comes in, then of course I'll go willingly, but in the meantime we both felt that I was of more use to the business.'

When the plates had been cleared away, Fiona excused herself and left the table, her flared skirt, silk overlaid with chiffon and embroidered at the deep hem, swishing softly as she moved across the room.

'I'm sorry to have put you in such a difficult position, Alex,' Angus said almost as soon as the door had closed behind his daughter's slender back. 'I'd no knowledge of her arrival until she appeared on the doorstep; if I had been forewarned I'd have sent word.'

'It's of no matter, sir. Time has brought a lot of changes,' Alex said through stiff lips, and saw relief light up his father's face.

'I'm glad to hear that the sorry business is over and

done with.' He fetched a bottle of port and a box of cigars from the sideboard and put them on the table. 'Since it seems she'll be under my roof for a few months, it's as well that the two of you met tonight. I couldn't be expected to keep you apart from each other forever.'

'No.' Alex selected a cigar.

'The whole business was most unfortunate,' Angus went on, dismissing the love his son and his daughter had known for each other before discovering that they shared the same father. 'But you've both moved on considerably since those days.'

'Yes, sir.'

'Water under the bridge,' Angus said, settling back in his chair, beaming, the matter over and done with. 'I shall rather enjoy spending time with Fiona again. I've missed her.'

Since Murdo's intervention, Rowena had gone off to school every morning without further protest, though she didn't enjoy the experience. She refused to walk beside the Highlander, who waited for her every morning at the corner of the pend, but that didn't seem to bother him. He walked behind her, made sure that she went into the playground and was always waiting by the gate at the end of the day to see that she got home safely.

'He strolls along like a gentleman with the whole day to himself, looking everywhere but at Rowena, while she marches ahead like a wee terrier and never gives him as much as a glance,' Rose told Caitlin with amusement, after cycling past the two of them one morning on her way to Harlequin.

At first Rowena refused to tell any member of her family about her school day, though every afternoon on returning home she closeted herself in the weaving shop. Caitlin suspected that Murdo Guthrie was hearing about what went on in the classroom, but it was some time before Rowena began to demonstrate to the others how she could draw, form a few letters and read a word or two from her school book.

She wasn't the only one doing homework at the kitchen table, for Mary, her mind still set on office work, had enrolled in bookkeeping classes at night school in September.

'I'd have thought you'd be glad of the chance to stop studying,' Kirsty told her daughter, but Mary shook her head.

'I like learning, and I need my diplomas if I'm to be considered seriously for office work. Anyway, it'll encourage Rowena if I'm working at my books along with her.'

In October, reviving an old family tradition, Caitlin and Mary, with Murdo and Lachie in attendance, took the little girl out into the countryside to pick brambles from the hedgerows.

'I don't know why I'm doing this,' Mary protested, trailing along behind Caitlin. 'I get more than my fill of fruit at work!'

'It's not for you, it's for Rowena,' Caitlin told her, knowing full well that the attraction for Mary was Lachie's presence. 'Anyway, it's enjoyable.' She managed to untangle a long branch laden with the sweet black berries, very similar to raspberries, and stripped it into the tin can she had brought, then she straightened up as Mary, spying a branch further along, gave a yelp of triumph and ran to claim it before the others did.

When the containers were full, they found a clearing where they could sit on the short, strong grass to eat the sandwiches Mary had prepared and drink from bottles of cold tea. Then Mary and Lachie and Rowena played tig, racing after each other with screams of laughter, while Caitlin, who had brought her notebook and crayons, tried to capture something of the browns and golds and oranges of the autumn bracken, interspersed with streaks and clumps of purple heather. Murdo perched on an outcrop of rock a few feet away, staring down over the town.

After a while Caitlin closed the book and rested her chin on her cupped hands, watching the others. It was grand to see Rowena enjoying herself. She had topped off her meal with a dessert of blackberries, which had left purple stains on the lower part of her face and her hands. Shrieking with pleasure, she was trying to catch Lachie, who kept dancing out of reach just as she got to him. When he judged that the little girl was growing frustrated, he let her touch him on the arm, so that it was then her turn to dance away from his outstretched fingers.

'You'd think they were all the same age,' Caitlin said, laughing as Mary and Lachie accidentally ran into each other and landed in a heap of grass. Rowena instantly threw herself on top of them, and the three rolled down a small hill, arms and legs sticking out in all directions.

'Once an adult, always an adult. They're right to enjoy their youth for as long as they can.'

'Did you enjoy your youth, Murdo?' The question was out of her mouth before she had time to think of it. He got to his feet without answering.

'Time to turn for home,' he said, and went to untangle the mass of humanity on the ground.

Watching him, she wondered if he had been a silent little boy, old before his time. If not, some outside influence must have made him the enigma he was.

*　　*　　*

They had descended the hills and were back among the streets, Rowena asleep on Murdo's shoulder, Mary and Lachie whispering and giggling a few yards behind, when a voice rang out from a knot of women on the opposite pavement. 'It fair sickens me tae see strong healthy men cowerin' at home when others are away doin' their fightin' for them!'

Shocked, Caitlin whirled round and stared across the road. Far from hiding, the woman who had spoken detached herself from her friends and advanced to the edge of the pavement. 'Aye, hen, it's your man I'm talkin' about,' she called, while her friends gathered behind her. 'It's time ye carried yer own wean an' telt him tae get a uniform on his back!'

Several passers-by, alerted by the shrill voice skewering the air, turned to look for her victim. Some of them nodded, while others simply gaped, awaiting a reaction, or glanced away and tried to pretend that they had heard nothing.

'My man's gone off tae God knows where.' Another woman stepped out from the group, shaking her fist. 'An' me wi' weans tae feed an' not knowin' if he'll come back dead or maimed. Why should the likes o' you walk the streets when the likes o' him's fightin' yer battles for ye?'

Mary and Lachie hurried up, their young faces pale with shock, but Murdo, ordering, 'Pay no heed,' kept walking, looking straight ahead. It was hard to do as he said. Caitlin was afraid that the women would follow them to Espedair Street, but to her relief the catcalls and jeering faded once they had turned the corner. Even so, she found herself walking faster and looking into the faces of the people they met. There was no doubt at all that some of them, as they drew near, measured the height and breadth of Murdo with a glance and a tightening of the lips as though they, too, were wondering why he was not in uniform.

She said nothing to Kirsty or Todd about the incident, and Mary, who had gone off somewhere with Lachie instead of going into the house with the others, was also quiet when she came in.

That evening Kirsty, already making the bramble jelly, looked from one daughter to the other. 'Did you not enjoy being up the braes today? You're both awful quiet.'

'It's the smell of the jam,' Mary said at once. 'It reminds me of work.'

Later she tapped on Caitlin's bedroom door and went in to talk about the incident. 'Poor Lachie was mortified. He's only fifteen, and there's scarce a pick of flesh on his bones as it is. He'd not have the strength to carry a rifle,' she said fiercely. 'Those . . . witches had no right to frighten him the way they did!'

'It was Murdo they were shouting at, not your Lachie.' Caitlin wondered how often he had had to endure such scenes before.

'D'you think Alex is having to put up with that sort of thing in Glasgow?'

'If he is, I'm sure he's able to deal with it, and so is Murdo.'

'It was . . . I felt dirty!' Mary shook with a sudden, violent spasm, and Caitlin sat on the bed and put her arms about her sister.

'Don't you fret yourself. Remember that words can't hurt anyone.'

'That's not true,' Mary said into her shoulder. 'They can!'

15

Alex knew as soon as he let himself into the flat that there was something wrong. The square carpeted hall looked just as it always did and, as usual at that time in the late afternoon, the place was fragrant with the smell of cooking, but there was something out of place somewhere.

A glance into the kitchen showed that it was empty, which was not unusual; Mrs Harkins often left for her own home two streets away before he returned, leaving him to dish up his own meal. Frowning because he was unable to put his finger on the problem, he hung up his hat and coat, put his cane into the coat stand and opened the drawing-room door.

The room looked inviting with the curtains drawn against the chill November night. A fire burned brightly in the grate, the electric lamps at each side of the mantelpiece were lit and Fiona half sat, half lay on the sofa, a magazine open on her lap. She looked up with a warm smile.

'Alex, I was beginning to think that you'd been delayed.' She put the magazine aside and flitted across the carpet to reach up and drop a swift light kiss on his cheek before drawing him to the armchair. 'I've made up the fire and put your slippers to heat.'

'What the . . . What are you doing here?'

She was at the sideboard, pouring whisky from a decanter. 'I've come to call on my brother,' she said over her shoulder.

'I don't recall inviting you.'

'Oh dear, you sound very cross.' Fiona bustled back to him, carrying a small silver tray bearing two glasses. She put it down on the low table by his chair, then straightened to face him, her lovely face alight with amusement. 'Are you going to stand to attention all night? It will make eating your dinner difficult.'

Over her head Alex caught sight of himself in the mirror, bristling like a turkey cock. He sat down suddenly.

'That's better.' Fiona took a glass from the tray and went back to the sofa. 'Just a little whisky and a lot of water,' she explained, lifting her glass slightly as though proposing a toast, then sipping the pale gold liquid. 'I sometimes drink it at home before dinner. I've noticed that, like George, you would much prefer your whisky on its own.'

'Does Father know that you're here?'

Her long lashes swept down to cover her eyes, then came back up. 'I confess that I told him a very little white lie and said that I was dining with the Matlocks. If I'd told him the truth he would have expected to come with me, and I thought that it was time that we spent a little time together. You didn't come to dinner last Friday.'

'I had another engagement.'

'I wondered if you might be staying away because of me. Because of . . . what we once were to each other. You haven't changed into your slippers.'

'I'm comfortable as I am.'

'You don't look very comfortable. I always put

George's slippers on for him.' She put her glass down and began to rise. 'Do you want me to—?'

He shook his head, and began to unlace his shoes. 'I can manage. Where's Mrs Harkins?'

'I sent her home after she had prepared dinner for us.' She settled herself against the cushions, totally at home. 'Do you realise that I've been in Glasgow for a month at least and you haven't even invited me here for a meal?'

'There's plenty food in my father's house,' Alex said shortly. 'And I have work to do. I don't entertain.'

'Not even your young lady?'

Alex's collar felt very tight, but he daren't let her see him put a hand up to ease it. 'I have no young lady.'

'So Papa told me, but I found it hard to believe. You're a personable man, Alex, as I know from my own experience,' she added sweetly. 'Dare I wonder if it's simply that you haven't found anyone to care for as much as you cared for me?'

Looking at the slow smile that curved her mouth he realised, too late, that he had fallen into a trap she had set for him.

'It has nothing to do with—' he bit off the word us, and finished, 'anything that went before. I'm simply too busy to socialise.'

Fiona, having achieved her aim, glanced critically round the room. 'I should have realised that you have no lady visitors. This place is far too masculine and uncomfortable. Perhaps I could improve it for you.'

'I prefer my home as it is.'

'Oh dear,' she said softly. 'If you're not careful, Alex, you'll turn into a dull, pompous old man interested in nothing but keeping his nose to the grindstone. You used to be so . . . ,' again, there came that pause that said far more than words, 'interesting,' she finished, running the tip of one finger lightly round the edge of her glass.

'Life has changed for us both since then, Fiona.' He had intended the words to be sensible and down-to-earth, but to his own ears his voice sounded artificial and, as she had already said, pompous. He felt warmth surge to his face and knew by the sudden lift of her eyebrows that he had indeed reddened.

'You were so young, that first time we met at the exhibition centre. So shy.' She looked down into her drink then added, her voice dropping to a near whisper, 'So kind and gallant. Neither of us dreamt that day that you were going to do as well as you have.'

'We've both done well. You have a husband, a new home.'

Fiona suddenly drained her glass, the muscles working smoothly beneath the creamy skin of her throat as she swallowed. 'Time to eat,' she said, standing up and taking his glass from him. 'I'm very hungry.'

Today she wore a dress of pale gold, almost the colour of her hair; as she walked ahead of him the honey-coloured silk seemed to caress her back and waist and legs, and her perfume wafted back to him.

She had found a candelabra in some cupboard and set it on the table. They dined by the light of the candles, with the rest of the room in shadow. The tiny flames winked and glittered on snowy napery, glasses and cutlery, and caught flashes of light from Fiona's rings and the single crystal hung around her neck on a fine gold chain. As she manipulated her knife and fork, her discreetly varnished fingernails gleamed occasionally in the light, and now and again, when she looked up at Alex, gold flecks seemed to dance in the depths of her velvet-brown eyes.

Mrs Harkins was a superb cook and the food was,

as always, delicious, but he ate automatically, scarcely aware of flavour or texture, while Fiona, seemingly unperturbed by his silence, chattered lightly about nothing in particular, springing up every so often to change courses or to pour more ruby-red wine from the bottle on the sideboard. She was, he thought, drinking more than was good for her.

When the meal was finally over, she offered to make coffee, but Alex shook his head. 'I think it's time I took you back to Pollokshields.'

'Already?' She screwed up her face. 'But the evening's young yet.'

'I've work to do and an early start in the morning. Where did you leave your coat?' He realised that he hadn't seen it on the coat stand in the hall; if it had been there, he would have been forewarned, and the entire evening would have taken a different course.

'In your bedroom.'

Her fur coat had been arranged across his bed, the high collar opened out over the pillow and the sleeves spread to either side. Alex gathered it up and turned to find Fiona standing just inside the door.

'I thought we could have coffee and brandy and talk about the old days.'

'There's nothing to talk about.'

She raised her eyebrows. 'That's not very gallant of you, Alex. Once you would have given everything you had to spend some time alone with me.'

'We had no idea then that we were brother and sister.'

She leaned against the doorframe. 'What if we hadn't found out, Alex?' He saw a tingle of excitement come into her eyes, while her lips parted to allow the tip of her tongue to slip through and moisten them. 'I've often wondered about that. Haven't you?'

'No.'

'If we had married, d'you think we would have been happy together in our innocence?' A shudder of sheer horror ran through him at the thought, and as she recognised it, her eyes narrowed. 'Does the thought of marriage to me disgust you so much?'

'It would have been like taking Caitlin or Mary for my wife.'

'But if we hadn't known, would it have been so wrong?' Before he realised what she was about, she had switched off the light, plunging the room into darkness. Silk rustled across the carpet towards him, then the coat was twitched from his hands and Fiona's hair was against his cheek, the smell of her in his nostrils, her hands on his shoulders and her body pressing itself against his. 'In the dark,' she whispered against his throat, her lips moist and warm, 'all cats are alike.'

'For God's sake!' Alex pushed her soft body aside and heard her give a gasp, then a brief cry, as he fumbled his way towards the door. He stumbled over the discarded coat, which slipped beneath his feet and almost brought him down. He kicked free of it, then blundered painfully into a piece of furniture before his outstretched hands touched something larger. Recognising it as the corner of the big mahogany wardrobe, he felt round it to the wall, the door and, finally, the light switch.

The light was dazzling after the darkness; blinking, Alex turned and saw Fiona half sitting on his bed, rubbing her shoulder.

'You hurt me!'

'And you disgust me!'

'How dare you say that to me after the way you've ruined my life! D'you know what it was like to be sent

175

away from my father's house then to find out that you were being made welcome in my place?'

'Fiona, I have never taken your place in our father's affections. As for sending you away, he thought it best for you to get out of Glasgow at the time, and you've made a good life for yourself in Fort William.'

'I had a better life here!' To his astonishment, she launched herself from the bed and rushed across the room to rain blows on him with clenched fists. 'I wanted to stay in Glasgow with Papa!'

Even when Alex managed to trap her wrists she kept struggling, only stopping when he shook her so hard that her head flopped on her long slim neck, strands of hair coming loose from her combs. 'For pity's sake, you've still got your father, and a husband.'

'Husband!' Fiona spat the word into his face. 'A man as dull and boring as you are!' Then her face seemed to shimmer and crumple, and she fell against him as though unable to support herself any longer, her body so limp that he had to release her wrists and put his arms around her to prevent her from sliding to the floor. 'Why did you ever come to Glasgow?' she wept. 'I hate you so much . . . I hate you!'

It was like holding a child. Her tears dampened then soaked his carefully starched shirt front, and her entire body shook as though in the grip of a fever. Alex freed one hand to stroke her hair, appalled by her utter misery. The desire she had kindled in him years before came surging back, and he recognised with shock that it was not, and perhaps never had been, a physical longing, but merely a desire to protect and shelter her.

Her sobbing finally slowed and stilled. She drew back from him, then turned without a word and left the room. The bathroom door opened and closed. Shaken, Alex picked her coat up and took it into the drawing room, where he poured whisky into two glasses, holding one out to Fiona when she finally came out of the bathroom.

'Drink it,' he urged when she shook her head. 'It'll do you good.'

She had tidied her hair, and although her eyes were red and her face pale, she looked as beautiful as ever. But her voice was still venomous when she said, 'I don't want it!'

She looked about for her coat, and when he held it out for her she slid her arms into the sleeves then pulled away from him and made for the door. Downstairs she waited in silence while he summoned a cab and followed her into it. Throughout the journey she stared out of the window, presenting the back of her head to him, and when they reached Angus MacDowall's house she got out at once and left him to pay the driver.

'I would prefer to go into the house alone,' she said coldly when he caught up with her at the gate. He watched until she had let herself into the house, then, although it had begun to rain, he sent the cab away and walked home, arriving chilled and soaked to the skin.

He drank her untouched whisky then stripped his clothes off before climbing naked into bed. Her perfume was still on the pillow and the sheets.

When Alex forced himself to go to his father's house on the following Friday evening, he found Fiona playing hostess to about a dozen people in all. She claimed him as soon as he went in and insisted on taking him from one group to another, her jewelled hand on his arm, while she introduced him to everyone as 'my dear brother'. After dinner, when the party settled down to play cards in the drawing room, he and Angus, who had clearly found it difficult to cope with so many people in his home but had done his best to be a good host, escaped to the study on the pretext of business.

'It's dull for Fiona to have nothing to do and no friends after the life she's been used to in Fort William,' the older man explained as he closed the door on a babble of voices and laughter. 'She needs to have folk about her. We must both make sure that she enjoys her stay here.'

From then on Fiona treated Alex with a cloying sweetness that stuck in his throat. She announced her intention of calling on his mother and sisters, and when she heard about Harlequin she determined to go and see the place for herself. Her father hired a motorcar for them, and after leaving Alex in Espedair Street with Todd, Fiona drove on to the old mill, where she advanced on Caitlin, hands outstretched. 'My dear girl, how grown-up you look – and how well you have done for yourself!'

Rose came into the fitting room to be introduced, bringing with her John Brodie, who had called on business. Caitlin, who had first known Fiona as Alex's sweetheart, remembered her as a sweet-natured young woman with an open interest in everyone she met. Now she was mature, confident and the openness was still there but, Caitlin thought as she watched Fiona charm John, there was a certain calculation in it, as though the brain behind the lovely brown eyes was appraising and weighing things up.

'Alex has told me all about your new venture,' she said sweetly when John had gone, 'and hearing about you both has made me feel that I've done nothing at all with my life. But all that will change, I promise you. Now, the clothes that stood me in good stead in Fort William will most certainly not do for Glasgow, so I must begin at the beginning.'

While Caitlin went upstairs to fetch some materials and to summon Grace, Rose showed the new client sketches of some of the clothes they had supplied.

'Caitlin is so talented, but then so is Alex.' Fiona paused, glancing at Rose from the corner of her eye, then asked, 'Do you know the family well?'

'Quite well.'

'Then you're no doubt aware that although Caitlin and I are not related, we share Alex as a brother?'

Rose picked up a magazine. 'Yes, I know. This draped wrapover skirt has become very popular with some of our clients. It's a style that would suit you.'

Fiona tossed a glance at the sketch. 'Yes, I rather like it. Alex and I are very close, although neither of us knew anything of the other's existence for many years. When we first met it was as complete strangers, as unrelated as you and I.'

'Indeed? This long jacket would also suit you.'

'It's very fetching,' Fiona said casually. 'Even although we were unaware of our shared blood, we took to each other instantly. There seems to be a bond between us.'

'As there is between Alex and Caitlin.'

'But they always knew each other as brother and sister and have therefore always behaved appropriately towards each other, whereas Alex and I . . .'

To Rose's great relief, Caitlin and Grace arrived, and they settled down to discussing Fiona's new clothes. She was a demanding client, and by the time she left to visit Kirsty and collect Alex for the return trip to Glasgow the three of them were exhausted.

'That one's a right madam,' Grace said flatly.

'Grace,' Rose protested, 'if you're to work with the clients, as we hope, you'll have to watch your tongue.'

'As long as I don't say it to them, where's the harm?'

'Just because they're wealthy it doesn't mean they're daft as well. They can read your thoughts in your face.'

'In that case,' said Grace, scooping up bales of cloth, 'p'raps I should come intae the fittin' room with a bag over my head.'

'She'll never do for the clients,' Rose said in despair when the woman had departed upstairs.

'She's an excellent seamstress with a good brain. And she's tired. We all are.' Caitlin looked about the room, strewn with magazines and sketches, and began to tidy it up.

'Was that woman always so demanding?'

'Not that I recall, but I only saw her once or twice when Alex brought her to Paisley. Marriage has changed her.'

'I can't understand what a man like Alex ever saw in her.'

'She was very lovely – she still is.'

Rose shrugged. 'If you like that sort of prettiness.'

'All that matters to us is that she wants us to make clothes for her,' Caitlin said firmly.

Kirsty had noticed little difference in Fiona. 'She's a woman now but still nice enough and just as interested in other folk as she ever was,' she said, but Todd disagreed with her when he came in for his evening meal.

'There's a calculatin' sort of look in her eye that I don't mind seein' there before.'

'You're havering!' his wife said, but he shook his head.

'I met her when I was a journeyman here and Alex brought her to the workshop to meet the men there. She was an open, honest sort of lass then, and poor Alex was fair cross-eyed with love for her. It was a sad business altogether.'

'And not one that any of us cares to remember,' Kirsty said tartly. 'It's over and done with long since.'

'Mebbe so, but if you ask me, it's left its mark on both of them. They're harder, but in Alex's case he's made good use of the strength he had tae find in himself. As to Mrs Chalmers, I think her sorrow turned in on itself, and that's never a good thing.'

To her annoyance, Mary had missed seeing the visitor, while Rowena had kept well out of the way, eeling from the weaving shop as Fiona and Alex entered and slipping back in there to hide after they had gone into the house for tea.

16

Far from being over by the New Year, the war seemed to be settling in. Although enemy troops had been prevented from taking Paris, they gained Belgium's main cities.

On New Year's Day, Rose, Caitlin and John Brodie attended a party held by Fiona Chalmers at her father's home. Neither Caitlin nor Rose was enthusiastic about accepting the invitation, but as John pointed out, it was a matter of business, since it gave them the opportunity to meet potential clients.

Fiona, in a rose-pink velvet and lace evening gown that Caitlin and the seamstresses had worked through several evenings to complete in time, fluttered like a butterfly among her guests, making a point of introducing Rose and Caitlin to her friends, whom she advised to visit Harlequin.

'Do you work there too, Mr Brodie?' one woman asked archly. 'I know that in Paris and London men design divine clothing for ladies.'

John turned pink with embarrassment. 'Oh no, I'm just a lawyer!'

'Now don't be so modest!' Fiona tucked one hand into the crook of his arm and told the people around them, 'Mr Brodie attends to all the tiresome financial business while Rose . . .' with her free hand she drew Rose, stiff and awkward with humiliation, to her other side, 'looks after the clients, and Caitlin makes wonderful clothes for them.'

Knowing Alex's dislike of social events, Caitlin wasn't entirely surprised to see that he tended to hover in quiet corners with his father. He and Rose had scarcely exchanged a word, but he finally came to Caitlin when she was on her own to say gloomily, 'I suppose you're having an enjoyable time.'

'Quite, although I scarcely know anyone.'

'Neither do I.'

'Never mind.' She slid her hand into his, squeezing his fingers. 'It will soon be over.'

'Did you design that frock Rose is wearing?' he asked. When she nodded, he said, 'It suits her.'

Rose's gown consisted of swathes of chiffon in varying shades of gold, bronze, deep glowing red and pale brown, falling to handkerchief points at the hem. As she moved through the crowd the skirt flowed and swirled about her long legs.

Alex's gaze followed her. 'It reminds me of autumn bonfires in the country.'

'The idea came to me when I saw the autumn colours of the bracken one day when we were blackberrying on the braes,' Caitlin told him, pleased that he had recognised something of the thought behind the design.

'Are she and Brodie seeing much of each other these days?'

'They still go to functions together, and John comes to the fashion house about once a week.'

'He's quite smitten with her.'

'Do you think so?'

'Surely you can see it for yourself. Is she taken with him, do you think?'

Caitlin remembered what John had said to her at the fashion house launch but decided to keep it to herself. For one thing, it had been said in confidence, and for another it was clear to her from the way Alex watched Rose that he himself was smitten. She had even seen Fiona Chalmers glance, narrow eyed, from him to Rose, as though she too had recognised his feelings. 'I don't know,' she said lamely.

'It must be good to feel sure of yourself and know who you are. Sometimes,' Alex suddenly said, startling himself as much as Caitlin, 'I feel as though I'm neither one thing or another. Not a Lennox or a MacDowall.'

She understood. 'Has Fiona's coming made such a difference to you?'

'Yes, it has, but not because of what went before,' he added hurriedly. 'The difference is in me. I feel as though I belong nowhere. Even my sisters are half-sisters, not related to each other yet sharing a parent with me.'

'You have Mam, and your father.'

'Do I? I feel as though I'm moving apart from them, or them from me. I wish to God, Caitlin,' he said passionately, 'that they had never set eyes on each other!'

'If you mean that, you're wishing your own life away. For my part I'm glad they met and that they loved each other, for otherwise I'd never have known you, and I'd have hated that.'

There was cynicism in the amused twist to his lips. 'You can't miss what you never had,' he pointed out. 'But you're right, there's no sense in thinking of what might have been. The thing to do is to shape what we've been given to suit ourselves.'

Then Fiona swooped down on them, insisting on introducing Caitlin to someone else, and Alex returned to his father, leaving Caitlin wondering, uneasily, what he meant.

Several of the women who had attended the New Year party found their way to Paisley over the next few months, and some of them put in orders. Caitlin wondered, since the war seemed set to continue, if the fashion house could survive, but Rose dismissed her doubts.

'The women we cater for have money, and war makes little difference to their lives. Oh, thcir menfolk might go off to fight, but our clients'll want to look specially nice when they come home again,' she said cynically. 'You've no idea how many young men I know who've taken advantage of this war to persuade their sweethearts to become engaged so that they have someone to fight for.'

Caitlin thought fleetingly of Bryce urging her to wear his ring.

'Or to marry them, just in case,' Rose went on.

Within a month Rose was proved right when Harlequin had to deal with no less than three hurried weddings before fiancés were sent overseas.

Tidying the fitting room after a hectic session with a tremulous young bride to be and her overexcited mother, Caitlin said, 'I don't think I could bear to marry a man who was going off to fight and mebbe to die.'

'That's not the way these lassies see it.' Grace shook out a petticoat and hung it up. 'Most of them cannae bear tae send their men away without givin' them all the comfort they can.' She sighed and stopped work to gaze at the far wall. 'I was like that mysel' when my man went tac fight the Boers. That's how I fell wi' my first, daft fool that I was. There's more than one left wi' a full stomach an' no ring on her finger down our street at this very minute. I was luckier than most, for my man came back and wed me. And I lived tae regret that an' all.'

Bryce came home in March, changed in a way that worried Caitlin.

'War's bound to mature him,' Kirsty soothed when her daughter tried to explain her thoughts. 'He went away a laddie and now he's a man.'

As Caitlin saw it, Bryce had hardened rather than matured, spending his afternoons in public houses and complaining because she was unable to be with him every evening. 'It's not as if I'm home for long,' he girned. 'If Alex had only got the mill and Todd had taken charge there—'

'And if the moon was only made of cheese we could toast it for our suppers every night,' Caitlin said, exasperated. 'Nobody can turn the clock back, Bryce. Things are as they are and we'll just have to wait to find what the future holds.'

'I want my future tae hold you. Come to think of it, I want tae hold you right now,' he said, wrapping her tightly in his arms and locking his mouth onto hers. He had drawn her round a street corner and into the deep shadow of a factory wall where even the thin pale light from the street lamps couldn't reach. At first she responded, then as he tried to back her against the brick wall she began to struggle, for even his kisses were different. Bryce had always been demanding, but now it was as though his sole intention was to pleasure himself, with no regard for her feelings at all. When he paid no attention to her struggles but only pinned her body closer to his with one arm while his other hand began to grope and knead, she fought back in earnest, finally managing to force him away.

'Now what's botherin' ye?'

'For pity's sake, man,' she said when she could speak, 'what has the army done to you?'

'What d'ye mean?'

'You're . . . different.'

'Of course I'm different! So would you be if ye'd lived in muck and filth and seen what I've seen. Come here.' He made another grab for her, then swore as she danced back, out of reach. 'You think I'm the only one that's changed? Look at you, all mealy-mouthed and "don't touch",' he jeered, his voice harsh and ugly. 'Is that any way for a woman tae behave when her man's back from the fightin'?'

'You're not my man, Bryce Caldwell!'

'Then who is?' His hand shot out and seized her wrist, the fingers digging in as he dragged her close. 'Who's been pleasurin' ye while my back was turned?'

'Nobody. I don't need to have a man in my life.'

Bryce laughed shortly, 'Of course women need men – what else are they for?' he asked. Then, breathing cheap whisky fumes into her face, he said, 'It's not thon Highlander, is it? Thon weaver?'

'It's not anyone!'

'I've heard about him, still hiding behind his loom, hopin' that the army never sends for him, takin' advantage of lassies whose men've gone to fight for them.' He was close enough now for his spittle to moisten her dry lips. 'If he's been puttin' his filthy hands on ye, he'll . . .' The words became a wet mumble as his mouth smothered hers again, his tongue probing deeper until she felt herself choking.

The need to gulp in air was great enough to give her fresh strength; recalling a crude piece of advice she had once heard Grace give to the younger seamstresses, Caitlin brought one knee up sharply between his thighs. He gave a muffled exclamation then staggered a few steps along the length of the wall before fetching up against its bricks, clutching at his groin.

'Bitch,' he choked, his back to her. 'Fuckin' wee bitch!' Then she heard the splatter of liquid on the ground as he vomited up his afternoon's drinking spree.

'Bryce . . .' She was more frightened for him than for herself now, convinced that she had done him terrible harm.

'Get away from me!' As he swung round on her the moon appeared from behind a cloud; in its light, still crouched over, eyes glaring and a thread of mucus drooling from his lips, he looked like some misshapen goblin. 'Get out of my sight before I . . .'

She fled down the road and around the corner, and kept running until she reached Espedair Street, where she stopped before the tobacconist's shop, using the window as a mirror while she tidied her hair and scrubbed tears of fear from her cheeks.

Something moved behind her reflection, and she jumped back and spun round, fearful that Bryce had followed her and come up behind her. There was nobody there, and looking back at the window she realised that Annie Mitchell was standing in the darkened shop behind the banked shelves of pipes and packets, watching her with cold eyes.

Her heart thundering, Caitlin turned away and hurried across the street, grateful when she went into the house to find that the others had gone to bed.

Kirsty had left a stone bottle in her bed; it was comfortably warm beneath her bare feet, but even so Caitlin shivered beneath the blankets for some time before falling into a restless sleep, plagued by dreams of Bryce chasing her through cobbled streets while Annie Mitchell watched from darkened windows, her eyes flat and dead.

Caitlin plucked up the courage next day to ask Grace, under the roar of the sewing machines, whether she might have done Bryce a serious injury.

'Ye mean ye . . . ?' Beneath the shelter of the cutting table, where they were both working, the older woman lifted one knee slightly. 'Ye did that tae a man?' When Caitlin nodded, biting her lip, Grace gave a shriek of laughter.

'What're you talkin' about?' Iris asked at once, while Lizzie, always ready for a gossip, stilled her machine.

'Nothin' at all – get on with yer work,' Grace snapped, and they obeyed, exchanging exasperated glances, as she went on, low voiced. 'I never thought ye had it in ye, hen. Ye're such a prim wee thing.'

'I had to do something. But now I wish I hadn't, for he was in terrible pain.'

Grace's large plain face began to break up, and she turned away hastily, a hand to her mouth and her shoulders shaking. 'Sometimes,' she said when the bout of laughter was over and she had turned back to the table, 'ye have tae dae more than keep yer hand over yer ha'penny.' She picked up the cutting shears and began to slide them deftly through the material on the table. 'Ye did the right thing, hen, for at times like that we've got tae put ourselves first.'

'Mebbe I should go and see him after work to make sure he's all right.'

'You keep away,' Grace ordered at once. 'If ye go tae him all worried in case he's been hurt, he'll just try tae take advantage again. He'll be fine. A nudge wi' a knee can bring tears tae a man's eyes, but they're made of strong stuff – more's the pity. He'll be fine,' she repeated reassuringly. 'The only thing is, ye'll no' be able tae catch him unawares again. Next time he'll be ready for ye, so ye'd best watch yersel'.'

'I'll not be going out with him again.'

'Best not,' Grace said briskly. 'Not unless he's the one ye want.'

As usually happened these days, Caitlin worked late at the fashion house, walking back home through the busier streets and avoiding dark corners just in case Bryce was looking for her. She arrived home to find Murdo Guthrie in the kitchen, holding a reddened cloth to his face while Kirsty attended to a cut on his forehead and Mary fussed round the stove. Rowena was leaning on the weaver's knee, anxiously staring up into his face, and the room smelled strongly of carbolic.

'It's nothing much,' Kirsty said as soon as her daughter came in. 'It looks worse than it is. Hold still now,' she added sharply, clapping Murdo's hand back in place as he tried to remove the pad covering his nose. 'Fetch some fresh water, will you, Caitlin? Someone found him just round the corner,' she went on as Caitlin took the basin from the table and emptied the bloodied water down the sink, then refilled it with hot water from the kettle. 'They brought him here, since they knew he worked in the weaving shop. Mary, I'll need another clean rag and you can bring the vinegar bottle while you're at it.'

Caitlin cooled the basin's steaming contents with water from the tap and took it over to the table. Beneath his tumble of dark hair, Murdo's face – what she could see of it – was ashen. One eyelid was swelling and blackening, and blood still welled from the deep cut Kirsty was attending to just above his brow. Caitlin, remembering the days when Alex and Ewan used to come home from play covered in scrapes and bruises, took the bottle and clean rag from Mary and shook vinegar over the rag before applying it to the swollen eyelid.

'Not a sign of anyone, but I didnae expect them tae hang about,' Todd announced from the back door. 'How are ye, lad?' He laid aside the stout walking stick he had been carrying and came over to inspect the patient.

'I'm fine.' Murdo's voice was thick and muffled. Despite Kirsty's protestations, he sat upright, pushing the ministering hands aside and taking the bloodied cloth from his nose. At the sight of his face, Rowena began to cry. 'I'm fine,' he insisted again through swollen lips, speaking directly to her, putting one finger beneath her chin so that her face was tilted up towards his. 'See? I've still got two eyes and a nose and a mouth.'

'Mebbe so, but they've a right second-hand look to them,' Kirsty said bluntly. 'You've taken a terrible thrashin'.'

He had. His nostrils were crusted with blood. There was another cut and a livid bruise along the cheekbone below his blackening eye, and a nasty raw scrape across the opposite cheek from ear to jawline, as though that side of his face had been rubbed along rough ground. Caitlin exclaimed at the sight of him.

'Have ye still got yer teeth?' Todd asked. The weaver nodded. 'And what about yer ribs?' Murdo put a hand to his chest and nodded again.

'Then ye'll live – unless ye get smothered tae death by the womenfolk,' Todd added as Kirsty began to protest. 'Ye've done all that needed doin', lass. What he needs now's a dram.'

'A cup of tea would be better.'

'With split lips?' Todd said from the cupboard where he kept his precious bottle of whisky. 'He'll no' be able tae take hot liquid.'

He poured a generous dram for Murdo and one for himself.

Kirsty, concerned about Rowena's schooling the next day, persuaded her to go to bed.

'You'll fetch me in the morning for school?' the child asked Murdo as Mary led her to the hall door. He nodded.

'If you're not up to it, I'll take her,' Caitlin said, and he looked levelly at her with his one good eye and said, 'I'll manage.'

When Murdo had downed his drink and Kirsty had bandaged the cut on his head, which was still bleeding, he got to his feet. Caitlin noticed him wince, and Todd wanted to walk with him to his lodgings, 'just in case'. But Murdo refused the offer.

'Did you see the way he got up from the chair? I don't doubt there's a rib or mebbe two been cracked for all that he said no,' Kirsty fretted when he had gone. 'Who could have done such a thing to the poor man?'

'It was mebbe a thief,' Mary suggested, and Todd gave a derisive snort.

'It took more than one man tae dae that tae a big laddie like Guthrie. Anyway, who'd want tae steal from him? A blind man could tell that he's not got more than a penny or two in his pockets.'

Todd was right. Murdo's clothes were always clean, but they were shabby.

'Come on now,' Todd urged his womenfolk, 'it's

time we were all in bed. We've had more than enough excitement for the one night.'

For the second night in a row, Caitlin found it hard to sleep. Kirsty's 'Who could have done such a thing to the poor man?' echoed in her skull over and over again.

She thought that she knew the answer, and hoped that she was wrong.

17

After some coaxing, Rowena agreed on the following morning to let Caitlin walk with her to school, but only on the assurance, made with crossed fingers, that Murdo, who she accepted needed to rest his poor sore face, would be waiting for her as usual by the school gate in the afternoon. When they went into the pend and found him waiting there, Rowena gave a whoop of joy and ran forward to throw her arms about his legs.

His face reminded Caitlin of the colourful map of the world that had hung in her school classroom. His left eye and the cheekbone below were badly swollen and bruised, and the scrape on the right side of his face was now an angry scarlet. He had washed his face and taken the bandage from his forehead to reveal a blood-encrusted gash that still looked nasty, and as he untangled Rowena from his legs, Caitlin saw that the knuckles of both hands were scraped and bruised.

'Are you all right?'

'I'm fine.' The expected words were spoken through swollen and broken lips. 'Come on now, you'll be late for school.' He gave the child a slight push towards the pend entrance, but instead of running ahead as she usually did, she put one hand in his and they walked out onto the pavement together.

At midday Caitlin took time she could ill afford from her work and walked swiftly to the street where Bryce lived with his parents and a clutch of younger brothers and sisters. The tenements here were old, and the close smelled sour and stale. As she climbed the stairs she saw that here and there on the small-paned landing window cardboard had been wedged into the square frames. The windows must have been broken some time before, because most of the cardboard patches were soggy.

Mrs Caldwell's eyes widened then almost immediately hardened as she recognised her visitor. 'It's you,' she said flatly. 'What d'ye want?'

Once or twice when she and Bryce had been walking out together in the innocent days before the war, this woman had made Caitlin welcome when she'd visited the flat. Now it was clear from her belligerent stance and the way her body barred the entrance to the flat that she knew of the quarrel between Caitlin and her son.

'Is Bryce in?'

'Mebbe.' Although it was after noon, Mrs Caldwell's hair was still entwined in paper curlers. After a night's sleep, some of them had almost unwound themselves and clung precariously to the ends of her hair. The large floral apron that almost engulfed her skinny body was badly in need of washing, and a cigarette heavy with ash hung between two nicotine-brown fingers.

'I want to talk to him.'

'I didnae say he was in, I just said mebbe. And if he is, mebbe he doesnae want tae talk tae you. It's a fine thing,' the woman had got over the surprise of seeing Caitlin and was snatching at the chance to air her grievances, 'when a laddie that's volunteered tae fight

195

for his king and country comes home tae find that his wee sweetheart doesnae even want tae know him!'

'Mrs Caldwell—'

'Think yersel' better than us now, dae ye, just because ye've found work in that fancy clothes shop down by the river? Well let me tell you, milady . . .'

The ash on the end of her cigarette tumbled onto the faded linoleum floor as Bryce, in a singlet and trousers with the braces dangling round his hips, shouldered her aside.

'What d'ye want?' He put both hands on the doorframe, his burly body all but hiding his small, skinny mother from view.

'Whatever it is, ye're no' bringin' her intae this house,' she quacked from beneath his arm. 'I say who comes in here, and she's no'—'

'Shut it,' Bryce said quite pleasantly, his bloodshot eyes still fixed on Caitlin. He reeked of stale drink from the night before, and he had been in a fight; she noticed that the brow above one eye was thick with congealed blood and a blue knot disfigured his jawline beneath the stubble on his unshaven chin. The big hands he rested on the doorframe were skinned at the knuckles, like Murdo Guthrie's.

'Away an' make us a cup of tea,' he commanded his mother. As she slunk away he eased his body slightly to one side. 'Come on in.'

In order to accept the invitation Caitlin would have had to squeeze past him, ducking beneath a hairy armpit. She shook her head. 'I've not got much time, Bryce. I just wanted to know why you and your friends attacked Murdo Guthrie last night.'

His eyes widened in mock surprise. 'The Highlander? Did someone give him a beating? Oh my,' he said, unable to hide a smirk.

'You know very well that he got a beating, and one he didn't deserve.' She clenched her fists tightly by her sides. 'I came here to tell you what I told you already, though it seems you didn't understand me. I've not been walking out with Murdo or with anyone else, and even if I was it's no longer any of your business. So you can just leave him alone in future.'

'I've not laid a finger on the man!'

'No? Then what happened to your face and hands?'

'My . . . ?' he looked at his hands, then stuck them into the waistband of his trousers. 'Nothin' happened,' he said swiftly, then wheedled, 'Ach, Caitlin, come on in and have a cup of tea and we'll go back tae the way we were.'

'I'm not coming in today or any other day, Bryce. I've finished with you once and for all – and you just leave innocent folk alone or I'll get my stepfather to you,' she said in a rush of words, then turned and fled down the stairs, fully expecting him to follow. Instead, he shouted 'Fuck you, you bitch!' after her and slammed the door with a crash that must have shaken the nails half out of the hinges.

One of the doors in the close creaked open as she reached the bottom of the stairs, and she caught sight of a waxen face peering from the gloom beyond the gap. Just as she gained the pavement a window somewhere above squeaked open, and a sudden avalanche of water crashed onto the pavement to her left, splashing her skirt, ankles and feet. As she whirled round, a knife bounced on the flagstones dangerously close to her shoe then clattered into the gutter. Potato peelings and several whole potatoes, some peeled and some still in their jackets, littered the wet pavement.

'Ye daft lummox!' she heard Mrs Caldwell screech

from above her head. 'That's the dinner ye're throwin' out of the windae!'

'Bitch!' Bryce's infuriated roar drowned out his mother's voice. The window slammed down, and Caitlin took to her heels and ran, her breath catching in her throat. She didn't stop until she was near enough to the river to feel safe, then she halted to put her hat straight and examine her skirt and stockings. The water splashes had dried during her headlong flight. During the rest of the walk back to Harlequin she kept breaking into giggles as she played the scene back in her mind. She longed to tell Grace all about it, but at the same time she knew that she couldn't. It would never do for Grace or anyone else to know that Harlequin's dress designer had just had a basinful of dirty water and potato peelings thrown at her.

Alex was furious when he discovered, on questioning his housekeeper, that Fiona had been in the habit of calling at his flat while he was out.

'I thought there was no harm in it since she's your sister,' the woman protested. 'She just wants to make sure that you have all you need, and she only stays for the time it takes to drink a cup of tea.'

'Even so, I would prefer it, Mrs Harkins, if nobody was allowed in while I'm absent.'

'And how am I to tell Mrs Chalmers that she's not to be allowed into her own brother's home?'

'I'll tell her myself, and I'll see to it that you're not troubled again,' Alex assured her grimly.

'Mrs Chalmers is in the dining room, sir,' the maid said when he arrived at his father's the following afternoon, assured that Angus was at the emporium. 'She's entertaining her sewing circle ladies.'

He had forgotten about the women's groups Fiona had organised to knit and sew clothing for the troops.

'How much longer will they be here, Ellen?'

'Only another five minutes, sir.'

'Then I'll wait in my father's study and you can tell Mrs Chalmers that—'

'Who is it, Mary?' Fiona called from the dining-room door. 'My goodness – Alex!' She came into the hall. 'What a pleasant surprise.'

'I've just heard that you're entertaining friends. I'll wait in the study until they've gone.'

'Not at all.' She took a firm grip on his arm. 'You must come and bid them good afternoon. They were just about to leave in any case. Ellen, we'll have more tea in the drawing room when the ladies have gone, if you please.'

The eight or nine women gathered round the dining-room table clucked and fussed like a hutful of hens when he was thrust unwillingly into their midst. 'Such a treat to speak to a young man these days,' one middle-aged woman gushed at him. 'So many of them are away now.'

'It's becoming quite impossible to arrange a decent party, let alone a dance,' complained another. 'I'm at my wits' end wondering how I'll ever manage to give Kate a decent eighteenth birthday party.'

'There's a war on, Margaret,' a white-haired woman dressed all in black boomed across the table. 'Our very lives are at stake, and the country has more to do than mess about with birthday parties!'

Margaret bridled. 'I'm quite aware that we're at war, Janet, but it seems wrong to deny Kate when both her sisters had such fine eighteenth birthday parties. If I could only be sure of exactly when her cousins expect to be home on furlough it would help. Officers have very smart uniforms . . .' Her voice trailed off as the white-haired woman gave her a scathing look, then turned to fix her eyes on Alex.

'While we work at our sewing we like to discuss the latest news, Mr MacDowall. Just before you came in, we were discussing the struggle to gain ground at Ypres. A sorry business!'

'It is indeed.'

'Have you yourself enlisted, Mr MacDowall?'

'Father needs Alex here,' Fiona said at once. 'And my dear husband, George, is already representing the family somewhere at sea.' She bit her lip and added in a lowered voice, 'I can scarcely sleep at nights for worrying about his safety.' Then, acknowledging the murmurs of sympathy with a delicate inclination of the head, she said, 'I couldn't bear it if I had to fret over Alex as well.'

The older woman tightened her lips and said nothing more, but Alex could read her thoughts as clearly as he had read the thoughts of most of the folk he had encountered over the past seven months – a fit young man like himself should be in uniform instead of lurking around at home.

The group broke up almost immediately after that, despite Fiona's protests. Alex helped to gather up sewing bags, materials, scissors and tapes, then to hunt for elusive needles, pins and reels of thread that had rolled beneath the furniture.

'So kind,' the woman who had been addressed as Margaret murmured as he handed over a long and lethal needle he had found on the seat of the chair his father normally used. 'You must come to Kate's birthday party.'

When Fiona came back from seeing them out she closed the door and leaned back against it, smiling at him. 'I thought they would never go! Shall we go into the drawing room? Our tea will be served in a moment.'

'I must get back to the store. I just came to say that I would appreciate it, Fiona, if you would stay away from my flat in future.'

'Oh dear.' Her eyes mocked him. 'I rather enjoyed talking to your housekeeper. Do you feel that I get in her way?'

'Not hers, mine. I had already noticed on more than one occasion that papers and files on my writing desk had been disturbed. I presume that that was you?'

She shrugged. 'You don't keep anything private in there, do you? Only papers to do with the store and the factory. And as Papa's daughter, I have every right to look at them.'

'Not when you're doing it behind my back.'

'Are you frightened, Alex?'

'Frightened?'

'In case I try to take the business away from you.'

'Don't be ridiculous!'

Fiona was still leaning against the door, her hands tucked behind her back. Today, in deference to the war work being carried out by the group, she wore a demure white broderie anglaise blouse and plain green skirt. The simple outfit made her look very young and innocent, but the gleam in her eyes belied the overall picture.

'I'm so glad that I've had the opportunity to meet your sister Caitlin again and to make Rose Hamilton's acquaintance. I admire Rose in particular, for she has no need to earn her living and yet there she is, doing so well. You like Rose's spirit too, don't you, Alex? I could tell by the way you looked at her at our New Year party.' She waited, then as Alex said nothing, went on,

'Some men would find her rather too bold, but not you, or John Brodie. He adores her. They would make a very suitable couple.'

'I've told Mrs Harkins that you are not to be admitted to my flat when I'm out. I trust you won't embarrass her by trying to gain entrance.'

'I wouldn't dream of it. After all, Mrs Harkins is a working woman too. This very afternoon we were talking about how this war has resulted in women taking over men's work. I'm quite sure that running a large furniture store must be easier than carrying coal or operating machinery in a factory.'

The maid tapped at the door. 'I've put the tea tray in the drawing room, Mrs Chalmers.'

'Thank you, Ellen.'

'You must drink it on your own, Fiona. I have to get back to work.' Alex swept past the two women and let himself out, slashing angrily at the shrubbery with his stick as he strode down the short driveway.

'The truth of the matter,' John Brodie told his fellow partners bluntly, 'is that Harlequin is in difficulties.'

It was mid-May. Caitlin, looking through the upper part of the nearest window at small white clouds floating in blue sky, had been fretting over a report in Todd's newspaper that the Germans had started wafting clouds of chlorine gas towards the British lines. Ever since, she had been wondering fearfully if Bryce was among those men choking and blinded by it. It was terrible to think of someone she knew suffering like that.

John's words brought her back to Paisley with a bump that made her heart lurch. 'You mean that we might have to close Harlequin down?'

'That's exactly what I mean.' He spread his hands

wide to indicate the building around and above them. 'When this place opened for business you both knew that there was very little money left. You've done well to keep it going for over a year – mainly because you've taken very little out of it, Rose.'

'The important thing is to repay Kirsty and Todd. I can afford to wait until we're bringing in more money.'

'But you shouldn't have to.' Caitlin felt guilty at taking a wage when her partner didn't, but unlike Rose she wasn't living with wealthy parents.

'Caitlin's right. All you're doing at the moment, Rose, is playing at running a fashion house.' John hastily lifted both hands, palms out, as she turned on him. 'You can bluster all you like, but you have to face the truth. If Harlequin can't support its staff, including you, while at the same time repaying investors, then it might as well close down.'

'No!'

'You knew at the beginning what you were taking on. You can't run away from it now.'

'But we've got as many orders as we can cope with.' Caitlin's mouth was dry at the prospect of failure. 'I often have to work into the evenings, and so do the women upstairs. In fact, I was about to ask if we could employ another seamstress.'

John shook his head. 'We couldn't possibly afford to meet her wages. You must understand that business consists of balancing outgoing costs against income. There must always be more coming in than there is going out. Unfortunately in your case you have to pay for your materials before you can make the garments, and you must pay your bills promptly if you want the warehouse to go on providing materials. Your clients, on the other hand, are under no such obligation to you.'

Rose began to pace the floor. 'But there must be something we can do.'

John tapped the end of his pencil on the table as he studied the rows of figures before him. 'Could you buy cheaper materials?'

'If we do that we'll lose orders,' Caitlin said at once. 'The women we cater for won't accept anything but the best.' Car tyres crunched on the gravel outside and she jumped to her feet. 'That's Miss Langmuir for her fitting. I must go.'

Rose continued her pacing when Caitlin had gone. 'John, there must be something I can do!'

She was wearing one of Caitlin's designs, a high-waisted costume with a wrapover skirt draped with such skill that, though narrow, it allowed the freedom of movement Rose needed. Caitlin had scoured Glasgow's shops to find the right material, silk patterned with varying shades of green in such a way that the suit seemed to flow around its wearer's long slim body. She looked, John thought as he watched her, as though she was walking in a forest with dappled sunlight shining on her through the trees. Then he coloured slightly, embarrassed by such poetic, unlawyerlike thoughts, and sat upright, riffling through the papers before him.

'You could let me put more money into the business.'

'No.'

'Why not? I could afford enough to help you over this patch.'

'I don't want the responsibility of using your money.'

'You keep telling me that I'm too stuffy,' John pointed out. 'I believe that I would rather enjoy taking a risk. Not that it would be, since I have every confidence in your ability. If I hadn't, I would never have agreed to you buying the mill in the first place.'

'You had little choice,' Rose told him dryly, 'since my heart was set on the place from the moment I saw it.'

'Will you accept my offer?'

She reached the window and turned, her silk jacket and skirt swirling about her body. 'I'd worry about you losing your money because of my hot-headedness,' she said, and John took a deep breath.

'If you married me it would be our money, and I could keep a closer watch on how it's spent.'

Rose stared at him for a long moment. 'That's the most unlawyerlike thing I've ever heard!'

'I mean it.'

'You can't possibly!'

'I most certainly can. Dammit it, Rose, I'm twenty-nine years of age, a bachelor in my right mind.' It was his turn to get up and start pacing, while she stood rooted to the spot. 'And I've just asked you to marry me. Why won't you take me seriously?'

'But you're . . . we're . . . friends,' Rose said feebly.

'We used to be friends, after we became business partners. Now we've – I've – moved on. I've been wanting to propose to you for weeks now . . . months.'

Rose looked about her, as though seeking help, then said, 'But the thought of us marrying is preposterous!'

'Why? Am I so unlikeable?'

'Of course not, it's me. Why should anyone want to marry me?'

'Because . . . for God's sake, woman,' John said angrily, 'don't ask such stupid questions. I want to marry you because I happen to love you. And before you say I can't love you, I can. I can do anything I want.'

'And so can I.'

'So . . . you're turning me down.'

She spread her hands out helplessly. 'John, I don't want to marry anyone.'

'I see.' He began to gather up his papers. 'I'll still lend you the money, of course.'

'I couldn't let you do that.'

John stuffed the papers willy-nilly into his briefcase and snatched up his hat and cane. 'Sometimes, Rose,' he said without looking at her, 'you infuriate me!'

18

True to her word, Fiona didn't call at Alex's flat again, but she did start visiting the store every day, working her way through one department after another, getting to know the staff and meeting some of the customers. She spent entire mornings in the offices and questioned Alex and his father at the dinner table during their Friday evening meetings. Angus was pleased with her interest.

'She never used to bother her head about the place,' he told Alex over their after-dinner brandies, 'but she's older now, of course, and no doubt marriage and learning how to run a household have given her an insight into the value of money. In any case, it keeps her occupied and takes her mind off fretting over George, so we must encourage it.'

Early in May the Cunard liner *Lusitania* had been sunk by torpedoes with great loss of civilian lives, and those few people who still clung to the notion that the war would be brief began to realise they they were mistaken.

Alex knew utter despair as he read about the drowning of innocent men, women and children. It wasn't just his own life that had fallen apart, but the entire world. Only the day before he had had to visit the confused and bewildered mother of a former employee of his furniture factory, a cheerful apprentice who had been among the first to enlist, convinced that after a few months in uniform he would be back at the workbench, a hero in the eyes of his less courageous mates. Instead he was lying in some makeshift grave in France. Alex had taken the mother a sum of money donated by those who had worked with the boy and a larger sum from himself and his father.

'Enough tae pay for a decent burial,' the woman had said when he'd spread the notes and coins before her, 'except that I don't think we're goin' tae be allowed tae bury him, for this is all they've sent me.' She'd indicated some possessions lying on a table by the window – cigarettes, matches, an open razor-blade, a notebook, some well-handled letters and, most poignant of all, it seemed to Alex, a clean, folded handkerchief.

'He was just seventeen,' she'd said, over and over again.

'Can we do anything to help you?'

She'd shaken her head. 'Not unless ye can turn the clock back . . .' Her voice had trailed away, but the red, swollen eyes raised to his face had asked why he was standing before her while her boy's lifeless body lay in another country, denied the comfort of being buried by the folk who had known and loved him.

It was a look that Alex had even begun to see when he looked into his own shaving mirror in the mornings. He could no longer believe that his father had more need of him than his country had. He finished reading about the *Lusitania*, folded his newspaper, went to the nearest recruiting office and enlisted.

He told nobody what he had done but began to spend what time he had left making sure that the factory supervisor knew enough about the business to look after it in his absence and that everything he had been dealing with in the store was in safe hands.

Early in June Fiona received word that her husband's ship had put in at Portsmouth and left hurriedly to spend some time with him before he returned to sea. The day after she left, Alex's papers arrived. He told his father first.

'Aye, well, I knew it was bound to happen sooner rather than later,' Angus said heavily, 'though I'd hoped that it would have been a while yet.'

'This war's dragging on too long, Father. There's no sense in fooling ourselves any longer that it's going to end soon. Best get over there and get on with it.'

'Aye, I suppose so.' Although they admired and trusted each other, Angus MacDowall and his son had never been close, probably because Alex had been a grown man by the time they'd found each other, and a harsh childhood and youth followed by a long, hard struggle to improve himself had leached away any emotions that Angus might once have had. There must have been some warmth there once, Alex sometimes thought, looking at his father's stern, lined face, for how else had he himself come into the world? His mother was a warm, caring woman, and the Angus she had known all those years ago must also have had warmth; Alex couldn't imagine her giving herself to a cold and unloving man.

Kirsty must have known the best of Angus MacDowall, but for Alex and Angus there were no memories of childhood and fatherhood to share and to bind them closer. All Angus's paternal love had gone to Fiona and was still hers.

It was a relief to both men when they were free to settle down to the practical side of things. Alex explained how he had left matters in the small factory and on his side of the store management.

'I'll go to Paisley tomorrow to see Todd and Murdo and my mother. Todd can run that side of the business easily enough, and I've arranged for the factory supervisor to keep in contact with him and with you.'

'Your mother'll be grieved.'

'Yes, she will.' Alex wasn't looking forward to breaking the news to her. 'But she's got Todd and Caitlin and Mary with her. She'll be fine.'

'Give her my regards when you see her. You'll have a dram . . .' Angus poured two generous tumblerfuls of malt whisky and raised his glass to his son. 'To your health, and to your safe return.'

'To the end of the war,' Alex acknowledged. They were in Angus's small study, the room he preferred to use when on his own in the house. Angus stared into the fire he always insisted on having, even in warm weather, then said after a long pause, 'It's too bad that Fiona's away. You'll not have the chance to say goodbye to her.'

'You can do that for me.'

'It's a blessing that Fiona's been taking such an interest in the business,' Angus said. 'She'll mebbe be able to help out a bit while you're away. And it'll give her something to do.'

Alex went to Paisley the following afternoon, when he was certain that the house would be empty and Todd closeted in the workshop at the end of the yard. He went straight to the weaving shop, where Murdo worked at his loom, and tested the new cloth between finger and thumb, enjoying as always the texture of strong, well-woven material. 'It's good.'

'They're coming for it tomorrow afternoon. I'd

already decided to work on tonight, so you can be sure it'll be finished in time.'

'That's not what I came about.' Alex pushed his hands into his pockets. 'I came to bid you goodbye, for I've enlisted.'

The Highlander turned to sit sideways on the saytree, facing his employer. 'I thought it would come to it.'

'I knew it must, sooner or later. I go tomorrow.'

'So soon? Have you told your mother?'

'Not yet. I'll come back tonight to see her and the others. I don't want you to say anything in the meantime.'

Murdo nodded. 'Am I to go on with the weaving?'

'Of course. Our customers have been pleased with their chair coverings, and Todd and Jock Beaton from the Glasgow factory'll let you know what's wanted. I've told my father that you'll be here for as long as you can.'

'You know that I'll certainly not be enlisting like yourself.'

'I'd not expect you to, Murdo. You stay here for as long as you like – or as long as you can.' Alex took a bottle from his pocket. 'I thought you might drink my health before I go.'

'It would be an honour, Mr MacDowall.' Murdo got up and went to a shelf at the back of the weaving shop.

'Alex,' Alex corrected him.

The weaver, returning with a tin mug in one hand and a china mug in the other, gave him a long steady look. 'As I've said before, I'm not comfortable with calling my employer by his given name. I'd as soon stay as I am.'

'You're a stubborn man, Murdo Guthrie.'

A faint smile flitted across Murdo's broad face. 'I've

been told that many a time.' He held the mugs steady while Alex poured the amber liquid into them, then offered him the china mug. Alex studied the farmyard scene painted on it with raised eyebrows.

'It's Rowena's mug,' the Highlander explained. 'She likes to keep it here for when we have a wee drink of tea.' He raised his tin cup to Alex and said something in Gaelic. 'That's a wish that the world treats you well and sends you homeward at the end of the day.'

Alex nodded and drank. 'Rowena's not getting in your way?'

'Oh no, I like to hear her talk and see her wee face about the place.'

'My mother says she's doing well now. Caitlin says it's thanks to you.'

'I'd not say that at all.'

'That Highland dancing you introduced her to seems to have settled her.'

'She's a rare wee dancer, and she loves the ceilidhs. She's doing fine at the school, too.' Murdo paused, then said carefully, 'I know that she seems difficult at times, but she's known more hardship than a bairn of her age should be expected to carry.'

Alex nodded. 'We can just hope that she has a better life to come.'

'Oh, she'll see to that.' The smile crossed Murdo's face again. 'She's got a strong will, has Rowena, and a determination that'll stand her in good stead throughout her life. It's just now, when she's wee and helpless, that she needs the strength of others.'

Alex left soon after and wandered round Paisley, revisiting old haunts. He walked along the banks of the River Cart until he had almost reached the old mill, then found a patch of shrubbery where he could watch without being seen. A car stood in the flagged forecourt, and after a while another drove in and a uniformed chauffeur helped two women out. They went into the building, then Rose Hamilton escorted another woman and a man out. They got into the car and she stood talking through the window for a few minutes. She was wearing a slim dark skirt and the long harlequin jacket Alex liked. When the car had gone, she stood for a moment, studying the outside of the building, then went back indoors.

He wandered into the town again and bought two pies, eating them while he walked back towards Carriagehill. The gates leading to the Hamiltons' long driveway were open, as always; Alex stepped inside and walked halfway to the house before stepping into the shrubbery. He leaned against a tree and waited, hearing the distant hooters of factories and mills marking the end of the working day. In the streets men and women would be hurrying along the pavements and queuing for trams and buses to take them home, but here it was peaceful, with only birdsong and an occasional rustle in the undergrowth. Time passed, but there was no sign of the bicycle Rose usually rode home from the fashion house. After a while, a motorcar turned in from the road, and Alex, recognising Mr Hamilton's car, peered through shielding branches to see if she was in it but could only make out one figure in the back seat. At last he made his way back down the drive and set out for Espedair Street.

Rowena had had a dancing lesson that day and came home impatient to show off her latest steps. After the evening meal, she coaxed Murdo from the weaving shop to play for her while she performed on her dancing stone. Shy though he was at being among them, he agreed on that particular night, and after

Todd had set chairs in the back yard for his wife and stepdaughters, the weaver came to the end of the pend, where he leaned against the wall.

Rowena seized the hem of her smock in both hands, her wrists delicately raised and fingers spread as she had been taught, and nodded at him. 'Now, Murdo.' He began to play, and she began to dance, twirling and spinning and leaping, light as thistledown and placing her feet, heel down and toe up, with practised precision.

There was no doubt that she could dance. Even Kirsty clapped enthusiastically when she had finished, and Rowena's grin almost split her small face in two.

'Another one, Murdo,' she called as the Highlander began to edge back towards the safety of his weaving shop.

'It's almost time for your bed,' Kirsty began.

'Please, just one more . . . please!'

Todd couldn't resist the pleading in Rowena's eyes and in her voice. 'It'll not hurt to let the bairn show us one more dance, Kirsty. It's a fine night tae sit out in – and ye've earned a rest, surely.'

It was a lovely evening. 'Just one more, then,' Kirsty agreed, and Rowena ran to drag Murdo back. This time, although the others watched Rowena again, Caitlin found her gaze travelling to Murdo. His waistcoat was unbuttoned, his shirt open at the collar, and his sleeves rolled up to above his elbows. His eyes were fixed on Rowena, but the lids drooped half over them, as though he was seeing other things besides the small figure dancing before him. His broad hands cupping the small mouth organ almost hid it from sight, and his fingers manipulated it deftly as he blew sweet music into it, music that she knew could change in an instant from merriment to sadness.

214

All too soon it came to an end and Rowena, after a final leap, drooped low on the flagstone in a graceful curtsey, accepting the flurry of applause just as Alex came through the pend and into their midst.

'A back yard concert, is it? You've got a fine night for it.'

'I'll get back to my work,' Murdo said, and was gone almost before the final word was out. Kirsty scooped Rowena into the house and her daughters followed, while Todd drew Alex down the yard and into the workshop to show him the work in progress.

Rowena was in her bed by the time the men came into the kitchen, Alex first and Todd following with an expression on his face that had Kirsty immediately demanding to know what was wrong.

'Nothing at all, Mam.'

'There is so. Todd Paget was never able to hide his thoughts.' She looked from one to the other. 'Is it the business? Has something gone wrong with it?'

'Ye'd best just tell her and get it over with, lad,' Todd advised his stepson, reaching as ever for his tobacco pouch.

'I've enlisted, Mam.'

Her face crumpled with shock. 'Oh, Alex! When d'you go? How long do we have you with us?'

'I've to report to Maryhill Barracks tomorrow.'

'Tomorrow?' Kirsty dropped into a chair, her hands to her mouth. 'So soon?'

'I've known for a week or two.'

'And you never said a word to us?' Mary asked in disbelief.

'I never said a word to anyone. I didn't want a fuss.'

'But . . . tomorrow! Oh, Alex!' Kirsty said, and burst into tears. He knelt by her side, pushing a handkerchief into her hands, trying to soothe her, while Mary and Caitlin automatically set about making tea.

When it was ready, Todd announced that he had forgotten to do something in the workshop. 'Mebbe,' he said awkwardly to Mary and Caitlin, 'yer mother and Alex should have a wee minute tae themselves.'

They took the hint, carrying their cups into the front room, where Mary perched on the edge of Kirsty's good couch and Caitlin stood at the window, looking out at the folk who passed by, wondering what difference the war had made to their lives.

'How'll we manage without Alex?' Mary asked from behind her.

'It won't be for long. He'll come back soon.'

'I hope so,' Mary's voice, usually so confident, was small and wobbly. 'I know he's not been living here for a long time, but he was always here in spirit, if you know what I . . .' She began to sob, and Caitlin put her cup down on the sideboard, heedless for once about the danger of leaving a mark, and went to sit by her sister. 'How's Mam going to manage without him?' Mary sniffled damply into her shoulder. 'He was always her favourite. If anything happens to him I don't know what she'd—'

'Nothing's going to happen to him! Nothing could happen to Alex. Of course he'll come back!'

When Kirsty called them back into the kitchen her face was swollen, but her eyes were dry. 'Alex has to go back to Glasgow now. I'm walking to the station with him.'

'Me too,' Mary said quickly.

'I'll stay with Rowena, just in case she wakens,' Caitlin offered. Like the others, she desperately wanted to be with Alex until the last possible moment, but someone had to stay behind.

Her mother summoned up a grateful smile. 'I'd be happier in my mind if someone was here with her. Mary, go and fetch Todd, he'll want to come with us. I'll just go upstairs and get my good hat and coat,' she added as Mary darted into the hall for her jacket then hurried back through the kitchen and out into the yard, pushing her arms into the sleeves.

'What'll happen to Murdo with you gone?' Caitlin asked Alex.

'Nothing,' Alex said with some surprise. 'My father appreciates his worth as much as I do, so his job's safe.'

'Unless he goes into the war too.'

'He won't, unless he must. Murdo Guthrie and the army have little time for each other.'

'So you do know more about him than you've let on?'

He smiled faintly. 'Even if I do, it's still his business and not mine to go telling to folk.'

'Did he do wrong? Can you tell me that much?'

'He did nothing wrong,' Alex assured her, then spoiled things by adding, 'not in my eyes, at least.'

'What about Rose?' she remembered suddenly.

His eyelids flickered, then stilled. 'What about her?'

'Are you going away without a word to her?'

'I'm certainly not going to her house with her parents there.'

'She's not at home tonight,' Caitlin suddenly remembered. 'John called for her at the fashion house. The two of them were going to his parents' house for their evening meal, then to a meeting in the town hall.'

'In that case you'll just have to tell her tomorrow.'

'D'you want me to give her a message?'

'You could tell her that . . .' Alex began, then

217

stopped. 'Just say that I hope Harlequin continues to do well, for both your sakes.'

Kirsty came in, dressed in her best hat and coat, her eyes bleak but her head held high, just as Todd and Mary arrived from the workshop. There was a last-minute flurry of goodbyes before they went out.

After they had gone, the kitchen seemed small and airless. Caitlin escaped into the yard for a breath of fresh air, walking over the grass to stand on the dancing stone where, less than an hour before, Rowena had been giving an impromptu concert and everything had been fine.

She tried a few tentative steps on the flagstone, then a few more. The lilt of Murdo's mouth organ came into her head, followed by the fine, clear notes of a fiddle then the rapid, light beat of the small drum.

Caitlin started dancing in earnest to the music in her head, her feet twisting and turning, heel and toe, her skirt flaring out around her as she spun and leaped, the tears on her uplifted face shining in the twilight.

19

—————◆—————

'What do you mean, Alex has gone?'

'He's volunteered for the army.'

'So he'll still be in Glasgow for a few weeks before he goes.'

'Rose, he volunteered weeks ago and didn't tell anyone. We didn't know until he came to tell us last night that he goes today.'

Rose's eyes blazed like sapphires set in white satin. She snatched her hat from its peg and jammed it onto her head, then made for the door while still struggling to get into her coat. 'There's one appointment for this morning and another for early afternoon,' she said breathlessly. 'They're in the book on my desk, but you'll need to keep a lookout for them. They hate it when nobody's on hand to open the door when they arrive.'

'Where are you going?'

'To Glasgow, of course, to see Alex before he leaves.'

Caitlin pursued her into the foyer. 'It's no use, Rose. He had to report to the barracks first thing this morning.'

Rose, one hand outstretched to open the door, rounded on her. 'Are you telling me that he left without even saying goodbye to me?'

'He did ask if you were at home, but I knew that you'd gone out with John. He left a message for you.'

'What is it?'

'He . . . He hopes that Harlequin goes well,' Caitlin said, and watched a tide of red suddenly flame into Rose's ashen cheeks.

'Is that all?'

'He had very little time. And you know Alex, he hates a fuss.'

'Oh yes, I know Alex!' Rose almost threw herself past Caitlin and back into the office, tearing the coat off as she went. 'Alex, the friend who can't even take the trouble to say goodbye!' She tossed her coat at the stand and missed.

'Rose . . .' Caitlin gathered it up, and hung it on its peg, then picked up the hat that hurtled down at her feet. 'I'm sorry. I wish I'd insisted on getting a proper message from him.'

'It's not your fault, it's his!' Rose was staring at one of the walls, her arms clamped tightly across her chest, her back to Caitlin. 'Just . . . go and see that the women are getting on with their work, will you?'

It was a very difficult morning. The client who had insisted on being seen at exactly ten o'clock failed to turn up until twenty minutes to eleven and was dissatisfied with almost every aspect of the coat that was being made for her. Rose made matters worse by treating the woman with a brittle formality that almost ended in a quarrel between the two of them, only averted when Rose left, pleading essential work waiting to be done in the office. Once she had gone, it took Caitlin and Grace all their time to smooth the client's ruffled feelings and win her approval of the work they had already done.

'I'd as soon volunteer for the French trenches as for another morning like this,' Grace said flatly when Caitlin returned to the fitting room after seeing the woman out. 'What's the matter with Miss Hamilton?'

Caitlin, too weary to prevaricate, explained briefly about Alex's hurried visit the evening before. 'Rose was out, so he didn't see her to say goodbye.'

'Is that all?'

'They were good friends.'

Grace raised an eyebrow at her. 'More than friends, if she's that upset about him going.'

Caitlin sighed. 'There was a time when I thought they might mean more to each other, but ever since Alex wanted this place and Rose bought it instead, there's been a coolness between them.'

'On the surface, mebbe, but underneath that madam's coolness there's a furnace blazing, you mark my words. D'ye think he feels the same way about her?'

'It's hard to tell with Alex.'

'And what about Mr Brodie? He's near daft with love for her.'

'You think so?'

Grace gave her a pitying look. 'I know so. Down our street the folk live so close together that you cannae sneeze without your neighbour blowin' his nose. It gets so's it's easy to read faces and voices, whatever words they might be using. Who'd have thought a plain stick like Rose Hamilton would have two nice-lookin' men daft about her?'

Caitlin snapped out of her reverie about Rose and Alex when Todd said during the evening meal, 'Young Bryce Caldwell was at the workshop this afternoon.'

She felt a sudden nervous thrill run through her. 'Did he mention me at all?'

221

'He was too busy braggin' about him an' his mates in the trenches. A right hero, that one.' Todd shook his head tolerantly. 'If half of what he says is right, he'll have the Germans skelpin' back tae their mams by Christmas.' He helped himself to another slice of bread. 'An' the things they get up tae when they're allowed time off would make yer hair curl.'

'What sort of things?' Mary asked at once, and her mother glared at her then at Todd.

'Never you mind, miss – and we don't want to know, Todd Paget.'

'I wasnae goin' tae tell ye. He was makin' out that he's above the rest of us now that he's in uniform and trusted with a rifle, but come the end of the war he'll be in that yard, cap in hand, lookin' for his job back.'

'And lucky if he gets it, the cheeky wee upstart,' Kirsty snapped.

'Ach, there's no harm tae him or any of them. They've got tae keep their spirits up somehow, and sometimes braggin's the only way tae keep goin'.'

'Did he go into the weaving shop?' Caitlin wanted to know.

'I made certain tae walk with him tae the road when he left, just in case. I know you think it was him that attacked Murdo thon time, lass, but I'm not so certain of it. Still, I thought it best tae make sure he was off the premises.'

Caitlin saw Bryce once during his furlough, when he passed by on the other side of the road one evening when she was walking back from the fashion house. There was a girl with him, and when Bryce saw Caitlin he gave her a long hard stare then put his arm about his companion, pulling her tightly to him and nuzzling her ear. Possibly he wanted to show her that there were other, and more malleable, fish in the sea, but all she felt was that a weight had been lifted from her shoulders and that both she and Murdo were surely safe from Bryce's attentions in the future.

John Brodie enlisted in July and left Paisley almost at once. The day before he went, he and Rose were closeted for an entire afternoon in the small office going over all the Harlequin books, which John had brought with him.

'Keep an eye on Rose for me,' he said to Caitlin when he was saying goodbye. 'And try to prevent her from doing anything that might harm the business.'

'She wouldn't do that. She's just a bit impetuous at times.'

A shadow crossed John's face. 'Unfortunately not all the time,' he said enigmatically, and left.

Rose had remained in the office; when Caitlin went in she was sitting at the desk, her head in her hands. Caitlin thought for a moment that she was weeping, but when she looked up her eyes were dry.

'Has he gone?'

'Yes.'

Rose heaved a great sigh, then asked, 'Can I eat at your house tonight? My mama will be in a terrible pet, and I don't want to face her.'

'You know you're always welcome. What have you done to annoy her this time?'

'Sent John off to fight.'

Caitlin sat down suddenly. 'You told him to enlist?'

'Of course not. I don't even want him to go.' Rose sighed again, then said, 'You might as well know. John asked me to marry him and I refused. And I think that that's why he decided to enlist rather than wait to be called.'

'And your mother knows.'

'Unfortunately he told his mama, and she immediately told mine. Apparently she had set her heart on getting me off her hands and onto John's, and she's been going on about it ever since.' Rose thumped a fist on the desk. 'I really must try to find enough money to do up that gatehouse! But the only way I can do that is to let John invest more in Harlequin, and then I'd have to agree to marry him.'

Caitlin was scandalised. 'Are those his terms?'

'No, but how can I turn down his proposal and yet take his money? Oh, Caitlin, what a mess I've got myself into. And now,' Rose thumped her fist down again, this time onto the ledgers on the desk, 'I'm left with all these dratted books to see to!'

Fiona Chalmers came to Paisley to see Todd on her father's behalf and to order a new gown from Harlequin. When the design had been agreed and the materials chosen, Rose brought tea in. As soon as she set the tray down, Fiona jumped up and took both Rose's hands in hers.

'My dear, Caitlin has told me about John.'

Rose shot an astonished glance at Caitlin, who said hurriedly, 'I told Fiona that he had enlisted.'

'And so suddenly, too. You must miss him dreadfully.'

'No more than you must miss Alex.'

Fiona gave a musical little laugh. 'There's a difference. Alex is my brother, whereas John is—'

'A friend.' Rose freed her hands. 'Do you take milk?'

'Yes, I do.' Fiona stirred her tea, sipped delicately, then beamed at them both. 'I can't tell you how grateful I am to you.'

Caitlin and Rose exchanged puzzled glances. 'Grateful?'

'Now that Alex has gone, it falls to me to help my father in his business. And I could never have found the courage to do that if I hadn't met you and seen this place.' A sweep of a gloved hand indicated the building around them. 'I told myself that if you two could become businesswomen, then I could too. And I've found that it can be very soothing to have something positive to occupy one's mind at a time of such worry. This war has been a blessing to women.'

'I doubt if women with families to raise and no man to support them would agree with you,' Rose said dryly.

'I'm talking about women like us, who have been set free to find their real potential.' She beamed from one to the other. 'Life will never be the same for us again, and that, I believe, can be nothing but a blessing.'

'The more I see of Fiona, the more I dislike her,' Rose said ten minutes later as they stood together on the steps watching Fiona leave for Espedair Street. 'She makes me itch.'

'She's a good customer.' Caitlin waved as Fiona's hand fluttered a farewell through the open car window.

'Don't you think that there's a sly look about her? She reminds me of a cat that's found all the cream and lapped up every drop.'

'You're being unfair!'

'Mebbe so.' Rose turned back into the building. 'But when I look into those wide, innocent eyes of hers, I get the feeling that she's up to something, and that whoever gets hurt, it won't be Mrs Fiona Chalmers.'

Caitlin arrived home that evening to find an air of mourning about the kitchen. Kirsty looked upset. Todd, who was usually the last to arrive home after work, was sitting at the kitchen table with a face like a thundercloud.

'Thon Fiona Chalmers was in today.'

'I know, she came to Harlequin to order a gown. Did she find fault with the workshop?'

'No, she seemed satisfied enough with that . . . for the moment at least. But she's turned Murdo Guthrie off.'

'What?'

'Told him and me that MacDowalls' can't afford their own weaver and from now on they'll be buyin' their cloth from a factory.'

'After the man stayin' up half the night to finish off the cloth he was working on so that the order'd be ready in good time,' said Kirsty, who had changed her opinion of the weaver.

'But what'll Murdo do now?' Caitlin asked.

'God knows. I cannae take him on for her father's my employer too.'

'We must write to Alex.'

'What can he do, away in England? In any case, it seems that the lassie's got Angus MacDowall's permission to do as she pleases.'

'What about Rowena?' It was the school holidays, and the little girl had spent the day at the shop with Kirsty.

'She's upstairs, putting her doll into a wee dress Teenie made for it today. She doesn't know yet, and I'm dreading the moment when she finds out.'

'I'll fetch her down and tell her in the weaving shop,' Caitlin offered.

The former storeroom in the pend was empty, the loom bare. On the shelf where Murdo's battered tin cup and Rowena's china mug normally stood side by side, the mug was on its own. Caitlin took it down and gave it to Rowena. 'We'll take it back into the kitchen, will we?'

'Where's Murdo?'

'He's finished his work and gone home.'

'Is he coming back tomorrow?' Rowena asked anxiously.

'No, pet. There's no more cloth to be woven.'

'When's he coming back then?'

Caitlin knelt down on the solid earthen floor and took the child's face between her palms. 'He's not coming back, Rowena,' she said, and watched the tip-tilted blue eyes blink rapidly several times as the little girl tried to take in the thought. Understanding dawned, and with it the realisation that for the second time in her short life Rowena had been deserted by the person she most trusted. Her face began to melt as tears filled her eyes then spilled down her cheeks. 'I want Murdo!' It was a cry from the heart.

'Rowena . . .'

'I want him,' she insisted, stamping her foot. She broke away from Caitlin and ran to the saytree, thumping at it with her fists. 'I want him here!'

When Caitlin picked her up she resisted at first, turning her fury and her small knotted fists on her aunt until finally, worn out, she collapsed against Caitlin's shoulder, sobbing over and over again, 'I want M – Murdo!'

Caitlin sank down onto the saytree, rocking the child, feeling her grief soak into her own skin, and she too cried for the loss of Murdo Guthrie, with his square, expressionless face and his hooded dark eyes beneath the tumble of hair, his kindness and his deep loneliness and his beautiful music.

* * *

She went in search of him the next day, sending word to Rose by a young lad willing to run a message for twopence that she would be late. Since nobody seemed to know where Murdo lived, Caitlin started with the Highland woman who was teaching Rowena to dance. From there she was directed to Mhairi's spotlessly clean single-roomed home in Orchard Street. Fortunately, the woman was home when Caitlin knocked at her door.

'Murdo? He lives in a wee lodging house down by the river, near Abercorn Street. But he'll not thank you for disturbing him. Murdo likes to keep himself to himself.'

'I must speak to him, Mhairi. He's just been turned away from his work.'

The woman shook her head. 'Is that right? Ach, poor man, he never seems to get the best of things. Aye, well, if you think you can help him I'd be glad to tell you how to find him.'

Her directions took Caitlin into a part of Paisley she had never visited before, where a warren of small factories and old tenements clung to the banks of the River Cart. Here the roads were narrow and the pavements clung to the building walls, with scarcely room for two people to pass. There was no indication as to the names of the lanes or the numbers of the closes, but just as she thought that she would never find Murdo's home, a woman passing by said inquisitively, 'Are ye lost, hen?'

'I'm trying to find a man called Murdo Guthrie.'

'Would that be the big Highlander?' The woman pointed at the next close. 'In there, and it's the door to this side of the close.'

The tenement was much older than the place where Bryce Caldwell lived with his family, and made their home seem like a palace. It was a relief to know that Murdo lived on the ground floor and she didn't have to attempt the stone steps leading up into darkness above.

There was no answer to her knock. She waited, knocked again and finally had to accept the fact that he wasn't at home. Slowly she turned away, just as what little light shone into the close was blocked by a tall figure. She peered at it. 'Murdo?'

'What are you doing here?'

'I came to see if you were all right.'

'I'm fine. Why wouldn't I be?' he asked abruptly, angrily.

'Can I speak to you?'

He hesitated, and for a moment she thought that he was going to refuse then he said reluctantly, 'If you must.'

The room was small, its sagging ceiling so low that Murdo had to stoop slightly when walking about. There was a small table, two straight-backed chairs, a sagging cupboard and, Caitlin saw when she peered into the shadowy bed recess, a low narrow cot. There was no fire in the small range, though even on that warm August day the room was chilly with the damp that came up from the creaking floorboards and probably permeated the entire building.

'Sit down.'

She sat in one of the upright chairs, noting that it and the rickety table were both well scrubbed. The range had been blackleaded recently, and the curtain at the small window was clean. Murdo stayed on his feet, head bowed beneath the flaking plaster ceiling. Caitlin wished that she hadn't come; she could almost feel his pain at having to watch her in it, aware of the poverty he had to live in.

'I'm sorry that you were turned off. We all are.'

Then, when he said nothing, she struggled on, 'Alex would never have allowed it to happen.'

'As he's not here any more it's not his concern.'

'It will be when he finds out about it. What are you going to do?'

'Look for work.' Although there was no change in his tone she sensed the dryness of the remark and flushed.

'In Paisley?'

'Wherever I can find it.' He paused, then said with patient courtesy, 'It's not your concern.'

'But it is. It concerns all of us – my mother and my stepfather and my sister.'

'You've no obligation. I'll manage.'

'And there's Rowena. Murdo,' she said on a sudden whim, 'you could live in Espedair Street, in the loom shop. There's room for a cot and chairs, and you could eat your meals with us.'

'I'll not take charity, however well meant it is.'

'It's not charity, it's what Alex would want us to do. He's bound to come home on furlough soon, and when he does he might be able to find you other work or persuade his father to take you back.'

'It's meant kindly, I know, but I'd as soon see to my own affairs.'

'But you can't go on living in this place!' she burst out, and regretted it as soon as she saw his face tighten.

'I've managed until now,' he said stiffly, and she had no option but to leave him alone in his tiny damp-smelling room with only his pride for company and comfort.

20

The key was stiff, and Rose had to use both hands and all her strength before it finally turned in the lock. 'All it needs is some oil,' she said as she pushed the door open and led the way into the gatehouse.

The place smelled stale and dusty. They groped their way along the hall and into the room on the right, where they managed to wrest the shutters from the windows. Light flooded in to reveal a fairly large square room.

'Big enough for a loom,' Rose said with satisfaction.

'There has to be a space in the floor for the treadles. That's why most loomshops have earthen floors.'

'Then we'll have some floorboards taken away. At least the loom belongs to Kirsty and not to that dreadful Chalmers woman, so we know we'll be able to move it here. Look, there's a cupboard and some shelving, and a fireplace to heat the place in the winter.'

They explored the rest of the ground floor, opening the window shutters as they went, then mounted the stairs to inspect the upper floor.

'It's waterproof, and snug enough,' Rose said at last when the two of them had gone back downstairs. 'We needn't bother with upstairs. We could put the loom in that front room, and Murdo could live in the kitchen.

There's even a range and a sink and a cold-water tap, and a privy out at the back.'

Hope tingled through Caitlin, but she pushed it away. There were too many obstacles. 'We'd have to clean the place out.'

'That wouldn't take long.'

'And furnish the kitchen.'

'He could bring furniture from the place where he lives now, and we'll buy anything else he needs from a second-hand shop or a pawnshop. We'll buy some material too so that the women can make curtains.'

'But can we afford to employ Murdo?' Caitlin voiced her greatest worry.

'We'll manage somehow. You've always wanted to have material woven to your own designs, haven't you?'

'Yes, but—'

'Now's the time to do it. If we don't move now,' Rose said, eyeing Caitlin closely, 'he might have to leave Paisley to find work.' She examined her hands. 'I'm covered with dust, and so are you. We'd better get ourselves cleaned up.'

On the way back across the courtyard she said, 'I'll go to see Murdo this afternoon to ask if he'll agree to work for us.'

'I'll do it.'

'Best leave it to me,' Rose advised. 'From what you say he's prickly about accepting anything he considers to be charity. As he scarcely knows me, I can keep things on a business footing. You care too much for the man to be properly businesslike.'

'What nonsense!'

'Is it?' Rose asked, with a gleam of amusement in her blue eyes.

*   *   *

There was little laughter in Rose's face when she returned to the fashion house that afternoon. 'You said that the place he lived in was poor,' she said when she swept into the design office to find Caitlin working there, 'but I didn't realise it was as bad as all that. I have friends who wouldn't let their dogs or their horses live in such conditions! You were absolutely right, Caitlin, we must get him out of there.'

'You spoke to him?'

'Yes.' A marble-topped washstand stood at one end of the room; Rose poured water from the flower-patterned ewer into the matching basin and reached for the scented soap, then washed her hands vigorously. 'I shall have a bath as soon as I get home. How can anyone live in such squalor?'

'Murdo keeps the place as clean as he can,' Caitlin said, on the defensive.

'Indeed he does, though I don't know how he manages it – or any of the other poor souls. It should have been pulled down years ago!'

Caitlin was almost dancing with impatience. 'What did he say?'

'He was suspicious at first – convinced that I was just being kind. But I wore him down in the end.' Rose took the towel from Caitlin and proceeded to dry her hands. 'He's agreed to work for us and live in the gatehouse.'

Despite her efforts to remain calm, Caitlin felt a huge smile of relief spread across her face.

'We don't even have to pay him all that much since he doesn't have to pay rent. He's offered to keep an eye on the place in return. So now we must set about getting the gatehouse ready and the loom moved. It pleases me,' she added with a gleeful smile, 'to know that I've managed to do something that would annoy Fiona Chalmers!'

*   *   *

Rose Hamilton wasn't one to drag her heels once she had decided on a course of action. Two scrubbing women arrived the next day to clean out the gatehouse, and a joiner of Todd's acquaintance came in two days later to make a well in the front-room flooring to accommodate the treadles of the loom.

'So much for your plans to live here,' Caitlin said when he had left and the two of them had crossed the courtyard to inspect his work. The place smelled of carbolic instead of dust and neglect, with a pleasant underlying aroma of new timber.

'Once we're really successful we'll build a loom shop and a nice wee house for Murdo in the ground between Harlequin and the river, then I'll get this place back. The floorboards can be replaced easily enough. In fact,' Rose said thoughtfully, 'I could keep that well as a sort of priest's hole to hide in when annoying people like my mama come to call. Now . . . ,' she dusted her hands together in the brisk movement Caitlin had come to know well, 'we must get the walls whitewashed here and in the kitchen, and curtains made for the windows, and move Murdo Guthrie in.'

Rowena soon learned the way to the gatehouse. The school year had started again, and with Rose's ready permission Murdo continued to meet the little girl at the pend each morning and walk with her to school before settling down at his loom. Not that she needed to be shepherded to school any more, but after the shock of almost losing him, Rowena liked to confirm that he was still in Paisley at the start of each day. After school she walked down to the gatehouse instead of going back to Espedair Street and stayed with Murdo until Caitlin took her home.

Despite Rose's insistence that it cost very little to

house and employ Murdo, Caitlin had her suspicions, fuelled by Rose's bouts of unaccustomed silence and the worried frown that was beginning to sketch fine lines between her eyebrows, that all was not well financially. Caitlin had always been content to leave that side of the business to John, and then to Rose, but a week after the weaver moved in, she insisted on being shown the books.

Even she, with her rudimentary understanding of finance, could see that matters were becoming serious.

'I'll have to put in another order for materials soon, and how are we going to pay for it?' she asked. It took time to weave cloth, which would only be used for special orders anyway. They still had to buy almost all of their materials from the Glasgow warehouses.

Rose jutted out her chin. 'I shall write to John. He told me that his offer of investment still stood.'

'And his offer of marriage? Does that still stand?'

Rose bit her lip. 'As a matter of fact, it does.'

'You said that you couldn't take one without agreeing to the other.'

'I know what I said. And don't look at me like that, Caitlin. There's a lot to be said for being Mrs John Brodie.'

'If it's what you really want.'

'What I really want,' said Rose fiercely, 'is to keep Harlequin going.'

'At any cost?'

'There's no hardship in marrying John. He's a fine upstanding man and he knows how much this place means to me. He would never try to make me sit at home and hold tea parties and talk about how difficult servants can be.'

'We're talking about marriage, Rose, not a partnership.'

'A good marriage should be a partnership, and I shall have a good marriage with John,' Rose snapped, and left the room, refusing to discuss the matter further.

Caitlin went over the figures before her again, but they refused to change. She wished that Alex was only a train journey away in Glasgow, for it would have eased her mind to be able to talk over the situation with him. He was still training in England, and his letters to his mother tended to be brief, giving little information. Kirsty clung to the hope that he would be allowed home on furlough before being sent away, but as yet there had been no word of it. Nor had he replied, as yet, to the letter Caitlin had written, telling him about what had happened to Murdo.

That night, she sat at the kitchen table when the evening meal had been cleared away and wrote to him again.

The maid's mouth fell open when she opened the door. 'Mr Alex!'

'Good afternoon, Ellen. Is Mr MacDowall at home?'

'He's out for the evening, sir, but Mrs Chalmers has some friends in for dinner. They're in the drawing room at the moment.'

'I hope there's plenty to eat, for I'm very hungry. Perhaps I could just eat in the kitchen,' Alex began to suggest.

'Oh no, sir, Mrs Chalmers wouldn't like that, sir. She'd be ever so cross if she found out you were here and she hadn't been told!' Ellen's alarmed expression added, *I don't want to have to entertain the master's son in my private kitchen.*

'You're quite right. I'd best show my face,' Alex said with considerable regret.

The drawing room buzzed with animated conversation. It died when he walked in, and the half-dozen people in residence turned to stare at the figure in the doorway. Then Fiona ran forward, both hands outstretched. 'Alex! Oh, Alex!' She threw herself into his arms, and he held her awkwardly, aware of the heady scent of her usual perfume and aware, too, of the flash of jealousy in the grey eyes of the uniformed young man she had deserted to rush to him.

'Why didn't you let us know you were coming?' She pushed herself back from him, still holding his arms.

'I'd no knowledge of it myself until yesterday.'

'Where's your uniform?'

'I went straight to my flat and changed.'

'Oh, Alex! How could you deny us a sight of you in uniform?'

'Very easily. It's not in the least comfortable, nor does it fit me very well.'

Fiona pouted at him, then said, 'Papa's out for the evening.'

'So Ellen told me.'

'Come and meet my friends.' She turned back to the group by the fire, sliding her arm into his in a way he remembered vividly, and drawing him forward to meet them, announcing proudly as she did so, 'This is my very dear half-brother, Alex MacDowall, home from the war!'

All Alex could think about as he shook hands with a clutch of men and women he had never seen before was that his stomach was in imminent danger of proclaiming its emptiness with a loud rumble.

'Fiona's brother, eh?' The young man in the uniform of a captain of the Royal Scots Fusiliers shook his hand heartily, clearly relieved that Alex wasn't a rival.

'Half-brother.'

'On furlough?'

'For four days.'

'Expect to be travelling across the water soon?' he asked. Alex nodded. 'I'm not long back from France myself. Which lot are you with?'

'The Argyll and Sutherland Highlanders. A private,' Alex added deliberately. He had begun to find a perverse pleasure in seeing officers' lips curl, as this man's were doing at that very moment, when they discovered that they were in the presence of the lower ranks.

To his great relief, Ellen announced dinner just then, and Fiona claimed Alex. 'Walk into the dining room with me,' she demanded, and the captain's cold eyes grew even colder. Alex, placed between two young women, was content at first to concentrate on his food and leave the others to chatter. When he did take time to listen, the talk was so boring that he tuned it out again.

Fiona occupied her father's seat at the head of the table, bestowing most of her attention on the Royal Scots captain to her right. The overbodice of her yellow-and-brown-striped dress led the beholder's eye from her creamy neck to a gold silk rosette at her trim waist, which was snug in a brown velvet cummerbund that matched her eyes perfectly.

After dinner the others played cards while Alex prowled the room restlessly, wishing that his father would come home. But Angus had still not returned when the guests left.

'Did Harlequin make your gown?' he asked when Fiona came back into the drawing room after seeing them off.

'How observant you are. Yes, they did.' One beringed

hand smoothed her skirt, gathered in soft folds at the knee in front, then falling to a scalloped hem that just revealed her slim ankles. 'Isn't it lovely? Your sister is very talented.'

'How is George?'

The fingers of her right hand automatically flew to the handsome diamond and sapphire engagement ring and the broad gold wedding band that George Chalmers had given her. 'Very well, as far as I know.'

'You must miss him a great deal.' Alex was on the couch at one side of the fireplace; when Fiona eyed the cushions beside him he turned slightly, stretching his legs out towards the fire and blocking any thought she might have had of sitting by his side. She took the seat opposite. 'It's fortunate that you have . . . friends like Captain Gibney to comfort you.'

She coloured. 'Martin Gibney is the brother of a dear friend of mine, nothing more!'

'Indeed. I believe that Murdo Guthrie has been dismissed.'

As he had intended, she was taken aback by the sudden change of subject. 'Who?'

'The weaver we employed in Paisley.'

'Oh, that Highland man who never had a word to say for himself? We decided that we couldn't really afford him.'

'We?'

She shrugged. 'I decided.'

'Does Father know that you turned the man off?'

Fiona smiled across the carpet at him, a small, malicious smile. 'Things have changed since you left, Alex. I know that Papa had decided to leave the house to me and the business to you, since you are his son and I'm only his daughter and he believes that women know nothing about business. But he's quite wrong;

women can deal with business just as well as men, and it's my view that Papa needs one of us on hand. So I've taken over some of the less important business matters, although, of course, I confer with him before making final decisions.'

'But he usually lets you have your own way.'

'Usually.'

'Murdo Guthrie cost MacDowall and Son very little, Fiona.'

'But probably more than it costs to simply buy in the small amount of material we need. I really don't see why you're making such a fuss over one man, Alex.'

'I'm making a fuss, as you put it, because I installed him in Paisley myself, and I introduced the use of specially woven cloth in our furniture. It was a factor that pleased many of our clients.'

'And you introduced hand-painted furniture too, but now that you're in the army that side of the business has had to go into abeyance. We must cut our cloth to suit our purse, Alex.'

'And now we have to buy the cloth first instead of having it woven,' he said dryly.

She shrugged the matter aside. 'Have you visited your mother yet?'

'I came straight to Glasgow. I'll see her tomorrow.'

Fiona's eyes narrowed. 'Then how did you know that the weaver had been dismissed?'

'Caitlin told me in a letter. Fortunately she and Rose Hamilton have offered him work and moved his loom to Harlequin.'

She shrugged, a movement that momentarily raised the upper curves of her breasts over the low-cut underbodice. 'So you've no need to worry about him,' she said. Then, with a hint of malice, she added, 'I thought you would have rushed straight to

Paisley to thank your friend Rose for rescuing your protégé.'

'I will, tomorrow.'

'Do give her my regards. She's a fascinating woman, don't you think?'

'I admire her compassion, and her sense of honour,' he said deliberately, and two angry spots of colour flared over Fiona's cheekbones.

'So, do you intend to run to Papa to complain about the high-handed way I've treated your favourite employee?'

'I haven't decided yet.'

Fiona got up and with an angry flounce walked to the window. 'Who owns that loom?' she asked after a pause.

'My mother, and my great-grandfather before her. So you can't claim it back as MacDowall property, Fiona. Such a pity.'

'Indeed.' She turned and came back to stand over him. 'But I can make life difficult for your stepfather if you keep trying to anger me,' she said, her voice suddenly venomous.

Alex leaned forward, all his pleasure at teasing her gone. 'You try that, Fiona, and you'll be very sorry!'

'My dear, what can you do about it? You'll be too far away to trouble me.'

It was perhaps as well that Angus MacDowall arrived home just then, his normally sombre face lighting up at the sight of his son.

Fiona went to bed soon after, leaving the two men to talk late into the night over a bottle of whisky.

'You'll have heard that Fiona's taken some of the burden of running the business from my shoulders during your absence?' Angus asked eventually.

'She said something about it.'

'She's surprised me in the past week, Alex. I'd never have thought that my daughter would have such a wise head on her shoulders. She's good with the staff as well as the clients. And having something to do keeps her contented, which is the main thing.'

Alex took a long drink of whisky and said nothing.

21

Alex spent the following morning at the emporium and the factory, where the supervisor seemed to have everything running smoothly. He had lunch with his father before catching the train to Paisley, where he went first to the shop. He was cheered to encounter Aggie, the old dressmaker's dummy, in her usual place on the pavement, chained to the wall so that no passing youths could whisk her away. Today she wore a high-necked pale blue blouse with frills round the neck and the three-quarter-length sleeves and a dark-grey serge skirt with a blue sash tied round her ample waistline.

Alex gave her an affectionate pat, feeling that as long as Aggie stood sentry in Causeyside Street, nothing too terrible could happen to his world.

Jean, busy behind the counter, gave such a scream when he walked in that the woman she was serving jumped a good six inches into the air and another customer browsing through the pattern books on their stand spun round and knocked the lot down.

'You near frighted the life out of me,' Jean squawked, rushing round the end of the counter. He barely had time to drop his bag to the ground before she threw her skinny arms about him. 'Where did you spring from? Does your ma know you're home?'

'I thought I'd surprise her.' He hugged her, then squatted to gather up the pattern books.

'Do me a favour, son,' the customer by the counter advised, her hand over her heaving bosom. 'Make it a gentle surprise. Ye just put ten years on me!'

Kirsty and Teenie were so busy that the thunder of their sewing machines had drowned out the commotion beyond the curtained doorway. Teenie saw him first and slammed her hand hard on her wheel to stop it. Any other woman would have taken the skin from her palm on the racing wheel or had her fingers jerked from their sockets, but Teenie, who knew what she was doing, hung on, although she was almost jerked out of her seat before the wheel stopped.

'What's amiss?' Kirsty, working with her back to Alex, peered up at her friend, letting her own machine whir to a halt more slowly. Teenie's eyes were like saucers, and when she tried to speak her mouth opened and shut like the trout Alex had once guddled for in the burns up in the braes as a youth. Speechless, she pointed, and Kirsty twisted round in her chair, then came out of it with a rush that took her straight into her son's arms.

'Alex! Oh, Alex!' She laughed and cried and hugged him and clutched at him as if trying to convince herself that he was really there. Teenie clasped her hands and twittered like a nest of birds, and Jean, who came in as soon as she had disposed of her customers, stood beaming, tears in her eyes.

'When did you get here? How long do you have? Are you staying the night?' The questions poured out of Kirsty when she finally released him from her grip.

'I came from England yesterday and stayed the night at my place in Glasgow. I've to start back to the camp

244

tomorrow morning, but I'll sleep in Espedair Street tonight, if there's room.'

'There's always room for you, son, you know that.' She mopped her eyes with her apron then said with a half-laugh, half-sob, 'Will you look at me, crying like daft bairn. It's the surprise that's done it.'

'A woman's got the right to have a good greet when her son comes back from the wars, hen,' Jean assured her friend. 'I'll away and put the kettle on.'

Alex would rather have gone straight to Espedair Street to see Todd and find out what had been going on in his absence, but Jean and Teenie were so thrilled to see him, and so full of questions, that he stayed for a while, drinking a mug of strong tea sweetened with condensed milk and telling them about the training camp.

'What happens when you go back?' Kirsty asked anxiously.

'I don't know, Mam. They'll probably move us out now that our training's over.'

The three women looked at him with frightened eyes. 'Will you be going abroad?'

'Probably,' he said reluctantly, then, at the panic in his mother's face, he added, 'I'll be fine. It'll take more than a few enemy soldiers to best me.'

Jean reached out to clasp one of Kirsty's hands. 'He's right,' she comforted. 'Alex knows how tae look after himself.'

'Mam, Caitlin wrote to tell me what happened to Murdo Guthrie,' he said as they walked to Espedair Street, Kirsty clinging to his arm.

'She told us she had. Poor lad, it was a sad business, but there was nothing Todd could do to help him.'

'I know that.'

'We offered him a home in the loom shop, but he'd

have none of it. Rose was grand, though, having the gatehouse cleaned out so that he could work there.'

'It was good of you to let them move the loom.'

'It was the least I could do for him. I always thought Fiona MacDowall to be a nice lassie,' Kirsty said after a pause, 'but it wasn't kind, what she did to Murdo. He never did anyone any harm, and though I wasn't altogether happy about Rowena taking to the man so much at the beginning, he's been grand with her.'

They had reached the pend; when they had walked through it she gave him a push in the direction of the workshop. 'Away and give Todd a surprise,' she urged, 'then come to the house.'

She hated to be away from him for a single second of the short time he had in Paisley, but she was also glad of the chance to get indoors on her own so that she could have a good weep and get it over with in private. By the time she had finished and washed her face and patted some flour round her eyes in an attempt to disguise their redness Mary and Rowena had come home.

'Away down to the workshop and see who's there.'

Mary looked at her mother blankly, then her eyes widened. 'It's not—' She stopped abruptly, glanced at Rowena, then turning so that the child couldn't see her face, she mouthed the word, 'Ewan?'

'God save us, of course not!' Even Kirsty had given up all hope of seeing Ewan at her door.

'It's Alex?'

'Of course it is.'

'Come on, Rowena,' Mary caught the little girl's hand. 'Come and see Uncle Alex!'

By the time her family had returned from the workshop, Todd wearing a broad grin, Kirsty had the preparations for the evening meal well in hand. Mary

246

started Rowena on her homework, then began to help her mother.

'When's Caitlin due home?' Alex asked.

'She's working on tonight,' Mary said. 'That's why I fetched Rowena from the gatehouse.'

'I think I'll just take a stroll down to the fashion house and have a word with Murdo.'

'Mind and get home in time for your dinner,' Kirsty called after him as he went out.

He stopped at the gatehouse first. Murdo Guthrie opened the door to him, beaming when he saw who the visitor was. 'Mr MacDowall, you're back home.'

'Only for a day or two, Murdo. I thought I'd look in to see your new place.'

With a certain pride, Murdo showed him the loom shop, with a stretch of cloth on the rollers bearing the pine-cone pattern made world famous by Paisley shawls the century before.

'Caitlin was always anxious for you to weave cloth for her, so she'll be pleased now that it's happening.' Alex followed the weaver into the kitchen, where something simmered in a pot on the range. 'I didn't mean to break into preparations for your evening meal.'

Murdo lifted the lid and gave the pot's contents a quick stir. 'There's enough for two if you'd care to join me.'

'I've to go back to Espedair Street for my dinner. Are you contented here, Murdo?'

The man ducked his head in a quick nod. 'I wasn't certain at first that I should accept Miss Hamilton's offer, but I want to stay in Paisley. There's nowhere else I can call home,' he added with not a trace of self-pity in his voice.

'I'm glad you did accept, for you're as good as one of the family now and we'd have worried if you had disappeared, especially Rowena.' Alex held out his hand.

'She's a good bairn,' the other man said as he clasped it. 'She keeps me in mind of what might have been.'

'I thought you'd want to forget that.'

'A man should never forget his past,' Murdo said gravely as he accompanied his former employer to the door, 'for it shapes his future.'

Caitlin, working on a sheet of paper in the design office, threw herself into his arms when he walked in. 'Alex – I'm so glad you're back!'

'Only until tomorrow, but I've said I'll stay the night in Espedair Street.' He held her at arm's length so that he could study her. 'You look bonny, and successful.'

'I've never been busier or happier. You've seen Murdo?'

'I have. It was good of you to give him work and a place to stay.'

'It was Rose who thought of it, and I'm glad she did, for I've always wanted our own woven cloth. You got my letter?'

'I did, and I'm glad you told me what Fiona was up to. Not that I can do anything about it, having to go back to England tomorrow night. But at least I know that Murdo's found a safe haven for the time being.'

She was searching his face. 'Did you mind me asking about the money?'

'What money?'

'The investment we need for Harlequin.'

He frowned down at her, puzzled. 'You never mentioned money in your letter about Murdo.'

'You didn't get my other letter, about Harlequin running short of money and Rose agreeing to marry John?'

His face went suddenly blank, as it always did when

he received a shock. 'No.' He guided her into a chair and then perched on the edge of the desk. 'You'd better tell me what you're talking about.'

As Caitlin explained about the cost of renovating the gatehouse's lower floor, the investment John had promised and the proposal of marriage that Rose had turned down, he listened without comment. When she had finished, he asked, 'And has she written to him?'

'I don't know. But I thought that if you could invest some money in Harlequin – if you were willing – it would be better than Rose agreeing to marry John. She's very fond of him,' Caitlin hastened to add, 'but I know she's putting Harlequin before her own wishes . . .' Her voice trailed away as Rose burst into the room.

'Caitlin, where's—' she began, then stopped abruptly, still clutching the door handle, as Alex jumped to his feet and turned to face her. The colour fled from her face then returned in a rosy tide. Caitlin closed the sketchbook she had been working on and reached for her jacket. 'I'd best get home. I'll see you there later, Alex.'

He nodded, his eyes on Rose. 'Tell Mam I'll be there directly.' Then, as the outer door closed behind Caitlin, he asked Rose, 'D'you happen to have any of that fine malt your father gave you?'

Rose swallowed, then said calmly, 'There's some left.'

He watched as she crossed to the corner cupboard. He could hear the neck of the bottle clattering softly against the tumbler as she poured the whisky, and as she brought the drink to him he saw that a tremor in her hand made the amber liquid tremble. It was only when he took the glass from her that he realised that his hand, too, was shaking.

'Thank you.'

She nodded, and went back to the cupboard to pour whisky into a second tumbler. 'I didn't know you were in Paisley,' she said, her back to him.

'I'm on furlough, just till tomorrow.'

'Does that mean that you're going to be sent abroad?'

'I don't know yet. Probably.'

She had only put enough drink into her own glass to moisten her lips. She swallowed it down in one draught then crossed to sit behind the desk Caitlin had been working at. 'Sit down.'

He sat on the edge of a small armchair. 'I hear that John Brodie enlisted.'

'Not long after you left.' She was wearing a dark green skirt and a high-necked pink blouse with three-quarter-length sleeves tight to just above the elbows, then spilling in a loose frill halfway down her forearms. She looked tired; there were violet shadows beneath her vivid blue eyes and strands of hair had come loose from the knot at the back of her head to fall in soft ringlets about her cheeks. To his surprise, Alex discovered that he was having to fight back the desire to tuck the curls back and smooth the weariness from her face.

'You'll be missing him,' he said instead.

'I miss his ability to deal with ledgers. I don't have that gift.'

'But you always kept the books for the shop, surely.'

'They weren't as complicated as Harlequin's, and John was always there to fall back on.'

A sudden mental picture of Rose falling back into John Brodie's welcoming, cushioning arms turned the taste of good whisky sour in Alex's mouth. 'I looked in on Murdo Guthrie on my way. He seems very comfortable.'

'I believe he's settled in well enough.'

'It was good of you to assist him when he lost his position with MacDowalls'.'

She looked at him searchingly. 'Did you know that it was going to happen?'

'I did not! It came as a shock when Caitlin wrote to tell me. It was Fiona's doing – she has my father wrapped about her little finger, and at the moment there's little I can do about it.'

'She has a gift for wrapping men about that little finger,' Rose said dryly, and he felt colour rush into his face.

'Until they find out the truth about her,' he said stiffly, and a hand flew to her mouth.

'I didn't mean . . . I forgot that you and she had . . .' She stopped, then said formally, 'I'm sorry, Alex, I shouldn't have said that.'

'It's all in the past now.' He leaned forward, elbows on knees. 'About Murdo, it must have cost you to get the old gatehouse habitable for him, not to mention his wages.'

'He takes very little, since he can live rent-free now.'

'Even so, I'd like to make a contribution.'

'There's no need.'

'I'm the man who brought Murdo to Paisley in the first place, and I feel responsible for the way my half-sister has treated him. At least let me show my appreciation for what you and Caitlin have done for him.' He took out his cheque book and moved purposefully to the desk.

'If you insist.' Rose relinquished the chair to him and moved restlessly about the room while he wrote the cheque and blotted it before handing it to her.

'I'll give you a receipt, of . . .' She broke off, staring

down at the slip of paper, then said, 'This is far too much. I . . . We can't possibly accept it!'

'Look on it as an investment, if you prefer.'

'I can't accept it,' she repeated. 'I won't.'

'You would if I was John Brodie.'

'What has John got to do with it?'

'For God's sake, Rose, we've known each other for too long to play games. You had to spend money in order to save Murdo, and it was money that Harlequin could ill afford. It makes more sense for me to replace it than John.'

Her face was white now, her eyes dazzling in their anger. 'What has Caitlin been telling you?'

'That Brodie offered to invest money into the business, – money that you need badly, – and you refused because he also asked you to marry him. She also told me that now Harlequin is in such a precarious situation you've decided to take up John's offer – both his offers.'

'That,' Rose told him icily, 'is my business. It has nothing to do with you or Caitlin.'

'If it concerns Harlequin it's Caitlin's business as much as yours, and if you're being forced to take steps you don't want to take just because of your compassion towards Murdo Guthrie, then it's my business.'

'You make marriage to John sound like a fate worse than death!'

'It could be, if you don't go into it with all your heart. Is that fair to him, or to you?'

'I adore John Brodie!' Rose stormed at him.

'Then marry the man, with my blessing,' Alex shot back at her. 'But at least get rid of your financial concerns first. Don't just sell yourself to him.'

'That's a disgusting thing to say!'

'It's a disgusting thing to do, especially to a man who cares for you as much as he does.'

She stared at him, white to the lips, then tore the cheque into shreds, tossing the pieces on the ground between them. Alex immediately returned to the chair and began writing out a second cheque, the pen biting into the paper.

'I won't take it!'

'You will.'

'Why should I accept a penny from you?'

'Because we both understand business. I know a good investment when I see one, and after all you've done for Harlequin you're not going to be daft enough to throw away the chance to stay solvent.' Once again he blotted the cheque, then he added, 'And because I care about what happens to you.'

'Care?' Rose asked scathingly. 'Is it caring to go off to join the army without a word?'

'I didn't tell anyone until just before I went.'

'You didn't tell me at all!'

'I waited for an hour in your father's shrubbery for you to come home on that bicycle of yours, but you didn't arrive because you had gone out with John.'

'You didn't write.'

'Because you didn't write to me.'

'Because you'd gone off without—'

'Rose, I've learned two things in the past few weeks apart from how to march and hold a rifle and shoot it,' Alex interrupted, suddenly tired of pretence. 'One is that when life's as uncertain as mine is right now, only the important things matter. And the other is that I love you more than I will ever love any other woman – though God alone knows why. That's why I want to help you.' He got to his feet and picked up his hat.

'Caitlin will give you the cheque in the morning, when your temper has had a chance to cool.'

'Alex . . .' She said when he had reached the door. He turned, his fingers on the handle. 'Don't go.'

He crossed to her, and reached out to her and knew the physical pleasure of smoothing her hair back and kissing the shadows from beneath her eyes. And, finally, he knew the ecstasy of kissing her lips and holding her, and knowing that at last he had found out who he really was and where he belonged.

22

The evening meal, which Kirsty had delayed until the rest of the family began to complain, was long past when Alex finally came through the back door.

'Sorry, Mam, I got on the crack with Murdo and the time just ran by before I knew it.'

'As long as you're here now. I've kept your dinner hot for you.' It had long since dried up, but he wolfed it down as though he hadn't eaten for a week, finally pushing the plate back with a satisfied sigh. 'Nobody cooks like you, Mam!'

'Away with you,' Kirsty said, delighted. Todd had fetched in bottles of beer, and some lemonade for the womenfolk, and they sat late into the night for once, talking and reminiscing but never mentioning the future. Once or twice, when Caitlin caught Alex's eye, he winked at her; there was no opportunity to get him on his own to find out what had transpired between him and Rose after she had left the fashion house, but she was certain, from the sparkle in his eyes and his ready laugh, that the two of them had finally settled their differences.

Kirsty was tearful when he left immediately after breakfast, clinging to him until he had to ease himself free of her embrace.

'I must go, Mam. My uniform's in my Glasgow flat and I have to change into it before I catch the train south.'

'You'll take care of yourself?'

'I'll take very good care,' he promised, adding, as his gaze met Caitlin's over his mother's head, 'for I've got a lot to come back to after this business is over.'

Rose was later than usual; when she finally came in it was to find Caitlin gathering up scraps of paper from the design room floor and studying them with a puzzled frown.

'This has got Alex's writing on it,' she said when her partner arrived, 'and so has this bit. Look, there's part of his name.'

'It's just some scribbles.' Rose plucked the shreds from Caitlin's fingers and tossed them hurriedly into the wastepaper basket by the desk.

'It looked to me like pieces of a cheque.'

'As a matter of fact, he did invest some money in Harlequin.' Rose produced the slip of paper from her bag and handed it over. Caitlin's eyes opened wide. 'This is enough to make him a partner!'

'He doesn't want to be, at least not yet.'

'What happened to the other one, the pieces on the floor?'

'He made a mistake while he was writing it,' Rose said airily.

'So you won't be asking John to invest money in Harlequin after all?'

'There's no need, thanks to Alex's generosity.'

'Giving money away seems to suit him,' Caitlin observed. 'He was glowing like a street lamp when he came home last night.'

'Was he?' Rose concentrated all her attention on

taking off her hat and stabbing the long pins into it before hanging it up.

'You're doing a bit of glowing yourself.' The previous evening's weariness had vanished from Rose's face and had been replaced by a sparkle in her eyes and pretty colour in her cheeks.

'It's riding my bike that does it – all that fresh air.'

'Mmmm,' Caitlin said, and left it at that, but as she went upstairs to start work she envied Rose and Alex. It must be a grand feeling, she thought, to love someone with all your heart and to be loved in return.

When the ceilidhs began again in the autumn, Rowena clamoured to be taken to them. Mary needed little urging, for it meant that she could spend time with Lachie, and Caitlin, who had begun to love the gatherings and the music, was happy to return to the Gaelic church hall.

Rowena had become something of a celebrity among the Highlanders. Her dancing lessons and the hours of practice she put in had developed her natural skill, and she often danced on her own in the midst of an admiring circle of adults and children. She was happy to do it, too. Watching her spin and twirl and step around the floor, hands tucked in at her waist or poised lightly above her head, Caitlin marvelled at the confidence that dancing had brought to the stormy rebel who had once insisted on sitting beneath the kitchen table or in a corner of the room.

Fewer people attended the ceilidhs now, since most of the young men had gone and the dancers mainly consisted of women, children and older men. One young couple who had always been among the first to take the floor was no longer to be seen; the man, Mhairi whispered to Caitlin and Mary, had been among thousands killed during the assault on Gallipoli, and his young widow had left Paisley to stay with relatives in Inverness.

'Folk she scarcely knows, but they're all the kin she has now and she couldnae stay here with the memories of Colin. Like the rest of us, they had to come south because there was work to be had here.'

Murdo and the other musicians struck up a lively tune, and Lachie immediately arrived to claim Mary as his partner.

'Did Colin and his wife come from Inverness?' Caitlin asked when her sister had been whirled onto the dance floor. Mhairi shook her white head.

'They're from the Black Isle, like me and Murdo. Have you ever seen the place, lassie? Oh, it's beautiful, just! It was because Murdo knew Colin and Peggy and me from there that he went to Glasgow when the army freed him. It was good that he found work right here in Paisley after a time, for it comforted him a little to be near folk from his own place. And now there's only me and him left.'

'Murdo Guthrie was in the army?' Caitlin asked, astonished.

'Did you not know that? I suppose there was no reason why you should, for it's not a time that he'd care to speak about, poor man.'

Mary danced by with Lachie, still too young to enlist and impatiently counting the months until his sixteenth birthday.

'If he was a soldier, why hasn't he gone back to it now we're at war?' Caitlin wanted to know, and Mhairi sucked breath in sharply through her teeth, making a hissing sound.

'After what they did to him? He'll not go until he

has to, and there isn't a soul here who blames him, not even the lads that have already gone.'

To Caitlin's annoyance, a stout middle-aged man claimed her as his partner at that point. It was a dance she knew, so her feet followed the music automatically, and her mouth smiled at her partner, but her mind was fixed on Mhairi's words. Alex must have known about Murdo's army days, but had not told her.

As soon as she could, she rejoined Mhairi, but by that time she was chatting to someone else, and Caitlin had to bide her time until after the interval before she got the old woman to herself again.

'You were telling me about Murdo—'

'I was mebbe talking out of turn, lassie, for it's his story to tell, not mine. But at the same time,' Mhairi leaned closer and peered into her face, 'mebbe you should know, for you've been kind to him, and you care for him.'

'Yes, I do,' Caitlin heard herself say, and realised with sudden shock that she was speaking the truth. 'I do,' she repeated slowly, and Mhairi nodded.

'I thought so. I hoped so, for he needs someone to care for him, though he'd never expect it, or even seek it. But that's all part of his sorrow.' She patted Caitlin's hand. 'Well now, it was when work was scarce just before the turn of the century that Murdo went off to join the army – not because he wanted to leave his home but because he'd a family to support.'

The room swayed around Caitlin, then steadied. 'Murdo had a wife?'

'Of course he did.' Mhairi gave an amused chuckle. 'D'you think a fine-looking young man like that would be single? If I'd been nearer his age, I'd have set my cap at him myself – not that Elspeth ever chased after him, for they'd had an understanding since they were wee bairns together. Murdo was a different laddie then, full of laughter and hope for what was still to come.'

Mhairi's eyes were dreamy as she looked back into the past. 'I mind the ceilidh we had when he and Elspeth were wed – it was grand! Then just nine months later the wee laddie was born, the spit of his father. They named him Dougald. Then the work got scarce, so several of the young men went into the army together, Murdo and Colin among them. They were sent to South Africa to fight against the Boers there. It was while Murdo was far away that his wee laddie got drowned playing in a burn by himself. He hadnae long since learned to run about, and he was full of mischief, just like his father.' Tears filled her pale-blue eyes at the memory. 'There was no consoling poor Elspeth; she got it lodged in her mind that the blame of it was hers, though it never was. I mind Murdo's own mother worrying about him when he was that age because he was so adventurous. Not long after the bairn went, Elspeth took a chill, and since her love for life had gone with her wee laddie, the chill went into pneumonia and she died of it.'

The music stopped, then started again, a slow sad air that suited the story Caitlin was hearing.

'Word had been sent to Murdo when the bairn was lost, and again when Elspeth followed him, but seemingly the army refused to let him come home, so he took matters into his own hands.'

'He deserted?'

'That's what they called it when they caught him. But what man wouldn't try to get home at a time like that?'

'What happened to him?'

'Oh, they put him on trial, then into an English prison for some years. By the time he came out, his mother had passed away and there was nobody left for him to go home to, so he came to join us in Paisley. And now,' said Mhairi, 'he's determined that he'll not fight for the King or any other man until he must, and who could blame him for it?'

'I wouldn't.'

'You'll not let him know that I told you, lassie, for he's a proud man and the last thing he'd want is anyone's pity.' Again, Mhairi laid a hand on Caitlin's. 'I only said because it seems to me that someone should know.'

Mary and Lachie went off together, as had become their habit, as soon as the ceilidh ended, while Murdo escorted Caitlin and Rowena back to Espedair Street. Rowena, still fired with excitement, ran on ahead, whirling out of sight at street corners then sticking her head round to see where the adults were. As sometimes happened now that he was working for Harlequin, Murdo talked about the cloth he was weaving and asked about Caitlin's plans for future designs. Tonight, her head buzzing with the story she had just been told, she found it hard to concentrate on work.

When, as always happened at some point, Rowena's energy suddenly ran out, she came back to walk between them both, holding their hands, leaning more and more heavily on them until the Highlander finally swung her up against his shoulder, where she fell asleep almost at once. Caitlin, loitering a step or two behind, watched his broad back as he strode along, trying to picture the younger man Mhairi had described to her, laughing and carefree, with a small boy's head in place of Rowena's tucked trustingly into the hollow of his neck and shoulder and a shadowy unknown woman by his side, her arm touching his.

*   *   *

'What was Mhairi saying to you last night?' Mary wanted to know over the breakfast table.

'Nothing in particular.'

'It didn't look like nothing. She was talking away, and your eyes were like saucers.'

'She was just telling me about something that had happened to her when she was younger,' Caitlin said firmly, and would say no more.

September brought heavy rain in France, or perhaps it was Belgium; geography had never been Alex MacDowall's strong point at school, and he had long since lost any sense of direction. To tired men one trench seemed much the same as another, and the same went for the enforced marches along country roads, through lanes deeply rutted from cart and wagon wheels, past the skeletons of trees stripped of their branches and leaves by shelling or destroyed by fire, and sometimes past worse sights than devastated countryside without hope.

Occasionally on their marches they had come on villages or solitary farmhouses long since deserted by their original occupants and pounded to ruins by heavy artillery from the Allies or the Germans. Sometimes, when a halt had been called, shelter of a sort had been found among the walls still standing.

Now, wedged into a trench hacked out from the clay, with a constant drizzle of rain descending from the low grey clouds above, Alex looked back enviously on those moments he and his comrades had spent in ruined buildings, with the stone walls and partial, sagging roofs providing some shelter from the elements and the opportunity, if sufficient timber could be found nearby, of a fire to huddle round.

Somewhere close by machine guns were chattering

nervously, accompanied by the frequent dull thump of heavy artillery. Today, the worst of the fighting was somewhere to the west of the trench where Alex stood on duty. Thankful for small mercies, he rested one shoulder against the wet clay wall and set his mind to what had become one of his favourite pastimes these days, designing and decorating furniture for the house he hoped, one day, to share with Rose.

The daydream had first come to him on the ship bringing him and his mates over from Britain, as a way of taking his mind off what was to come. It had started as a single room, but as the days dragged by and life became more confusing, frightening and fragile, the house had grown until now it was the size of his father's. If this bloody war didn't end soon, Alex thought with a grim smile, he would soon find himself mentally working on Buckingham Palace.

By the time his relief came splashing along, Alex was stiff with cold.

'Fuckin' hell,' the man said, squinting up at the lowering sky and blinking the raindrops away. 'It's not just the Almighty pissin' on us today, he's got the whole band of bloody angels at it too.' He stuffed a cigarette into his mouth and searched his pockets for a packet of Lucifers. 'Cup o' cocoa waitin' for you back there, you lucky bastard.'

Icy rainwater, yellow from the clay, had gathered almost ankle deep in the trench, splashing over Alex's puttees as he trudged back to the dugout he knew as home these days, round corners, up earthen steps, along again and down more steps. Some men had managed to gather together timber to make doors for their dugouts, others had scrounged real doors from derelict buildings, but a tarpaulin was all the privacy that Alex and the handful of men he shared with had.

The floor was wet in here too, but at least it wasn't raining. He dropped his kit into a corner, sloughed off his raincoat and rummaged among his possessions for his precious towel.

'You'd think we'd all be dead of pneumonia, living like this,' he said as he scrubbed the worst of the rain from his face, hair and neck.

'Death by pneumonia isn't allowed in the British Army, pal,' a man stretched out on one of the camp beds said laconically. 'Cocoa in the jug if you want it. I'd've made tea, but we're out of Darjeeling and the missus just wouldnae go out into the rain tae buy more. Anyway, a passin' rat asked tae borrow the lemon slices and I didnae have the heart tae refuse it.'

'Cocoa'll do me fine.' It tasted like nectar, and it was still hot enough to spread some warmth through his limbs. Alex settled down on his camp bed and unfastened his tunic, pulling a small bundle of letters from an inside pocket. He knew them off by heart but rereading them was his greatest joy. Caitlin, his mother and Rose were regular correspondents, while his father wrote once every fortnight. Angus MacDowall's letters tended to be dry single-paged missives, mainly concerning business, but Alex treasured them as much as the others, knowing that his father felt more comfortable with ledgers and invoices than letters.

Kirsty's letters, too, were fairly short, her fears for Alex and her determination not to voice them almost leaping from the pages. Caitlin, on the other hand, wrote freely and with confidence about her everyday life, the ceilidhs and the walks up the braes with Rowena and Murdo and, sometimes, Mary and Lachie, and she wrote with news of Harlequin. Now and then she included a note from Mary, mainly about her work in the jam factory.

He always kept Rose's letters till last. She wrote as she tended to speak, in short no-nonsense sentences, telling him amusing stories about Harlequin and about herself and her parents; but always, towards the end of each letter, came the section written from her heart for his eyes only. He read each letter thoroughly, word by word, then put them carefully away before lying back, hands behind his head, returning in mind if not in body to that evening in the design office when he and Rose had finally stopped sparring and faced the truth about themselves. It had been a long time in coming, but as she had said in several letters, it had been all the sweeter for the delay.

He recalled the taste of her skin and her mouth, and the sheer, unexpected femininity of her. He remembered how he had waited on the pavement by the station steps the next morning and how Rose had come careering down the street on her bicycle just as his train had been signalled, skidding to a halt and wrestling it across the pavement. He had taken it from her and carried it down the steps, propping it against the wall, then, suddenly nervous, had turned to see that she was equally hesitant.

'Did it really happen?' she had asked. 'Did we really . . . ?' And when he'd nodded she had launched herself into his arms, heedless of the folk on the platform.

'Let's not tell anyone,' she had said as he leaned his head through the open carriage window. 'Not until you come back. Just in case we change our minds.'

'We won't!'

'I know we won't,' she had said, running alongside the train as it gathered speed.

He fell asleep smiling at the memory, and almost immediately a hand shook him awake for his next spell of duty. Outside it was dark, but the rain was still there, and so were the machine guns and heavy artillery. The night above was frequently shattered by brilliant white star-shell flashes, and now and again the entire sky seemed to burst into scarlet flame as a bomb or a land mine exploded. As Alex took up his position again, there was a sudden commotion further up the trench.

'Some bloody idiot decided tae have a look tae see what was happenin',' he was told by a soldier hurrying past. 'A sniper took his face off, stupid bugger. Now they'll all start aimin' at us.'

A stretcher party went by at a run, returning some time later with their burden. A sheet had been tossed over the body. As they went by the light from a star shell showed that over the area where the man's head should have been the sheet was defiled by a great wet splash of crimson.

As the soldier had prophesied, the enemy's attention suddenly focused on their section of the trench, and for several days their eardrums rang to the constant chatter and thud of machine guns and artillery as well as the crack of rifles. They went over the top in an attempt to gain ground, running through mud and jumping over barbed wire cut by an advance party, but the heavy artillery hadn't destroyed the enemy after all, and the German lines held firm, forcing those still on their feet to retreat to their trenches.

After listening all day to the cries of the wounded who hadn't managed to get back, they had to go back out at night, falling into water-filled craters, tramping in the dark over dead men and scrabbling in the mud for wounded they could drag back to precarious safety.

It seemed to go on for ever, but at last it was their turn to be relieved and marched back behind the lines to rest for a few days in a makeshift tent village.

Crowded in with a dozen other men, Alex slept for a full twenty-four hours and awoke starving. He made himself take time to shave and to bathe in a tin hip bath, which brought back nostalgic memories of the proper bathrooms with proper baths in Espedair Street, his father's house and his own flat. Then he put on fresh clothing and walked to the mess tent, where he ate until his stomach felt as though it was about to burst. Unlike most Scots, he hadn't taken up the cigarette habit until now. Since enlisting, he had come to appreciate the comfort of tobacco. He fetched a second cup of coffee and lit a cigarette, drawing the smoke deep into his lungs.

A noisy group of Australians sat at the next table; he glanced at them, then looked again as the man facing him whipped off his distinctive wide-brimmed hat, pinned up at one side, and waved it in the air to illustrate the final line of his story. For a moment Alex stared at the familiar rugged features beneath short-cropped brown hair, then he leaped to his feet, pushing past a group of men walking between the two tables. He put his hand on the other man's shoulder, stopping him in midsentence.

'Ewan?'

Ewan Lennox turned, brows furrowed at the interruption, and blinked up at his stepbrother.

'Christ, Alex,' he said. 'A fellow can't get away from his family anywhere!'

23

'D'you know what you've put Rowena through, sending her to Paisley on her own and leaving her there without a word?'

Ewan shrugged and took a mouthful of beer. They had found a table in a corner of the big mess tent, away from the worst of the noise. 'She's all right, isn't she? I knew Mam and Dad would look after her, and I couldn't take her with me.'

'Ewan, your father died not all that long after you . . . went away.' Part of Alex wanted to throttle Ewan for all the misery he had caused, but at the same time he knew that now that he had made contact with the man he had to handle the situation fairly cautiously for fear of losing him again before he had heard his story.

Ewan took the news of his father's death calmly. 'That's too bad, but he was in a pretty poor way when I last saw him. Mam's still at the house?'

'Yes. She married Todd Paget a few years after she was widowed.'

Ewan stared, then threw back his head and roared with laughter. 'That's rich,' he gasped when he began to sober up. 'Me and Beth run off together just before she was supposed to marry Todd, then Mam marries

268

him instead. Beth'd love that one – if I only knew where she was.'

'She's still alive, then?'

Ewan took another deep drink. 'As far as I know,' he said, then added with an ugly downward twist of the mouth, 'not that I care if the bitch is rotting in hell with her fancy man!'

'What happened?'

It took some time, and several drinks, to get the entire story out of Ewan. He and Beth had gone up north and had married when they discovered that Rowena was on the way. At first, as far as Alex could make out, things went fairly well for them.

'We ended up working for this rich man with an estate out in the country. I worked with the outdoor staff while Beth was employed in the kitchens; they gave us a cottage to live in, and they didn't mind the kid. Sometimes Rowena was in the kitchens, sometimes she was out on the moors with me. She's got guts, that kid; she should have been a boy. Then,' the downward twist marred his pleasant mouth again, 'there was a big shooting party, out on the moors every day, banging away with their guns. Not like this lot we're in among,' he added sarcastically. 'They had motorcars and picnics brought from the big house, and chairs to sit on and plenty to drink. I've often wondered how many of them ended up here, popping away at Germans instead of pheasants and grouse and having to drink from puddles instead of opening another bottle. I wish I could meet some of them; I'd show them a thing or two. If they are here they're probably wearing officers' gear, holed up in some comfortable château with manservants to look after them. Did you know that the really rich don't even know how to wipe their own arses? They need servants for everything.'

'What happened to you and Beth?' Alex asked patiently.

'What d'you think? I was one of the beaters and she was among the women bringing the nice lunches out to the moors and setting the tables, putting out the knives and forks and the glasses. And this man got his eye on Beth.' He sneered. 'He wasn't even a man, just a kid not long out of university. He hadn't even started shaving yet, which was just as well since he didn't have a chin anyway. You know the type – a youngest son, all set to be pushed into some nice job hand-picked for him.' He paused for a while, his face tight with anger, his fierce eyes fixed on patterns he was drawing with one finger in some spilled beer. 'And when the birds had all been shot out of the sky and they all got into their motorcars and went home, Beth went with him.'

'What did you do?'

Ewan looked across the table, his gaze hard. 'What else could I do but go after them? I should have said good riddance to bad rubbish and left them to it. He'd have got tired of her – or she might have got tired of him first and asked to come back to me. Who knows? But I went after them with some idea of dragging her back where she belonged with me and Rowena. Or beating the hell out of her. One or the other, it didn't matter much at the time.'

He hadn't changed all that much. The Ewan that Alex had grown up with would never have let anyone take anything away from him. 'You caught up with them?'

'I did, and the silly little fool tried to protect her. Can you imagine that?' Ewan asked with amusement. 'I was bigger and fitter and older, but he had some daft idea in his bird-sized brain that it was his place to defend her. So he got it instead of her.'

'Did you kill him?'

Ewan stubbed out his cigarette and lit another. 'No. I could have, without thinking twice about it. But the very first blow bloodied his nose, and that sent Beth screaming for the law and the army and God knows what. So I had to get out of there and go on the run. Me and Rowena.'

'You took her with you?'

'I'd no choice. Beth had left her behind – she didn't want to be lumbered with a kid. I could have just left her too and hoped that somebody would see to her, but it didn't seem fair. She's always been a decent brat, and she favoured me more than her mother anyway, so I went back to where I'd left her waiting and we went off together.' He shrugged. 'I didn't mind trailing her along. She'd spent most of her time with me anyway, in the gardens or out on the moors. Beth didn't have much time for her once she got past being like a doll to play with and began to get into mischief and ask questions and talk as if her mouth had forgotten how to stop. With me, she learned fast enough when to shut up and keep out of my way, so I didn't mind her.'

'So you went on the run with a little girl?'

'No other choice. But things got difficult. The law wouldn't let up – they're like that when folk like us have the nerve to hurt folk like them – and once or twice we nearly got caught. Rowena was slowing me down, so I found a carter to take her to Paisley and I told her I'd come for her when I could. Right after that I heard about a ship heading for Australia, and I thought that'll get me away from the lot of them once and for all. So I managed to get work aboard and off I went. I found work easily enough when we got there, and things were working out fine when this lot started up. Next thing I knew, I was back on a ship, in uniform.'

'You'd no intention of getting in touch with Mam, had you, or your daughter?'

'I might have,' Ewan said evasively, 'once I'd got on my feet.'

'You might at least have written to let us know that you were still alive. Do you have any idea what that wee girl's gone through, waiting for you to come back for her and not knowing what was going on?'

'I knew Mam'd look after her.' Ewan fumbled for another cigarette and muttered a curse when he found that the packet was empty. Alex laid his on the table.

'You'll go and see her on your next furlough?'

'Best to leave things as they are. I'll only unsettle her.'

'Go and see her, Ewan! You owe her that, at least.'

'I'm a wanted man, remember?'

'With a war going on the police'll not be likely to be looking for you that hard. Besides, you'll only be in Paisley for a day or two. I'm going to write home and tell them I've met you, and I'm going to promise Rowena that you'll see her on your next furlough.'

Ewan finally agreed, adding, 'But I can't take her back to Australia with me, for I've been living in a bunkhouse with the rest of the men. It's no place for a kid.'

'Mebbe one day, when you're more settled. She's started school now, and she's doing well from what I hear.'

As the men who had been sitting with Ewan came by on their way out of the mess tent, one laid a hand on Ewan's shoulder. 'All right, mate?'

'Just coming.' Ewan picked up his hat. 'Our rest period's over and we're heading back to our lines.'

'Where are you?' Alex fished in his tunic pocket and pulled out a notebook. When Ewan told him, he said,

'We're just a bit to the west of you. Give me your army details and your address in Australia.'

'Think I'm going on the run again?'

'You've done it before,' Alex said levelly, and Ewan shrugged and told him what he wanted to know. Alex scribbled it down, then flipped to an empty page and pushed notebook and pencil over to his stepbrother. 'Write a note to Rowena, and I'll send it with my next letter.'

'For Christ's sake . . .'

'Do it! It'll mean a lot to her.'

Ewan sighed and scribbled a few words. '"Dear Rowena, hope you're well and being good. I'm fine,"' he read aloud, then said, 'I'm not a letter writer – I don't know what else to say.'

'Write, "I miss you, and I'll come and see you on my next furlough."'

'For—'

'Just do it, Ewan!'

When Ewan had gone Alex, unable to settle, walked round the camp, stepping over guy ropes and tramping along duckboards laid down over the soft, sticky mud. He found a lane and followed it between scraggy bushes until it ended at a ruined farmhouse, its windows gone and its front door hanging drunkenly by one hinge. The farmer and his family must have left hurriedly; the remains of a doll lay in a sheltered corner of the courtyard, half of its china head missing and one glassy blue eye staring up at the sky. He picked it up, wondering what had happened to the child who had played with it, then laid it back on the ground gently, smoothing its limbs and its clothing, and walked back to camp to write to his mother to tell her that he had found Ewan.

*   *   *

When his unit returned to the lines, its numbers replenished, the bombardment was still going on.

'It's been hell on earth,' someone told Alex. 'Dave McGill's gone, and Mack Polmont . . .' The air above screamed as a heavy shell ripped through it, and they both ducked automatically. The scream cut out, then came the explosion. A great fountain of earth, mud and water shot up towards the sky before showering back onto them.

'And Robbie Ballantyne lost a shoulder,' the soldier went on, brushing mud from his tunic. 'Shrapnel. They took him off to the sick bay, but he was losing blood fast and I reckon he'll be gone by now.' He recited the casualties in a flat voice, name after name after name, ending with, 'And I've heard that a bunch of Aussies further along had an even worse time, poor bastards. Scarcely one of them left.'

Alex's captain, considered by the ranks to be a decent bloke, promised to do what he could to find out what had happened to Ewan. Alex decided not to mention the Australian casualties in his next letter home, for there was no point in alarming Kirsty with rumours.

Twenty-four hours after returning from the rest camp, he felt as though he had never been away from the trenches. His Paisley family, his father and Fiona, and even Rose, were like a dream he had once had. It was as though he had spent his entire life being deafened by guns and blinded by the flash of explosions and star shells. The rifles he and the other men fired in return felt as puny and as useless as children's toys. He had never known such exhaustion, despair or sheer bone-dissolving terror. He couldn't remember the pleasure of eating food that wasn't cold or didn't taste of mud, or the joy of walking on dry firm ground, free of rats. The wet-walled trenches were the only home he had ever known, and the only escape he could hope for lay in climbing out into the wasteland beyond and walking into a bullet. He began to like the idea of death and found himself hoping that the chaplain's pictures of heaven and the angels were wrong. All he asked of death was blessed silence and darkness, peace and rest.

The rain seemed set for the winter, or perhaps forever. When he was despatched to the captain's dugout with a message, it took him a long time to get there, stopping every now and again to haul one foot or the other from a particularly gluey patch of mud.

'Just a minute,' the captain said as he turned to go after making his delivery. 'MacDowall, isn't it?'

'Yessir.'

'Didn't you make enquiries about a cousin fighting with the Australians?'

'My stepbrother, sir.'

'Oh yes. Got a note here.' The man, probably younger than Alex, rummaged through a pile of papers on his desk then brought one out and peered at it. 'Ewan Lennox – that right?'

'Yessir.'

The man's eyes were red rimmed with exhaustion, but even so there was sympathy in them. 'I'm afraid he didn't make it. There doesn't seem to be any doubt, for he's listed here among the dead. Sorry.'

'Yessir. Thank you, sir.' Alex saluted and made for the door. As he reached it the world suddenly exploded in a blinding flash and a noise that split his head open. Then, at last, the wonderful, welcome darkness took mercy on him and came to fetch him.

24

Rowena was delirious with joy when Alex's letter arrived. Even though she was doing well with her reading, Ewan's brief scribble was beyond her, so she insisted on having it read out to her over and over again until she had learned it by heart. She took the single page with her everywhere she went and tucked it carefully beneath her pillow every night before settling down to sleep.

'She's fair worn the entire household out with her excitement,' Kirsty told Jean. 'And she's going to wear that dancing stone of hers out too, the way she thumps and birls on it all the time she's at home.'

'She's bound to be excited, hearing from her father after such a long silence.'

'Aye.' Kirsty's eyes misted over. 'It's a miracle, Ewan going away to the other end of the world then our Alex finding him in the middle of all the fighting. It'll be good to see him again.'

She and Todd agreed that there was no point in letting Mr Laidlaw and his daughter know about Alex's meeting with Ewan. The Laidlaws had made it quite clear when they rejected Rowena that they no longer considered Beth to be part of the family, and in any case, as Mary pointed out, not even Ewan knew of Beth's whereabouts.

'I doubt if they'd want to hear that she'd deserted her lawful husband and her wee daughter and run off with another man,' she said, and they agreed.

Since her husband had enlisted, Annie Mitchell had become even more sour faced and irritable with her customers. It seemed to Kirsty, when she went into the tobacconist's shop, that Annie was becoming more like her grandmother every day.

Each time the thought came to her, she vowed to herself that, whatever happened, Rowena, who after all had old Mrs Laidlaw's blood running through her veins, would not follow the same bitter, twisted road as she grew up.

Caitlin and Murdo took Rowena brambling on the braes in October and, as had happened the previous year, the little girl ate most of the sweet black berries and ended up with purple stains about her broad grin. While she ran off to explore, the adults studied the sketchbook Caitlin had brought with her, discussing the possibility of Murdo weaving some of her cloth designs. Now and again he took the pencil from her hand to sketch deftly a more workable variation of one of her ideas. It was a mellow, pleasant late-autumn day, and they were sitting comfortably side by side on a large rock; occasionally Murdo's sleeve touched Caitlin's, and once, when he bent over the book, his hair brushed her cheek. For a man, he had surprisingly soft hair, with a pleasant soapy smell to it. His soft, deep voice was pleasing to her ears and she liked the way his square, blunt-fingered hands moved swiftly, confidently, across the pages on her lap. She felt safe with this man, much safer than she had ever felt with Bryce Caldwell.

As soon as the thought came to her mind, she scoffed at it, for after all Bryce had wanted to be her sweetheart, while Murdo was just a friend. But the sensation persisted. She did feel safe with him, and at home with him. Just then, Murdo turned his head to ask something, and when she looked into his deep-brown eyes, so close to hers, her reply died on her lips and the pencil fell from her fingers. He immediately stooped to pick it up and return it. When she took it from him, their fingers made contact for a brief moment, and she felt her cheeks grow warm. He seated himself beside her again, and she answered his question, looking at the sketchbook, speaking to it, longing to look into his face again but unable to. Almost immediately afterwards she snapped the book shut and announced that it was time they started for home.

Rowena was nowhere to be found, and when Caitlin called her name there was no answer. Caitlin called a second time, then again.

'She'll be hiding somewhere,' Murdo said easily.

'She'd have answered if she'd heard me, surely. She might be anywhere – she might have fallen over an outcrop of rock and been hurt, or . . .' She could hear the panic in her own voice. What if something had happened to Rowena while her aunt, who was supposed to be looking after her, had been thinking of her own pleasures instead of the child's safety?

'Rowena?' Murdo didn't even raise his voice much. 'Behave yourself now, and stop worrying your Aunt Caitlin.'

Immediately a bush some fifteen yards away rustled, and Rowena's purple-stained face appeared at knee level. 'I'm in my wee house,' she called. 'Come and see!'

The thicket looked impenetrable, but Murdo pulled the branches aside and bent to look through the gap. When he straightened up, he was grinning. 'She's found a wee house right enough. Give me your book and see for yourself.'

Caitlin gathered up her skirts and crawled between the branches he held back for her to find that the thicket was in fact a tight ring of bushes, with a space several yards in diameter within. A young tree grew in the middle of the open area, its branches entwining with the lower bushes to form a fairly thick ceiling. The sunlight that filtered through revealed Rowena squatting on a dry floor spread with dead leaves, hands linked around her knees.

'See?' she said, delighted. 'This is my own wee house.' When Murdo crawled in she insisted that they sit down on either side of her, then took their hands in hers.

'Now you're visiting me. When my daddy comes to see me we'll live here, him and me, and nobody can visit us but the two of you.' She tucked their hands into her lap and began to play with their fingers, so that all three hands became entwined.

When they started back towards Paisley Caitlin lagged behind, as she often did, to watch Murdo and Rowena, hand in hand, stepping confidently down the tussocky hill. Murdo's jacket, well worn and neatly darned, was a little too tight for him. It clung to his broad shoulders, and when he put his free hand up to brush hair back from his face, she thought for a moment that the arm seam might split, but it didn't. She felt a sudden wave of tenderness for the man. Rose had been the first to tell her that she cared for Murdo, and she hadn't denied it. Now, watching him walk away from her, she knew that Rose had been right, and that she

did care, probably far more than was good for her,
for Murdo Guthrie had already chosen his woman and
loved her and given her his child. Since he had lost
them both, it seemed unlikely to Caitlin that he would
ever want to walk that road again.

Kirsty was worried about Alex. He hadn't written for
several weeks, and the silence wasn't like him. She
had wondered aloud on a few occasions if someone
should go to Glasgow to ask if Angus MacDowall
had heard from him, but she wouldn't go herself, and
Todd, Caitlin and Mary were all reluctant to make the
journey since none of them knew the man well.

Rose had become quieter than usual, and somewhat
withdrawn, and Caitlin suspected that it was because
she hadn't heard from Alex either. Although neither
of them had mentioned it, she was fairly sure that
her half-brother and Rose were now corresponding.
Finally, when Kirsty's concern began to reach the
stage of panic, Caitlin asked Rose point-blank.

'I haven't heard from him for several weeks, and
it's not like him.' Rose was too worried to prevaricate.
'D'you think something's happened to him?'

'If it had, if he'd been wounded or . . .' Caitlin
couldn't bring herself to say the word, so hurried on,
'I'm sure that Mam would have been notified. If Mr
MacDowall's down as Alex's next of kin, I'm sure
he'd have let Mam know if he'd had word.'

'If anything's happened to him, Caitlin, I couldn't
bear it,' Rose said fiercely.

'It hasn't. Alex wouldn't let anything get in the way
of his future!'

Just before Kirsty had reached the stage of insisting
that one of them go, Fiona paid a visit to the workshop
and to Harlequin for a fitting for her new coat.

'I don't believe that Papa has received a letter from Alex for some time,' she said vaguely.

'Then he must just be busy, for the War Office would let us know if anything had . . . happened,' Caitlin said, with one eye on Rose. Fiona, too, was watching Rose closely.

'Has he not even written to you, Rose?'

'Why should he?'

'I thought that you two were such friends.'

'Men fighting the war have more to do with their time than write to every last acquaintance,' Rose said dismissively, then remembered some urgent business in the office.

'I couldn't bring myself to admit that Alex and I are exchanging letters,' she told Caitlin when Fiona had gone. 'There's something about that woman that makes me reluctant to let her into any part of my life.'

One morning in early November, Kirsty ran into the workshop waving a letter in Todd's face. 'It's Alex – he's been hurt, and Ewan's . . .' She burst into tears, and it took some time before Todd could calm her down. When he finally read the letter, he took her back into the house and made her a cup of tea. Kirsty wrinkled her nose at the first sip. 'It's terrible, and there are tea leaves floating on it. You've not let the water boil properly!'

'I'm a cabinet-maker, no' a cook.' He fetched the whisky bottle and tipped a generous dose into the cup. 'Here, this'll make it taste better.'

'Todd Paget, you're just wasting good whisky – and good tea!'

'Take a mouthful of it at least,' he insisted. 'It'll help to calm you.'

When she had recovered her composure the two of

them walked down to Harlequin to tell Caitlin and Rose that Alex had suffered severe concussion in an explosion that had killed his unit captain, only feet away from him at the time, and that Ewan was dead.

'Are you sure Alex is all right?' Rose asked, white faced.

Kirsty handed over the letter. 'See for yourself. He was expecting to return to the lines within the next day or two. He'll be there now,' she added despairingly. 'To think that he was safe in the base hospital and we didn't even know it! And poor Ewan—' She stopped short, then said firmly, 'Rowena mustn't know about her father, not after getting that letter.'

'But she's expectin' the man tae come here on his next furlough,' Todd protested. 'She'll be lookin' for him.'

'Todd, I couldn't bring myself to tell her what's happened. She's too wee to bear so much grief!'

'Mam's right,' Caitlin said. 'It would break her heart to hear that he's dead. We'll just have to keep saying that he's not been able to get away, at least until she's a bit older and more able to understand.' And so it was agreed, though they found it difficult to listen to Rowena wondering aloud if her daddy might be allowed to come to Paisley for the New Year celebrations.

John Brodie was among those who were able to get back home at the turn of the year. He visited Harlequin and expressed his satisfaction with the ledgers. 'But you'll need to do something about getting folk to pay their bills in better time.'

'It's not easy since most of them are friendly with my parents. You can't ask a man you're sitting beside at a dinner party when he's going to settle the account for the frock his wife's wearing further along the table.'

'I know. I had the same problem myself when I was seeing to your books.' John turned a page, then paused. 'This investment . . . Alex MacDowall?' He looked up at Rose. 'So that's why you didn't take up my offer.'

'Alex was . . . generous.'

'So I see.' There was hurt in his eyes, and in his voice. 'I didn't know that you were going to approach him.'

'I didn't. Caitlin told him that we were having financial problems, and he . . .' Rose faltered to a standstill, then said in a rush, 'To tell you the truth, John, I think that Alex MacDowall and I will get married when the war's over.'

His face went blank. 'I see.'

'I'm sorry.' She put a hand on his arm, but he pulled away at once.

'Sorry? I wish that you'd at least have had the decency to tell me about MacDowall before I made a fool of myself by proposing to you.'

'I didn't know, then. At least, I didn't realise—'

John got up and held a hand out to stop her. 'Save your breath, Rose, I'm not really interested,' he said coldly, and walked out, brushing past Caitlin in the foyer, without a word. She went into the office to find Rose slowly gathering up the ledgers.

'What's amiss with John?'

Rose didn't turn round. 'He found out about Alex putting money into the business.'

'But why should that make him so angry?' Caitlin asked, confused, then as her friend said nothing, 'Rose?'

Rose gave an almighty sniff and swung round to face her. 'If you must know, he also found out that Alex and I are planning to marry.'

'Oh, Rose!' Caitlin flew across the room and hugged the other girl. 'I'm so pleased for you both! I've always known that you were meant for each other, but at times I was beginning to wonder if you would ever find . . .' Realising that her friend was as stiff in her embrace as a clothes-pole, she stepped back. 'Aren't you happy about it?'

Tears glittered in Rose's eyes. 'John was so angry, Caitlin. He thinks I've deliberately deceived him, but I haven't. Alex and I didn't even know until the end of his last furlough. That's why we didn't tell anyone, but now John's found out and . . .'

Her voice broke, and again Caitlin put her arms about her. This time Rose gave in and leaned against her. 'Oh, Caitlin, why does happiness have to cause so much misery?'

'It's just the way things are.'

'The last thing I wanted to do was to hurt John. I should have found a better way of telling him.'

'He'll learn to accept it, in time.'

'But I don't have time,' Rose wept. 'We're both going to a dinner party tonight . . . it'll be dreadful!' She snuffled, then pulled away from Caitlin, sudden horror in her face. 'Mama will be there . . . you don't think he'll say anything to her, do you?'

'Of course not. John would never do anything to hurt you or your mother, no matter how upset he might be,' Caitlin reassured her.

She was right. On the following morning Rose reported that John had kept out of her way at the dinner party and had said nothing to betray her.

'But Mama smelled a rat, and I had to go through a Spanish Inquisition on the way home as to what I had done or said to annoy him.'

'At least he kept your secret.'

'And so must you, until Alex's next furlough. We'd better confess then, for I couldn't bear to go on like this.'

'Not a word will pass my lips,' Caitlin promised.

When John returned to the office that afternoon he found Rose alone. She jumped nervously to her feet, fingering the brooch pinned to her bodice, and he gave her a wan smile.

'It's all right, I'm here to apologise.' He put his hat on the desk and squared his shoulders. 'It was wrong of me to lose my temper yesterday. I realise now that that's not the answer.'

'It was all my fault. I should have written to you as soon as I knew.'

'I'm quite glad that you didn't. Better to get bad news in the comfort of my own home town than in the thick of battle. Not that your news is bad,' he hastened to add, 'At least, not for you or Alex MacDowall.'

'John, Alex and I didn't realise . . . not until his last furlough . . .'

'I should probably have guessed that this might happen. The two of you quarrelled rather too much. I take it that your parents don't know about this?'

'Nobody knows except Caitlin. John, I wish I could have said yes to you when you asked me.'

He forced a smile. 'Don't be daft. Think how much more difficult things would be for all of us if you had accepted me then realised that you really wanted him. At least I can't fault his choice in women.'

'I can, but then I always said that there was something wrong with Alex MacDowall.' Rose tried to return the smile, but failed.

'It seems to me that there's very little wrong with

him.' He gave her a long look, as though memorising her features, then said, 'So there's nothing left but to wish you both well.'

'I wish . . .'

'So do I, my dear, but there we are.' He went to the door, then hesitated and turned. 'Tell Alex that if he's looking for a best man at his wedding, I'm willing.'

'D'you mean that?'

'Why not? If I can't have you then he's my next best choice for you.'

Rose went to him and kissed him on the cheek. 'You're the kindest man I know, and the most honourable.'

'Oh, I'm well aware of that,' John said wryly. 'Perhaps if I'd had more fire in my belly you'd be marrying me instead of Alex MacDowall.'

Shortly after John returned to his unit, a crisis hit Harlequin when Iris, who had recently become engaged to be married, left the sewing room to work in a factory. As soon as Lizzie heard what her friend was being paid in munitions she, too, handed in her notice, and Rose and Caitlin had to advertise for two new seamstresses. They appointed two older women, one of them a skilled embroideress as well, but it took a while for the newcomers to settle into the work, which meant that Caitlin had to spend more time at a sewing machine for several months, just when the fashion house was busy.

In deciding not to let Rowena find out about her father, they had forgotten for once the thriving grapevine that carried news throughout every community. One afternoon early in December Mary fetched Rowena from her dancing class and brought her home to Espedair

Street because Murdo was busy completing a piece of cloth. The little girl spent some time practising on her dancing stone, then wandered into the kitchen, where Mary was preparing the evening meal, and asked if she could play hopscotch on the pavement.

'As long as you don't wander off. There's a bit of chalk in that drawer.'

Rowena found the chalk and and went through the pend. She was missing her usual visit to Murdo, and on that day even a game of hopscotch seemed tame and uninteresting. For devilment, knowing that Mrs Mitchell hated children to play on the pavement outside her shop, Rowena hurried across the road and began to draw on the pavement.

In no time at all the shop bell pinged and Annie Mitchell appeared on the step. 'What d'ye think you're doin'? Go and defile the pavement on your own side of the street!'

Rowena, at a safe distance, stuck out her tongue, and the woman's face crimsoned. 'Don't you dare to cheek me, ye wee bizzum! Bad seed, that's what you are, no better than your father!'

Rowena felt her own cheeks burn. Nobody insulted her daddy! 'When he comes here he's going to break your window!' she shrilled defiantly.

'I've no doubt he would if he could. He's already broken my poor father's heart, so why not his window as well? But luckily for us all he can't, now he's dead and gone.'

The words hit Rowena with such force that her eyes almost popped out of her head and her mouth fell open. Then she pulled herself together.

'He's not dead!'

'Aye, but he is – killed in the war, and good riddance tae bad rubbish!'

'He's not, he's not!' All Rowena wanted to do was to hurt the woman who was hurting her. She threw the chalk at Annie Mitchell then charged, head down. Her skull and the woman's stomach smacked together with a force that sent Annie reeling against her shop wall, the breath sucked out of her lungs. For good measure, Rowena kicked her in the shins then whirled, her head still down, and ran blindly along the pavement with no thought of making for home. Even though it was getting dark, all she wanted, at that moment, was to get away from Espedair Street and from Paisley and all the nasty folk who lived there.

Kirsty came home to find Mary and Annie Mitchell shouting at each other on her doorstep.

'For pity's sake, what's going on?'

'Well might you ask! That wee tinker of yours needs a right good thrashing!'

Kirsty's heart sank. She was tired and cold, and looking forward to a quiet evening in her warm comfortable kitchen. 'Rowena? What's she done now?'

'Playin' hopscotch right outside my door, she was, and when I told her tae get back tae her own side of the street the wee bizzum started on about gettin' her father tae break up my shop!' Annie sniffed loudly and folded her arms across her flat bosom. 'I told her he'd not get the chance, seein' that he's been killed in the war.'

'You told Rowena that her father's dead?'

'Next thing I knew she'd butted me.' Annie foamed on. 'It's a mercy I'm still on my feet!'

Kirsty turned her back on the woman and raised her voice above the whine. 'Mary, where's the bairn?'

'I don't know, Mam.' Mary was near to tears. 'She asked if she could play hopscotch, and I said she could if she stayed on this pavement. But there's no sign of her.'

'Run to the workshop and see if she's hiding there. As for you, you evil, foul-tongued witch,' Kirsty rounded on Annie, 'get off my doorstep and out of my way!' And she pushed the woman aside then went into the house and slammed the door in her face.

Rowena wasn't in the workshop or in the room that had been the weaving shop.

'She'll have run to Murdo,' Todd said, 'I'm certain of it. Don't you worry, lass, I'll just away and fetch her home.'

'She'll be making for the bushes on the braes,' Caitlin said when Todd and Murdo came looking for her.

'Up on the braes?' Todd shook his head. 'She'd not go there in the dark.'

'I think she would, for she called the place her wee house.'

'You're right,' Murdo said. 'I'll go there now.'

'I'll come with you.' She snatched up her jacket. 'Todd, let Kirsty know.'

With every corner turned, Caitlin strained through the darkening winter evening, hoping to glimpse a small figure trudging just ahead, but it was never there.

'How long ago was it that she met up with Annie Mitchell?' she asked breathlessly, half running to keep up with Murdo.

'About half an hour, as far as I can judge. If she ran, she could be quite far ahead of us.'

They reached the town's edge and struck out along country roads, leaving street lights and houses behind. They were climbing now, and Caitlin soon got a stitch in her side. She struggled on, pressing her hand tightly against her waist to hold the pain at bay. Once, stopping to catch her breath, she saw the town sketched below by street lamps and house lights. The wind sighed and murmured in the trees, and when she turned back to look at Murdo his sturdy figure was just a shadow in the night, moving away from her and leaving her on her own. She pressed her fist hard against the sharp pain and struggled after him, suddenly afraid to be alone. How much more frightening this place must be for someone the size of Rowena, she thought, as she fought her way through a clump of broom that seemed to have risen up from nowhere to entangle her.

When he stopped she almost ran into him. 'I think it was near here,' he said. 'It all looks different in the dark.' Then, with concern, he asked, 'Are you all right?'

She was almost too breathless to speak. 'I'm fine,' she started to say, then suddenly she wasn't fine at all, for the tears were pouring down her face and she could do nothing to prevent them.

'It's all right.' Murdo gathered her into his arms. 'Hush now, it's all right. We'll find her.' For a moment he held her close, stroking her hair with one hand, then he eased her back and fumbled in his pocket, bringing out a handkerchief to mop her face. He must have spread it on the bushes behind the gatehouse to dry after washing it, for it smelled of fresh air.

'Mebbe you should sit down on this bit of log and wait while I go on.'

The sharp pain of the stitch was subsiding now. 'No, I have to find her!' Caitlin insisted. He took her hand and drew her to his side without wasting time on an argument.

As he had said, the area was quite different in the

dark; they stumbled around together, changing their minds several times and trying another direction. Occasionally Murdo called Rowena's name, but the darkness around them seemed to absorb his voice like blotting paper, and there was no reply. They heard the sound of rushing water, and Caitlin felt Murdo's hand tighten painfully on hers before he let her go.

'Stand by that tree over there and wait for me.'

'Murdo . . .'

'Do as I tell you!' he shouted at her and disappeared into the night, heading for the sound of the water. As she fumbled her way to the tree she could hear Mhairi's lilting voice telling her of how Murdo's little son had drowned in a burn.

She waited for some time before he finally came crashing back over the grass. 'There's no sign of her by the water. Come on.' The hand that caught at hers was wet; he must have been feeling his way along the bank, dreading what he might find.

She had only gone a few steps when something caught at her free hand, digging into her skin with tiny needles when she gasped and tried to pull away. 'Bramble bushes!'

Murdo released her hand again and moved past her. 'And a dry-stone dyke beyond,' he said. 'There was a dyke by the brambles we picked, wasn't there?' Then the moon slipped for a moment between the overhead clouds. 'There's the rock we sat on. This way.' He caught at her arm and pulled her after him, slipping and stumbling on the rough ground.

'And here . . . ,' his breathless voice was rough with triumph, 'are the bushes. Wait.' He stooped, then disappeared into their midst. Caitlin knelt down, praying that they had been right in their guess as to where Rowena might have taken refuge, and almost immediately Murdo's face appeared right in front of hers. 'She's here!'

Caitlin pushed through the bushes, heedless of the way they caught at her hair and her clothing, and he guided her hands until they touched a small cold face, wet with tears.

'Oh, Rowena!'

'I want my daddy!' Rowena whimpered against Caitlin's fingers.

25

Murdo wrapped Rowena in his jacket and carried her all the way home. At first she struggled against him, then she gave in and wept hopelessly. Then she slept, worn out by grief and her long, lonely trek through the dark.

Caitlin thought at times on the downhill journey that they were never going to reach home. Several times, tripping over unseen obstacles, falling, picking herself up again, she wondered if they would have been better to have stayed in Rowena's wee house until daylight, huddled together for warmth.

Finally they gained the streets, where cobbles and flagstones under their feet instead of grass and stones made the walking easier. And at last they reached Espedair Street and trudged through the pend. Kirsty, alerted by some sixth sense, threw the back door open just as Caitlin was about to lift the latch, and at last they were in the warm, gaslit kitchen.

Rowena, wakened by the sudden light and the clamour of relieved voices, woke and began to cry again for her father. Kirsty, clucking and fussing over the little girl's filthy appearance, tried to take her from Murdo, but he shook his head and said firmly but courteously, 'If you please, Mrs Paget, I think it would be as well if we just got her into her bed. If you'd show me the way?'

Flustered, she went ahead of him into the hall while Todd guided Caitlin into his chair and Mary ran to ladle soup from the pot on the cooker.

Kirsty came back into the kitchen almost at once. 'He wants to stay with her for a wee while, till she's asleep.' She looked at her family, bewildered. 'I didn't know whether it was the right thing to do, but he was so insistent, and Rowena wouldn't let go of him.'

'Ye did the right thing, pet,' Todd assured her. 'The bairn trusts him, and at a time like this he's mebbe the best person for her. You can make a fuss over Caitlin instead – and I've no doubt that Murdo'll be ready for a meal when he comes downstairs.' He eyed the bowl of broth in Caitlin's hands hungrily. 'I know I am.'

'She's sleeping now,' Murdo said when he finally came downstairs. 'I think that'll be her till the morning.'

For once it wasn't difficult to persuade him to stay to eat with them. First, despite his obvious exhaustion, he insisted on taking a lamp into the wash house so that he could clean himself up. As his clothes were splashed with mud and torn from struggling through bushes, Kirsty fetched some of Todd's clean clothing for him.

Dour man though he'd been, Kirsty's father had adored his wife and had converted an upstairs bedroom into a proper bathroom for her – one of the first to be installed in Paisley. As Caitlin bathed in warm water in the comfort of the house's four walls, she was grateful to her grandfather for his foresight. She changed out of her blouse and skirt, as muddy and torn as Murdo's shirt, into clean clothes and brushed twigs and leaves from her hair before tying it back with a ribbon. Her hands and, she saw when she looked in the bedroom mirror, her face were covered with tiny scratches from the bushes on the braes, particularly the bramble bushes.

When Murdo came back into the kitchen he, too, carried scratches and tears that stood out against his scrubbed face and neck and hands. He had washed his hair, towelling the worst of the water from it then combing it with his fingers so that it lay sleek and shining over his skull, back from his forehead for once and emphasising the strong bone structure of his face. He didn't speak much during the meal, leaving it to Caitlin to tell the others how they had found Rowena.

'How could that Annie Mitchell have done such a wicked thing?' Kirsty fumed. 'Rowena could have died up there if you'd not known where to look for her. I'm going to go over there first thing tomorrow and—'

'Ye'll do nothin' of the sort,' Todd told her firmly. 'Ye'll let the matter drop, for it'll only make things worse for Rowena if ye start a quarrel with Annie Mitchell. Anyway, the woman's not worth it.'

Caitlin glanced across at Murdo. As the warmth of the room dried his hair it had begun to curl slightly, and the lamplight, catching the soft wisps at the ends, framed his head in a soft golden halo. His hands, as he spread margarine on a slice of bread, were calm and capable; she lowered her eyes to her plate, remembering the feel of those hands on her back and on her hair in the brief moment when he had held her in the darkness of the braes. She wished that he wasn't so set on keeping his own company, for it was good to have him there, a part of her family for once.

None of them was the worse for their journey to and from the hills, but to Kirsty's distress Rowena slipped back somewhat to her earlier days, retreating into silences and occasional tantrums.

'The bairn's got tae get the shock over Ewan's death out of her system,' Todd told his wife. 'Just leave her, however hard that might be. She'll sort herself out, given time.'

He made a frame for Ewan's letter, and Rowena kept it by her bed along with her father's photograph. She spent a lot of time with Murdo, who seemed to be the only person who could soothe her.

Alex came home for a few days in March, looking older and thinner and very tired. Caitlin, knowing how desperate Rose was to see him again, invited her to the house, where she hung back a little while Alex hugged his mother and his half-sisters and Rowena.

'Hello, Rose,' he said then, almost shyly.

'Hello, Alex.'

Caitlin, looking from one to the other, longed to shout out their news, but clamped her mouth shut, knowing that they themselves would decide when the time was right. Kirsty yearned to hear about Ewan, but nothing could be said in front of Rowena, so while they ate their evening meal they talked about the shop and Harlequin, and Todd enquired after Angus MacDowall's health. As before, Alex had gone to Glasgow first.

'He's fine. How are things in the workshop?'

'Everything's grand. Mrs Chalmers seems pleased enough with what we're doin', so she's made no more changes.' Todd said nothing about the anxiety he had suffered after Murdo had been turned off, wondering if he or his journeyman and apprentice would be next to meet with Fiona Chalmers' disapproval.

While Kirsty put Rowena to bed Alex and his step-father went to the workshop.

When they returned and they had all gathered round

the table again, Kirsty finally gave free rein to her curiosity. 'How did Ewan look?'

'Just the same – a bit older, mebbe, but as jaunty as ever, despite what he'd been through. I think he liked it in Australia.'

'Did he ask about us?'

'Of course he did,' Alex lied. He wasn't about to tell them that Ewan, as before, had shown little interest in any of his family. 'He was pleased to hear that everything was going well and that Rowena was happy here and doing well at the school. He said that he'd come and fetch her once the fighting was over and he had made something of his new life.'

'Poor laddie.' Ready tears rose to Kirsty's eyes. 'Mebbe Australia would have been the making of him.'

'We'll never know now,' Todd said enigmatically.

'We won't, but I'm sure that Mam's right and it would have worked out well for him. At least we know what happened to him, thanks to my captain. Not every officer would have taken the trouble to do what he did for me.' Alex paused, staring down at his hands, then said, 'And not a minute after he told me about Ewan he was dead himself, poor man.'

'And you almost gone with him,' Kirsty said with a shiver.

'If the shell had landed in the trench a few seconds later, I'd have been blown to kingdom come,' Alex agreed, 'but it happened just as I was on my way out. The door blew right off its hinges and smacked straight into me, and I was thrown into a corner with it on top of me, sheltering me from the worst of the blast. The captain and his aide caught the full force while I escaped with a cut face and concussion. I was very lucky.'

Rose could contain herself no longer. 'That's it, then,

Alex MacDowall,' she announced. 'I'm not going to let you go back to the fighting without putting a ring on my finger first!' Then, appalled by what she had just said, she stared round the circle of astonished faces and added, her voice wobbling, 'It's time everyone knew that you're mine.'

Kirsty gave a little scream, while Mary gasped and Caitlin yelped, 'At last! I thought I was going to burst!'

Todd puffed a cloud of tobacco smoke and said, round his pipe, 'I thought somethin' was goin' on between you two.'

Alex looked as astonished as the others. 'You might have told me first instead of blurting it out like that.'

'I told them because it's just occurred to me that if you walk into any more shells I'll at least have a ring to pawn. Do you have any objections to making our engagement official?' she challenged him, her eyes very bright.

He got up, walked round the table, drew her from her chair and kissed her full on the lips. 'No objection at all,' he said. 'But I warn you, if you insist on getting that ring then find someone better while I'm away, I'll be able to sue you for breach of promise.'

Kirsty burst into tears.

Alex felt more alive than he had for months as he marched up the Hamiltons' long driveway the following morning. Once again he was going into battle, but this time it was on a more level footing than the military struggles he had been involved in for so long. This time he wasn't a nameless, unimportant part of the whole, but a man in his own right, determined to win against all the odds.

Rose, who had stayed at home instead of cycling to

Harlequin, opened the door to him, drawing him into the hall and into her arms.

'You've told them?'

'I have.' Her blue eyes danced. 'Mama took an attack of the vapours, but that's only to be expected. Papa humphed and grumbled a bit, but I think he's willing to give us our blessing. He's waiting for you in his study.' She led him over to the door and straightened his tie. 'Be firm, and don't take no for an answer.'

'I don't intend to.'

Rose's father was a neatly built man, smaller than Alex but with the air of authority expected of a man who was partner in a well-established Glasgow firm. He shook Alex's hand firmly then nodded him towards a chair on the other side of the desk.

'I'll be blunt with you, young man. I've been through this same business twice before, with my two older daughters' suitors, but at least I knew them and their families. I know nothing at all about you, other than what Rose has said, and she's naturally biased.'

Alex was fully aware that Mrs Hamilton must already have given her husband a damning report on his background and his suitability as a husband for their youngest daughter. He was also certain that he had only been granted this interview because of Rose's insistence and perhaps her father's curiosity to see the applicant for himself. Attack, in this case, might well be the best form of defence, and if his judgement was correct, he had nothing to lose and everything to win.

'If I may, sir, I'll be equally blunt with you. My mother was your wife's sewing woman at one time and I only met my father a few years ago, but even so . . .' he began flatly then plunged on, as the older man's eyes widened and his jaw dropped, into a detailed description of his work as a cabinet-maker, the discovery that he had a talent for hand-painting furniture, and the results that had come from meeting his true father.

'If you're about to tell me that I have entirely the wrong background to be a fit son-in-law, I would be the first to agree with you – although I must say that I'm proud of my family and what they have all achieved. I should also point out that I only hold the rank of private in the army. But now that we've got my unsuitability out of the way I'd like to concentrate on my assets,' he said smoothly, and went on to list them, throwing false modesty to the winds and ending with, 'And as for your daughter, I love her deeply, and it's my intention, should I be spared, to make her the happiest woman in the world and to ensure that she will never want for anything for the rest of her life.'

'So . . . Your mind's quite made up, is it?'

'It is, sir.'

'Mmm. You're aware, I suppose, that my daughter is not the easiest person to live with.'

'I am, sir, but I'm determined in any case.'

'And you know as well as I do that if I withhold my consent she'll go ahead and marry you anyway?'

'Yes, sir.'

'You'd marry her in the face of our disapproval?'

'I would, Mr Hamilton, for her wishes are far more important to me than yours.'

'You put me in a very difficult situation, MacDowall.'

'I regret that, sir, but there's little either of us can do about it.'

'I suppose not. You'd best come with me to face her mother, then,' said Rose's father.

Angus MacDowall held a hurried dinner party on the following night, the night before Alex returned to his unit, to mark the engagement. Kirsty, terrified at the thought of going into Angus's home, would have stayed behind to look after Rowena, but both Alex and Rose insisted on her presence.

'If it hadn't been for you we'd never have met each other,' Rose protested, while Alex, who had already arranged with Jean Chisholm to stay with Rowena so that the rest of the family could travel to Glasgow, said firmly, 'This is the most important moment of my life, and I want both my parents to be with me.'

Once the first five minutes or so were over, Kirsty began to relax and enjoy herself. Angus treated her as he would have treated any other guest, and Fiona, as his hostess, was at her most charming. When it came down to it, Todd was more intimidated by the size of the house than his wife was.

'I can't help thinking,' he murmured when they had a moment to themselves, 'that if things had turned out differently, you might have been the mistress of this place instead of sitting in Espedair Street with me.'

In his eyes she recognised the doubts that she herself had known just after Rowena's arrival, when she had realised that if his marriage to Beth had gone ahead as planned, Todd could have been the child's father. She reached for his hand and squeezed it. 'You're wrong, I'd never have been mistress of a grand house like this. If things had been different and . . . ,' she hesitated, then used the name she had known Angus MacDowall under, 'if Sandy and I had been able to marry when Alex was on the way, he'd have stayed on as my father's apprentice and I'd still have ended up in Espedair Street.' Then she leaned over to whisper in his ear, 'But I'm glad about the way things turned out, for I'd much rather be there with you than with him.'

Mrs Hamilton, who had had to struggle to maintain a pretence of pleasure over her daughter's choice of fiancé, was considerably relieved when she saw his father's handsome, comfortable home. Her husband and Angus, both silent men, took to each other from the first and disappeared into Angus's study not long after dinner to smoke and drink brandy and talk in peace.

Rose was radiant in a long tunic patterned with intermingled blues and greens, worn over a hobble skirt in sea green. The outfit, designed as usual by Caitlin, went well with the emerald and diamond ring she and Alex had chosen together that afternoon.

'I can see that I'll be paying large amounts of money over to you when I'm married for my wife's clothes,' Alex told Caitlin.

'We don't charge much.'

'You deserve more, and you'll get it once the war's over – if it ever is over,' he added grimly.

'It will be one day.'

'I hope you're right, for all our sakes. But when the day comes Harlequin will do well for itself between your talent and Rose's determination. In fact I wouldn't be at all surprised if Fiona doesn't soon put in an order for an outfit very similar to Rose's. She's been eyeing it all evening.'

'Has it bothered you that Fiona has become so involved in your father's business?'

'Not at all,' Alex said, though she saw a muscle along his jawline suddenly tense. 'It keeps her busy and my father happy.'

Caitlin let the subject drop, but she had noticed that he tended to avoid speaking to Fiona and had seen the malicious glances the woman shot at him when she believed she was unnoticed. Once they had believed that they loved each other, but now . . .

Caitlin shivered and put the thought out of her mind. There was no point at the moment in brooding over a future that might never come for any of them.

26

In May 1916 compulsory conscription into the armed forces was brought in, and for the first time since taking up residence in the gatehouse Murdo Guthrie came to the main building. He told Rose and Caitlin that he was leaving. 'I'm sorry about the cloth still on the loom, but they've not given me time to finish it.'

'Don't you worry about that. It'll stay where it is until you can come back to complete it,' Rose told him briskly, adding, 'You will be coming back to work for us when you can, I hope?'

'If it's your wish.'

'It certainly is. And in any case you'll be returning to the gatehouse when you're on furlough.' She shook his hand heartily. 'Good luck, Murdo. We'll miss you.'

When Rose had gone upstairs to see Grace, Murdo said to Caitlin, 'I'm going to fetch Rowena from school and bring her back here for a wee while. I'll try to explain what's happening and why I have to go away.'

Caitlin swallowed to ease the sudden dryness in her mouth. 'She'll miss you very much.'

'And I'll miss her.' Fumbling in the old canvas bag he carried over his shoulder, he produced two thick exercise books. 'Could I leave these with you?'

'Of course.'

'They're letters to Rowena,' Murdo said. 'I'll write to her, of course, but just in case . . . If anything should happen to me and my letters stop coming, I thought mebbe you could post these to her, one by one. I know how much she treasures the one letter she got from her father.'

He held the books out to her, and she thrust them away, appalled. 'How can you talk about the possibility of your own death so calmly?'

'Because whether we like it or not, men are dying in their hundreds on both sides.' For once, there was an edge to his soft voice. 'Rowena's had a hard time of it, poor wee lassie, with losing her father twice over, and it'd be cruel for her to lose someone else to this war. She's got the right to feel sure of the other folk in her life, at least until she's old enough to understand the ways of the world better. And . . .' He paused, then said, 'I thought that you'd be more able to understand my thinking than anyone else.'

Caitlin held her hand out for the books. 'I'll make sure she gets these if they're needed,' she said through stiff lips.

'I'm grateful.' He hesitated before saying awkwardly, 'I'm expecting a lot of you . . .'

'If there's anything else I can do, I will.'

'Mebbe your brother's told you something of what's happened to me.'

'Alex hasn't said a word, but I did hear something from Mhairi.'

He smiled faintly. 'That old woman worries over me as if I was her own. Since you know, I wondered if you would keep this for me.' He delved into the bag again, this time bringing out a framed photograph. 'It's of Elspeth, my wife, and the bairn.'

Caitlin looked down at the formal portrait of a thin young woman, her dark hair drawn back, her large eyes anxious, although her mouth was curved in a smile. Her arms were around the child on her lap, still in the long dress some little boys wore until they were 'shortened' and put into trousers at five years of age. His long, dark curly hair stood out around a chubby face, and his eyes, also dark, were alight with the glee of being alive. It looked as though he had worked one arm free of his mother's grasp, for he brandished it triumphantly in the air, short fingers outspread as though reaching for freedom. He was so like Murdo that Caitlin caught her breath.

'I don't want to take it with me in case it gets lost or damaged, but I don't like the thought of leaving it behind on its own,' Murdo was saying earnestly. 'I'd feel better about it if I knew someone was looking after it for me.'

'I'll take good care of it,' Caitlin promised, and he nodded, then held his hand out. 'I'd best say goodbye, then.'

They shook hands formally, then as he turned to go, Caitlin asked, 'Can I . . . Would you mind if I wrote to you?'

He gave her a smile that lit up his whole face and briefly emphasised the similarity between himself and his long-dead son. 'I'd like that,' he said.

When he had gone she opened the exercise books. Every page contained a short letter that began 'Dear Rowena' and ended with 'From your friend, Murdo Guthrie'. Between, in a strong, clear hand, were a few lines about the weather and how busy Murdo was, and how everything was fine, and he hoped that Rowena was doing well at school and keeping up with her dancing practice.

Caitlin found a sheet of paper to wrap the books and the photograph in. By leaving them with her, Murdo had made her guardian of the people he held dear: Rowena and his dead wife and son. She supposed that she should feel pleased and honoured by his trust, but part of her wanted desperately to be among their number and not just the outsider appointed to look after them.

When she went to the gatehouse to collect Rowena at the end of the day, Murdo said, 'I'll walk with you to Espedair Street, if I may, and make my farewells to your mother and Todd before I go on to see Mhairi and some of the folk from the ceilidhs.' He put a hand on Rowena's head. 'We're going to write to each other while I'm away, aren't we?'

The little girl, who looked as though she had been crying, nodded, her eyes on the floor.

Murdo put on his jacket, then patted the pockets and looked around the kitchen. 'Did you see where I put my mouth organ, Rowena?'

'No.' Her voice was deep and grumpy.

'You'll want to take it with you.' Caitlin glanced around, but the place was so neat that it was easy to see that the instrument wasn't there.

'Ach well, mebbe it's as well to leave it behind, for I doubt if I'll have much time to play it and I'd not like to lose it,' Murdo said, and shepherded the two of them towards the door.

He didn't stay long at Espedair Street, and when he turned to go Rowena, sulking in a corner, suddenly ran to him and threw her arms about his legs.

'Don't leave me! Take me with you!'

He picked her up and held her tightly for a moment. 'Sweetheart, I have to go, but I'll be back. I promise you that I'll be back,' he said, then pushed her into Todd's arms and left.

Caitlin lay awake for most of the night. When she went to work in the morning, the gatehouse had an empty, deserted look.

Rowena treasured the letters she received from Murdo, guarding them jealously from the rest of the family and refusing to let anyone know what was in them. She herself wrote to him every day after school, sitting at the kitchen table with her tongue sticking out from between her teeth and her head so close to the paper that the pen sometimes got tangled in her long hair. She kept up her dancing classes and still spent a great deal of her spare time on her dancing stone in the back yard, moving to music that only she could hear.

Murdo wrote regularly to Caitlin as well, short formal letters at first, but gradually developing into longer missives revealing glimpses of his life and his thoughts. As with her letters to Alex, she wrote about Harlequin and her family and life in Paisley.

Some of the men and boys who had flocked off to war so enthusiastically in 1914 had returned to the town, all their dash and glory gone. Those able to get out and about were to be seen on the streets, some on a crutch to compensate for a missing foot or leg, others with empty sleeves pulled inside out or pinned out of the way. Some bore scars, some had been blinded; some coughed and wheezed, their lungs destroyed by chlorine gas.

In August it was Mary's turn to start worrying when Lachie finally achieved his sixteenth birthday and went off to don a uniform. As had happened with Alex and John, he was allowed a short furlough between completing his army training and being sent overseas, but to Caitlin and Rowena's bitter disappointment Murdo was packed straight off to France from his training camp.

'In view of my past record as a soldier, I think they're afraid to let me go in case I don't return,' he wrote to Caitlin. 'And instead of trusting me with a rifle they are sending me to serve with the Medical Corps. This suits me very well, as I would rather do what I can to help wounded men than add to their numbers.'

On a pleasant breezy day in early September, Caitlin set about the task of bringing the brown-paper parcels that held the family's winter clothing from the top shelves of the wardrobes and carrying them to the back yard to be unpacked and pegged on the clothesline to air.

Every spring for as long as she could remember, her mother had made a point of wrapping the winter clothes in paper with camphor in the pockets to deter moths. It was a custom that had led to many protests in the past, for it meant that in early autumn every garment had to spend several days on the clothesline to let the fresh air remove, as much as possible, the strong smell of camphor. If for some reason the clothing couldn't be sufficiently aired, such as during a wet autumn when it was impossible to hang clothes outside or a sudden early cold snap that meant that the coats and jackets had to be worn, the wearers exuded a pungent smell that caused heads to turn and noses to wrinkle. When that happened the entire family complained loudly, but Kirsty paid them no heed and refused to give up her custom. 'I'd sooner have a smell of camphor about my clothing than have holes in it,' she insisted.

When she opened the wrappings round Rowena's warm coat, which would certainly need unpicking and lengthening before it could be worn again, Caitlin dipped her hand into the pockets to remove the camphor and brought out a familiar object instead. She stared at it, then turned to Rowena, who was sitting on her dancing stone, talking earnestly to her doll in a low voice.

'What's this?'

The child tossed a casual glance in her direction, then her small face went blank and she jumped to her feet. 'It's mine.' Whipping the mouth organ from Caitlin's palm, she pushed both hands tightly behind her back.

'It's not yours, it's Murdo's mouth organ, the one he thought he'd lost just before he went away.'

'He gave it to me!'

They faced each other challengingly, then Caitlin said, 'Come in here,' and led the way into the wash house, where they were less likely to be overheard. She had half expected Rowena to take to her heels, but the child followed her, and Caitlin closed the door behind them. 'You took it without Murdo knowing, didn't you?'

'I'm looking after it!'

'Did he ask you to?' When Rowena shook her head, staring at her shoes, Caitlin went on, 'So he still thinks it's lost, and he's still wondering what happened to it.' The child said nothing, and for a moment Caitlin looked at her bent head helplessly, unable to judge how to deal with the matter. Then she said tentatively, 'You shouldn't take things that don't belong to you, Rowena.'

Rowena, chin well down, muttered something into her chest.

'What did you say?'

Rowena took a deep breath. 'He'll have to come back for it now,' she said, and suddenly it all made sense.

'You took it because you knew he'd want it back?' Caitlin asked, and when the copper head nodded she knelt down on the flagged floor and tipped Rowena's chin up so that they were eye to eye.

'You'll have to write to Murdo and tell him it's safe – and tell him you're sorry you took it without asking.'

'Can I keep it?'

'Until he comes for it. But put it in a better place this time,' she added when the child's face lit up. 'In a drawer, mebbe.'

'If I do that Granny'll see it.'

'We'll tell her that Murdo asked you to keep it safe for him – but you must tell him in your next letter, mind.'

When Rowena had taken her precious burden into the house Caitlin went back to the clothesline. It occurred to her, as she worked, that there was little difference between herself and Rowena. They both nurtured the superstitious hope that one day Murdo must return to claim his possessions – the mouth organ from Rowena and the framed portrait of his dead wife and child from Caitlin.

In January the members of the Gaelic ceilidh band, invited to play at a concert to raise funds for the war effort, asked Rowena to acompany them and give a dance demonstration. To her family's surprise, she agreed. Kirsty made her a ruffled white blouse and a tartan skirt and almost burst with pride at the applause the little girl received.

'I just wish her daddy could have seen her,' she said emotionally as they walked home later, Rowena skipping ahead.

'I wish Murdo could have seen me,' Rowena said sleepily to Caitlin when she was in bed.

'I'm sure he wishes it too.'

'I'll tell him all about it in tomorrow's letter,' Rowena said, and was asleep before Caitlin reached the door.

*   *   *

'We can't allow matters to go on like this!' Rose brandished a fistful of pages at Caitlin during their usual monthly business meeting. 'Look at these unpaid bills. No wonder we're finding it difficult to pay our debts.'

'Write and ask them to settle.'

'I've done that already, but most of them ignored the letters.' Rose sank into a chair on the other side of the desk. 'And several assured me that their outstanding accounts would be dealt with when they next came in to order a dress or a jacket or a skirt. Only they weren't.'

'Is there nothing else we can do?'

'Not that I can think of. Some of them have even used the war as an excuse – their husbands are in uniform and they themselves know so little about how to deal with the household finances.' Rose flapped her hands and fluttered her eyelashes and dropped into a childish voice, '"And it's such a burden, my dear, with the servants just flocking off to work in those nasty factories without so much as a thought for all we've done for them in the past. My poor little head was simply not made to deal with nasty things like cheque books and accounts and handing money over to people who need it and have earned it. Why else do you think I got married in the first place?"' Then, reverting back to her own voice, she said, 'The next time some silly little powder puff of a woman says that to me I shall point out that even society women are possessed with brains and that their only problem is that they choose not to use them.'

'Then they'll take umbrage and you'll lose most of our clients.'

'We might as well not have them, since they cost us in time and materials yet give nothing in return. I do wish that John was here!'

'D'you want me to try writing to them?' Caitlin suggested, very much against her will.

'You're our designer. You shouldn't have to do that,' Rose protested, though hope gleamed in her eyes.

'As you say, John can't do it for us any more, and you know most of these people too well socially to dun them for money. I could try it.'

Relief radiated from Rose as she scooped up the bills and handed them over. 'You are a darling!'

After the meal had been cleared away that night, Caitlin spread the invoices over the kitchen table, turned to a blank page in her sketch pad and began to note the various amounts down.

Mary, helping Rowena with her homework at the other side of the table, craned her neck inquisitively. 'What have you got there?'

'Unpaid invoices.' Caitlin completed the list and added it up laboriously, then added it again, tutting her irritation when the totals differed.

'Here, let me.' Before she had time to object Mary had spun the book round, whisked the pencil from her hand and had begun to move the point briskly from total to total, muttering under her breath. 'There.' She turned the book back to face Caitlin, who saw that Mary's total was different from her two.

'Are you certain?'

Mary, who had taken over Jean's shop books after gaining her diploma in bookkeeping at night school, eyed her sister scathingly. 'Of course I am. Look.' She deserted Rowena and came to stand behind Caitlin, the pencil deftly skimming up and down the page as she chanted numbers. 'No doubt about it,' she said, then whistled softly. 'Are you and Rose owed all that money?'

Caitlin nodded. Now that the total was before her in black and white, she too was horrified to discover how much was owed to the fashion house and how few people had paid their accounts promptly.

'How on earth can you keep going if people don't pay you?'

'We can't, that's why I said I'd try to collect the money.'

'But you're supposed to be designing clothes.'

'I know, but Rose has already done all she can, and there's nobody else.' Caitlin thought longingly of the shop days when all she had been expected to do was make alterations to second-hand clothing.

'I could do it.'

'You?'

'Why not? None of your clients knows me, so I can be as firm as I like.' Mary swept the invoices together. 'I'll begin by writing to them.'

'Rose has already done that.'

'I,' said Mary grandly, 'will write a different sort of letter. And if they ignore it I shall call on them after work and on Saturday afternoons.'

'You don't think she'll be too hard on the clients, do you?' Caitlin worried to Rose the next day.

'I don't know, and frankly I don't care. Somebody needs to take these women in hand, and if Mary's willing to do it then I'm behind her.'

'But if she offends them they'll go elsewhere.'

Rose raised an eyebrow at her. 'That would be their loss, for you're an excellent designer and we charge less than anyone else. And they all know that.'

Within three weeks Mary's letters, written in her clear, firm hand and signed 'Miss M. Lennox, Accounts

Department', had resulted in settlement of more than half of the delayed accounts. After she had called at their homes, dressed in her best clothes, all the others paid the money owing, apart from one extremely difficult young woman.

'And she can find some other fashion house,' Rose stated. 'She won't be missed, and when word gets out, as it will, it will teach the others a lesson for the future.'

'Can we afford to turn anyone away?'

'Caitlin, the woman was never satisfied with anything we did for her. I think we've reached the stage where firmness is advisable.'

'I would certainly prefer not to deal with Mrs Clark again if I could help it.' The woman had indeed been very difficult to please and had at times driven Caitlin and Grace almost to distraction.

'So would I. Even with the war we're doing quite well for clients, and now that we're being selective those who do stay with us will feel quite privileged. It might even bring in some new clients. Do you know that two people even apologised to me for having taken so long to settle?' Rose added gleefully. 'They'll respect us more now that we have an accounts department run by our very capable Miss M. Lennox. That's the way business works.'

She gloated again over the ledger before her. 'D'you think Miss M. Lennox would allow us to use her services again? We will, of course, be paying her commission for what she has already done for us.'

27

Mary was delighted to receive her commission and to agree to continue dealing with any clients slow to settle their debts.

'I don't know how you could face folk in their own homes and ask them for money,' Caitlin shuddered. 'I'd be too nervous.'

'Each to her own. I'm not able to design clothes, like you. To tell the truth, I enjoyed it. I was polite, but firm.'

The two of them had taken Rowena to the braes to gather brambles. Their containers filled and the picnic lunch they had brought with them eaten, the sisters were sitting on a grassy hillock while Rowena gathered an arrangement of ferns to take home to Kirsty.

Mary pulled a grass stem and began to chew it, staring thoughtfully into space. 'I shall put the money into a bank account,' she announced finally.

'A bank account?' Caitlin twisted round to gape at her sister.

'Why not? My money's as good as anyone else's. I don't see the bank turning up their noses at it.'

'But folk like us don't have bank accounts!'

'I'm not folk like us,' Mary said serenely. 'I'm me. And since I've no intention of spending the money and

316

I'm certainly not going to keep it in an old sock beneath my mattress, it'd be as well in a bank. I've been reading about such things, and it means that the bank will pay me for the privilege of holding my money. It's called interest. It's a good way of saving up.'

'What are you saving up for?' Caitlin asked, then sat up abruptly when her sister said, 'Mebbe for a place to live once this war's over and Lachie comes home.'

'The pair of you are thinking of getting married?'

'I doubt if he is, but I am.'

'Mary Lennox, you're only sixteen, and Lachie's just seventeen!'

'I know, but we won't be sixteen and seventeen forever.'

'You're too young to think of settling down. You might meet half a dozen other lads before you find the right one.'

'Mam was my age when Alex was born.'

'That was different.'

'Mebbe so, but sometimes you just know when you've found the right man. At my age,' Mary said earnestly, 'you think you'll live forever and there's always going to be plenty of time to do all the things you want to do. But war soon teaches you that things might not go on forever after all, so then you have to grow up faster.'

'What if Lachie doesn't come home?' Caitlin asked tentatively. There was a long silence before Mary spoke again.

'If he's killed I'll still need money to live on, and there'll mebbe even be more reason for me to provide it, since I might not find another man that I like as much as I like him. So,' she ended triumphantly, 'whatever happens, I'm bent on putting my commission in the bank.'

As Mary went to help Rowena, who had entangled her skirt in a thorny bush, Caitlin sat up and wrapped her arms about her knees. Her mother had always said that Mary was an old head on young shoulders; watching her sister's deft movements as she freed Rowena and the serenity in her face when she walked back towards Caitlin, she felt at the moment as though she, and not Mary, was the sixteen-year-old.

'In any case,' Mary picked up the conversation as though it hadn't been interrupted, 'Lachie will come home. I've set my mind on it, and if you want something badly enough you're bound to get it. Look at Rose, getting the old mill and starting up her own business.'

'Rose had money behind her.'

'Even if she hadn't she'd have found some way of earning it.'

'D'you know how to go about setting up a bank account?'

'No, but Rose will. I'll ask her to go with me the first time.'

In April of 1917 America had entered the Great War, and with the influx of its young, eager servicemen it began, in the following months, to look as though the battle might turn in the Allies' favour after all.

But the way ahead was still hard, and local newspapers throughout Britain continued to carry long lists of dead and missing servicemen. Todd always made a point of reading the names and one evening in spring, Caitlin came home to find him waiting for her, his normally cheerful face grave.

'Ye'd best see this, lass.' He thrust the *Paisley Daily Express* into her hands. Halfway down a list of names, underlined in pencil, was Bryce Caldwell's name.

Caitlin sank into a chair, staring in disbelief. It had

been hard enough to imagine the world without Ewan, let alone Bryce, with his strength and his swaggering and his utter confidence in himself.

'Are they certain?'

'They must be, or he'd not be listed as killed in action.'

'His poor mother,' Kirsty said tremulously. 'I'll go along and see her after Rowena's gone to her bed. D'you want to come with me?'

Caitlin thought of her last meeting with Bryce, and the splash of water and potato peelings on the pavement, and doubted if Mrs Caldwell would be pleased to see her. 'I'd best leave it, Mam.' She put the newspaper aside and went upstairs, in need of time to herself. All at once it seemed to her that the world had shifted slightly, and would never be quite the same again because Bryce was no longer part of it. She wished that she could have been kinder to him in the past, but at the same time she knew that that hadn't been possible. They had each had their own paths to walk.

She had slipped into the habit of opening up the gatehouse once a month to dust what little furniture Murdo possessed and making sure that everything was as he had left it. On the following day she found time to take the key down from its hook and hurry across the yard.

Seventeen months had passed since she had last seen Murdo, and now the suddenness of Bryce's death wakened within her the fear that she might never see the Highlander again. In the kitchen, she ran her fingers over the things Murdo had touched, then settled herself in his fireside chair, laying her arms carefully along the rests and leaning back against the wooden strap that had supported his head. For a few minutes she stayed where she was, eyes closed, pondering over Mary's firm views on life and envying her sister's certainty over her feelings for Lachie, then she leaped to her feet as the outer door opened and Grace called her name.

'In here!' Caitlin shouted back, applying the duster vigorously to the chair. 'I'm just keeping the dust away,' she explained when Grace put her head round the door.

'Mrs Langmuir's arrived early for her fitting. I'll finish this off for you,' Grace said, whisking the duster from her hand.

In July the staff and pupils of the South School held a small concert for parents and friends to mark the end of the term. Following her success in the fund-raising concert, Rowena was invited, to Kirsty's delight, to demonstrate her dancing skills. On the night Kirsty insisted on bustling her daughters along the road a good forty-five minutes before the concert was due to start; as a result they managed to get seats in the front row, where they sat listening to mysterious thumps and footsteps on the other side of the dusty curtain, laced with the occasional squeal of juvenile excitement and sharp adult reprimand and the ripple of keys from the piano that bulged out of the curtain at the front of the stage. Behind them the hall began to fill until every seat had been taken and the walls vibrated to a buzz of excited conversation.

Rowena had been placed quite far down the programme, so they had to wait for some time while children of various ages sang songs, recited poems, fumbled their way through musical items and gave a demonstration of physical exercises. Although there was a shortage of almost everything because of the war, parents and teachers had managed, by utilising old clothes, cardboard boxes, empty tins and what coloured paper they could find, to improvise some splendid costumes.

'Poor wee soul,' Kirsty whispered as they waited for the curtain to open on Rowena's performance. 'She'll be that nervous, having to wait for so long.'

'Not Rowena,' Mary whispered back, leaning across Caitlin. 'She'll be loving every minute of it!'

'Shh!' her mother told her sharply as the curtain began to part in the middle and jerk back towards both sides. The stage was empty, but before Kirsty could begin to panic a small, familiar tartan-clad figure marched confidently in from one side, stepping up to the centre of the stage then bowing briskly. The audience applauded warmly, and Caitlin felt her mother swell with pleasure as someone behind them said in a loud whisper, 'That's the wee lassie that danced at the concert tae raise money for the soldiers. Awful good, she is.'

A skirl of music came from the wings, and white-haired Hamish from the Gaelic church strode on stage with his accordion to take his bow. When the last clap had rung out from the audience, he settled the accordion more comfortably into place over his round stomach and looked across at Rowena, who carefully placed her feet in position and lifted her thin arms above her head in a graceful pose. She gave a brisk nod of the head, then sprang into action as Hamish began to play.

The applause at the end of each of the three dances proved beyond doubt that she was the star of the show, which ended with all the children squeezed onto the stage in red, white and blue costumes, singing patriotic songs. When the curtain finally closed and the lights went up, tears were streaming down Kirsty's face.

'The wee souls,' she choked, fumbling in her bag for a handkerchief. 'The wee, innocent souls!'

She wasn't the only one in tears; the hall was filled with the sound of snuffles and the blowing of noses. When, after a moment, the curtains opened again to let the young performers flock in a colourful stream down the wooden steps to join their families, they were greeted by another hearty round of applause.

Rowena was one of the last to come onto the stage, her face flushed with excitement, her eyes searching the thronged hall for familiar faces. Waving to her, Caitlin saw the child, about to step onto the highest step, suddenly stop, staring wide eyed at the back of the hall. Then, with a piercing scream of 'Murdo!', she hurled herself down the stairs, narrowly avoiding a collision with some of the children already on their way down, and started struggling through the crowd, passing her grandmother and aunts without a glance, even when Kirsty called to her.

'What's amiss with the bairn?' she asked in astonishment, while Mary wanted to know, 'Was that Murdo's name she shouted out?'

'It couldn't be! Caitlin, what d'you think you're doing?' Kirsty squawked as her elder daughter scooped up her skirt with both hands, heedless of whoever might be looking.

'Hold me, Mary,' she said, and scrambled onto the chair she had just vacated to get a better view. Not meant for such use, it wobbled beneath her and she had to put all her faith in Mary, who gripped her with one arm while trying to hold the chair steady with her free hand. Peering above the milling, bobbing heads, Caitlin almost lost her balance altogether when she saw Todd beaming and gesticulating at her from the back of the hall. Beside him, in army uniform, Murdo Guthrie ducked down into the crowd, both arms outstretched, then straightened up and hoisted Rowena high into the air, the red paper skirt she had worn for the final number flaring out around her thin body.

Caitlin tried to jump down from the chair, but Mary's tight grip forestalled her. 'Get me down!' she commanded, and after a clumsy struggle the solid floor was beneath her feet again. 'It's Murdo, he must have been allowed home!'

'Only for two days,' he explained when the three women had finally managed to reach the outside door, where he and Todd and Rowena were waiting.

'I got the surprise of my life when he arrived at the door,' Todd chipped in, beaming. 'Then I decided that the best thing was tae fetch him along tae the school.'

'Did you see me?' Rowena, still in Murdo's arms, was clamouring into his ear. 'Did you come in time to see me?'

'I did, and you were a grand sight!'

Hamish arrived, the shabby case that held his accordion helping him to forge a way through the people who still stood in chattering groups in the small foyer. He and Murdo greeted each other warmly in Gaelic, while Kirsty began to organise her family.

'We'd best get home and out of this cold night air. It was that warm in the hall that we could all catch our deaths if we don't walk fast. Murdo, you'll follow along and eat with us?'

'Of course he will,' Todd said heartily when Murdo began to shake his head. 'We all want tae hear what ye've been doin'. Yer friend an' all,' he added, grinning at Hamish.

'Of course,' Kirsty chimed in, though Caitlin could see her eyes narrow as she tried to calculate whether or not the meal keeping hot in the oven could stretch to feeding two unexpected guests.

Hamish explained that his wife was expecting him home and would worry if he was late, but Murdo agreed to follow them back to Espedair Street in a few minutes. Rowena wanted to stay with him and clung to him when Todd tried to lead her away. When Murdo said quietly, 'No, do as you're bid, Rowena,' she stopped struggling and went quietly along the footpath.

He arrived just as Mary and Caitlin had finished setting the table and he insisted on having a wash before joining them for the meal. Murdo looked tired, Caitlin thought when he came indoors again, but even so he wasn't as reticent as he had once been. No doubt that came from being with people all the time. From what Alex had told her, soldiers had few opportunities to be on their own.

He didn't say much about his duties, other than that he and his colleagues were kept busy most of the time. He ate hungrily, leaving it to the others to do most of the talking. Rowena chattered happily about school and the ceilidhs and going to the braes with Caitlin and Mary to collect brambles for jelly.

'But I didn't eat so many this time because I'm older and more sensible,' she explained, yawning hugely.

Kirsty pounced. 'Time for bed, young lady.'

'But . . .' Rowena began, then slid a glance at Murdo from the corners of her slightly slanted eyes and changed the sentence to, 'Can Murdo come and say goodnight when I'm in bed?'

'If your grandmother allows me to. Then I must be off to my own place.'

'You could stay here,' Todd offered, but the Highlander shook his head. 'I'll be fine at the gatehouse.'

'Can I come and see you tomorrow?' Rowena asked at once.

'You can, but right now you're going to your bed.' Kirsty held out her hand. 'Come along.'

'Don't forget to come up and say goodnight, Murdo.' Rowena widened her eyes and lowered her voice dramatically. 'I have something for you.'

When they had gone, Rowena's voice receding as she mounted the stairs, Todd got to his feet. 'You'll have a glass of beer with me before you go. Sit yourself down by the fire, man.'

Murdo drank his beer, then spent five minutes upstairs with Rowena before thanking Kirsty and Todd for their hospitality and departing.

When Caitlin left for Harlequin the following morning, Rowena insisted on going with her.

'Murdo might still be in his bed,' Caitlin protested. 'He'll be tired after all his travelling to get here.'

'Then I'll stay with you until he wakes up,' the little girl told her, but when they reached the gatehouse they found Murdo, in his usual clothes, working at the loom.

'I've been thinking of this unfinished cloth all these long weeks and months,' he said when Caitlin protested that he should be enjoying his free time instead of working, 'and looking forward to sitting at the loom again.'

He ate his midday meal at Espedair Street, and afterwards he took Rowena with him while he visited his old friends. The ceilidh that night became a celebration of his homecoming, with even the oldest Highlanders coming along to welcome him home and hear about his time away from them.

'You'll have to excuse us our rudeness in speaking Gaelic,' Mhairi said to Caitlin and Mary. 'It's not the right thing to do at all when there are those among us who only know English, but there's some things that come from the heart that can only be said in our own tongue.'

'We don't mind at all. It's a beautiful language,' Caitlin assured her, but there were times, as she listened to their laughter and studied their animated faces, when she did feel left out and longed to know just what they were saying to each other.

Murdo took his usual place on the dais with the other musicians when the dancing started, but after a few dances Mhairi jostled her way to where the band stood, calling, 'Now, Murdo Guthrie, it's not seemly for you to go hiding behind that mouth organ of yours when the place is filled with women wanting to dance with you – even old bodies like me!'

'Ach, Mhairi, I've never been one for the dancing, for I'm too clumsy. Why else d'you think I learned to play this thing?' He held the instrument up, but she flapped her arms at him.

'Stop your excuses, man, and take me round the floor this minute!'

He shrugged, smiled and, after a word with Hamish, stepped down and took Mhairi's hands in his. After that he alternated playing with dancing with every woman and girl in the room. It was true what he said, he wasn't a good dancer, but nobody cared, for pleasure was all they were after.

Caitlin was his partner for the last dance, a delicate strathspey that was one of her favourites. When it was over he walked with them back to Espedair Street as he had always done. Dusk had fallen, and as they turned into the street the lamplighter was at the far end, lighting the last gas lamp. Murdo shook his head when he was invited in.

'You're all tired after the dancing. I'll get back to the gatehouse.'

'Can we go up the braes tomorrow?' Rowena wanted to know.

'We could bring some food for a picnic,' Mary chimed in eagerly.

Murdo glanced at Caitlin, who nodded. 'It would be nice,' she said.

'I'll be here at ten o'clock, then.'

'We'll be ready.' Mary seized Rowena's hand. 'Come on, it's long past your bedtime.'

The two of them scurried through the pend, but Caitlin lingered to watch Murdo walk away. As he passed beneath one of the lamps, its light haloed his hair, now much shorter than before, as befitted an army man, and edged his square shoulders in soft warm gold against the darkness. The sight triggered off a memory; for a moment she couldn't think why, then she recalled the night she and Bryce had been kissing in the pend and she had almost fallen in through the door of the weaving shop when Murdo had opened it.

The moment was so far in the past that it seemed to belong to another life. That was the night, she remembered, that Alex had come to Paisley to ask Todd if he was willing to take over the new factory he had intended to set up in the old mill.

Murdo turned the corner without looking back and disappeared from her sight. Slowly, she walked through the pend, but instead of going into the house she stepped off the path and onto Rowena's dancing stone as the memories came flooding back. Since that night Rowena had come into their lives, and Ewan and Bryce had been obliterated from the world like stains wiped from a kitchen shelf, their lives ended cruelly and suddenly in a country far from home.

She and Rose had come to own a business, Rose and Alex had at last found each other, and Murdo, a stranger that evening, had become as much a part of her life as the yarns he wove together on his loom to make cloth. She did a few steps of the strathspey they had danced together, humming the music softly, then jumped as the back door opened and Mary put her head out.

'Are you coming in or not?'

'I was just having a look at the night sky,' Caitlin apologised, and hurried into the house.

28

The four of them spent the entire day on the braes behaving, as Mary said to Caitlin later, 'like daft bairns'.

'I think it was a good thing for all of us. I've never seen Rowena enjoy herself so much.'

'You're right,' Mary admitted. 'It was grand to be able to stop fretting about what folk might think and just make fools of ourselves.'

They played childish games, ran races and even took their socks, stockings and shoes off and paddled in a fast-flowing burn so cold that it numbed their feet and legs. Even Murdo joined in, and Caitlin felt that day that she had finally caught a glimpse of the carefree young man that Mhairi had once described to her.

As usual, she had brought her sketchbook and coloured crayons with her, and eventually she settled down with them, while the others crouched by a pool below a waterfall where Murdo was supposed to be teaching Rowena how to guddle for trout. After a while Rowena and Mary began to walk along the river while Murdo came back to where Caitlin sat, using his handkerchief to dry his hand and arm, which he had plunged into the water as he demonstrated how to tickle a basking trout before deftly whipping it from a pool and onto dry land.

'Did you catch any?'

'There were none to catch, but at least Rowena knows now what to do if she ever does finds a trout.' He settled a few feet away, elbows on knees.

'I noticed last night that she had returned your mouth organ.'

'Aye. She'd already written to confess.'

'It was wrong of her to take it.'

'Mebbe, but it's understandable. The lassie had nothing to remind her of her father, other than that photograph your mother gave to her and then the letter he wrote just before his death. I should have thought to leave something of mine with her. I'll give the mouth organ back to her before I go, to keep for me.'

'Then you'll have to do without it again.'

'To tell the truth, I have another that I got when I thought that one lost. But I'll say nothing of that to Rowena.'

Caitlin suddenly remembered the portrait he had entrusted to her care. 'If I'd know you were coming back, I'd have set your family's photograph in the gatehouse.'

'No matter. I carry its image with me wherever I go,' he said shortly, then lapsed into a brooding silence. Reluctant to break into his thoughts, Caitlin went on trying to capture the different shades of the bushes and grass and wild flowers, occasionally slipping a sidelong glance at his profile. After all these months she was scarcely able to believe that he was really there, sitting close to her. But only for a short while, for tomorrow he would be gone. There was so much she wanted to ask and to say, but the day had been perfect and she didn't want to do anything to spoil it.

It was Murdo himself who finally broke the silence. 'It's knowing that places like this exist that's kept me in my right mind over the past year.'

'It's been bad, then.'

'Aye. You couldn't know unless you saw it with your own eyes what metal can do to a human being. And anyway, I'd not want you or anyone else to see what—' He bit off the final word sharply, as though slamming a door against his own thoughts, then said after pause, 'I'll tell you one thing, though, spending day after day in the presence of death makes a man realise that life's meant to be lived looking forward, not back. Even when it seems that there's not much ahead.'

'The war must end one day.'

'God willing.'

She was unable to hold her tongue any longer. 'Will you come back to Paisley when it does?'

'Where else would I go?'

'You didn't go home to the Black Isle when you last left the army.'

He shot a glance at her across his shoulder. 'I see old Mhairi's tongue's been clacking again.'

'She spoke as your friend.'

'Aye, I know she did. I didn't go back because there was nothing left for me there. In Paisley there's unfinished cloth waiting on the loom, and there's Rowena.'

Caitlin's heart had begun to rattle about beneath her ribs as though it had broken loose. She drew a deep breath to calm it, and set her sketchbook aside. 'Rowena's not the only one who wants to see you come back, Murdo, . . .' she began, then all at once Rowena herself came running up the hill, Mary behind her, calling to them to come and see a little waterfall they had found, and the moment was lost.

*　　*　　*

After her success in getting clients to settle their bills, Mary had taken over total responsibility for Harlequin's invoices and collections in her spare time. When she suggested that those women who objected to settling their bills within a reasonable time should be given to understand, politely but firmly, that they could no longer expect to continue as clients, Rose applauded the idea, but Caitlin was horrified.

'They'll complain to their friends and we'll lose everyone, and then where will we be?'

'Folk value a service more if they think it might be taken away from them,' Mary said implacably. 'Anyway, they'll be too embarrassed to tell anyone.'

'Mary has the right idea, Caitlin. I know these women, and most of them are terrible snobs. They'd clamour to buy a duster if they thought that there was some privilege in owning it.'

'I don't want to take the risk of losing clients.'

'Caitlin,' Rose said firmly, 'you're a better designer than you realise. Why else d'you think we've done so well for clients? They like wearing your clothes, and they'll not want to lose you. Apart from any other consideration, we're the only fashion house in Paisley. It would be different if we were in Glasgow, where the clients would have a wider choice.'

As it turned out, she was right; the understanding that if they were lax in settling their accounts they would be required to find someone else to design their clothes made most of the clients eager to settle their accounts, and Harlequin continued to thrive, so much so that a few months later Rose suggested to Caitlin that Mary should be invited to become Harlequin's bookkeeper.

'Thanks to her efficiency we're making enough to support another wage, and it means that there'll be someone else here to meet clients if we're both busy. Mary's good at dealing with people, and she can go on doing the shop accounts, since the businesses are connected anyway.'

It was agreed, and by Easter, Mary, to her delight, was well settled in the small office, while Rose moved her desk into the design office.

By the autumn of 1918 the Allies had begun to make notable advances, forcing the German troops back step by step. The enemy was being defeated at last, but by that time another enemy was on the loose in the form of a virulent influenza epidemic that swept through the Western front, killing hundreds of troops on both sides, then stepping effortlessly across the Channel to invade Britain. The Espedair Street household was fortunate, for it passed them by, but it claimed a number of Paisley folk, including old Mr Laidlaw in his flat above the tobacconist's shop and Mhairi, the kindly Highland woman Caitlin had come to regard as one of her dearest friends. Caitlin found it hard to find the right words to tell Murdo of the woman's death.

Shortly after she wrote to him with the news, the influenza claimed another victim; having come unscathed through the entire war including the Battle of Jutland, George Chalmers, Fiona's husband, fell ill on the ship bringing him home and died in an English hospital.

In November church bells pealed, firecrackers were let off and the people of Paisley and every other town, city and village in the country flocked onto the streets to celebrate the end of a long and bitter war, the war to end all wars.

'No more having to order yards of black to make

mourning clothes!' Rose exulted as she and Mary and Caitlin struggled through the crowds to reach the Cross. 'Just you wait and see – we're going to be rushed off our feet making clients look stylish now that their menfolk are coming back home! But first,' she stopped and caught Caitlin by both hands, swinging her round so that they were face to face, 'comes my wedding dress, for after all the waiting I've done I'm determined to marry that brother of yours as soon as he sets foot in Scotland!'

Her predictions were correct. Within two weeks they were inundated with orders, and Rose had to bring in another sewing machine and appoint another seamstress to operate it.

Alex came home in January, and he and Rose set the date for their wedding for February. Mrs Hamilton would have much preferred to have had the time to organise a big wedding, but Rose refused to wait.

'Now she's in a terrible pet about the whole thing because she says that all her friends will think we're having to hurry the marriage along in order to make room for a christening,' she told Caitlin and Grace as they worked on her gown, adding, 'I hadn't realised how boring fittings were. How can women go through this for pleasure?'

'For some of them, it's their main pleasure. We won't be much longer,' said Caitlin. With Rose's approval, she had designed an ivory satin gown in the tunic style that suited her friend so well, overlaid with Chantilly lace falling in folds from the plain square neckline to end in handkerchief points just above the ankles. A broad satin sash encircled Rose's hips, and the lace veil, also falling to points, was to be held in place by a tiara of orange blossom.

'Mind you, if Mama had got her way and we'd to

wait for several months, there may well have been a christening to follow.'

'Rose!'

'Don't be such a prude, Caitlin. Alex and I have known each other for years and yet we've scarcely had half a dozen hours together since we became engaged. Is it any wonder that I, for one, feel completely frustrated?'

'It's only human nature,' Grace agreed placidly. 'Separation does that to folk.'

'Mama should just be grateful that Alex is willing to take me off her hands at all now that I'm over thirty. I'm sure my papa is. This war's going to result in hundreds of elderly marriages. You'll have to hurry up, Caitlin, if you don't want to find yourself on the shelf.'

Caitlin rearranged the lacy folds then stepped back to study the effect. 'I'm happy enough as I am.'

'No you're not. You're longing for Murdo Guthrie to come back.'

'Rose!'

'No point in denying it, my dear. Is it, Grace?'

'Not to us,' agreed Grace, who was kneeling behind Rose and pinning up her hem. 'But don't let us fret you, hen, we've neither of us said a word to anyone else.'

'Not even to Alex, though it's been hard to keep my mouth shut. My skin's beginning to itch – can't we stop for today?' Rose appealed.

When the fitting was over and she was getting dressed again, Rose waited until Grace had left the room before saying, 'There's another reason why I want to marry Alex as soon as possible. Oh, this dratted skirt!' She peered over her shoulder, trying to match the fastenings. 'Now that she's widowed, Fiona has decided to stay on in Glasgow with her father.'

'Turn round.' Caitlin slotted hooks into eyes with precision. 'What does that mean for Alex?'

'That's just what he's wondering. At the moment she's in mourning, but she's been getting more and more involved in her father's business during Alex's absence, and he has a suspicion that she intends to continue along that path.'

'But Mr MacDowall took Alex in as his heir. He'd not turn his back on his own son after all Alex has done for the business.'

'Of course not, but when he first approached Alex, Angus MacDowall's intention was to leave the house to Fiona and the business to Alex, with the money divided between them. In those days Fiona had no interest in the business and he wanted it to go to someone of his own flesh and blood who would continue to run it after he was gone. In any case, Fiona married soon afterwards and settled in Fort William. If it hadn't been for the war she might have stayed there and things would have remained as they were. But Fiona's changed a great deal since then, and there's no knowing what way the wind will blow. As I see it, the sooner I'm Alex's wife and able to support him in whatever he may have to face, the better.'

She smoothed her hair before the mirror then turned to smile at Caitlin. 'It's a good thing that Mary's with Harlequin now,' she said. 'It means that if need be I can spend more time in Glasgow.'

The light of battle gleamed in her eyes, and Caitlin saw a familiar bounce in her step as she left the room. There was nothing Rose relished more than a challenge, and clearly she sensed one in the air. At least, Caitlin thought, watching her friend's straight back as she left the room, Rose and Alex were on the same side this time.

* * *

Despite what Mrs Hamilton referred to disapprovingly as the speed of her daughter's nuptials, the church was almost filled with well-wishers when Rose and Alex married. John Brodie was best man, while Caitlin and the daughter of one of Mrs Hamilton's closest friends were the bride's attendants in dresses of dark-blue lace over ivory satin, with flowers in their hair.

The weather was cold and the sky grey and lowering, but when Rose stepped from the car that had brought her to the church she was so radiant in her happiness that she seemed to light up the day. She could scarcely contain her impatience as she waited in the porch for Caitlin to arrange her veil and for her father to smooth his hair and straighten his jacket. When the organist, after a dramatic pause, broke into 'Here Comes the Bride', she seized her father's arm and almost whisked him up the aisle, though at least she remembered to match her step to his instead of striding out. In the grey stone church, Alex's red hair glowed like a beacon, drawing his bride straight to him. Following Rose along the aisle, Caitlin kept her gaze fixed on her half-brother and was rewarded by the expression in his eyes when he turned and saw Rose approaching in her wedding finery. When she reached him he took both her hands in his and gave her such an adoring look that his mother and his future mother-in-law, in the front pews, both started weeping.

'Possibly for different reasons,' Alex told Caitlin at the reception in the Hamilton's house. 'Mam was always soft-hearted, but I have a suspicion that Rose's mama might have been sobbing because it was me standing beside her daughter and not John.'

'I don't think it'll be long before she starts singing your praises.'

'I don't care whether she does or not.' Alex, restless

when he and Rose were apart, turned to search the crowded drawing room for a glimpse of her. 'All I care about is making sure that Rose never regrets her choice.'

Kirsty had dreaded having to attend the reception in the very house where she had once worked as a sewing woman, but once the elaborate meal laid out in the huge dining room was over she began to feel more comfortable. Mr Hamilton had gone out of his way to make Todd and herself welcome, and his wife, while a little stiff, had been courteous. Now that Alex and Rose were safely wed, and clearly delighted to be so, Kirsty's nerves began to subside. She even slipped out of the drawing room when everyone was occupied and went along to have a look at the small room, little more than a cupboard, where she had once worked and where she and Rose had first met.

It hadn't changed at all, nor did it hold any memories for her, happy or sad. It was simply a room that belonged in the past. Recrossing the hall, she sat down on a straight-backed chair for a moment, unwilling to face the crowd in the drawing room. Her new, stylish shoes were cutting into her ankles, and she tried to ease them away with one finger, then jumped as Angus MacDowall said from above her bent head, 'Mrs . . . er . . . Kirsty, are you all right?'

Embarrassed, Kirsty wrenched her finger out of her shoe, which, tight though it had been, promptly popped off her foot and clattered onto the parquet flooring. 'I'm fine.' She looked up at him, her face burning with embarrassment.

'Allow me.' He went down on one knee and slipped the shoe back on as easily as picking up a dropped glove, then glanced up at her. 'Would you like a glass of sherry?'

'To tell the truth, I'd prefer a nice cup of tea.'

'Why not? Wait here.' He went unhurriedly into the dining room, while Kirsty, flustered, wondered how a woman should behave towards a stranger who also happened to be the father of her first-born. She cast an imploring glance at the drawing room door, hoping that Todd, Caitlin or Mary might come through it and save her, but it remained closed, and she felt that it would be rude to scurry back into the room and let Angus return to an empty chair.

'Here you are.' He was back, followed by a capped and aproned maid holding a small tray set with tea things and a glass of some pale amber liquid. Angus set a small table close by Kirsty's chair then positioned another chair for himself while the maid poured tea into the single cup.

'Will that suit, madam?'

It was far weaker than Kirsty liked, but she nodded.

'Have lemon instead of milk,' Angus advised, taking the glass from the tray and seating himself beside her. 'You'll find it refreshing.'

She didn't care for the idea at all, but she didn't like to argue. To her surprise, she found when she sipped at the cup that he was quite right. 'How's your daughter?' she asked tentatively when the maid had gone. A shadow passed over his face.

'Grieving, and there's so little I can do to help her.'

'There's not much anyone can do. You'll have to let her take her own time.'

'So I'm told. But at least Alex is happy. You've got a fine lad there, Kate.' He used the name that only he had called her when they were both in their teens, and when she allowed herself to look at him she saw that his expression held more than a hint of the orphaned boy she had once known and loved.

'We both have a fine lad there, Sandy.'

'The way things turned out, it's you that had all the worry of raising him.'

'Mebbe so, but you've not done so badly by him yourself.'

He leaned over and touched her cup lightly with his glass. 'To both of us, Kate, and to our boy and his new wife,' he said.

When he finally rose to return to the drawing room, he almost bumped into Mary in the doorway. She beamed at him, as she had beamed at everyone, friend and stranger, since receiving word the day before that Lachie was on his way back to Paisley.

'There you are, Mam.' She settled herself in the chair Angus MacDowall had vacated and reached over to the tray for a biscuit. 'What were you and Mr MacDowall talking about?'

Kirsty smiled at her daughter, thinking that the path that had started with Alex's conception had just completed its full circle.

'Just about old times,' she said.

29

It was April before Murdo Guthrie returned to Paisley.

On the day before he was due to arrive Caitlin, Kirsty and Mary gave the gatehouse's ground-floor rooms a thorough spring-cleaning and stocked the kitchen cupboard with food, then Kirsty, admitting freely that her nose was bothering her, insisted on a tour of the upper floor.

'I know I've seen through the place before, when Alex was thinking of buying the old mill and he wanted us to live here, but to tell the truth I was in such a state that day that I can't mind what the place was like.'

Caitlin, too, got a chance to have a proper look at the place, and was surprised by the size of the rooms which, despite their thick coating of dust, were elegant and airy.

'It's a shame that such a bonny place isn't being put to its proper use,' Kirsty said when they arrived back in the entrance hall. 'You'd have thought Rose and Alex would have wanted to bide here instead of renting that flat out along the Glasgow road.'

'The flat's handy for Alex's work in Glasgow and Rose's work here, and if they'd taken this place over we'd have had to find a new weaving shop and some-where else for Murdo to live.' Caitlin opened the front door while Mary gathered up the bag containing their dusters and scrubbing brushes.

'I suppose you're right.' Kirsty cast a final glance round before following her daughters into the yard. 'But mebbe one day it'll become a home again. A bonny place like this deserves to be lived in properly.'

That evening Caitlin walked back to the gatehouse. She set paper and sticks in the kitchen grate, made certain that the coal scuttle was full, then took the framed portrait Murdo had entrusted to her care from her bag and sat on Murdo's fireside chair, studying the photograph as she had studied it so often in the two years it had been in her possession. His small son beamed back at her, while the child's mother still stared from the frame with anxious eyes.

Having heard from Mhairi how some Highlanders possessed second sight, Caitlin wondered if Elspeth had had it and if she had known, or guessed, that her happiness was not to last.

After a while she set the portrait on the dresser and went home.

Murdo's letter had simply said that he would be travelling by train from Glasgow and expected to arrive in Paisley before midday. Caitlin, suddenly anxious and apprehensive about seeing him again, would have gone to work as usual, but Rose would have none of it.

'The man's been away for two years. Surely someone should be there to welcome him back.'

'It doesn't have to be me. Perhaps Mam or Mary.'

'He didn't leave his most precious possession with Kirsty or your sister,' said Rose, who knew about the photograph and the letters in the exercise book. 'And he didn't write to them either. Of course you must go. You want to, don't you?'

'Yes . . . no . . . I don't know, Rose. He might not want me to be there, and anyway I won't know what to say to him.'

'"Welcome home" would be nice after what he's been through. You're going to Gilmour Street Station to meet him, and no arguments.'

'Would you come with me?'

Rose sighed, then said, 'If it's the only way to get you to go, I will – but it's not me he'll want to see, it's you.'

'You don't know that.'

'I think I do. Mary can be left in charge while we're away. I don't know how we managed before she came to Harlequin.'

Mary had certainly settled smoothly into her duties. Adult and sophisticated in discreet, smart outfits supplied by the fashion house, she had swiftly acquired the art of greeting each client with just the right mixture of respect and friendliness for that particular individual and of making sure that their every need was catered to. John Brodie, who was once again supervising the bookkeeping, was impressed by her efficiency, and she got on well with Grace and the other sewing women. For her part, she said that she was quite pleased to be free of the smell of jams and marmalades.

Rowena, determined to meet Murdo's train, refused point-blank to go to school that morning, so a welcoming party of three waited on the platform for him. He wasn't on the first train to arrive.

As the guard's van disappeared from view, Rowena surveyed the empty platform stretching out before them. 'You don't think he's changed his mind and gone to live somewhere else?' she asked anxiously.

'Of course not,' Rose told her briskly, while Caitlin

assured the little girl, 'He'll come on the next train,' though she herself was beginning to worry.

Rowena's well-shaped brows, so like her mother's, drew together above her neat little nose. 'Perhaps he's arrived at Canal Street Station and he thinks we don't care because we're not there to meet him.'

'He said he'd be coming in at Gilmour Street. We'd best wait here.'

They waited while the minutes ticked by and the platform began to fill again with people preparing to board the next train from Glasgow and travel on it to Ardrossan. It seemed to Caitlin that hours dragged by before the signals finally rattled then collapsed into a new position, though when she glanced at the platform clock she saw that less than thirty minutes had passed since the last train.

When the engine finally appeared from round a bend it seemed to take a long time to puff into the station and grind to a halt. Caitlin and Rowena, hand tightly clutching hand, studied the windows that flashed by.

'Did you see him? Did you see Murdo?'

Caitlin shook her head, and Rowena danced with impatience. There seemed to be a lot of folk disembarking at Paisley and a considerable number of travellers anxious to board. Rowena would have darted up the platform, but Caitlin kept a grip on her fingers, worried in case the child got tangled in the throng and swept onto the train by accident. They stayed where they were, jostled by people hurrying to the entrance and by late-comers running to catch the train. Doors had begun to slam shut along its length when Rose, taller than Caitlin and standing on tiptoe, her neck stretched to its full extent, said, 'There he is!'

'Where?' Rowena wrenched her hand from Caitlin's and scrambled up onto a nearby bench.

'Right up at the top. He's been in a carriage just behind the engine.'

'I see him! Murdo!' Rowena leaped from the bench, landing on her feet with a thud that must have sent a shock wave up through her entire body, and began to run, heedless of her aunt's call and narrowly avoiding a collision with a woman making her way down the platform.

Now that almost all the travellers had either boarded the train or gained the exit, Caitlin could see Murdo's tall figure at the far end of the platform. He was carrying a suitcase in one hand and a kitbag in the other, and as Rowena hurtled towards him he put them both down and opened his arms wide. Although she was now nine years of age, more than halfway to adulthood and almost up to Caitlin's shoulder, she launched herself from the platform when she was yards away and flew through the air into his embrace. As she landed he took an involuntary step back, then steadied himself and spun her round, her long black-stockinged legs flying out behind her.

'Her dad just back from the wars, is he?' The woman Rowena had almost bowled over reached Caitlin and Rose and paused, turning to look at the reunion.

'He isn't—' Caitlin began, then as Rose's elbow dug into her ribs she amended it to, 'Yes.'

'God bless the wee soul – and God bless you too, my dear.' The woman put a hand on her arm. 'It's grand to see a family reunited after all we've been through.'

'Isn't it?' Rose agreed warmly.

Murdo had put Rowena down; she caught his hand and tried to tug him towards the exit, but he resisted. The stretch of platform between himself and Caitlin made it difficult for her to make out his expression

345

in detail, but she sensed that he was hesitating, just as uncertain and apprehensive as she was herself.

'Go on – go to him,' Rose urged. 'He's waiting for you to make the first move.'

'What if he isn't. What if he's wishing Rowena had come to meet him on her own?' Now that the moment had come Caitlin's throat muscles were so stiff that she could scarcely get the words out. Her heart thundered in her ears and she felt as though she was about to burst into tears, though whether of joy or fear she didn't know.

'For goodness' sake, d'you want the four of us to stand here for the rest of our lives?' Rose asked impatiently. 'Someone has to make the first move. The poor man needs to know how you feel about him. Show him!'

Caitlin took a tentative step forward, then another and another, until she was walking then running along the platform. Her skirt caught about her legs, and she knew that her hat was coming adrift and her hair loosening from its pins, but now that she had made her decision she no longer cared.

Murdo freed his hand from Rowena's and began to move forward, his hands reaching out to her. Close enough now to see the smile spreading over his face, she knew that everything was going to be all right for the two of them, today and tomorrow and for always.